"YOU'VE NEVER
READ ANYTHING LIKE IT."
Joseph Di Sabato, *The Village Voice*

"To learn so much about homosexuality
during the Vietnam war is a rare
opportunity."
Edmund White, author of *States of Desire*

"Sexual tension among the men in war is
surely the most important part...Most other
writers didn't dare to even mention it, but of
the few who tried, nobody has succeeded so
well as Nelson in telling such a complicated
story."
Perry Deane Young, *Newsday*

"Explains why the marines on Capitol Hill
have a rage against the macho-oriented gay
men in their midst."
Jim Marks, *The Washington Blade*

"A brilliantly written novel."
Ray Howe, *Chattanooga Times*

"Sensitive, funny, fast-moving."
Richard Hooker, author of M*A*S*H

The Boy Who Picked the Bullets Up

CHARLES NELSON

AVON
PUBLISHERS OF BARD, CAMELOT, DISCUS AND FLARE BOOKS

Poems by Arthur Rimbaud from *Arthur Rimbaud: The Complete Works*, translated by Paul Schmidt (New York: Harper & Row, 1975), Copyright © 1967, 1970, 1971, 1972, 1973 by Paul Schmidt. Reprinted by permission.

AVON BOOKS
A division of
The Hearst Corporation
1790 Broadway
New York, New York 10019

The William Morrow and Company, Inc. edition contains the following Library of Congress Cataloging in Publication Data:

Nelson, Charles, 1942–
    The boy who picked the bullets up.

    1. Vietnamese Conflict, 1961–1975–Fiction.
I. Title.
PS3564.E458B6   813'.54   81-9438
                                    AACR2

First Avon Printing, August, 1982

AVON TRADEMARK REG. U. S. PAT. OFF. AND IN
OTHER COUNTRIES. MARCA REGISTRADA, HECHO EN U.S.A.

Printed in the U.S.A.

WFH   10   9   8   7   6

To PAUL SCHMIDT

Who advised me to write,
   Showed me how it was done,
Flattered, cajoled, ranted, and raved,
   Took abuse
                  and gave it,
      And still remains a friend.

                  and

To LAURA MORLAND
   Who supported me.

The Boy Who Picked the Bullets Up

PART ONE

✪ ✪ ✪

DEMOCRACY

Toward that intolerable country
  The banner floats along,
And the rattle of the drum is stifled
  By our rough backcountry shouting . . .

In the metropolis we will feed
  The most cynical whoring.
We will destroy all logical revolt.

On to the languid scented lands!
  Let us implement industrial
And military exploitations.

Goodbye to all this, and never mind where.
  Conscripts of good intention,
We will have policies unnamable and animal.
Knowing nothing of science, depraved in our pleasures,
  To hell with the world around us rolling . . .

This is the real advance!
                Forward . . .
                        March!

                        —ARTHUR RIMBAUD

My dear Paul,

The Post Office returned my last letter after a note had been added: WRONG PAUL CARROLL. "Had there ever been a right Paul Carroll?" I wondered. "And where has he been?" Months of intermittent speculation followed; then, last Sunday evening, I finally found you out. I was strolling through the Fenway when a dark shape glided across the path in front of me and slipped behind a tree.

"Terry!" I cried. "How are you?"

"Shh!" hissed the shape.

I ambled over to the tree. "Hello, Terry. Where ever is Paul?"

"In Morocco. Please go away." He stared beyond me at some bushes, where another dark shape stood among piles of soiled Kleenex.

"What ever is Paul doing in Morocco?" I asked.

"Teaching, for God's sake." He tried to push past me, so I stifled an image of your teaching for God's sake, grabbed Terry by his scented scarf, and dragged him to the pool of light under a nearby lamppost. He had aged brutally.

"What are you doing now?" I asked.

"Acting," he said.

Aren't we all?

Morocco! And up to no good, I'm sure, riding upon magic carpets, dancing with houris, and comparing swords with ruthless infidels. My "Uncle" Ralphie has long dreamed of retiring to Tangier, where he'd heard that little girls and boys could be rented for a nickel. Is that true? Have you ever? What's it like?

My life-style is less exotic. And it's on your head. Remember? "Do it, Kurt. Enlist. You might find the Armed Services amusing." You set a gallon of vodka martinis on the table and told me tales of your hitch in the Army that gave visions of myself among stouthearted men tramping arm in arm along a dusty trail and crouching knee to knee in a damp fo'c's'le. I told you what Mother had said. "Join the Navy, Kurt. You'll eat three hot meals every day and sleep in a warm bed every night. And girls look twice at a good-looking man in a sailor suit. I always did." You agreed. The next day I visited your friendly neighborhood recruiter. Did I ever tell you how friendly?

I arrived at Great Lakes Training Center with several hundred other recruits. We were herded into an auditorium and ordered to relinquish any weapons carried upon our persons. Brass knuckles, blackjacks, switchblades, and revolvers appeared on all sides of me. A tyranny of shaven heads, extracted teeth, and bloody inoculations followed. I had entered a brave new world.

After Boot Camp, I asked to be sent to Aviation Ordnance School, where I could learn gunnery. I knew about gunnery from reading comic books. A gunner's mate squeezes into a little turret upon the deck of a big ship and shoots down kamikazes. Sounds rugged, doesn't it? Well, that Navy employment counselor wasn't stupid. He looked me over and assigned me to Hospital Corps School, where I could learn to be a mininurse.

I spent three months digesting medical terminology and hospital procedures. Despite my good intentions, I ranked fifty-ninth in our class of sixty.

I was graduated, nevertheless, and requested Boston, the home of my old pal Paul, as a duty station. To my astonishment, my request was granted; to my dismay, old Paul had vanished. I decided to lose myself in my work. I was assigned to the Urology ward in the hospital below Bunker Hill, where my duties were simple. I had only to bear witness that the bed-wetters and the newly circumcized ate their meals, slept between clean sheets, swallowed their medications, peed with regularity, and didn't read *Playboy*. (Hard-ons break the stitches.) I pushed piss for three months; then I was transferred to Pediatrics, the most coveted duty in the hospital. The nurses on Peds were either local civilian ladies who gave no rousing damn about rules and regulations, or young lieutenants j.g. who were looking among the doctors for husbands instead of over my back. Pleasant working conditions with bed and board provided; a cultural bonanza of museums, theaters, and libraries; and a profusion of students, sailors, and Irish-Italian laborers contributed to a rich, full life in Boston.

And I'm leaving, by my own choice, for an assignment in Vietnam. As the old lady spy said, after pushing a little maid out the window and drinking a vial of poison, "Fools! Fools! The world is full of fools."

Relentlessly,

Kurt

CHELSEA NAVAL HOSPITAL
BOSTON, MASSACHUSETTS
3 August 66

Arch,

Orders arrived last week. I go to Vietnam. I've a chance at last to prove myself a deserving son of the glorious Confederacy. Although I'll serve beneath a Union flag, I shall fight to protect the South against Carpetbaggers. And that's good enough for me.

I'll be assigned to the Marine Corps, should you mistakenly conjure an image of me on a battleship sailing up and down the rivers of the Mekong Delta. The Marine Corps was formerly a branch of the Navy; because marines must travel on the Navy's ships to establish their beachheads, the two services still maintain close ties. One of these ties that bind is the Medical Corps, trained by the Navy and donated to a Marine Corps that has apparently expended its educational energy converting punks, rascals, and fools into tough, slavering killers.

I have yet to be apprised of my future duties. I'm agreeable to accompanying the marines whatever their destination, but how many beachheads do you suppose they must establish in Vietnam? Perhaps there is no destination; perhaps I am to be packed inside the hold of a Landing Ship Tanker as it circles aimlessly about the Pacific. Preparing for such a circumstance, I've been poring over *Asia from A to Z* in an attempt to discover possibilities for debauchery in various Oriental ports. Do you think that their pussies actually slant?

I don't lack enthusiasm for this year abroad. Can you recollect the itch we once had to become super jocks? I'm preparing for Vietnam as diligently as we did for baseball.

STEP NUMBER ONE: Get in Shape. I'm doing that by jogging and vigorous calisthenics.

STEP NUMBER TWO: Make the Team. I've done that.

STEP NUMBER THREE: Avoid Injuries. You couldn't imagine the enormity of my desire to do that.

In my fantasies, I'm already an All-Star.

Relentlessly,

Kurt

CHELSEA NAVAL HOSPITAL
BOSTON, MASSACHUSETTS
4 August 66

Chloe dear,

I'm going home for a few days of leave before I head for Vietnam. I'd like to sit on the verandah and sip fine bourbon while chatting with family and friends, but strife runs rampant. I should forget *Little Women* and reread *The Sound and the Fury*. In our family, turmoil is a part of gracious living.

Mother has been quarreling with my granny. It's all very vague, but their letters of late have been disquieting. Granny's letters usually open with a description of dinner and close with her menu for supper; now they begin with reminiscence and end with despairing postscripts. Instead of being riddled with platitudes gleaned from the *Reader's Digest*, Mother's letters are now laced with hostile stray phrases directed against my granny.

A few days ago I received a letter in which Mother casually mentioned that "the old mule died." I doubted she could be so hard, but with Mother one never knows. I called home immediately. Mother told me that DT had responded to rising fuel costs by acquiring a mule. It died. When I divulged my misapprehension, Mother chuckled malevolently. I realized then that I can't go home again.

Yet I will. After all, rashness is a better fault than fear.

Relentlessly,

Kurt

Dear Mom,

Mother is no longer your little girl; she attained her full growth years ago. Her hair is a nest of writhing snakes and her face turns men to stone. She shall plunge the venom of a cottonmouth, two of your snow-white hairs, and the yearnings of a hundred sailors into a cauldron of seething swamp water, utter several blasphemies, consult the horrid bubbling of her mind, and pronounce the panacea for all your problems. Every night before you say your prayers, you should repeat one hundred times: Phyllis is always wrong. When you believe her, I shall know you approach senility.

They served an excellent dinner at the hospital on Sunday: cauliflower soup, a cucumber salad, roast beef, mashed potatoes, peas, and for dessert, a plentiful helping from a watermelon carved into the shape of a basket and filled with little balls of fruit.

You may recognize a nose plastered against a window of the Saturday bus. It will be mine. We should have little difficulty sneaking away from Mother; she'll have planned a homecoming feast for me and will be examining pork chops as carefully as the witch did Hansel and Gretel. We'll drive to your house, and while I'm gorging myself with the cornbread and buttermilk you'd best have ready to hand, you can tell me all about it.

Love,

Kurt

BELLE OMBRE
DEAD RIVER ROAD
BONIFAY, LOUISIANA
9 August 66

My dear Paul,

I found a letter from Morocco dated December and another from Denver dated July that Mother had thrown into my desk after she'd read them. Thank you for couching your obscenities in a literary language so obscure that she couldn't puzzle out a word. How do I know she couldn't? I'll tell you. She didn't forward the letters to me after underlining significant passages in red ink and writing "Ah, ha!" in the margins. Can life be all bad for orphans?

How ever do you do it? Paris...Prague...Tangier... And now the Colorado Rockies. Your life is a succession of Marlene Dietrich films. You should only exist on the silver screen and then only in the Thirties. If, as I believe, you aren't just a figment of my imagination, I'd love to meet whoever dreamed you up.

Marlene would feel at home here, slinking about the old plantation and gazing through louvered windows at the gloomy confluence of Dead River and the Bayou Louache. Emerging from the snake-ridden swamps by both river and bayou are knolls of comparatively dry land called hummocks. DT, my stepfather, grows fern on these hummocks: twenty-five acres planted in Plumosus, which is a brambly branch of the Asparagus family rather than a fern, and another five acres in Leatherleaf fern. The dark-green plants are cut, packed in ice, shipped to wholesale florists throughout these United States, and sold to retail florists, who use them to garnish bouquets and corsages.

My brothers and I went waterskiing on the Bayou Louache today. Neil piloted the boat while Ricky and I skied. As I swung out recklessly on one side of the wake, skimming next to water hyacinths and old cypress stumps, Ricky tried to ski on one foot, his other foot holding on to the tow rope. He fell and Neil slowed the boat; I sank gently into the warm murky water, next to a clumb of rotting stumps surrounded by thick aquatic plants, a likely playground for water moccasins. (How ever did the Indians wear those things?) I kicked off my skis in terror and swam for the boat. Neil stood with an upraised oar.

"Go get the skis, Kurt."

"You've got to be joking. That place has to be alive with snakes."

"I paid too much money for those skis. Get away now. You try to get in, I'll bash your brains in."

"I'll get you for this, Neil."

"You gotta catch me first."

Whatever happens in Vietnam, nothing can frighten me more than fighting my way through those hyacinths to gather Neil's skis. And I'll never be more exhausted. Neil was too fearful of my revenge to let me into the boat; I had to ski the five miles back to our dock.

So now I sit, bone-weary, in a room Mother decorated in Depression Renaissance. Paint-by-number portraits of swamp birds glare beadily from chocolate walls onto an aquarium shared by three razor-fanged fish I suspect to be piranhas. Writhing vines creep through French doors to catch the flies my brother Ricky brings into the house to feed his chameleons. The dampness has etched mildew stains upon the walls, termites have done considerable damage, and the floor is neither level nor secure. It is a room assembled from a nightmare.

Malevolent piranhas appear to be no more disposed to ill will toward me than my parents, who seem cheered by the idea of seeing me off to war. Patriotism aside, they believe combat will make a man of me. I fear bloody battles and numerous medals would serve insufficiently toward attaining that goal; nevertheless, I am determined to be gallant and butch and a glory to the marines.

Whom the gods would destroy they first make mad.

Relentlessly,

Kurt

BELLE OMBRE
DEAD RIVER ROAD
BONIFAY, LOUISIANA
10 August 66

Arch,

I should have thought painting sawmills all summer at $5.50 an hour would have left you with a savings account sufficient to meet the necessities of a lazy winter in Mazatlán: tequila, tacos, and penicillin. DT, my stepfather, always needs steady help, however, and would hire you on sight. Most of his white workers are alcoholic and undependable; the niggers are in and out of jail. You could make a little money cutting fern—fifteen cents for each bunch of twenty-five. But it's boring, backbreaking work and despite your ability to withstand the damp weather of the Pacific Northwest, you've never undergone the debilitating sultriness of a Louisiana summer or the bone-chilling drizzles of winter. If you're game, notwithstanding, you can live for free in an old cabin we own by the Bayou Louache, with nothing between you and the Gulf of Mexico but sixty miles of swamp, rife with repulsive things. I wouldn't live there on doctor's orders.

A thunderstorm played havoc with Belle Ombre last night, so my brothers and I spent the morning picking up soggy clumps of Spanish moss and heavy branches before they could crush and discolor the fern. Horseflies and red ants bit us. Mosquitoes drew blood. Swarms of gnats flew into our eyes and ears. Countless other insects distracted us from the business at hand. Distraction could prove dangerous, because coral snakes, cottonmouths, and rattlers had crawled up from their flooded burrows to make temporary homes underneath the refuse. I watched the ground so carefully for slithery, squirming things that I neglected to look up. I should not have neglected to look up; I plunged face-first into several cobwebs shared by immense spiders.

When we finished picking up debris, DT handed us hoes and pointed to the fern beds under the slat house. This is the oldest section of the fernery, built where few trees grow. Ancient posts hold up ceilings of weathered gray slats that protect the fern from the sun. Many sections of this roof have collapsed, which makes working there perilous. Hundreds of rusty nails stick up from fallen slats, which conceal scorpions and poisonous centipedes that congregate under them. Hundreds of rusty nails stick down from the slats that have yet to fall. These slat houses were built forty years ago by DT's father to accommodate his height of five feet four. I am six feet three. I would forget that my height was not accommodated. I would stand up straight to ease my back and drive my skull into a rusty nail. Lockjaw would probably become me.

After we finished under the slat house, we chopped weeds growing around the bases of the fernery's 20 million oak trees. We prefer hoeing weeds to any other job in the fernery; we can stand erect, and we hold weapons lethal to serpents. We chopped from tree to tree, arguing about which of us did the most work or playing such games as "I Went to the Store and Bought an Apple, a Banana, and a Cherry." Neil can't work and talk at the same time, but he loves to play these games;

he leaned dreamily against his hoe as he conjured up his shopping list.

DT drove by at one such conjuration. He has never understood our need to make work fun, and he hates games. He yelled at us. He sent Ricky to the packing shed to build crates, left Neil to hoe alone, and took me to a distant hummock to cut old Asparagus fern with the Gravely tractor.

A Gravely tractor is like a large power lawn mower and is used to cut thick weeds. A Gravely functions badly where ruts abound—places like the fernery. Whenever it hits a rut, a Gravely twists around and stops dead, driving a steel handle into the groin of the unwary operator trudging behind it. The Gravely passes through innocuous-looking clumps of vegetation, which prove to be hillocks of dirt that burst into clouds of dust, raising havoc underneath contact lenses. Today I drove the Gravely into a stump, which broke the blades of the infernal machine. I felt guilty, but guilt seemed better than the festering bitterness that was leading me to contemplate DT's destruction.

At that, I accomplished more than Neil. He passed the afternoon watching two snails fuck.

Relentlessly,

Kurt

BELLE OMBRE
DEAD RIVER ROAD
BONIFAY, LOUISIANA
11 August 66

Chloe dear,

Mother and Mom greeted the bus. Mom appeared prim and trim in an expensive beige suit with hat and gloves; Mother looked breezy and sleazy in a cheap sun dress of brown and orange. We drove home, where the two ladies vied for a moment alone with me. Mother won; my granny has a weak bladder. As soon as she heard the click of the lock on the powder room door, Mother said, "Kurt, you haven't seen my flowers." She hustled me outside to show them off.

Mother enjoys working with plants, unlike her sons, and I must give the old she-devil credit; her flowers are lovely. I told her so. She basked for a moment in the glory of her green thumb; then she fixed her eyes upon me as if she were the Ancient Mariner and I the Wedding Guest, her voice dropped into the tragic tone that bodes no good for someone, and she said, "I don't know what to do about Mom." She sighed and gazed at her dahlias.

I distrusted involvement—even an earthworm can learn—but I was curious. So I said nothing. And got involved. Mother recognized my silence for the irresolution it was; after all, she'd nurtured it. She plunged into the heart of the matter. "Oh, Kurt, it's so sad. Mom's getting old. I think we're going to be forced to put her in a rest home." And allow Mom to depend on the kindness of strangers. Mother is always up to something.

"I've tried, God knows. I'm even willing to have her live here with us, although she would drive me crazy. We'd build a garage in the fernery. DT could park his tractors and trucks on the ground floor, and Mom could have her own little apartment upstairs. But she doesn't want to give up her house in town. It's like talking to the wall."

Mother eased me behind the gazebo, where we couldn't be seen from the house. The Dobermans followed us. "Her mind is going fast. When you're around her like I am, day in and day out, you realize just how bad off she is. Now she's saying she should never have left the ranch. How on earth could she manage things alone, in the middle of winter? She's nuts."

I listened intently as I examined the Dobies for ticks. "Of course, I'm the villain in the piece. I forced her to sell the ranch. Ha! She'd have crawled on her hands and knees all the way from Montana to get away from those damned turkeys. But I forced her. I'm the villain. Just like I want her to live with us so I can keep an eye on her. But she's got to have her own home. She doesn't realize she's nearly seventy years old. She could fall down and break her leg again and lie there in pain for days before anyone would find her. She's my mother. I couldn't stand that. But I don't care about her; I just want to get my hands on her money. As if she had that much."

I was enjoying myself. I rather miss seeing Mother in action. She pulled a pack of matches out of her pocket and burned two ticks off Cougar. "She's crazy as a loon, Kurt. Wait until you hear her new idea. She's going to have her hair dyed blond." Mother looked at me through narrowed eyes. I was aghast. Gratified, she went on. "That's right. Blond! As it is, she spends half the day in beauty parlors and dress shops. She's

12

so vain. And at her age. It's sad, watching her lose her dignity."

Mother deserved a point for the image of Mom as a blonde, but I've learned never to give her an advantage. I waved a stick above my head. Cougar and Puma barked expectantly. Mother looked at the house, grabbed my throwing arm, and dragged me into the grape arbor. She continued, "And she spends a fortune on clothes. She dresses so that everyone will think she's rich. I know what she's doing. She's trying to catch a husband. She's always had to have a man around, and she's willing to marry anything wearing pants to get one. Wait until you see her new boyfriend. He's so broken down he can hardly drag himself over to her house for a free meal. His wife's dead; he almost is. He's just the old fool to believe Mom's loaded. I wouldn't be surprised if they plan to get married." Mother tightened her lips in disgust at the idea of anyone's marrying for money. I thought of short, chubby, bald, ugly, rich DT. "Mom says she just dates Howard for companionship. Shit! She's got us for companionship. She's senile, Kurt, like her friends. Playing silly games all day—they're worse than kids. All they think about is having fun. Fun fun fun! Well, somebody's got to give up his fun to face reality, and as usual, it's me. Mom will marry this old fart or the next one that comes along, he'll be sick all the time, and she'll wear herself out taking care of him. All her money will be drained paying for his doctor bills and she'll be so overworked, she'll have a stroke herself. That's when the old goat will hobble out to find another dumb old bag who'll kill herself taking care of him. And Mom will be left all alone."

When we reached the center of the arbor, I saw a Monopoly board set upon a bench, decorated with green houses and red hotels. I knew that two faces peered at us from behind the thickest vines; Neil and Ricky were hiding from Mother and DT when they were supposed to be toiling in the fernery. The dogs wriggled with delight and crashed through the vines. I took Mother by the arm, and we strolled past the Monopoly board. "And do you know who's left to carry the burden? That's right. Me. Yes, me. Selfish Phyllis. The one who loves people for their money. I'll have to bring her here. I'll be the one who will have to take care of her. I'll be the one who will have to wipe her ass for her. You've got to think ahead. Things like that happen." Mother appeared grim, staring "things like that" in the face. "We'll put her in a nice home with people her age. She'll be comfortable and have security. It's the only thing to do."

We arrived at the pool, currently a home to Ricky's ducks, Bonnie and Clyde, and stood under a willow tree to escape the heat. As we slapped at mosquitoes, Mom joined us. "There you are. I've been looking for you everywhere." A silence ensued; then Mom spoke of the convenience of an air-conditioner during a Louisiana summer. Mother spoke of thinning the grape arbor, too handy for sons addicted to games and sloth. I spoke of Mother's hibiscus. Mom then exclaimed, "Do you know, there is the most terrible rattle in my car." She sighed and studied the hibiscus.

Mother said, "I'll have DT look at it when he comes in."

"Oh, no!" Mom exclaimed. "He'll be wore out after working hard all day." She sighed. We admired the oleanders. "I think the prices those men charge at the garage are just awful, don't you?"

"I'll have DT look at it when he comes in," Mother said.

"Oh, no!" Mom exclaimed. "He needs his rest. It's probably some little thing any man would know how to fix." She gazed wistfully at me.

"Would you like me to look at your car, Mom?" I asked.

"Oh, Kurtie, would you?" She smiled sweetly at Mother, who conceded the point, and carefully avoiding the peacocks, we walked up to the driveway. I started the motor. I heard no rattle. Mom did. "Doesn't it sound just awful?" I lifted the hood of the car and peered at the mess therein. I twisted a greasy lump, I turned an oily knob, and I slammed the hood shut. I cleaned my hands with the dust of the driveway. I started the motor again. The rattle remained inaudible.

"Isn't he the smartest thing," Mom observed. "I've always said that Kurtie could do anything he set his mind to. Why, he's so smart, I'll bet he could even fix my air-conditioner at home. It rattles, too."

"I'll take a look at it tomorrow, Mom."

"Oh, Kurtie, I'd hoped so that you would fix it today. I won't sleep a wink tonight if you don't. We have time before supper, don't we, Phyllis?" Mother appeared dubious. Mom smiled sweetly. I agreed to go just to spite Mother—she was beside herself with the desire to accompany us, but the roast needed basting. I drove, and we tore off in a cloud of dust that settled on Mother who, I noticed in the rearview mirror, glared after us until we turned onto Dead River Road. Mom sat back in the seat, heavy with victory; then she turned to look at me. She smiled. She looked out her window. She sighed. "Oh, Kurtie, I should never have sold the ranch. I loved that place. I wish we were still there."

"You've got to be kidding," I said. "Don't you remember those terrible winters? Those sorry turkeys. You'd be alone. And scared to death."

"One of you boys would come stay with me. You loved the ranch, too."

"Hardly enough to dig in for the winter."

"I was happy there. I used to go out on the porch and look at the mountains. They always inspired me."

"You hated it while you lived there. That's what you told me."

"I never told you any such thing. I loved Montana. I should never have let Phyllis talk me into selling." Mom lapsed into a reverie. "Kurtie, do you know what your mother wants me to do? I like to died when she told me. She wants me to sell my little home and move out to the fernery. Heavenly days! I don't want to live over a garage. I was stuck on that ranch for years with only those goofy turkeys for company, and I'm certainly not going to bury myself in a swamp now. I'm still young; I want to have fun. Wouldn't you?"

"Of course."

"I'd be scared to death out there alone in the night with the snakes and the bugs."

"And the gators."

"And the alligators."

"And the scorpions."

"I think it's just awful, don't you?"

"And the rats and the centipedes."

Mom leaned across the seat and peered at me. "What did Phyllis want to talk about during your walk?"

"She's worried that you won't have enough savings in case anything happens."

"Phyllis just wants to get her hands on my money. She says I spend too much. I don't. I still have twelve thousand dollars left from the ranch, plus my home and car. Promise you won't let on to your mother."

"I promise."

"That's three thousand for each of you kids. Dad worked

hard for that money, and he wanted you kids to get it—not DT. You're executor. You're going to have to take care of things when I'm gone. You'll be shed of me soon enough."

"You'll outlive us all, Mom." She enjoys hearing me say that.

"I hope not." She leaned back heavily. "I don't want to become feeble and helpless. Promise me you'll give me some pills when that happens."

"I promise."

"You just leave the pills where I can reach them."

"I promise. That's a nice-looking suit you're wearing."

Mom brightened. "Do you think so?"

"It looks real good on you."

"It should. It cost me two hundred dollars, but I think that if you want something nice, you have to pay for it, don't you?"

"I guess so."

Mom leaned forward to look into the rearview mirror. "Kurtie, I want to ask your honest opinion. Tell me the truth. How do you think I'd look as a blonde?"

I told her the truth. "Like an old whore."

She was sorry she'd asked. We drove into her carport. Nothing was said about the air-conditioner; although it was running full blast, I heard no rattle. Mom went to her secretary and pulled several folders from a drawer. "I want to talk business with you, Kurtie." I loathe talking business, but we went through everything: checking account, savings account, the titles to the house and the car, bonds, will, insurance policies (life, auto, fire, hurricane, and burial), and her record of expenditures. As I lingered over the fine print, Mom disappeared into the kitchen.

"Soup's on!" She began setting the table. "I've made all your favorites: cold ham, cornbread, apple butter, and sweet potato pie. And I bought a gallon of buttermilk, just in case."

"Gee, Mom. I'm expected home for supper."

Mom looked hurt. "I'd always hoped you would consider this your home."

"I do, I do. But I'm anxious to see Neil and Ricky . . . Listen, Mom, we could eat supper tonight at the house, and I'll come by tomorrow for lunch."

"And you'll stay for supper."

Shit! "I'll stay for supper."

With a martyred air, Mom put everything in the refrigerator;

then we returned to Belle Ombre. Supper brought back the memories: The roast was burnt. Mother lacks a light touch in the kitchen and prefers to serve hot dogs. Or spaghetti. Or peanut butter and jelly sandwiches. The Four Little Stroms and How They Grew. The dining arrangements hadn't changed; I ate with the adults, while Neil and Ricky messed in the kitchen. "They're nothing but pigs, that's why. If I had a trough, I'd feed them from that. It makes me sick to watch them eat." Mother bitched throughout supper, Mom exclaimed, and DT maundered. I should have preferred to slop with the hogs.

When the dishes were washed and put away, everyone gathered around the dining room table to play cards. Mother's slower now that she wears bifocals, and she's always been a bad sport; when even Neil scored higher than she, the games ended. After Mom went home, I followed the boys upstairs, where we talked deep into the night.

Everyone had gone to church by the time I woke up. I ate several bowls of Cheerios while catching up with my favorite series, "Can This Marriage Be Saved?" in Mother's back issues of *The Ladies' Home Journal*. At noon I borrowed Neil's car and drove to Mom's. She had set three places.

"Who's eating with us?" I asked.

The doorbell chimed. "Oh, good!" Mom cried. "That will be Howard." She opened the door to an elderly man in Bermuda shorts.

"Hello, darlin'," he said. They embraced.

"Howard, I want you to meet my grandson, Kurt Strom. Kurtie, this is Howard Smithfelt." Mr. Smithfelt looked me up and down, wheezed, hurtled over to the table, and began devouring the ham Mom had set out. I assumed from his grunting that he enjoyed it.

After lunch a lady with bright-blue hair dropped by. "So you're the grandson who's just dying to play bridge." I glared at Mom. She smiled sweetly. The four of us sat down to cards. Howard hawked moist and lengthy coughs in my face at three-minute intervals. Fawn tittered inanely throughout four rubbers. Mom batted her eyes at Howard. I kept score.

In spite of it all, I was glad to have stayed through supper. Mother had exhausted her culinary repertoire with the roast beef and had boiled hot dogs. (Not that I missed anything— she boiled some more the following night.) After the kitchen was cleaned up, Mother sent the boys upstairs to do their homework. School didn't open for another month, so I knew she wanted to talk. She led me into the living room. DT followed us. They settled on the sofa. Mother lighted a cigarette. She looked at me. "So how did you find Mom?"

I answered truthfully. "The same as always."

"Did you meet Howard?"

"Yes," I replied.

"What did you think of him?"

I thought it best to change the subject. "Mom doesn't know that you plan to put her in an old folks' home. She thinks you want her to live out here."

Mother put on her practical look. "We're only thinking of her own good. The way she's flinging her money in every direction, there isn't going to be a penny left. DT wants to put more land under fern. Mom's money would provide the capital. She'd get five percent interest. If she cared about anything besides having fun, she could see the wisdom of our plan."

I disagreed. "It seems to me that she can invest or spend her money as she wishes."

"You're just like her, Kurt. You live for today and to Hell with tomorrow. Well, somebody's got to think about tomorrow and, as usual, it's me. I'll bet a pretty penny that she doesn't have twenty thousand left in her savings. I know she shows her bankbook to you. Am I right or am I wrong?"

"Gosh, Mother. I never pay her no mind when she talks finances."

"I don't doubt it; you're so damn dumb about money. It's a crying shame, watching her throw away everything she got for the ranch."

I thought of my own savings account. I had never touched the ten thousand the Tigers gave me to sign with them, and working on the ranch all those summers, I had accumulated five thousand more. "Instead of making Mom unhappy, why don't you borrow from me?"

Mother snubbed out her cigarette. She glanced at DT; then she looked at me. "We already have."

"You're shittin' me." Silence. "How much?"

Mother went into a giddy Southern belle act, touching her hair and blouse with quick, limp wrists. She glanced at me to see if it was going over and gave up in mid-act. She lighted another cigarette. "All of it."

18

I'd wondered about the beach house in Gulf Shores and Mother's new Lincoln. "You withdrew my savings without asking me?"

"You didn't need it, off playing baseball. If you had gone to college, like I wanted you to, it would be a different matter. But no, you have to play games for a living. Fun fun fun! That's all you think about."

"You took my savings out of the bank and never even asked me?"

"Kurt, try and talk sense for once in your life. You should be glad you can help out. And your money is as safe as Mom's would be. DT and I feel it's best to get the affair done with. We've engaged a lawyer who has already begun proceedings. Reverend Clifton has expressed his willingness to testify to Mom's senility. Now, Kurt, don't you worry. Aunt Billie will take good care of her."

Aunt Billie! She manages a nursing home in Birmingham, a filthy old house with dingy little rooms that reek of urine and are filled with ancient, distracted people who wander off in search of long-dead husbands or wives. I should hate to think of Mom's being isolated among the toothless and the mindless. I gave an opinion. "I think what you're doing is wrong."

DT said, "It doesn't matter what you think. Your grandmother is going to be put away."

Mother spoke before I could. "This is hard for Kurt, DT. He remembers Mom as she was before Dad died. He understands what must be done." DT stroked the legs Mother had draped across his lap. She aired several personal grievances against Mom, the most outstanding being a lack of respect for DT, hardly a symptom of a deteriorating mind. Finally, Mother stated that Mom's incarceration was as good as done, and I might as well accept the fact. She leaned back against her pillows and smiled at DT, who continued to stroke her legs.

I recalled a maxim learned at Mother's knee: *Hit them where it hurts.* "Mother," I said softly. She glanced at me, studied my face, and sat up to do battle. "I believe we have before us an emotionally charged issue. We might do well to obtain an outside opinion or two. I'll list the pros and cons of stripping Mom of everything she owns before shipping her to Aunt Billie; then I'll send copies of the list to the minister of every church in Bonifay, to the president of each circle in the garden club, and to the Grand Worthy Matron of the Eastern Star. If the majority believes you're in the right, I'll help you pack Mom's bags."

Mother cursed. She wept. She threatened to hold her breath. "Viler than a serpent's tooth is an ungrateful child."

As I smirked, DT said, "And you can get your smart ass right the goddam hell out of my house."

Mother let out her breath and stared. "Your house. *Your* house!"

DT mumbled, "Aww, Hon, you know what I mean."

"Marry a widder woman, use her money to fix up your dump of a place, and then throw her children into the snow."

"Aww, Hon. Come on, now."

"Far be it from me to clutter up *your* newly painted house with my children. NEIL! RICKY! FRONT AND CENTER! You just wanted *your* house cluttered up with the furniture I bought with the money Will left for his poor orphaned children. *Your house!*" The kids appeared in the archway. "Neil, put the silver and the photo albums in the car. Ricky, gather up the dogs and cats. Everybody pack your bags. We're leaving DT."

The kids stood with blank faces as Mother swept past them and up the stairs. DT shuffled behind her, moaning low. "Aww, Hon. Don't get upset, Hon . . ."

Need I tell you that we're all still at Belle Ombre, although Mother has moved into one of the guest rooms, where she's enjoying herself, reading all night with a box of candy beside the bed. I must pack my bags anyway. I leave in the morning for five weeks in North Carolina, where I am to learn jungle lore, followed by a year in Vietnam and lots of fun fun fun.

Relentlessly,

Kurt

BELLE OMBRE
DEAD RIVER ROAD
BONIFAY, LOUISIANA
12 August 66

Dear Mom,

You demanded a copy of my will, so Neil will drop this by when I'm gone. I don't want to face your wrath. I should never have given Mother power as executrix. Such an absurd descent into filial faith obliges me to correction, but I haven't the time to spare.

All things considered, I believe Mother to be thoroughly cowed by the threat of social embarrassment, but you might do worse than putting your affairs in Guy Perrone's hands. A bachelor, Guy might come cheaper than your lawyer, who has four daughters to put through college. Guy and Mother are old adversaries and his documented interest in my baseball career extends to my personal well-being. Your happiness is part of my personal well-being.

And I'm laying said well-being on the line. I guess I enlisted in the Navy to honor Daddy, his brothers, and all those boys you and Dad and Mother hated to see going off to get killed. You mustn't worry; the Vietnamese conflict is hardly the holocaust of World War II. My job is to care for the sick and the lame. I doubt that I'll be in any danger, although I shouldn't mind a scratch on the arm got from some daring sally behind enemy lines. I'd walk into the house next September with my arm in a sling and decorations plastered across my chest. That would be nice, but I'm not studying wounds at all. Not my own.

Love,

Kurt

MOFFET POINT
CAMP LEJEUNE, NORTH CAROLINA
16 August 66

My dear Paul,

I've slipped again into the abominations of lust and lechery. And I try so hard.

During a farewell tour of Boston, I drifted into Sporter's Bar, a vile place filled with sin and temptation. Eyes smouldering with the coals of Hell glowered at me. A beautiful blond, blue-eyed angel wafted by with a suggestion that I leave the snake pit to enjoy the view from his high-rise apartment. "The nearer to Heaven," I thought, "and why not?" As we gazed over the lights of Nineveh, a demon within me whispered evil intentions into the ear of the angel, obviously of the fallen fraternity. Just as the fruit was ripening, the telephone rang. "My lover, the priest," murmured the angel. They chatted for an hour. "Yes, I am alone," lied my angel between his pretty teeth. I wished he was, and an interlude later, the wish became a fact.

Walking along, wrapped within a cloak of thought, I never noticed that Satan had led me back to Sporter's. A tall, lean, bearded student from Paris cajoled me into entering his apartment, a dungeon furnished with mirrors, whips, and a huge bed covered in black leather. The student uttered unprintable demands. I fell to my knees in supplication. The student took advantage of my position. He expressed his creed: chastisement. He slapped me. "Crawl across the floor, faggot, and kiss my ass." Although that is hardly my bag, I can get into it. Flushed with power, the student reached for a whip. I can't get into it that much. I slapped him, which couldn't have pleased him more. But whatever else could I have done? A man must either imitate the vicious or hate them. The student was so overcome by my unnatural brutality, he grabbed the whip and began to wield it. I felt that contrition had been given its due, so I knocked him down with my fist, wriggled into my whites, and walked out the door. The student leaned over the windowsill, butt-naked and blood streaming from his nose as he screeched, "Come back, sailor. I'm sorry. Come back." The good Christian people enjoying a balmy summer evening on Beacon Hill appeared horrified. I picked up my seabag at the bus station, climbed aboard an MTA bound for the airport, and bought a standby ticket for New Orleans.

After five days of Mother's Southern hospitality, I bought a midnight ticket for North Carolina via Greyhound and sat down in the middle of a sparsely populated bus. I noticed a sturdy soldier across the aisle perusing the novel *Candy*. Its degeneracy had aroused him. He became aware that I had noticed his arousal. Entangled within a web of lust, he scowled. He compounded his sin by reading further. He looked at me again, closed the book, and turned off his overhead light. No one sat near us. I moved across the aisle to share his seat and, after a brief introduction, offered to relieve the GI of his prurience. "The Lord moves in mysterious ways," I said to myself, as I unbuttoned his fly.

I changed buses in Atlanta. At the back of the bus, his face

22

hidden in shadow, sat a likely companion. As the bus roared down the highway, I rested my head upon my likely companion's broad shoulder. Against his strong chest. His flat belly. His hard thighs. His bulging lap. Touchdown.

Later, in the Charlotte, North Carolina, bus station, I saw my new friend emerging from the rest room. In the full light, his body remained admirable, but the spotted face should have strained a mother's love. As I walked up to him, his pale face flushed and his pink spots whitened, and he hissed, "Stay away from me, faggot."

I could only assume that he hoped to wound me.

Relentlessly,

Kurt

MOFFET POINT
CAMP LEJEUNE, NORTH CAROLINA
17 August 66

Dear Mom,

As the bus left the station, I curled up in the backseat and slept most of the way to North Carolina. You were correct in warning me against Greyhound terminal restaurants. I looked at the congealed salads, the congealed gravies, and the congealed pies; then I bought an RC Cola from the machine and retreated to the bus, where I dug into your most satisfying food basket. I'm much obliged.

I must agree with Mother when she protests your working among your flowers at high noon. You become dizzy; your cheeks flush scarlet. That would be very nice, your having a stroke and becoming paralyzed. What fun you'd be. You once said, to my dismay, that you wanted people to feel sorry for you. I prefer distance between me, the sick, and the lame. Work, if you must, in the cool of the morning.

It's never cool here, but I sleep every night between clean sheets and I eat three large meals every day. Although the food would ordinarily dismay anyone who has dined upon the splen-

23

dors of your table, I was raised on Mother's cooking, too, and I feel quite at home.

Love,

Kurt

Chloe dear,

I should have called when I passed through Atlanta, but I arrived at the bus station at 3 A.M. I've been taught never to telephone a lady after 8 P.M. Mother says that by 8 P.M., a lady has decided how she will spend her evening. Mother's certain that she is well versed in the etiquette for a Southern gentlewoman, another example of the distance between reality and illusion. Nevertheless, she's my mother, and I remembered her advice. And I had a vision of you spitting nails. I thought it better to refrain from an early morning call.

I have run into an old buddy, however, who brought his car to Lejeune. I chatted him into a tasteful fantasy sweetened by the charms of Georgia peaches. We'll arrive in Atlanta on Friday night.

I wish it were Friday now. This is a dreary place. Mom took a tour by bus through the Smokies last October to view the foliage. I must agree with her that autumn in the Appalachians of North Carolina ranks among Nature's masterpieces. Regrettably, it's summer, and I am situated at the opposite end of the state where Nature has been less inspired, in a desolate place halfway between Cape Fear and the Dismal Swamp. The colors here are not those God has wrought: the red puffy eyes of hard-ass lifers, the white strained faces of flabby sailors, and the drone of one thousand corpsmen moaning the blues. The barren landscape is a lifeless brown; the buildings upon it are a tattered gray. And olive-green is in overwhelming profusion.

The walls and ceilings of our ancient barracks were long ago and never again painted a sickly hospital-green. Our blankets are brownish-green. Our food bears a green, moldy tinge.

24

Green bugs share our food and blankets. The men surrounding me are green in complexion, attire, and years. I hate to complain, but after all those winters spent working in the fernery and all those summers trimming sixty-five thousand Christmas trees on the ranch, the color green is wormwood and gall to me.

> Relentlessly,
>
> Kurt

MOFFET POINT
CAMP LEJEUNE, NORTH CAROLINA
19 August 66

Arch,

Envy is one of the Seven Deadly Sins, good buddy. I'm flattered of course, but let's be completely fair about this, shall we? I can picture your reclining on an easy chair, a cold beer in your hand. You stare wistfully out the window at the splendor of Mt. Rainier and sigh, "Kurt sure is the lucky one. He's going to sail the ocean blue. Glamour and excitement! He'll surf off Diamond Head and dance the hula hula on Bora Bora. He'll see Fujiyama through the cherry blossoms and go to the supermarket in Old Peking."

Your envy, old sport, is misdirected. You've been taken in by my penchant for fantasy. Let's give a nod toward reality. My buddy Babich could enlighten you. He salaams to reality. My fantasies end happily, like fairy tales; Babich's reality plumbs the lower depths.

I met Babich in Corps School. He was a model for us all. A brewery invited everyone over twenty-one in our company to drink free beer at a polka party in Milwaukee. Four men out of a class of sixty were eligible; only Babich declined the invitation. He wanted to study. And he did. And without ever displaying any obnoxious smarts, he ranked first in the class.

"Where ever did all that work get him?" you may ask, and I'll tell you. He got to Boston, as I did, and an assignment on Orthopedics. He busted his hump under a squatty shrew of a nurse as he cared for his patients, many of whom had been badly mangled in Vietnam and were long-term, restless, and cranky. Babich's mercy, however, was strained only by Mr. Winston. A thirty-year-old man who looks sixty, Mr. Winston was dying of arthritis, of all things, slowly clenching himself into a tiny bag of painful bones. His fretful voice echoed in every corner Babich tried to hide in. Babich would snub out his cigarette, grit his teeth, and go to Mr. Winston.

"Corpsman, could I *please* have a glass of water?" Babich always went to the sink and brought a glass of water back to those skinny, twisted hands. Babich would hold the glass as Mr. Winston sipped. Babich begrudged Mr. Winston every drop.

"Kurt, I can't stand it," he would say. "I'll do anything. I'll empty their bedpans, I'll scrub their assholes, and I'll help the doctors change the dressings on their disgusting wounds; I don't mind any of that. But Mr. Winston and his glass of water . . . He drives me crazy. I want to ram a hose down his throat and turn on the water full force. I want to take his food and smear it all over his face. I hate him."

So Babich would work all day and then rush back to the barracks to tell me all about it: Mr. Winston, the shrewish nurse, his ill luck with women (no luck, really), and, above all, about Vietnam. Babich lived in a bleak world to begin with, and his coming encounter with Ho Chi Minh brought him to new depths of depression. After our orders arrived, he lay on his bunk, chain-smoking and listening to his jazz collection, and stared at the ceiling. A conviction developed; his demise seemed inevitable. His pessimism began to get to me, and I avoided him until one day, as I sneaked past his quarters on my way to supper, a nicotine-stained forefinger beckoned. Babich invited me to sit down; I squatted rather than risk having to change my whites after sitting on his gray sheets. He had solved his dilemma; he would barter with the enemy.

"Kurt," he croaked, "I can find no ecstasy in the idea of death. Can you understand that? I feel that to escape it, I must make an offering to the Cong. As you know, I am aware of my physical ugliness. Only too aware." Sadly, he shook his head. "Nevertheless, upon consideration, I find an affection for every repulsive part of my body. I refuse to give up my eyes, my ears, my vital organs, or my sex organs." He looked down at his decaying shorts and gurgled obscenely. "My arms are necessary for many activities; smoking cigarettes, changing records, finger-fucking . . . Heh heh heh. But I figure anyone

26

as lazy and unathletic as I could muddle along without his legs, although I should prefer to keep one as a souvenir. I've done some research and found that if I am right-handed, then I am left-legged, unless I am abnormal, which is food for thought. I am right-handed so, hopefully, my right leg is my most expendable portion. Therefore, so that I won't be killed, I am willing to donate my right leg to the Viet Cong."

His future settled, Babich stopped chanting "I Have a Rendezvous with Death" and began rereading "Howl," an old favorite; I skipped supper to lie on my rack and stare at the ceiling. My fantasies faded into a gray swirling mist. I could no longer envision myself as a shining knight setting off to defend the Holy Grail. Babich is a good guy and all that, but he does tend to take the ginger out of one's dreams of glory.

Relentlessly,

Kurt

MOFFET POINT
CAMP LEJEUNE, NORTH CAROLINA
23 August 66

Chloe dear,

Amid bawdy ballads sung fortissimo, Wendell would suddenly recall another specimen of your culinary skill, upon which he would rapture until his repertoire of superlatives was exhausted. I'd pass along his compliments, but I can't remember them; I was distracted by his determination to challenge every approaching vehicle to a game of "Chicken." No torture conceived by the Viet Cong could possibly compare with that test of my stoicism. Nevertheless, it was good to see you, gentle cuz.

Wendell was an excellent companion at Corps School. Every day he would add another chapter to the tale of his high school affair with a majorette. "Mandy was dynamite, Kurt. Just dynamite. She had short, thick, muscular legs. After her parents went to bed, we'd take off our clothes and get on the sofa. Mandy would wrap those muscular legs around me and turn into a passionate beast. I'd bring sex-technique books, and we would act them out. She was such a passionate beast."

27

Mandy, however, was back in Philadelphia, and Wendell trained at Great Lakes Naval Training Center. One time he accompanied three other corpsmen to North Chicago, a nearby conglomeration of dives and clip joints, where they met four sleazies. The men bought the sleazies drinks and eventually retired to an apartment. All but Wendell and his sleazy disappeared into bedrooms; she wouldn't cooperate.

"So what did you do?" I asked.

"He beat off all over the table," giggled one of the luckier men.

Wendell expostulated indignantly. "But I made her watch."

My best to Marvin.

Relentlessly,

Kurt

Dear Mom,

I visited Chloe in Atlanta this past weekend. She's picked up a little. I'd never met her husband Marvin: He's fat and jolly, too. You'd like him; he'd remind you of Dad. Marvin is an electrician, he enjoys sitting down to an ample table, and he's subject to getting drunk now and then. They held a party for me. Chloe sends her love.

I made the excursion with Mickey Wendell, a classmate last winter at Corps School and again here. He had such a good time in Atlanta that he has decided to spend each of his remaining weekends in a different Southern capital city. This coming Friday he leaves for Richmond.

My buddy Babich from Boston got orders for Nam, too. I've told you about him. He's from New Bedford, Massachusetts, the home of Captain Ahab. (Remember buying Neil and Ricky those drapes and bedspreads with whales all over them? Captain Ahab was the man with the pegleg and a telescope.)

I'm glad to hear that your blood pressure is down. Don't

work in your garden when the sun is high. I want you looking right smart when I come home next year.

Love,

Kurt

MOFFET POINT
CAMP LEJEUNE, NORTH CAROLINA
25 August 66

Arch,

I am a grunt. A reluctant grunt. A lot of grunts are reluctant. My buddy Babich is the most reluctant grunt of all.

A grunt is a marine, as a soldier is a doggie, an airman a birdie, and a sailor a squid. I live reluctantly among grunts of every race, color, and creed... I take that back. Only one creed inspires a marine: *A hard cock has no conscience,* unless one hails from the Deepest South where cock means pussy, but I think that's just a matter of semantics and not of religion, as Marinedom is.

A marine will answer to "grunt" and to "jarhead." I like "jarhead"; the word has a nice ring to it. But I prefer "grunt." I guess I prefer "grunt" because when a marine is nearby, grunts are the sounds I hear. Marines march past continuously, always in groups, and each marine is in step with the rest of the group; as they march, they grunt. As they pig down food in the mess hall, they grunt. They grunt their satisfaction after all that marching and eating. They grunt their contentment as they scratch their heads, their asses, and their balls. My buddy Babich and I have conjectured that after insufficient foreplay, a jarhead's lovemaking begins with a short grunt during primary penetration and ends fifteen pile-driving seconds later with an elongated grunt leading immediately into a woofing, leg-shaking slumber.

If they survive, little grunts mature into Red-Necked, Many-Medaled Sergeants. One recognizes a Red-Necked, Many-Medaled Sergeant by his grunt, which is deeper, hoarser, and even more penetrating than that of a little grunt. The Red-Necked Many-Medaled Sergeant's call goes, "You *WILL* get a *HAR*cut. You *WILL* get a *HAR*cut."

My buddy Babich and I undertook a promenade the other day. During our stroll, we came upon some little grunts at play. "Bang! Bang! You're dead," type of games. (Autumn moves anon, and the Marine Corps prepares to reap a muddy, bloody harvest of cannon fodder.) Silently, we viewed the spectacle for a few minutes. I was about to turn to Babich with a quip when suddenly a ferocious, slavering, red-eyed, Red-Necked, Many-Medaled Sergeant swooped down upon us.

"I am Sarge, the Great and Terrible."

Babich and I replied with one voice. "We are corpsmen, small and meek."

Sarge said, "You *WILL* get a *HAR*cut."

Babich flung himself to the ground, buried his head in the mud, and pretended he wasn't there.

Once more Sarge roared, "You *WILL* get a *HAR*cut."

I leaped over Babich's quivering body, sprinted to the base barber shoppe, hurled myself into a chair, and advised the barber, "You *WILL* give me a *HAR*cut." And he did. He shaved me bald. It was the most depressing thing that's even happened to me. But what's done is done, I always say, and whatever will be, will be. Like the song. Babich often worries about whatever is to be. He took one look at my *HAR*cut and crawled upon the barrack stove to moan.

Coming events cast their shadow before him.

Relentlessly,

Kurt

MOFFET POINT
CAMP LEJEUNE, NORTH CAROLINA
26 August 66

My dear Paul,

I'm hardly lonely—where ever did you get that idea? A thousand corpsmen and vast honks of grunts surround me. And my buddy Babich has accompanied me to this side of Paradise. Unwillingly, to be sure, although he volunteered, an action that appalls him for its stupidity. I talked him into it. I'll tell you how it happened.

When they asked us to put in for sea duty, they gave us a

globe and told us to pick a destination. Babich rested content in Boston, but if he had to leave, he desired safety and red-light districts. He decided to go to Southern Europe. He asked me how to get there. I swore to him that scuttlebutt had it that the surest way across the Atlantic was by volunteering for Vietnam; you were then dispatched immediately to the Mediterranean Fleet to regain your sanity. After living for a year under military thinking, it seemed logical, so Babich requested the Land of the Yellow Peril as his next duty station. Unfortunately, he was misinformed.

I tried to cheer him. "Look at it from a positive viewpoint, buddy. I do. I think of myself as Destiny's plaything, a piece of driftwood floating down the River of Life."

Babich looked at me through jaundiced eyes. "Kurt, you're fucked." Still, he did try to see it my way. It didn't work. It just gave him a new metaphor for misery.

"Kurt, your River of Life is like that Bayou Douche where you live. It doesn't go forwards; it doesn't go backwards. You just drift in slow circles. My River of Life is polluted and packed with treacherous ice floes. Rocks, snags, and whirlpools confront me. And now I'm poised on the edge of a bottomless waterfall."

Among the other tragedies of Babich's existence is that he will die unlaid. He lusts fervently, but is too sensitive to "...force such ugliness upon a woman." He has thick lips, buck teeth, greasy hair, an unwashed body...I suppose I should stop; after all, I am his best friend at the moment, but to those of us who study physical attractiveness, he is unsightly.

Babich suspects that his physical welfare ranks low upon the Marine Corps' list of priorities. He bunks below me, and every morning he shakes me awake. "Kurt! It's the beginning of another terrible day." He lullabies me to sleep every night. "Kurt! We're one day closer to Nam." We are together all the time.

Another man who worked in Boston was transferred to Lejeune with us, and Babich, who has a fierce loyalty to the known, has bound us together in a sad sack triumvirate. I hardly knew Stokes in Boston. He was assigned to a medical ward under a blob-nosed nurse with "sensual thighs" and hung out with a crowd of lumbering, bulky, thick-tongued men who flunked every test of their wit.

One day, and apparently out of the blue, Stokes invited me

to brunch with his mother at their summer place in Newport. I had nothing to do that morning, as he knew, but I declined the invitation. The main reason was sloth, but I felt the invitation to be bad form. Stokes had intimate friends among the proletariat, and as a comparative stranger, I was to be the first of his fellow corpsmen to make the excursion to Newport; furthermore, I'd once overheard his bragging about beating up queers on Boston Common. He continued to press the invitation, embarrassing me and an uninvited Babich. My refusal stood firm.

I think Stokes has yet to forgive me. Despite a great show of camaraderie—arms draped across my shoulders and intimate, roguish grins flashed my way—I feel uneasy with him. Physically, he attracts me: lean taut body, open intelligent face, pale hair and blue eyes . . . And he's rather dashing and carries an aura of ruthlessness. Were I to succumb to his charm, however, I'm fairly certain Stokes would feel duty-bound to inform Babich. I should hate to have my buddy hurt: His is an honest abhorrence of faggotry.

Here comes the old abhorrer now. We're due at the enlisted men's club for a couple of brews, and I've still got curlers in my hair.

Relentlessly,

Kurt

MOFFET POINT
CAMP LEJEUNE, NORTH CAROLINA
30 August 66

Dear Mom,

It has rained all week. The barracks smell sour and damp. I'm glad I brought a travel bag filled with paperbacks. Currently, I'm reading Henry James, who wrote long novels to be perused during inclement weather.

No, the food is the same, but I've grown accustomed to its taste. And I've learned to eat it as a marine. Firstly, one stands in line for an hour or so, whiling away the time with good chat. Secondly, one holds out his little metal tray and watches tidbits get slung upon it. Thirdly, one aligns himself with his buddies

32

in a V formation to push through the herd of corpsmen crowding the mess hall. If the offense is successful, the trio realigns into a pincer formation over a table being used by smaller and weaker corpsmen and threatens to spit into their dessert should they dawdle. (While hovering in expectant expectoration, it behooves one to guard his aforementioned little metal tray with arms and elbows, so that larger and stronger corpsmen cannot spit into one's own dessert or, worse, steal it.) After the smaller and weaker corpsmen have finally retreated, one sits and sticks one's face into the middle of the little metal tray, and he vacuums his food into his mouth. The food that clings to one's face is wiped off with the sleeves. One cleans his sleeves by rubbing them into his hair. The entire process brings back fond memories of Neil and Ricky.

Speaking of hair, I have none. I wanted to look like a marine, too, so I asked the barber to cut it short. He complied with fervor.

Mother wrote to say that she and DT plan to drive up to see me one last time. Now that I am bald, I look rather less than how I'd prefer to look when seen for the last time. My reply should discourage her.

Love,

Kurt

MOFFET POINT
CAMP LEJEUNE, NORTH CAROLINA
31 August 66

Chloe dear,

My buddy Babich cherishes jazz, but he can diversify into rock should a song tickle his fancy. For several days he has been croaking the opening lyric of a song by the Rolling Stones apparently entitled "My Dear Lady Jane." I'd accepted this devotion and his incessant repetitions as one of Babich's eccentricities, but last night the words registered. You must have read *Lady Chatterley's Lover*. The gamekeeper refers to his prick as "John Thomas" and to Lady C's pussy as "Lady Jane." Perhaps I'm wrong about that, but there aren't any reference books at hand. And who around here would know anyway? So that is what I told Babich. He was delighted. He considers it a good sign. I'd known that he feels music gives his thoughts form and content; I hadn't known that he feels music to be an equivalent to Tarot cards.

I find little content in jazz, so I've rarely listened to it. This ignorance flabbergasts Babich, but he feels that because I accept his flaws as a human being, can he do less? Nevertheless, his tolerance is strained by my penchant for musical comedy. I'd refrained from forcing this penchant upon him until today.

We were standing in the chow line. Babich was depressed—nothing unusual—and time passes during my attempts to cheer him. Today I tried by conceiving a musical comedy about Vietnam. Several titles occurred to me: *Hellzapoppin'*, *The Cong and I*, but I finally decided on *Maim*.

The three characters who head the cast are Blokes, a heroic tenor; Baldy, a stalwart baritone; and Cabbage, a beguiled and whimpering basso profundo who groans out plaintive dirges such as his swan song:

(To the tune of "Smoke Gets in Your Eyes.")

> *They asked me how I knew*
> *That my life was through*
> *To them I replied,*
> *"This bullet in my side*
> *Cannot be denied . . ."*

As a chorus of high-kicking grunts sings "God Bless America," little yellow angels wearing red, white, and blue robes descend to walk Cabbage up Jacob's Ladder to that Great Marine Base in the sky.

To my utter amazement, Babich failed to find diversion in *Maim*, but now that I think about it, perhaps it would work better as a movie.

Relentlessly,

Kurt

Arch,

We shall soon set out for Vietnam, unprepared for combat duty. Except for elementary calisthenics even my buddy Babich could surmount, our only physical training has been a three-mile hike to an overnight campout in the woods, where we played soldiers and Indians. I underwent more hardship carrying a trombone in the Bonifay Christmas parade. We do march briskly to classes: "Viper Identification," "Plague Symptoms," and "Corpse Care." (Step number two of "Corpse Care" instructs us to shove the dogtags belonging to the cadaver between its upper front teeth.) Then there is "Pitfalls of the Byways." Our very own Red-Necked, Many-Medaled Sergeant took us on a trip through a disturbing Disneyland of booby traps, none of which appeared conspicuous and all of them annoying. One I'd prefer to avoid is a cunningly camouflaged hole in which a sharpened stake covered with diseased shit awaits the unwary. This is called a punji stick. (Pungent? Punish?) Babich muttered to himself for hours.

To Babich's utter amazement, a few gung-ho guys have infiltrated the company. (Gung-ho = avid for punishment.) Most will be attached to the Second Marine Division in the Caribbean and are excited by the ordeal that impends for the rest of us. Their favorite class is "Field First Aid," during which they gallop about bandaging the artificial injuries worn by more lethargic classmates enacting battlefield casualties. Stokes, a friend of ours, caught the gung-ho fever and galloped about with the best of them. For a day or so, Babich felt betrayed by such unseemly enthusiasm; then he decided that Stokes was the exception that proved the rule. Babich's rule: *Discretion is the better part of valor*. He and I watch the activity as we lounge under shade trees, languidly disputing the details of hideous plastic wounds tied to our legs. We have our choice, but we prefer leg wounds. You must lie still for head wounds and are unable to brush away flies.

Yesterday we ran through an afternoon of battle conditions. Supposedly real bullets flew over our heads at a height of three feet, while we crawled through mud, under barbed wire, and over shell shocked comrades. I enjoyed it, despite Babich's

35

dark prophecies of things to come. Then we climbed a webbed net that hung from a high wall. We decided that the wall represented a ship, but why ever would we climb onto a ship in Vietnam? I liked climbing the net anyway, although the wall was twenty feet high and we had to jump off the other side into a pile of sand. I held my nose, took a breath, and paused to reconsider. Stokes, in a fit of impatience, pushed me over the edge; then he pushed a trembling Babich, yelled "TIMBER!" and jumped off after us, as Babich and I scuttled frantically out of his way.

We usually pass our mornings sitting in a classroom, just what I hated about school, except they provide neither textbooks nor study sheets at Lejeune. We must pick it up as they throw it at us. Babich and I have difficulty with the Grunt dialect, and we miss a word here and there. We are too shy to demand a repetition, and the men who do understand, or don't care, glare at anyone who asks a question. Babich and I never quite know what is happening. School has always been like that for me. I couldn't understand something that everyone else could, the class would move on as I fell steadily behind, and I would finally flunk the course. I don't want to flunk Vietnam.

The portents say I will. At the moment I am flunking "Backpack II." I did well in "Backpack I." The course curriculum consisted of unbuckling a large canvas sack, opening it, and pulling out all the stuff it contained. I was good at that. But in "Backpack II" you must put all that stuff back inside the canvas sack and close it up. There's the rub. I try, and try again, but I never have enough room for everything. Stokes can't bear to watch Babich and me fumble and grumble. He pushes us aside to put things to right. I don't think I'm going to learn anything that way.

"Rifling" and "Pistols" turned out to be a blast. (Ha ha!) After a lot of trouble taking them apart and putting them together (see above paragraph), we went to the firing range. The Red-Necked, Many-Medaled Sergeant in charge yelled at our ignorance of firearms and of the years of target practice needed to elevate us to mediocrity; then he threw up his hands and strode away in disgust. The Red-Necked, Many-Medaled Sergeant who replaced him told us that pistol practice is a farce— pistols have little range and are wildly inaccurate, unless used by an expert. And he told us that the VC feel very good when they kill corpsmen, and they can recognize a corpsman by the pistol he carries. We broke down and rebuilt our pieces several more times. A firearm, in Grunt, is a piece.

At night we spend stimulating evenings in the barracks, where one may read, talk, play cards, stare blankly, or clean his piece. Mild amusement can be got ragging those who will pass a soft year in the Caribbean. Witty cries of "Coward!" resound. Enthusiasm for such repartee has lagged, however, since an exasperated and very enormous "coward" loomed over a group of his tormenters to remark, "I don't want to hear another word from you, Dead Men."

Relentlessly,

Kurt

MOFFET POINT
CAMP LEJEUNE, NORTH CAROLINA
2 September 66

My dear Paul,

This huge base teems with spirited young men, and a person should think to revel in carnality. A certain solace is afforded by BAMs, but they dismay even the easily pleased. (A BAM is a lady marine. Try to imagine Ernest Borgnine with tits.) The privacy for self-abuse is impossible to find. What ever do they do with it? Something must be happening somewhere.

I try very hard to avoid thinking about sex. I read books. I write letters. I lie on my rack and make elephants and horsies from the mildew stains on the ceilings. I count sheep jumping over fences; the flock turns into a high school football team. "Maybe through activity," I think to myself. I can't go outside; a heavy drizzle falls upon Lejeune. I take a turn within the barrack. Men lie upon their racks and read, write letters, clean their pieces, or stare blankly. Should I stop to chat, I would only hear about home or of the heroes they will soon become. I walk through the passage connecting our barrack with that of our sister company. Men lie about in various stages of dishabille as they read, write, stare . . . I return to my barrack.

Babich sleeps off a depression—no chance of distraction there. Wendell sits immersed in an atlas; his current compulsion is to list all the towns in America that have names derived from European cities: e.g., Rome, Georgia, and Moscow, Idaho. I recommend Troy, Ithaca, and Syracuse, New York, before moving on to visit Stokes. He bunks in a small annex at the end of the barrack. He is alone in the annex. He lounges in his undershorts on an upper bunk. I lean against the bunk. My arms rest upon the mattress, and my head rests upon my arms. Stokes turns on his side to face me. His pelvis is six inches away. He smiles. I tear myself away. I try very hard to avoid thinking about sex.

So I take a shower. The water is cold, the better to make us grunt. I prolong my agony under the showerhead to converse with a stunning cowboy from South Dakota, while he washes several pairs of socks as well as himself. His attention is held by those soapy socks. We are alone in the shower room. I can rivet my eyes upon his desirability without his knowing.

Stokes enters, smiling. He watches me, but I refuse to let him catch my eyes off guard. I rinse off quickly and leave the shower room. As I resentfully dry myself, I notice several men on the floor of the washroom, poring over a sexy picture book. I squat behind them, peering over their shoulders at shots of undraped lovelies playing volleyball.

Stokes emerges from the shower and joins me behind the little group of lusting squids. After a minute or so, I look up to acknowledge him and find myself jowls to balls and in the shade of an unending erection. Feeling that its open display is for my benefit, I hesitate, and before I sneak another glance, I check the direction of Stokes' attention. He looks at neither the book nor me, but at a precise and excessively fastidious member of our company who shaves in a mirror opposite us. Miss Priss returns Stokes' grin. Stokes stands up and slowly wraps a towel around his waist, never taking his eyes from the mirror. The Master-at-Arms comes by just then and disperses us, and I can catch my breath.

Stokes and Miss Priss become inseparable. Good merchandise finds a ready buyer.

Relentlessly,

Kurt

Arch,

Several of us decided to get away from jarheads for a couple of days—we may have no further opportunities for a year. So we drove to Charleston, South Carolina. We got away from marines only to find ourselves surrounded by sailors. A capsule review of Charleston: tars and tar babies.

We disobeyed the rules: Charleston is off limits. Regulations state that written authorization is needed to travel more than a hundred miles from Lejeune. They prefer that we revel in nearby Wilmington, North Carolina. Scuttlebutt convinced me that Wilmington is as dead as Pinkville, Kentucky, on a rainy Monday night and though I fondly recall the scintillating midnights we spent after games in Pinkville playing the pinball machines at the bus station, I am more sophisticated now and look forward to baser pursuits. Wilmington may have all the depravity five servicemen could desire, but I fucking doubt it. And we had little time to search it out.

So what did we do in Charleston? We had no guidebook to depravity in South Carolina either, so we went for a few beers. And we passed the evening, you guessed it, playing pinballs, with shitkicking music insulting our ears. The grass isn't greener, Arch. You can't get away from yourself. I dropped quarters into the machine and shook it with the reckless abandon and the wild joy of yesteryear.

What fool said, "Youth's a stuff will not endure"?

Relentlessly,

Kurt

Dear Mom,

We've just spent our final weekend in the United States. Some of my barrackmates passed their time writing lengthy letters to loved ones; others went to the trouble and expense of flying home to see those loved ones. Such excursions entailed a flight aboard Cape Fear Airlines, which has a local monopoly and a dreadful safety record. Its planes are little propeller jobs rejected by the Wright brothers before their success at Kitty Hawk. The remains of those planes dot the landscape of the Dismal Swamp.

I prefer risking my life on the ground, so I set about convincing a buddy with a car and an obsession to visit Southern capital cities that Charleston is the capital of South Carolina. He elected to believe me. Three guys went with us.

We threw our money around as freely as sailors on liberty. After renting a room at the Heart of Charleston Motor Inn, we frolicked in the pool; then we ordered supper from room service. I chose fried chicken, candied yams, peas, and sweet potato pie. Supper was nearly worth the price.

Charleston is old and picturesque. We walked past antebellum houses painted in soft pastels and viewed Fort Sumter from the Battery. We'd hoped to view a few pliant Southern belles, but we ended up walking into a bar. As Ernest Tubb wailed "On the Wings of a Snow White Dove," we drank our beers and hearkened to my buddy Babich lamenting over his distant and beloved jazz collection.

Tell me what I hear about Karen isn't true. My sister consorts with the enemy? Say it isn't so.

Love,

Kurt

MOFFET POINT
CAMP LEJEUNE, NORTH CAROLINA
8 September 66

Chloe dear,

Karen has entered nursing school. "Good thinking," you say, as you nod over another rum and coke. "Unlimited opportunity. Positions galore." Perhaps, my dear Chloe, but would you really want your sister to be one?

I have a prejudice against nurses, engrained in me by Mother. She loathes them. It's true that Mother's likes and dislikes are generally no model for a sane approach to life, but I've worked under several nurses who have encouraged me to develop a yearning to commit genocide upon the profession.

There was our company nurse in Corps School, a snippy little blonde lieutenant with the regulation chunky calves. Her obvious disdain for enlisted personnel and her constant refrain "Quick! Like a bunny," made me want to load a hypodermic needle with arsenic and commit euthanasia.

The head nurse on the Urology ward in Boston was a tall, skinny disaster of a woman who flew through the door every day, bat-cape flapping in her acrid breeze, screeching heartless "Good mornings," and trailing long, bony fingers across the venetian blinds. "Men," she would nasally invoke, "look at this dust. Let's get moving, men, and get this ward in ship-shape." I felt drowning her in a pail of old urine would be an apt demise.

Just before we left Boston to become grunts, a passive urge to see all nurses extinct became a compulsion. A young lieutenant subbed on Pediatrics for the regular nurse. She was crinkle-haired, blob-nosed, flat-chested, and had ankles like Alley Oop, but I would never hold mere homeliness against her. What I didn't like was while I rushed from crib to crib changing diapers and sheets, holding bottles, inserting thermometers up tiny protesting assholes, and examining the turds of a tot that had swallowed half the thermometer some fool on the previous shift had left in its mouth, the bitch in white sat on her broad ass reading *Sue Barton, Registered Nurse, in Nicaragua*. When I finally had a free moment and sat down to fold some fresh diapers which would only too soon be needed, the bitch looked up from her book. (After five hours of uninterrupted reading, she had reached page 90, and Sue Barton books are written in LARGE PRINT.) She ordered me to bring her a cup of coffee. I didn't like it one bit, but I did it. I brought her the goddam coffee. But I stumbled just as I reached the desk, splashing the coffee upon her clean, white, starched uniform.

The next night my buddies, Stokes and Babich, joined me in the last of a series of going-away parties we gave ourselves. As we returned to the base smashed out of our minds, Stokes began gesturing obscenely at passing cars. One passing car screeched to a halt. It took some time for the screeching halt to register. When it did, I turned around to see offended sailors holding each of Stokes' arms as a third punched him in the stomach. I staggered back to help, but all I remember was a fist heading toward my face in slow motion. When I came to, I was walking down the sidewalk with my buddies. They said I'd fallen backward, and after what Babich had observed as a "sickening, crunching bounce" on the curb, my head landed just in front of the car's rear tire. After I fell, the sailors jumped into the car and tore rubber down the street. Stokes had the presence of mind to yank me onto the sidewalk by my legs, or my head would have been crushed. I thanked him, and in due course presented myself before the emergency room doctor, who admitted me to the hospital with contusions, abrasions, and a possible concussion.

Well, guess who stood duty when I awoke the next morning with a splitting headache and my possible concussion. Right! Sue Ammonia-Crotch Barton, RN, USN, with her mammoth ankles crossed beneath the slightly stained uniform that covered her "sensual thighs." She ordered me to make my bed, sweep down the ward, mop where I had swept, polish the sinks, and douche the toilets.

I lay back in the bed with my hands clasped behind my head and said primly, "Oh, no. Didn't they teach you in nursing school that a doctor pronounces a patient fit for duty? I'd be afraid to take an aspirin handed me by a nurse. I'm amazed when a nurse can find her nose to pick it." That I got a good laugh from the other patients proved small consolation for being put on report for disrespect and spending my final weekend in Boston waxing the halls of the hospital as I daydreamed of cutting off Sue Barton's nipples with garden shears.

And Karen plans to join the starched sorority. I should hate to admit to a sister with mutilated tits.

Relentlessly,

Kurt

My dear Paul,

I refused to spend my last weekend in the U.S. with Henry James and Jane Austen, so I lured several buddies to Charleston with vast promises of a wild weekend. Wendell, a humpy number from Philly, drove us down. He had been nagging me to join him for excursions each weekend to various Southern cities, but I had maintained my decorum with great difficulty when we slept in the same bed during a visit to my cousin Chloe in Atlanta. I have taken the vow, you know. Still, I figured there's safety in numbers, so with Babich, Stokes, and Miss Priss along for the ride, keeping my hands, etc., off the muscular cherubic Wendell would be easier. Nevertheless, as we climbed into his car, I had to bite my tongue when Wendell engagingly remarked that this weekend he was game for anything.

So was Babich. All the way to Charleston, he leaned over the front seat between Wendell and me, chortling and licking his lips over visions of the immorality before us. Then depression set in; he, of all persons, was unlikely to get laid. He would brood for a few minutes before declaring that there is always hope. A fit of elation would ensue. But no hope for him. New depression. Ad nauseam. As a result of his manic groaning, I could hear nothing of the quiet conversation held between Stokes and Miss Priss in the backseat throughout the trip.

When we arrived in Charleston, a debate commenced over the likeliest method of finding women. Wendell wanted to drive about the city yelling "Woo woo" at passing ladies. Stokes thought we should serenade the windows of a local girls' school. Babich held out for the bus station. Miss Priss and I seemed in silent agreement: Women were unnecessary. The five of us went to a bar to discuss our plans over a few beers. No compromise was reached, so after a stubborn Wendell drove off to go "Woo woo," the rest of us abandoned ourselves to Bacchus. We played pinballs and made merry until the bar closed; then I herded my drunken little flock back to the motel, clamping a steely hand upon Stokes' shoulder when he showed signs of provoking the boisterous sailors who emerged from taverns on every corner. At the motel, I poured a couple of fifths of Southern Comfort down the throats of my buddies. Within an hour Miss Priss had passed out, Babich was kneeling over the toilet as he puked, and Stokes sprawled across from me, coyly suggesting availability. Recalling that view of his elegant pecker, I considered the approaches I might attempt.

I had help from an adjoining room, where a couple was apparently consummating their passion. At first, we'd needed to press water glasses against the wall, but now the lady's wild cries were clearly audible. "Oh, Max! Oh, Max. Ohhh . . ."

I ventured an innocuous statement. "Listening to that stuff sure can get a guy horny."

"Yeah," said Stokes.

"Zzzzz," droned Miss Priss.

"Oh, Max!" the lady cried.

"Arghh," groaned Babich in the bathroom.

"I'd like to part those ruby lips with my prick," I noted, "and rape her in the mouth."

"Yeah," said Stokes.

"Arghh," groaned Babich.

"Max!" cried the lady.

"My nuts are so loaded, I'd blow her head off when I shot," I continued.

"Yeah," said Stokes.

"Oh! Oh! Oh!" exclaimed the lady.

"Shit!" I went on doggedly, "I'm so hot, I'd even let a queer blow me."

"Yeah," said Stokes.

I began to take heart. A shaft of light shone through the window. The shadows in the vicinity of Stokes' crotch gave me furiously to hope. I leaned over and dusted that bulge with my knuckles, lightly. Something stirred. Stokes smiled dreamily and closed his eyes. I sat up carefully, at which point an explosion of light hit us as Babich opened the bathroom door. "I feel so much better now," he said. He sat down next to me, eager to join our conversation. His unwashed body served better than a duenna.

Wendell woke us around noon; he had slept in his car and wanted to shower and shave. We passed the afternoon riding around and yelling "Woo woo." That evening I deserted the whole sick crew as they sat in a bar, solemnly burning their forearms with cigarettes.

I walked the streets for an hour, cursing the caution that had made me give away my *International Gay Guide* when I enlisted; then I saw a peroxided queen posing under a streetlamp. She saw me, too. She batted her eyes, licked her lips, and wriggled her ass. I hovered in the shadows across the street. She humped the lamppost. I stepped into the light, hesitantly. She drifted down the boulevard, casting lascivious looks over her shoulder. I followed, maintaining a half-block's distance between us. She sashayed into a tavern. This must be the place. I waited outside for a minute; then I entered. The queen stood at the bar facing the door, her head thrown back and her pelvis thrust out. Sitting at a table were three chubby, balding faggots. One screamed, "Oh, Mary! Would you look at that number in the doorway." I backed out of the place.

I flagged down a cab and asked the driver to take me to a more congenial spot. He dropped me before the door of an antebellum town house serving as a private club. A club packed with military. Gay military. As Loretta Young exclaimed upon accepting her Academy Award, "At long last!"

I bought a beer, found a wall to lean against, and surveyed the talent. It was considerable. As I began to compile a top-ten list, I was attacked by a colonel-type around forty, but boyish looking in a cold-blooded killer sort of way. Within thirty seconds, he had squeezed my ass, squeezed my crotch, and squeezed my hand against his crotch. He wanted me to go with him to the parking lot, but I pleaded a previous engagement. Following a few more minutes of squeezing, groping, and grabbing, he retired to the men's room to "take a whizz."

As soon as he disappeared, I eased to the side of a darkly handsome Celtic stud who ranked number one on my list and who had been studying me. I told him of the pressure exerted upon me by the colonel-type. He'd noticed. Would he mind helping a sailor out of a bind? No, he'd be glad to. When the colonel-type returned, I introduced him to my "lover." Colonel was taken aback, but inquired hopefully whether we would enjoy a threesome. Clutching my firm negative against his solid chest, he withdrew from the siege.

I asked my lover his name. Tim. He said he understood my predicament. He wasn't looking for sex himself; he had just wandered into the bar for a few beers.

"That's strange," I said. "What a coincidence! How bizarre!"

We enjoyed a couple of beers before the closing bell rang. Tim bought a fifth of bourbon from the bar and said, "Let's blow this joint." All right. "Would you like to drive around and see the city?" he asked.

"That would be very nice," I replied.

The tour ended at the Battery where Tim parked amidst a clutter of cars with steamy windows. He opened the bottle of Kentucky's finest, and we passed it back and forth as we gazed at the water and talked of Vietnam and baseball. Manners given their due, I got tacky, and Tim had to fend off my squeezing, groping, and grabbing. After a while, I ceased and desisted. He really did want to talk. And I'd heard a distant cry of "Woo woo!"

So we talked. Tim had attended Virginia Tech. We then talked of me. Where was I from? What was my background? He wanted to know all about my past, while I was aching for a hint about our immediate future.

The subject finally turned to sex. I felt as if I were being interviewed for a job. How old was I the first time? Did I like older men? Had I ever hustled? Well, if I am unable to do it, I can get into talking about it.

A sun slightly more red than our eyeballs emerged from the Atlantic to shine upon the only car left on the Battery. We were in it. The bottle was empty. I was chattering. Tim seemed dazed. A furtive groping sobered him up considerably. He drove me to the motel, where we shook hands and said goodbye.

I lurched into the room to find Stokes curled up against Miss Priss spoon-fashion, with his arm encircling Miss P's chest. Babich and Wendell slept noisly in the other bed. I stripped to my shorts, flopped next to Stokes, and passed out.

Tuesday evening, and back at Lejeune, I had a visitor. Tim. I asked him how he found me. "Dazzling," he replied. (I'll accept that.) He smiled dazzlingly himself, said he'd been thinking about me, that he liked my style (what style?), and would I come with him for a couple of drinks. Babich and Stokes walked up to us as I was checking my engagement calendar. I introduced my cousin Tim Strom to them. They were pleased to meet him. Tim was pleased to meet them, too. Babich was so pleased that Tim was pleased that he began to babble of his bargain with Ho Chi Minh. I dragged Tim outside. Babich followed us to the car. I rolled up my window in his face and Tim spun out. He stopped at the guard shack, where he showed his I.D. to the guard. "Thanks, Lieutenant. Have a nice evening." Lieutenant, huh? Nothing less than I deserve.

Tim drove to New Bern, a little town thirty miles or so to the north. I chattered inanely all the way. Tim laughed or replied accordingly; occasionally, he paid no attention whatsoever. My pride usually disappears when I'm confronted with matters of the flesh, so I took no offense. Assuming Tim to be a romantic, I took no liberties either; he'd need dim lights, soft music, and large cushions.

Tim pulled up before a small white frame house just off the highway. "Follow me," said the lieutenant as he got out of the car. Well, that's what they've been training us to do, right? I followed him. A light was burning in the sparely furnished living room. Cornball music blared from a radio. "Sit down," Tim ordered, before disappearing down the hallway to the back of the house. I heard muffled voices. Tim reappeared. "Come with me."

I followed him into a small room containing only a big bed and illuminated by a light bulb fixed in the ceiling. A tall, broad gentleman of fifty or so sat in his underwear on top of the bedspread. He had arrogant eyes. He looked me up and down with them. "Splendid!" he said.

Tim introduced us. "Joe, this is Kurt."

"Hi," I said.

The big man continued to stare at me. "Take off your clothes." I did as he advised. Against my will, an erection rose to meet those eyes. "Splendid!" said the big man. He motioned toward the door.

Tim said quickly, "Kurt, there's a head down the hall. Why don't you take a shower."

So that was the problem: Tim was a soap-and-water freak. Well, if it took germicide, Clorox, and a bit of ado with a comparatively unattractive third party to make the handsome lieutenant, so be it. But I was quick. Thorough, but quick.

When I returned to the bedroom, Tim was gone. My clothes were gone, too. Joe lay in his shorts on the bed. "Your clothes are in the next room. Put them on. You'll find a piece of paper on the dresser. Memorize what it says. Then come back and knock on my door. I'll say 'Come in.' You come in. I'll say, 'What can I do for you, son?' That's when you say what's typed on the paper. Got that?"

47

"Yes, sir."

"Good. Go to it."

I left the room, closed the door behind me, went to the other bedroom, grabbed my clothes, and ran to the living room. I didn't find Tim there. I dressed quickly and went outside. Tim's car was gone. I walked to the highway; it was too dark to hitchhike. A tavern splashed light upon the road about a half-mile away. I walked toward it. I got to thinking that I might be wiser to hide for an hour or two, should Joe or Tim come looking for me. I entered the tavern. Tim sat at the bar, facing the door. I walked over to him.

"What are you doing here?" he asked.

"Joe sent me."

"That was quick."

"After we finished, Joe seemed anxious for me to leave."

"Yeah, well, we'd better go back. He might want something else."

"He said to tell you just to carry me to the base." Tim nodded and returned to his drink. He seemed in no hurry to go. "You are going to take me back, aren't you?"

"Of course. That was understood." He studied the peroxided barmaid carefully and discouraged all my attempts at conversation. I bought myself a drink and studied my watch. It was lots of fun. After an hour, Tim called the barmaid over, bought a pint to drive on, and went outside. I followed him and got into his car. Tim roared out of the parking lot. He drove fast. I tried to converse. He was curt. I couldn't blame him; I was getting personal.

"You and Joe do this sort of thing often?"

"That's not any of your business, is it?"

"You and Joe lovers?"

Tim snorted. "Hardly."

I thought about our acquaintance. "You're not even gay, are you, Tim?"

"Not at all."

I pondered the night's events. "Joe wants me to come back next Sunday."

"He does?" Tim seemed surprised.

"Yeah. He said I did right well." Whatever I did.

"You must have." Tim chuckled. "When I saw you in that bar full of cocksuckers, I knew you'd be perfect. Jesus, I knew." He pounded on the steering wheel; then he took another

48

slug of liquor. "Kurt, would you like to get out of going to Nam? It can be arranged. He wants to see you Sunday, huh? Jesus, that would be great." He tipped the bottle again. "What time on Sunday?"

"Seven. Uhh, Tim. There's just one thing."

"Yeah? What's that?"

I hated to ruin his sudden good mood. "Joe liked me. A lot. He said I was splendid."

"So?"

"Well, I did it with Joe, but he doesn't really turn me on."

"As long as you did it."

"That's what Joe said."

"You told him?"

"Sure. He liked it better that way."

"Figures."

"But why should I do anything that turns me off? What would I get out of it?"

"You want money? I thought you said you never hustled."

"I don't want money."

"He hurt you pretty bad, huh?"

Hurt me! "Some. But I can take it."

"Well, what do you want then?"

"You."

"Me?" Tim laughed; then he said disagreeably, "You're not getting me, baby. You can bet your sweet ass on that."

"Joe asked me what it would take to get me again. I told him I wanted to make it with you in a bed. The works. Everything. If you refuse, I'm not going back."

"That's too bad."

"Yeah. Joe didn't like it at all."

"I'll bet he didn't."

"Anyway, he said for you to come back after you've dropped me off and tell him whether I'm coming on Sunday."

Tim looked sharply at me. "What?"

"If you and I have sex tonight, I'll go back next week to do anything Joe wants." My palms were sweating, my teeth were chattering, my knees were shaking, and my voice was unsteady. I sat trying to catch my breath. Would Tim recall that I was leaving for Nam on Saturday morning? And what was written on that sheet of paper?

A long silence ensued before Tim spoke, in a hard, cold voice. "What did Joe say to that?"

"He said you would do anything to make him happy."

Another silence. "He said that?"

"Yes. And he said to remind you that he thinks I'm splendid."

Suddenly, Tim swerved off the road, stopped the car, and sat rigidly at attention, his eyes staring straight ahead and his hands clenching the steering wheel. Was he going to beat me up? Was he going to kick me into the swamp? I thrive on danger.

We sat there for five minutes. I was afraid to move. Finally, Tim spoke. "That son of a bitch," he said. He took a deep draught from his bottle, pulled onto the highway, and accelerated to a hundred and ten. He maintained that speed for twenty or so miles; then, without any warning, he hit the brakes. I nearly went through the windshield. He pulled into a motel court. When he came out of the office, he drove to Room 6. Before turning off the ignition, he sat quietly for a minute or two. By the light of the dashboard, I could see tears in his eyes. He got out of the car and went inside the room. I followed him. Well, that's what they've been training us to do, right?

I was gentle. Thorough, but gentle.

Relentlessly,

Kurt

KADENA AIR FORCE BASE
OKINAWA
13 September 66

Chloe dear,

> When Karen and I were tiny tots
>   And life was a series of "No's" and "Not's,"
> We'd empty Mom's jewelry box on the floor
>   And when my granny walked in the door,
>
> She never screamed at our glittering stack;
>   Instead, she taught us how to play "Back."
> And back in the box went pendants and rings,
>   Necklaces and glistening things.

Daddy taught us the game of "Boo!"
  And Mother taught us "Hide the Shoe!"
Other kids taught us "Jump the Rope"
  When Baby Jim ate all that soap.

Before we grew up to games on shelves
  Or learning how to play with ourselves,
We were stuck on a lonely ranch with Mother;
  Naturally, we turned to each other

And played a game called "Desert Isle."
  We'd swim from a shipwreck with just a pile
Of necessities we strapped on our backs.
  What fun it was to load our packs
With life-supporting gear and toys:
  Dolls for Karen, cars for the boys . . .

But alas and alack! It's no game they play;
  I'm going away for a year and a day.
Upon my back, I'll tote a pack
  Crammed with things grunts shouldn't lack.
And attached with cord will be my hoard
  Of books I'll take so I won't be bored.

What books would *you* take to augment the dearth
  Of amusements to while away your days?
The Bible for solace? Thurber for mirth?
  For drama and poetry: Shakespeare's plays?

Robinson Crusoe for practical reasons?
  The Oz books for sentiment's sake?
My Life and Loves for the rutting seasons
  And when you've got a shit to take?

Well, Mom's made me liable to take the Bible;
  I've an old wish to read it through.
And your copy of English Poetry—
  For me, that's something new.

A book I borrowed from brother Neil
  Called *Animal Kitabu*
And my handy corpsman's manual
  Covered in navy blue.

So good-bye, dear heart, I go to war,
   A seabag slung over my shoulder:
Such a fool to love honor more;
   I'm daft, I'm dazed, my bowels grow colder.

And he sailed away
   For a year and a day
      In his durable olive-green suit.

Relentlessly,

Kurt

Cam Ranh Bay, Vietnam
14 September 66

Dear Mom,

I am in Vietnam. A Marine Corps transport carried me to San Francisco. I flew by TWA charter to Okinawa. The Air Force got me here. Other sky angels will take me to the successors of those who stormed the Halls of Montezuma and the Shores of Tripoli. Most of the other corpsmen have already joined them. I am in the last shipment.

After a direct flight from North Carolina to California with one stopover in Denver (at the edge of your beloved Rockies), we were supposed to depart immediately from San Francisco, but the plane developed a problem, gifting us with a two-day layover in that Baghdad-by-the-Bay. I presented myself as a tourist: riding the cable cars, taking in the view from Telegraph Hill, and dining on lobster at Fisherman's Wharf and roast duck in Chinatown.

We stopped for one hour in Honolulu. You've told me that you fancy visiting Hawaii one day, so I was disappointed that I lacked the time to obtain inside information for you. I did take notice of a soft, warm breeze blowing across the observation deck of the airport.

I reboarded the plane reluctantly and sat next to a young colored girl away from her home in a small Georgia town for the first time and bound to meet a husband stationed in Okinawa. She misgave our pilot's expertise. I told her about those small planes belonging to Treasure State Airlines in which

Karen and I rode when we visited you and Dad in Montana. I got carried away, I guess, and became somewhat sentimental in my reminiscence: the pilots who invited Karen and me into the cockpit, the stewardesses who sat with us for lengthy chats, and the passengers who bought candy for the tots traveling by themselves all the way to Billings. Evidently I reassured the colored girl; she fell asleep during my ramblings, and I was left alone with my thoughts.

The plane landed in Okinawa, and the civilians went their ways. Military personnel were hustled aboard a couple of buses and taken to the transit barracks several miles from the airport. The buses followed an irregular shoreline. Twilight gave the soft hills of dark green and brick red a deep and rainwashed aspect.

I stayed in the transit barracks for two nights and one day. With no duty and only obliged to form up three times daily with the other transit personnel for roll call, I passed my waking hours exploring the little settlements that crowd the gates of the huge compound. More color there of the local variety.

And now I am in Vietnam. The late afternoon is hot. A dusty breeze blows across the stony ground. We sit near a tin shed. Everybody appears busy. We must wait until our names are called to board a flight north. I've got one eye on Heaven and one on the main chance.

Love,

Kurt

CAM RANH BAY, VIETNAM
14 Setpember 66

Arch,

The past week has been hectic. Just before we left Lejeune, a dreadful rumor swept through the barracks: If a corpsman who lacks medical knowledge or battle courage is assigned to their unit, marines will shoot him in the back at the first opportunity in hopes of drawing a better one in the next lottery. I pulled out my navy blue corpsman's manuel and began to cram. During first-aid classes, I pushed my way to the front and took meticulous notes. I ran down hills, I ran through gullies, and I splashed through creeks, frantically following the cries of "CORPSMAN!" I bandaged imaginary injuries and I injected imaginary morphine. I strained my eyes poring over pictures of gunshot wounds, bayonet stabbings, snake bites, and syphilis chancres. I got out of bed an hour early to undergo the tortures of one hundred pushups, twenty-five chin-ups, and a three-mile run. I begged futilely for extra time on the firing range. I looked longingly at *Emma*. I am willing to bet Jane Austen never heard of Vietnam, and I wish to God I were one with her there.

My buddy Babich considered me a victim of a hysteria brought about by propaganda and continued to grandstand from behind large trees. He was convinced that someone will shoot him, and the sniper might as well be a marine as a VC.

Our journey to the Land of the Frenchman's Folly was by air. Because of a problem during take-off, they granted us two days of liberty in San Francisco, which I passed riding the cable cars up and down those lovely hills, my groin pressed against dimpled knees. When I finally arrived in Okinawa, Babich greeted me with ardor.

"Kurt, I've got to have ten dollars."

He had dived headfirst into the fleshpots of the island and spent his all upon the Golden Sisters of the Cross of Shame. The heavy load of his chastity had been lifted from him. He'd even pawned his watch in an effort to secure memories.

"Ah, Kurt. These women are really something. Such smooth skin. So clean. I eat out every one of them and lick their assholes." He admitted to a lack of discrimination; he was after quantity. I lent him twenty dollars and declined pressing invitations to join him in his pleasures. I was already too close to Paradise.

And I draw ever nearer. Everyone looks busy and efficient, dusty and grimy, and I wonder just what the hell I have got myself into.

Yet Caesar shall go forth.

Relentlessly,

Kurt

My dear Paul,

Our term of trial at Camp LeJeune climaxed with a bewildering lecture on masturbation delivered by a drunken admiral. Whether he stood pro or con was a matter of conjecture; whatever his position, the speech was superfluous. I'd hazard to guess that we all know how to do it and have little intention of stopping.

Half the class gathered in the auditorium. The admiral, a roly-poly Santa Claus of a guy, began the program with an exhortation for us to go over there and show those yellow devils just how tough the Navy is, and that some of us would be killed and others wounded and that our sacrifice would not be in vain. He left the stage to much applause. A movie was projected, an example of the work done by the Medical Corps during the Second World War. After a short subject of the American flag rippling and bluster about our Heritage, the main feature came on. It was shot during the invasion of some Pacific island or another. We were excited by the film. As marines were wounded, corpsmen treated them. Litter-bearers carried the wounded to Triage. Doctors operated on the beach. Bombs burst in the air. We identified with one or another of the doctors or corpsmen and cheered them on. I felt proud to be a member of the medical profession.

Suddenly, the screen went blank and the sound track went silent, and the narrator's voice informed us that this piece of film had been rescued after a mortar barrage had killed everybody we had been watching. The lights went up on a silent group of corpsmen.

The admiral staggered to the podium dragging a three-foot-long plastic penis behind him. He held it up for display; then he commenced his lecture. "This is something we've all got. You sure better not be in the Navy if you don't. Not this man's Navy." Laughter throughout the auditorium; the class liked this. So did I, figuring the admiral was talking along my line. But as he went on, I got lost. "The women of America want these to come home safe, and that means safe in every way. You don't want to disappoint the women of America."

Shouts of "No!" "Never!"

The admiral fondled the penis and continued. "It's awful

hot where you're headed and your scrotum hangs loose in the heat. This is a natural phenomenon, and your Navy drawers let it hang natural. So don't wear jockey shorts; wear your Navy drawers. Jockey shorts confine your scrotum and get it overheated. That makes you sterile.

"And don't forget to pack away Johnson's Baby Powder in your seabag. You can buy it here at the PX. You dust under your scrotum with Johnson's Baby Powder every day, and you won't develop a rash; you wouldn't want to itch so bad down there, you scratch if off. I've used Johnson's Baby Powder throughout my adult life, and I've never had a rash." It was a riveting moment of autobiography.

"Men, this is an organ vital to everyday life. You all like beer, don't you?" General assent. "Well, that beer might go in your mouth, but it comes out of this. If you're like me, you enjoy drinking, but you've got to pee. Mighty important little organ. Or mighty important big organ, as the case may be." He winked lewdly and stroked the gargantuan pecker he cradled in his arms. I steeled myself and looked around to see 499 men staring at the stage, contemplating the admiral and his plastic penis.

"You have to keep it clean," he was saying. "Wash it every day, but don't rub too hard. You wouldn't want *that* to happen, not with other real men in the showers. This is for the women of America." I decided I liked neither the man nor his message. He rambled on and concluded, "I want every swinging dick in this auditorium to come back to the States with this in his pants, not in his hand."

That was our farewell from America. The admiral was probably the sadist who ordered "Where Have All The Flowers Gone" played over the loudspeaker as we packed for departure. He waved good-bye at Cherry Point Naval Air Station to several Marine Corps transports carring eight hundred Navy corpsmen destined for dispersion and dismemberment in Vietnam. We changed planes at Travis Air Force Base, but as our fancy TWA charter took off, the cockpit window blew in on the pilots, giving us a two-day layover in San Francisco. An ill omen? I could stand it.

I rode the cable cars up and down those lovely hills, trying to exude the glamour of the doomed and thereby attracting avid glances from the light-footed masses. No one looked twice. Nevertheless, as I carefully dusted under my scrotum with

Johnson's Baby Powder in the shower room of the Turk Street YMCA, I rubbed too hard, and what the admiral had feared would happen, happened. The happening introduced me to a rangy soldier from Illinois, heroically hung and himself fresh from Nam. I had my way with him before learning that he was a romantic, so I wined and dined him in a dimly lighted restaurant in Chinatown. We brushed knees under the table and gazed into each other's eyes over sweet and sour chicken. My fortune cookie read, "You are going on a long journey."

I went. In Okinawa I lived for two days in a forlorn and tattered barrack. As I wandered through the maze of beer halls and whorehouses that crowded the gates of the transit compound, I bumped into Miss Priss. She was peering into murky doorways, searching for Stokes. The object of her search had returned for each roll call with a parboiled smile; I guessed he had been soaking at a disreputable bathhouse. Miss Priss never caught on; she kept plying Stokes with anguished questions as to his whereabouts. Stokes preferred his mystery and replied curtly. Miss P bought a bottle of saki and proceeded to give us just what the party needed: a crying drunk.

At the moment, we are outside the transit shed at the Cam Ranh Bay airfield, where we await the posting of billets. Babich squats in the dust and sun, distracted and incoherent. Stokes leans against a wall, lovingly stroking his piece. Miss Priss bites her nails between pleading glances at Stokes and, like me, stares nervously into what distances there are. My Bible is open to Lamentations.

If God had wanted us to be marines, we would have been born with red necks and tight jaws.

Relentlessly,

Kurt

Dear Mom,

Be of good cheer; I am safe. They have assigned me to the First Medical Battalion, a hospital that caters to wounded marines, the Royal Korean Army, and the Vietnamese: military and civilian. I have yet to meet a Vietnamese: wounded or healthy. I haven't entered the wards, and God knows I have no plans to leave the base. This is the time to stay close to where the home fires burn.

My buddy Babich was sent to a line company deep within the jungle. I won that lottery. Within me a bold, adventurous Kurt is anxious to sally forth into battle so he can exhibit the mettle of a Strom; also within me a prudent, trembling Kurt questions whether this particular Strom might prove himself an inadequate hero. I try to think of this interim at the Med Battalion as a period of reconnoitering the situation.

My fellow noncombatants often count the number of days that they can look forward to serving in Nam. I would have to count 389, had I enough fingers and toes. Because I have only ten of each, I won't think about it today; I'll think about it tomorrow. After all, tomorrow is another day.

Love,

Kurt

FIRST MEDICAL BATTALION
CHU LAI, VIETNAM
21 September 66

Arch,

An abundance of corpsmen has saturated the line companies, so I am temporarily assigned to the First Medical Battalion in Chu Lai until the VC thin out the surplus.

First Med is a hospital. Victims of warfare, accident, and intrigue are sent here to recuperate and move on, or to die. They are transported from their mishaps by choppers (helicopters) or ambulances (panel vans). The casualties are immediately taken to the Triage unit (the emergency room) where they are sorted out according to the priority with which they need treatment. Casualties come in three categories:

1. Those who are badly wounded but can be salvaged go immediately into surgery before their flight out of Nam.

2. The merely wounded (those who are still able to tote their pieces) convalesce on the wards until they are fit to return to duty.

3. The hopelessly damaged are left until last by which time, ideally, they have ceased to live. This may sound callous, but they would survive as either vegetables or small pieces of their original selves.

The site has a pleasant prospect overlooking the South China Sea. The monsoon, which arrived with the deluge of corpsmen, sweeps in each evening to drown us in mud; at dawn, a red sun erupts from a purple ocean to dry the mud to dust. Behind crescent beaches, green cliffs ascend to a plateau stripped of vegetation for half a mile inland to where traffic-clogged Highway 1 links the coastal fortifications that belong to us good guys. On one side of First Med is a chopper pad, where helicopters bring in and fling out the wounded; on the other side is a SeaBee encampment. SeaBees (C.B. = Construction Battalion) are hardworking sailors who build airfields, roads, and new bases according to the unaesthetic plans of Navy engineers. Their basic technique is to scrape the land bare, either raising clouds of dust or digging deep grooves in the mud; it all depends upon the time of day.

The nerve center of Med Battalion is a long, low, wooden building, which squats upon the crown of the bluff and is shrouded by black canvas flapping in the ocean breeze; it houses Triage, X ray, and the laboratory. A few feet away is a concrete and steel unit divided into four surgeries and a recovery room. Across the parade grounds and toward the sea are the wards and the public buildings, which include the mess hall, a chapel, and a library. Above the cliffs are the officers' quarters.

Behind the nerve center and down a muddy path toward Highway 1 are the enlisted men's quarters, a dozen 15 feet × 30 feet huts. If you escape being swallowed by the muck or suffocated by the dust, you can continue along the path to the conveniences: a cold-water shower, a pipe to pee in, and three metal drums half-filled with kerosene in which we poop.

They assigned me to a hooch already shared by nine men. In a living space of 6 feet × 4 feet, I must fit my cot, my seabag, my travel bag, and myself. Without sheets and under one damp blanket, I must try to sleep at night with the rain ripping through canvas flaps to splash upon me. Contrary to Mother's firm conviction, at least one of her sons is unhappy as a pig in shit. In the distance, beyond beautiful green mountains, flashes and booms illuminate our evenings. Babich and Stokes are out there somewhere.

And what should I do in Illyria?

Relentlessly,

Kurt

FIRST MEDICAL BATTALION
CHU LAI, VIETNAM
22 September 66

Chloe dear,

I arrive at First Medical Battalion. They assign me to a hut already shared by nine men. Three assholes have usurped one half of the hut, because they have been stationed here the longest. (Assumption #1: The longer one has been in Nam, the more likely it is that one is an asshole.) Six guys who seem more pleasant are crowded into the other half of the hut; they make room for the new guy. He is grateful that they hide their annoyance.

The three assholes in my hooch are nasty in different ways. One just ignores me, which suits me right down to the ground. The second complains about our environment and solicits my sympathy. As I have recently come from relative comfort in the States and feel strongly that following this purgatory come the fires of Hell, I withdraw from his tales of woe. He resents my withdrawal and damns me for my ignorance. The third man is actively hostile. "You Are Stupid Even for a Cherry, Everything You Do Is Wrong, and You Are Klutzy." He watches everything I do with repugnance, and under that malevolent glare, I become self-conscious and "Klutzy."

So there are assholes everywhere. The majority of your hooch-mates are nice guys; you should be thanking your lucky stars. Yes, I suppose I should. But the six nice guys have their peculiarities, too.

#1 Nice Guy is an E–6, hospitalman first class, and head honcho in the hooch. You feel he is judging you so he can report to his superior whether you should be kept or thrown away (i.e., sent to the lines). #2 is willing to spend all nonworking hours with you. He makes plans for showing you the local sights. He gives you his only deck of pornographic playing cards. He couldn't find his hands if they were in his pockets. #3 is friendly, too; then he mentions a temporary lack of cash. He borrows twenty dollars. You'll be lucky to see penny one of it. #4 sleeps day and night. Every time I walk into the hut, he is dozing nude on his cot, flies exploring his pubic and oral areas. (Assumption #2: Those are tse-tse flies and he has sleeping sickness.) You suspect #5 of being the thief who stole that watch you left on your cot while using the rest room facilities, and #6 is a trifle picayunish and wriggles his eyebrows a lot. (Assumption #3: I am a stranger in a strange land.)

Relentlessly,

Kurt

FIRST MEDICAL BATTALION
CHU LAI, VIETNAM
23 September 66

My dear Paul,

When I embarked upon this new program, I said to myself, "Kurt, you are going to show those people that you can exist for a year without sex." That's what I said. Those people found such a rash statement difficult to believe. And their doubts were well-founded. I'll amend that vow. I'll have sex only with anonymous strangers.

I must amend that vow. I've already had sex. On my first day in Nam. I'm so ashamed.

It happened at the airport in Cam Ranh Bay. They called for Stokes and sent him into the jungle. They called for Babich and sent him into the jungle. It seemed that Wendell had already been sent into the jungle. Miss Priss suffered acutely after Stokes' departure, and I found it difficult to maintain an optimistic outlook. I studied the handful of men who remained in the transit shed, looking for someone to take my mind off an unforeseeable future.

Sitting quietly by himself was a tanned marine with white teeth and eyes which were quite, quite blue. I threw my seabag by his bench and started a conversation with the dreary thing wearing eyeglasses who sat next to him. I find it easy to be natural and amusing with dreary things, and my marine hearkened to the conversation. He flashed those white teeth a couple of times at my bon mots. I included him in the conversation. He flashed those blue eyes. With forty men sitting around us, I would be hard pressed to work up something, yet work it up I would. My youth may wear and waste, but it shall never rust in my possession.

When darkness fell, everyone looking official left the transit shed. We assumed that no more flights were likely. As the flashes and booms in the distance were getting closer, I suggested we remove ourselves to a position that would protect us from enemy mortars. Gorgeous and Dreary agreed. We found an empty bunker across the road and piled our seabags in the middle, dividing it in two. I lured Gorgeous into one side of the seabags; Dreary and another parasite tried to make themselves comfortable on the other side.

Soon thereafter, Heaven helped me. It opened. When the first drops began falling, I pulled my poncho out of my seabag to cover us. As Gorgeous was supposed to catch an early morning flight to Bangkok for R&R (Rest and Relaxation), he wore khakis and shoes instead of jungle greens and boots. He carried no change of clothes in his travel bag. The trench began to fill with water. I voiced an opinion: To visit Bangkok in a muddy, wrinkled uniform might lack chic. I suggested that he take off his uniform and put it in my seabag, where it would remain dry; I would do the same with mine. He agreed. Shoes, socks, and underwear followed. We huddled under the poncho. My hand roamed. He rebuffed me. Twice. The third time was the charm.

The next morning, the sun shone upon the wicked. Gorgeous

told us how well he had slept, despite the rain; then he could hardly get away fast enough.

A cruiser and a destroyer passed in the night.

Relentlessly,

Kurt

First Medical Battalion
Chu Lai, Vietnam
27 September 66

Dear Mom,

To train as a corpsman, I attended three months of classes at Corps School at Great Lakes. I worked on several wards in the Chelsea Hospital, and I spent five weeks at Camp Lejeune ostensibly acquiring the skills needed to provide efficient first aid on the battlefield. Such an education costs the U.S. Navy $75,000. Fly that well-trained and expensive corpsman halfway around the world. Deposit him in a mess hall to wash pots and pans for thirty days. *C'est la guerre.*

I called Karen from San Francisco; she remains my sister, whatever her profession. She works six evenings a week as a nurse's aide to pay her tuition for the classes she attends every day and for the household bills. Instead of working to help with the bills, Reggie will sit at home with the babies, trying to find himself. Far be it from me to deny someone the opportunity to find himself, although I think Reggie could have chosen a better time. And what ever did he have to lose anyway?

Mother is not to know about Reggie's self-absorption. I've long marveled that she refrains from clipping wedding announcements out of the *Acadian*, comparing them with the birth announcements that appear during the following nine months, and sending all disgraceful ascertainments to Karen. To Mother's way of thinking, no woman would be good enough for me, and Reggie is not good enough for Karen. Mother's thoughts lack consistency. She's often accused Karen and me of being good for nothing. I should think then that she'd consider Reggie as a perfect mate for Karen. Then again, a foolish consistency is the hobgoblin of little minds.

Love,

Kurt

FIRST MEDICAL BATTALION
CHU LAI, VIETNAM
28 September 66

Chloe dear,

Two years ago, when I was young, I saw a Japanese movie about a couple who farmed a barren island. Whenever they needed water, they had to row their little boat across a bay to the mainland. They filled their jugs and returned to their island. They emptied their jugs and returned to the mainland. And back. And there and back again. The film was as boring as my life.

They put me on Kitchen Patrol my second day in Nam. Every morning at four, I ease into my damp greens and dash through the drizzle to the scullery. A huge pile of pans needs to be scraped of the previous night's baking. I stack them next to my tubs; then I carry several ten-gallon containers to the water buffalo. (A water buffalo, in this connotation, is a large metal drum on wheels with a spigot at one end.) I fill the containers with water and lug them back to the kitchen. After several trips, I boil the water in a fifty-gallon cauldron and fill my tubs.

As soon as the baking pans stand in their racks scrubbed shiny clean, the breakfast pots stack up: pots of grits, pots of oatmeal, and frying pan after frying pan caked with the remnants of eggs and bacon. I must use clean water to loosen the cement that the cooks mix into the Crisco, so I go into the storm to the water buffalo. And back. Lunch strikes before one knows it and then, in its turn, supper. And for every meal, it's thrice more into the breach, dear cousin. At seven, I pull myself erect, endure the evening inspection, and go home to watch my hoochmates play cards until a very late hour.

I have company by the tubs, a pimply, bespectacled youth

who washes the officers' dishes in a little sink next to the window. (We enlisted men eat off our very own little metal trays. The food, by the way, is excellent.) Oglesby is even a reader, although he reads only mysteries. We pass the dreary hours with literary discussions, comparing the merits of Sir Arthur Conan Doyle with those of Dame Agatha Christie. Neither Oglesby nor I have had the free time to cultivate friendships outside the mess hall, so, unfortunately, we can trade no gossip. We do spend delicious moments disparaging the Kool-Aid crew, which we hold in low esteem.

The head honcho of the Kool-Aid detachment is an ugly little grunt whose nose and chin meet in front of his mouth. The moronic martinet with the disposition of a hornet has two ill-tempered dwarfs serving as his mates. The trio usually works in Graves.

No one has anything pleasant to say about the jarheads who work in Graves, an isolated building at the far end of the compound. Except for grunts whose ambitions lie in the cold-storage business, Graves duty is a punishment for those who are too cowardly to serve on the lines and too stupid to do anything else. Every three months, they rotate to KP for thirty days. Kool-Aid is their inherited domain: All they must do is tear off the tops of those little packages and pour the contents into five-gallon pots.

Rain on the roof. Again. Brings to mind those stupid turkeys on Mom and Dad's ranch. They would inevitably look toward Heaven during a rainstorm to see where the water came from; they'd open their mouths to gobble about the phenomenon and drown. Come to think of it, I'd best bone up on artificial respiration. The grunts I've met seem unlikely to know enough to come in from the rain. I should hesitate before comparing marines with turkeys. And yet . . .

Relentlessly,

Kurt

Arch,

I've enjoyed an absolutely ripping week. I could barely find the time to fit everything into my schedule. Of course, shining those great pots at my wee sink from 4:30 A.M. to 6:30 P.M. every day on a tour of KP duty does fill the hours, but I'm ever so glad to be able to do my little bit for the boys in the field. Let's see. There's so much to tell you, I hardly know where to begin.

Last Friday Chief Hospitalman Hambsfetz, guest lecturer at our little academy during Orientation Day, had us new men rolling in the aisles. His best anecdote was about a tipsy marine so annoyed with the slow service at a local bistro that he summoned the five-year-old waitress to his table and, in a rowdy pique, used his bayonet to whack off a couple of her fingers.

Saturday night the Protestant chaplain spoke to us of God and Heaven and suggested that we should appreciate our nearness to both. The chaplain is a jolly fellow who apparently pictures God as a great scowling but benevolent general in the sky. He encouraged us to accept the same viewpoint.

We were urged to attend church services Sunday, but they preach the New Testament: with Christ from cradle to cross. I prefer plagues sweeping Egyptland, the earth swallowing Onan, and Elijah telling the bears to eat the nasty children. So I didn't go.

On Monday we attended the cinema. A Jerry Lewis movie played. Did you know that the French consider him a genius? Perhaps I lack the Gallic humor.

John Wayne starred in Tuesday's main feature. I've wondered whether the French consider him a genius, too. He's certainly the rage in this neck of the woods.

Wednesday. What ever happened to Wednesday? Fireworks! Behind the mountains across the way. People were careless with the explosives, however, and they treated lots of folks in the emergency room with hands blown off or eyes blown out.

Thursday I considered the "Big Bang" theory of the creation of the universe and there you have my life in a nutshell.

Relentlessly,

Kurt

FIRST MEDICAL BATTALION
CHU LAI, VIETNAM
30 September 66

My dear Paul,

I'm amazed at your feeling that my travels are exotic. That my removal to the Orient fascinates you. That the thought of me in the midst of tumult elates you. That Paul Carroll considers his friendship with a potential hero an honor, something to be toasted with mulled wine before a raging fire in his cozy cabin, while the autumn leaves drift past his window.

Unfortunately, heroism is as remote as Warren Beatty. Here on the underbelly of the world, I am at one with the tropical depression. My fantasies of gallantry are shattered. While all my buddies fight in the jungle for God and His country, I stand thirty days of duty with the Kitchen Patrol.

The worst of it is that I begin my day at 4 A.M., brutally awakened by a flashlight that could illuminate the nine Circles of Hell. Actually, I am usually awake before the sexy jarhead comes by to flash the light. As everyone in the hooch sleeps soundly at that hour, I am ready for my human alarm clock with my covers thrown back and my morning piss-hard revealed. The jarhead has begun to throw the light down there and lets it linger for several seconds before he shines it in my ostensibly closed eyes.

Half a loaf is better than none.

At times during the day, the sun shines. Or so I'm told. At night it rains incessantly. I am sweaty and greasy after a day with the pots, but as no one else bothers to shower, I have rested content in my own filth; subsequently, the chief man in the hooch, Jenkins, offered to show me around the conveniences. I knew where they were, but I think it was a subtle hint; we live in close quarters, and his bunk is next to mine.

Flattered that anyone took any interest in me, and despite my feeling that a cold-water shower during monsoon season was like shipping faggots to San Francisco, I peeled off my uniform, laid a towel across my cot, grabbed my flashlight and my soap dish, and followed Jenkins into that good night.

We carefully exercised the buddy system—that mud is deep! Jenkins had to see a man about a dog so we stopped by the shitter. As we entered, I shone my flashlight across the shitter's sole occupant. I had only a brief glimpse, but I could swear the man had an erection. And what better place to do it? I sat between Jenkins and the anonymous self-abuser for my own less exotic, although somewhat sensual, purposes.

For a person who has always preferred privacy on such occasions, I have become blasé about company. During Boot Camp, they expected six toilets to accommodate one hundred men within thirty minutes. A line of men stood before each of the toilets staring at the men squatting thereupon.

But that was long ago and far away. Here, despite the relatively unhurried atmosphere, Jenkins and I soon finished and left that man to his relief although, as several shafts of light were bobbing their way down from the hooches, I thought he'd best hurry.

On to the showers. Two men stood under one of the nozzles, giggling as they soaped down each other's backs. I tried to see who they were and what, exactly, they were doing, but circumstances frustrated me. Jenkins showered next to me, and I didn't want him to catch my peering at the couple with too much interest. The tiny, sputtering bulb that swung to and fro on a wire above us gave insufficient light to study them by; it was dim, having been shaded in hopes of spoiling the aim of snipers in the jungle across the road. The two men were still giggling when Jenkins and I left for home. On the way we passed by a hut where a startlingly handsome blond sat writing at a table, naked. Sport, it was an interesting excursion.

A couple of nights later, I sat alone in the hooch with Jenkins. As I browsed through some disgusting Japanese snapshots lent me by a lusty neighbor across the aisle, I got turned on. Jenkins, who was writing letters, noticed my tumescence. "Realizing" my indecent exposure, I modestly adjusted myself within my olive-green shorts, but my main man was quick. He joined me on my cot to see those photos for himself, at which point I was racked with indecision.

Jenkins is married with three children; ostensibly, he is straight. It has been my observation that sex with straight guys is often spontaneous. My natural reaction is to recognize my opportunity and seize it. Jenkins is plain, balding, and walks ungainly. I hate to lower my standards, but this is war. And he does have a hairy chest and a big piece of meat. As he tentatively reached out to measure mine, and I was about to break some ridiculous vow I'd made, another hoochmate burst through the door. We ceased our explorations before they began.

Manipulatis Interruptus.

Relentlessly,

Kurt

FIRST MEDICAL BATTALION
CHU LAI, VIETNAM
4 October 66

Arch,

It's ironic. I am more sailor in the Marine Corps than I ever was in the Navy. My entire life revolves around water.

I wake before dawn. During the night, the wind has invariably ripped through the canvas protecting our screen windows from the elements; my blanket is soaked. I slide into my damp greens and trudge through the rain to the chow hall; occasionally, a rift in the storm gives me a glimpse of the ocean. Until the sun comes out, I listen to the pitter-patter of the rain on the roof above my head. While the sun shines, my arms are immersed to my collarbones in the tubs. At midday, I skip over the puddles to the library to borrow a few soggy mysteries, which is all that I have the energy to read. At night I wade home. My only solace: He that is born to be hanged shall never drown.

My hoochmates view my little collection of books with suspicion.

"Is that a good book?"

"It's all right."

"What's it about?"

69

"An old lady who solves murders."

"Oh. You sure do read a lot."

"Yeah."

"I read sometimes."

"Yeah?"

"Reading helps me fall asleep."

And God help the salon that would depend upon the scintillating repartee that surrounds me. Picture, if you will, two men sitting on the end of their cots with heads, hands, and tongues hanging loose.

"Two hundred and twelve days to go."

"Yeah?"

"Yeah. Two hundred and twelve. You?"

"One hundred and sixty-four."

"Yeah?"

"Yeah."

"Getting down there."

"Yeah."

"You playing cards tonight?"

"Don't know. You?"

"Don't know."

"Me neither."

"Only an hour 'til supper."

"That all?"

"Yeah."

"An hour, huh?"

"Yeah."

"Wow!"

"Yeah."

Silence.

"Two hundred and twelve to go."

I have agreed with myself to speak only a small portion of my mind.

Relentlessly,

Kurt

Dear Mom,

Have I told you how well we dine here? The mess hall serves up meat at every meal; for instance, tonight I dined on steak, mashed potatoes, green beans, biscuits with butter and jam, and cherry cobbler. The potatoes, like the eggs we eat for breakfast, are powdered and nearly inedible, but otherwise the marine cooks deserve any compliment they receive.

At the moment (11 P.M.), I am tired. Although I enjoy writing to you, I should prefer to do so tomorrow. Nevertheless, that several of my hoochmates are using my cot as a card table works to my advantage. Were I to continually postpone the writing of my letter, I might have difficulty pulling out my pencil and paper again. I lack adherence to my resolutions.

The hut in which I would be sleeping were my bed not being used as a card table measures 15 feet × 30 feet. The lower half of each wall is wooden; the upper half is screen. Tarpaulins are tied upon the walls to protect us from the rain that beats down all night upon the tin roof. Yes, we have a floor and no, we don't have a television. My hoochmates bathe seldomly and reluctantly; as no Chinese laundry is nearby, our clothes remain unwashed. The odor inside the hut defies description. Nonetheless, I'll try to describe it. The stench is foul and pervasive.

My nine hoochmates work regular shifts from eight to four; they go to sleep around one o'clock. As I must arise at four-thirty, I should prefer going to sleep a few hours this side of midnight. That is impossible. The men talk loudly in hope of making themselves heard over the wind, the rain, and one another. This is a good time to write letters.

I wish I had something to write about. I work in the mess hall fourteen hours a day, seven days a week, for thirty days. This morning I arrived at work fifteen minutes late. I was punished for my tardiness by two hours of overtime spent cleaning the stoves.

I've had a gracious plenty of the nobility of labor.

Love,

Kurt

Chloe dear,

NOAH, HE WENT, AND HE BUILT HIM AN ARKY–ARKY

SETTING: A typical hooch in a typical medical battalion
during a typical monsoon in a typical Southeast
Asian nation in conflict.

The CURTAIN RISES on a room of modest proportions, packed
to the rafters with cots, seabags, footlockers, and corpsmen.
(NOTE TO DESIGNER: *Use olive-green profusely.*) A noise like
the beating of a thousand tom-toms added to three million
marbles dropping simultaneously into tin cans mixed with the
roar of Niagara Falls as heard from inside a barrel is audible
throughout the sketch. (NOTE TO ACTORS: *Speak loudly at all
times.*) Five men are playing cards. They sit upon two cots and
a footlocker pulled around a third cot they use as a card table.
Smoke rises from the third cot; someone's cigarette has rolled
out of an ashtray, setting a blanket afire. It is noticed. General
alarm. "Fire!" *"Zu hilfe!"* Someone pours the contents of a
beer can upon the blanket and douses the fire. A damage check
reveals a large hole in the blanket.

WIT: Is Strom going to be pissed or is he going to be
pissed?

Several shrugs. The card game resumes. (NOTE TO LIGHTS:
Flicker and dim at odd moments.)
In other parts of the hooch, other men do other things. One
pares his toenails with his knife and sniffs the scrapings. Another man picks his asshole with his fingers and sniffs the
scrapings. A third man stares vacantly into space and smiles.
A fourth man in red silk lounging pajamas lounges. A fifth
man lies nude upon his rack, flies swarming about his genitals.
(NOTE TO PRODUCER: *Check municipal morality laws.*) A sixth
man counts the days remaining of his tour of duty in Nam. A
seventh man sits perplexed over a crossword puzzle. He speaks.

WISDOM: Does anyone know a four-letter word?

The door opens before anyone can answer. Wind scatters the cards and rain bespatters the players. A very weary man dressed in drenched-green crawls through the door. He kicks it shut with a very weary foot.

CONCERN: Hard day, huh, Strom?

The man in drenched-green continues to crawl. Steam rises from him. (NOTE TO PROPS: *Everything should be moldy, clammy, and damp*.)

PRUDENCE: You don't mind us wallering all over your bed, do you, Strom?

The crawling man looks up. He obviously minds. Even so, the wallering continues. The man with the vacant stare rushes over to squat just in front of the man on the floor.

SIMPLICITY: Man, Strom, you look beat, you understand what I mean? Jeez. Wow! Man, I know how it is. Jeez. Tough. Wow! You understand what I mean? Jeez.

The man in drenched-green groans. Flies swarm over to alight upon his boots, eyes, and lips. (NOTE TO DIRECTOR: *The flies may present a technical problem*.) The man in the corner speaks.

FAITH: Hey, Strom! Two hundred and twelve to go.

The man in red silk lounging pajamas wafts over to stroke the hair of the man in drenched-green.

CHARITY: Kurt, darling, if you'd care to relax in my corner until the game is over, I'd be glad to have you.
HAPPINESS: I win again.
PERSEVERANCE: Let's play another game.
INNOCENCE: You don't mind us using your cot, do you, Strom? Strom?

Strom lies in a steaming puddle on the floor, unconscious.

FAITH: Two hundred and twelve. Two hundred and twelve. Two hundred and . . .

CURTAIN

Of course, it needs work.

Relentlessly,

Kurt

FIRST MEDICAL BATTALION
CHU LAI, VIETNAM
7 October 66

My dear Paul,

I come off KP next week and a hoochmate who supervises the booby hatch has offered me an apprenticeship there. I'd already accepted a job offer from Jenkins, who supervises the recovery room, but I was curious and dropped by to take a looky-see at the nuts.

The number one maniac was a simple-looking SeaBee who had bragged too long and loud of his devoted gal Sal back home. When she sent him a Dear John letter, his bored hoochmates serenaded him with "They Call Her Frivolous Sal." The SeaBee went berserk and shot six of them. Five died, the sixth was critically wounded, and a seventh who witnessed the massacre fell into a catatonic shock. Death by "Friendly Fire."

When I walked in expecting bedlam, the killer SeaBee was playing "Sorry" with a pair of tubby, middle-aged marine gunny sergeants. Several other men played cards. Only the catatonic seemed out of it.

The sergeants had been discovered on the floor of their hut in a soixante-neuf. It sounds comical, but after twenty years or so in the Crotch (the Marine Corps), they will spend several months in the brig at half-pay for the crime of sodomy, be issued an undesirable discharge, lose their pensions, and learn that their families have been notified of their proclivities. I wonder whom they so offended.

I was told that if I accepted the job, I would be trained to soothe the shell shocked during their occasional breakdowns. At other times I would play games with the loonies, the undesirables, and a couple of very pretty desirables who tried to do naughty things in the wrong places with the wrong people. It was tempting, but I'm afraid I couldn't have resisted touching the untouchables.

Still, without danger the game grows cold.

Relentlessly

Kurt

FIRST MEDICAL BATTALION
CHU LAI, VIETNAM
11 October 66

Chloe dear,

Late last night as I attempted to snuggle underneath a soggy blanket, an apparition bearing a startling likeness to the Frankenstein monster appeared in our doorway, where it stood steaming and streaming. "Which one is Strom?" it said. Everyone looked at me. I threw my blanket over my head, but it has a large hole in it. The apparition stuck its finger through the hole, poked me in the chest, and beckoned me to follow it into the storm. A patient in the recovery room wanted to see me. "Who can it be?" I asked myself.

Babich!

"Oh, Kurt, it's terrible. Just terrible. It's always dark and everyone shoots at you and you're always cold and wet and scared. The captain is a maniac and he sends everyone into the night to get killed and it's always wet and mines are everywhere, blowing people's legs off and I can't believe I'm not dead. Bugs crawl all over you. People scream all the time. It's terrible, Kurt, just terrible. Try not to go out there." He looked at me through drug-dulled eyes, as if he were seeing a dead man; then he shook his head despairingly and turned it toward the wall.

When his vital signs stabilized, I helped carry Babich to one of the wards. This morning a chopper flew him to the hospital ship *Sanctuary,* where the doctors will examine his leg. He may have nerve damage. After a short recuperation, Babich will return to his line company. The prospect leaves him cold.

Babich served under just one fanatical officer; another is a patient now on ICU, a handsome steel-eyed captain of thirty-five or so. He lost both legs when he stepped from his tent onto a land mine his own men had set up.

Relentlessly,

Kurt

First Medical Battalion
Chu Lai, Vietnam
12 October 66

My dear Paul,

Sensation within the perimeter last Saturday night. The marines of Motor Pool who maintain and operate the compound's trucks, jeeps, and ambulances got drunk and rampaged through the hooches looking for queer corpsmen. Their particular target was Alf, "The Big One," a huge, gentle fairy with a remarkable resemblance to the Frankenstein monster. They found him hiding behind his footlocker and dragged him off to an unknown fate.

Alf's little lover was frantic, I hear tell, and wanted to arouse the battalion commander to "stop it." Cooler heads persuaded Bernie to calmly await the Big One's eventual liberation. The vigil ended several hours later, when Alf stumbled in the door of his hut, subdued and reticent.

Alf and Bernie, who looks like Shirley Temple, enlisted together and have never been separated. The couple has partitioned off a quarter of their hut, pushed their cots together, and have hung velvet paintings of sad little girls on the partition. Although I'd stopped by their hut a couple of times to chat with an acquaintance from Lejeune, I'd never put two and two together—I'd never realized they were gay. I had to be told about them, and that's another story.

One midnight I slogged through the mud to the shitter. The man sitting next to me in the darkness moved his foot against mine. What followed is censorable. As I walked out the door afterward, the invisible man hissed, "Tomorrow! Midnight."

Curiosity got the better of me, and the following evening found me sitting over a hole, worrying about rats chomping down on my precious and waiting for my demon lover. He showed up on time: my hoochmate the lab technician, a prematurely aged nervous nelly. Hardly my type. Call it circumstance. Anyway, he filled me in about Who's Who, in which I am probably now listed. Sadly, my sisters rank among the homeliest of the battalion personnel; I cannot imagine being tempted again. But then, one never knows whom one will do, does one?

Babich came through the Med Battalion. He had been wounded in the right leg by one of our mortars. He was very depressed. I tried to cheer him but failed. I thought Miss Priss might help; Babich had a furious craving for the familiar. I went to Miss P's hut only to learn that she had gone to a line company. She'd volunteered. It takes all kinds.

Miss P had been assigned to one of the wards. I saw little of her, although she did wave prettily as she passed through the chow line. I learned from one of my hoochmates working in Personnel that Dana had attempted several times to get transferred to the boondocks. A few days ago a call came through for volunteers to go out. Miss Priss stood first in line.

Oglesby, my companion during KP, was second. As he put it, "I'd blow Rin-Tin-Tin if it got me out of washing one more dish."

To each his own. Greasy Joan doth keel those pots.

Relentlessly,

Kurt

FIRST MEDICAL BATTALION
CHU LAI, VIETNAM
13 October 66

Dear Mom,

Thank you for the cookies. I opened the package after work and passed it around the hut. I'd planned on setting the remainder aside to munch at my leisure, but cries of "We want more!" rent the air. The package was emptied within minutes. You have another success on your hands.

My buddy Babich passed through the compound; he was wounded in the right leg. Now he is somewhere out to sea. He wasn't severely hurt; there were a few holes where shrapnel had entered. I thought his mother might worry when she received that telegram the Navy sends, so I wrote her the details as I knew them; I remembered to include that his face was unmarked. (Only Babich's mother could care.) He will just have a few small scars, and they will be tiny things.

My hoochmates play a card game they call "Okinawa Gin." It's like "Oh, Hell," although it takes less skill, especially when playing with my hoochmates.

Of course, I dislike scrubbing pots and pans, but what ever can one do when he is in the Navy and dislikes his job?

1. He could throw down his scouring pad and throw up his hands, announcing that he's quit. He'd get thrown into the brig.

2. He could shrug philosophically and scrub those pots until his tour of duty in Vietnam ends. That occurs in 366 days.

3. He could do his job so poorly that he would be replaced. He would then be sent to the lines.

4. He could convince himself that he just loves scraping and scouring those pans, smiling all the while. He would be put on exhibition and hauled from town to town in an iron cage.

5. He could feign ill health. Unfortunately, he lives in a hospital complex where expert malingerers have failed to outsmart the doctors.

6. He could isolate a hepatitis germ and drop it into the oatmeal batter, closing the mess hall. He'd rather swab pots for the next twelve months than eat "C"-rations for two weeks.

7. He could exhibit his unmentionable to the sweet young Red Cross worker who visits the mess hall each week for Sunday dinner. But what ever would he do if she laughed?

No one lives content with his condition.

Love,

Kurt

Arch,

I'm becoming better acquainted with the men who share my humble home, so when I have an hour or two to kill between lunch and supper, I visit them at their jobs.

BEST-ALL-AROUND works in the emergency room. When the helicopters churn in with dead and wounded men, he rushes to the landing pad to help the marine litter-bearers carry them up to Triage (or Sorting). BAA records the patient's names, service numbers, injuries, and probable destinations: Return to Duty, Ward, Operating Room, or Graves. He sorts the men according to the degree of their injuries and cuts away their boots and uniforms. He treats minor wounds: disinfecting, debriding (cutting away dead and injured tissue), stitching, and bandaging. He aids the doctors with serious wounds: starting intravenous injections, handling instruments, and holding down limbs. He lays the dead men in a corner; they will be sent to Graves. During slack times, BAA will hose down stretchers and floors to wash away blood and debris, and he'll stock supplies.

In X ray is MOST TALENTED. He wheels the wounded from Triage to X ray, transfers them to the X-ray table, and photographs them. He develops the X rays, delivers them to Triage, and usually helps the doctor determine the extent of the damage to the patient.

MOST VERSATILE works in the laboratory. Should a wounded man be headed for surgery, MV draws his blood, types it, cross matches it with the blood and plasma he has in cold storage, and puts several pints on reserve. He spins a tube down to check for blood loss—a hematocrit (blood count). He places a drop of blood upon a slide, stains the slide blue, and counts under a microscope the ratio of white and red cells to blue cells—Hematology (the study of blood). He spins down a tube of piss, dumps the clear liquid, places a sample of the sediment upon a slide, and checks it under the microscope for white cells (infection) and red cells (blood)—Urinalysis. Other departments within the lab include Blood Chemistry, which tests such things as sugar or alcoholic content of the blood;

Serology—venereal disease; and Bacteriology—the study of spit and shit.

The head operating-room technician is MOST INTELLECTUAL. Besides assisting at operations, he prepares the injured for surgery: cleaning the wound, shaving the area around the wound, and injecting pre-op medications. He can act as an anesthesiologist and is responsible for the recovery room.

MOST DEPENDABLE controls the evacuation of the wounded from First Med to the airfields, where they are put aboard flights to the USA, the Philippines, Japan, or other parts of Vietnam. Vegies (brain-deaths) are sent to a hospital on the other side of Chu Lai. Crispies (burn victims) go to Yokuska, Japan; Cam Ranh Bay has a special hospital for scorched Vietnamese (Rice Crispies). The men who will return to tote their pieces again are carried by choppers to the hospital ships *Sanctuary* or *Repose*.

A sixth hoochmate is head corpsman on the Neuropsychiatric (NP) ward. His patients include the battle fatigued, druggies, perverts, and crazies. He plays games like "Monopoly" and "Sorry" with them to keep the nuts calm. I think he should be MOST FRIENDLY.

MOST LIKELY TO SUCCEED works in the base commander's office. LIK-SUC keeps personnel records, answers telephone calls, and makes coffee.

MOST ATHLETIC works in Supply, where he orders, unloads, unpacks, and stores supplies. He carries the supplies to the wards and departments as they are needed.

My ninth hoochmate is the chaplain's assistant. He sleeps most of the day and night. I haven't a glimmering of what his responsibilities may be. I suppose we should think of him as MOST RELIGIOUS.

Relentlessly,

Kurt

Dear Mom,

I'm glad life goes well with you. For goodness' sake, don't feel guilty that you're enjoying a pleasant existence while I suffer through "The Heat of War"; it's hardly that. You should be cheering me up instead of becoming maudlin. You'll soon be sending me cards edged in black, which contain locks of your hair. I don't need your hair; my own has grown back luxuriantly. Perhaps the moisture stimulates growth.

I've completed my thirty-day tour of KP duty. Now I work in the recovery room—the Surgical Intensive Care Unit. SICU is a tunnel-shape building of corrugated tin attached to the operating rooms. And heated. The work force consists of six men and is divided into two shifts; my shift begins at midnight and ends at noon. We nurse the post-operative patients until they stabilize; then they go to the wards or out-of-country.

You mustn't believe for a moment that Ricky is indifferent to your attending his football games. He'd never allow you to know how much he cares. Ask Neil. He goes to every game, come hell or high water. Even Mother and DT pry themselves away from the boob tube, although Mother's vexing in her lack of partisanship: We cheer only for Ricky's teammates; Mother hates to see any of the boys lose. Everyone knows his attendance is gratifying to Ricky, if unacknowledged. I would have been an All-Star every year that I played in the minors had I such support in the stands. You're Dad's proxy in a way. Ricky and Dad were awfully good buddies. I know how often I wished that Dad and Daddy could have been alive to see me play ball.

And don't worry about Ricky's getting hurt; a bevy of junior high school beauties will be happy to ease his pain with their attentions.

Love,

Kurt

Arch,

No one could fault you for preferring the sunshine of Mazatlán to the drizzle and hard work of the fernery. My stepfather is inured to the vagaries of his employees; he expects them when he sees them. Never apologize, good buddy, never explain.

I am working on the Surgical Intensive Care Unit, twelve hours out of twenty-four. I share the midnight-to-noon shift with Alf, who looks like the Frankenstein monster, and Randall, a short-timer with only a few weeks left in Nam. Randall seems enamored of machinery, and despite my meager flair for operating apparatus, he is determined to have me learn everything there is to know about the stuff. I push and pull intricate contraptions around the ward as wary of the evil looking things as the patients are, as I don't understand the theories behind the treatments any more than they do. "It's very complicated," I tell the simple grunts, when they are able to ask.

We have several kinds of suction pumps, which are used to clear away debris in various organs: lungs, stomachs, and windpipes. Did you know that stomach contents are dark green and look like liquid spinach? I didn't. We run the spectrum of the rainbow here. Blue? That's the color of the face of a heart attack victim; he looked like the mad curator in *The House of Wax*. He died. White? Tapeworms. One of our Vietnamese patients was in a double spica, a plaster cast covering the body from the lower ribs to the toes with openings for evacuations, and he had to evacuate. We lifted him onto a bed-pan and watched a long, white tapeworm poke its head out of his asshole. De-trashing a windpipe brings up a beige froth flecked with pink. And purple, lime green, and black for gangrene and brown for shit and yellow for piss and pus and oceans of red.

I lack the training for many of the procedures we use and I could err seriously. Watching a doctor draw blood from the femoral artery in a patient's groin, I marveled at the ease of such a method as compared with stabbing away at a guy's arm; the next time a blood sample was required, I decided to tap a femoral myself. Randall saw me. He said that arterial blood clots with more difficulty then venous blood, and hemorrhage could result.

I'll confess to a mistake I made with a Viet Cong prisoner whose legs were amputated. The procedure used here for amputees is primitive. We must make do with metal weights of varying poundages, which are strung together on ropes hooked to long stockings wrapped around the patient's stumps. Don't ask me why. I haven't an idea why they use such a treatment. And I should. I really should. I'll get some answers from Randall tomorrow. He takes things seriously and expects me to know this shit; happily, he has a lot of determination and patience.

Anyway, I was checking the VC's vital signs every fifteen minutes—temperature, pulse, and respiration. His blood pressure was slowly declining, but I hated to keep saying, "His blood pressure is getting lower"; it sounded so boring. So instead of watching him carefully, I passed the time of day with Alf; then Randall noticed that the VC had stopped breathing. We pounded his chest dutifully, but he was dead. Although I felt embarrassment, no one really cared; it was only a zip.

That was my first day on the ward. The following day I was assigned to a black marine shot in the chest, a fat and very stinky dude who has been having a hard time breathing—as a result, he's become greatly attached to an oxygen mask from which the doctors are trying to wean him. Whenever something bothers Sambo, he writes another illiterate message on his little note pad, a task he prefers to talking.

At one point, he wrote a message demanding the oxygen mask be placed over his face. As his doctor had left orders that Sambo had another hour to go until we put him back on the tank, I went to the other end of the ward to get Randall's advice. Randall needed help with one of his own patients, and a couple of minutes passed before I could return to the jig. He was bouncing up and down on the bed and scribbling furiously on his tablet that he wanted the doctor. I fetched his doctor from Triage. Sambo's message to the doctor was "Dat komen bees pregadeeced [That corpsman is prejudiced] an leafs me to die." That wasn't quite the truth, but I feared I would soon be back among the pots.

Randall told me to forget it; the spook had been an asshole ever since he'd arrived on the ward. Nevertheless, I fretted over the incident. I was slightly prejudiced, although more against his odor than his color: He wouldn't let anyone bathe him. And he was badly wounded. The following morning I went to the chow hall to fill the lunch buckets; while I was gone, Sambo stopped breathing. Randall gave mouth-to-mouth resuscitation and revived him. Had I been on the ward instead of Randall, I don't think I would have bothered.

Last night the men in the other crew stayed after their shift was completed to join Randall in an interrogation of an old man suspected to being a VC. He had a stomach tube down his throat that the guys kept pulling out and reinserting—an extremely uncomfortable procedure. "You VC?" Out with the tube. Gagging and choking sounds. "VC numba ten." (Bad!) In with the tube. Gagging and choking sounds. Repeat procedure fifteen times. I felt sorry for the old man, but after my boo-boos, I wasn't about to get anyone pissed at me by protesting.

And who am I to protest anyway? Alf told me that Randall's best friend entered a hut pointed out to him by an old Vietnamese farmer who said it contained VC documents; what the hut really contained was a booby trap, and Randall's buddy was blown to bits.

I fear that what's past is prologue.

Relentlessly,

Kurt .

FIRST MEDICAL BATTALION
CHU LAI, VIETNAM
20 October 66

Chloe dear,

I'd been reluctant to step outside the compound. Two conscious reasons affected my sense of adventure: 1. They might think I'd like it better out there. 2. They might not let me come back inside. One subconscious reason affected me: I considered the compound as a womb.

My buddy Randall scoffed at reason and dragged me kicking and screaming into the world. My first baby steps were directed toward the PX a couple of miles to the south. We toddled along the beach to get there. Randall bought a case filled with little cans of foul-tasting Mickey Mouse orange juice; I bought a tape recorder for $110, marked down from $225. We carried our prizes home along dusty Highway 1. I thought I'd experienced enough excitement to last several months; Randall had just begun my education.

The following afternoon, we strapped on the required .45 pistols and walked down the road to a small village. We picked up the laundry left there by our alternate shift and carried it to a tiny restaurant, where we ate dinner: rice with bits of pork and chicken. Good manners decree that a diner leave some food on his plate; otherwise, the Vietnamese feel they have failed as hosts by offering too little. Scuttlebutt has it that the Cong lace beer and soda pop with ground glass; they need do nothing so deadly to convince me of their shortcomings as hosts. When the waitress served my warm beer, I hesitated, but I feared Randall's scorn more. I drank three. Late that night, I whipped out of my hut and hurled myself into the storm several times, so I could pay emergency visits to the shitter; for three days, I suffered from a mild dysentery or a severe diarrhea. Whichever, the meal was delicious.

All this gadding about has inspired me to rent an elephant complete with howdah for an overland expedition into the mountains to shoot tigers.

Every dog is a lion at home.

Relentlessly,

Kurt

FIRST MEDICAL BATTALION
CHU LAI, VIETNAM
21 October 66

My dear Paul,

At one or two o'clock in the morning, the patients sleep. If Triage and the OR have shut down for lack of business, we douse the house lights and, sitting with our backs toward Stinky Lô Blô, resident zip and number one pain-in-the-ass, indulge in good chat.

During one of these interludes, I told everyone the plot of *Who's Afraid of Virginia Woolf* as I remembered it. Alf was enchanted. I ran to my hooch, brought my new tape recorder to the ward, and we improvised a script. Randall and I played the male roles, while Alf and Bernie played the female parts. Alf delighted in emoting such lines as "George! You are nothing but a dumb cluck. That's all you are, a goddam dumb cluck."

That was the first production of the Chu Lai Players—A Different Show Every Night. *Reeling Through Dixie:* a pitiful tale of the Old South starring Alf as Modess Tampax, a ruined belle; Bernie as her uppity free-issue serving wench Lavender Lou; Randall as Cap'n Randy; and me as General Lee Horney. *The Rise and Fall of the Third Reich* with Bernie as Hitler, Randall as Walter Pidgeon, Alf as the Whore of Babylon, and me as the beast that ate Europe. *Alice in Blunderland:* a wonderful tale of a girl who falls into a magic toilet. Bernie emoted Alice; Randall enacted the White Worm; I played the Mad Shitter; and Alf was the Black Queen.

Randall is getting good, and we may expand into Shakespeare, Chekhov, and Wilde. Unfortunately, Bernie is impossible as a thespian and quite temperamental. Nevertheless, he is married to the star.

The zips and marines are an inadequate audience and never laugh at our best lines. We are but caviar to the general.

Relentlessly,

Kurt

First Medical Battalion
Chu Lai, Vietnam
25 October 66

Arch,

An upswing in VC activity has many casualties coming through the Med Battalion. No new shipment of corpsmen has arrived; twelve-hour shifts are now the rule on the compound. This forebodes more men going to the lines to replace dead and wounded corpsmen. I evaded one call for volunteers two weeks ago. Those going left behind a compound short of fools, and when a second call came yesterday, no one held up his hand. Ten men of E-3 rank were to be sacrificed; eleven of us were assigned to Med Batt. (I'm not counting the three men exempted because of KP duty.) Because I worked ICU and the other ten worked the wards, I was the eleventh man. I am holding my breath and hanging by my nails until the new shipment arrives. When it does, I am safe for the duration.

Most of our casualties are Americans, but there are a few Koreans and Vietnamese. We transfer the Americans out of ICU as quickly as possible; the Koreans usually stay for a couple of days. They seem to be a rough lot and seldom report sick, unless they have five serious wounds and are perforated with holes. We have no interpreters, so communications between the Koreans and us are difficult. Post-operative procedures often include twelve hours of fasting, which is difficult to explain in sign language to a semiconscious and thirsty man. As a result, the Koreans have a distressing tendency to drink their own piss whenever we leave the ducks (portable metal urinals) within their reach.

The Vietnamese stay forever. ICU's mascot is Stinky Lô Blô, who has been on the ward for months. He suffers from a gangrenous leg, which the doctors hope to save. As the leg rots, the ward has developed a pungent atmosphere, the proverbial "sickly sweet odor of decay." The other corpsmen, all veterans, stay away from the poor guy, which is all right with him because I am he who Stinky loves. My daily appearance has him quivering with excitement as he tries to catch my eye. I am softer than the other guys; I must look at him. When I do, he greets me with his entire English vocabulary, "I shit, Doc." So I slide the bedpan under him. Several times a day. He enjoys saying that revolting sentence. And he adores shitting.

His greater need is owning two protection dogs like Cougar and Puma. Koreans loathe their fellow dinks, and the most comatose revive to snarl at him. The less critically wounded among the Koreans slide out of bed to crawl along the floor toward Stinky, hissing and spitting and dragging their tubes behind them. We wait until their machines are ready to topple before we call a halt to the procession. Stinky cringes in his low cot, watching them in wide-eyed dismay.

Stinky's female counterpart is Camille, an ebony-dentured mamasan someone shot in the belly. I must continually irrigate her stomach tube to rid it of innumerable foot-long tapeworms, hideous things slightly more repellent than Camille.

One morning, as I avoided her tubercular cough while fishing for worms, Camille half-consciously grabbed a tender part of my anatomy between her long, sharp fingernails. As I wear nothing beneath green operating-room pajamas, she got a firm grip upon my precious. The pain was exquisite. My pleas of "Let go, dear" went unheeded, so I hit her on the head with the basinful of worms I held in my left hand. The dear let go. Everyone laughed. People around here are easily amused.

Relentlessly,

Kurt

FIRST MEDICAL BATTALION
CHU LAI, VIETNAM
26 October 66

Dear Mom,

The monsoon has increased in force, volume, and duration. Only the afternoons remain sunny, if muggy. Before the rain falls incessantly, I intend to swim as often as possible. Every day after lunch, several of us pick our way down the cliff to a crescent beach. At either end of the crescent, rocky hills slope downward to meet the sea. The riptide has drowned several men; I am safety-conscious and paddle about in the shallows.

I received a letter from the mother of my buddy Babich. She has heard nothing from Jim since he's been injured. His silence troubles me; at Lejeune, he wrote his family several times a week. Jim's grandmother sent me a large package filled with cheeses, a ham, and four loaves of black bread hard enough to break teeth; his little sister sent several comic books about Sergeant Rock and Captain America. The food was devoured by my buddies on the ward; the comic books, by my hoochmates.

Ricky wrote, too. (Were you sitting down as you read that sentence?) He says Mother plans to cook Bonnie and Clyde for Thanksgiving. Besides saving money, Mother will be rid of the ducky-doo Bonnie and Clyde leave on the terrace as they watch television through the glass doors. Ricky is furious; Neil is brokenhearted. Neither of them will eat a morsel. I'll try to devise a rescue plan, although I'll feel like a hypocrite; I can hardly censure Mother's loathing of turkey.

Yes, I like my new job and no, I feel little regret that my training as a combat medic is going to waste.

Two capable and hardworking men share my shift: Randall instructs me with patience and tact; Alf makes me laugh. Both encourage me and neither becomes ugly when I err, despite awe-inspiring opportunities. They prefer to calmly demonstrate the theories behind the proper procedure, watch as I repeat their instructions, and either smile their approval at my success or quietly endure beginning the lesson once more. Alf stays equable throughout the day; Randall is more volatile. I've seen his temper explode at lazy or indifferent corpsmen and at the patients who hurt the least and moan the loudest.

If I make my life here sound dull, amends are forthcoming. I've nosed out a few extracurricular activities that pass the time well enough.

A SeaBee camp next door shows movies every night in a little hollow; I attend them two or three times a week. First Med shows movies, too, on the parade ground in front of the mess hall; I avoid these. The wind blows sand up from the beach, and I sit in a frenzy clawing at my contact lenses. The other night, as Natalie Wood ran hysterically into the rain, the breeze did a blowing, Kurt did a clawing, a lens did a slipping, and it was gone with the wind. I neither found my lens nor learned whether Natalie ever got dry. Happily, I'd brought three extra pairs with me.

I visit the library daily to read the *Stars and Stripes*, our Armed Services' newspaper. My visits are brief. As I've finished all the mysteries, I'm left with old *National Geographic* magazines and cowboy novels. (I read in a *National Geographic* magazine that the monsoon season takes place during April and May. Everyone who has been in Nam for several months says the monsoon season is just beginning. What ever is a person to believe?)

Mom, please put an end to these wistful yearnings for the ranch. You have the knack of recollecting only the pleasant parts of life; don't forget the harsh winters, the isolation, and, above all, the turkeys. Yes, think of those damned turkeys, so stupid they wouldn't come in from the rain. And always dying of something or other. And that incessant gobble gobble gobble.

Really, Mom, if you become sentimental about those turkeys,
I'll hand you over to Aunt Billie myself.

Love,

Kurt

FIRST MEDICAL BATTALION
CHU LAI, VIETNAM
27 October 66

My dear Paul,

Alf and I cohosted a going-away party for Randall last night.
I broke out two long-hidden fifths of rum, and Alf charmed
the cooks at the mess hall into letting him bake some inventive
and delicious hors d'oeuvres from a ham sent me by Babich's
grandmother. Bernie made decorations out of candles and beer
cans. Who throws better parties than faggots?

Although the festivities were in honor of Randall, I used
them as an excuse to woo a muscular, curly haired grunt recovering from an appendectomy. I'd begun my courtship the
previous night by escorting him to the SeaBee camp for a
movie: *The Ghost and Mr. Chicken* starring Don Knotts. My
jarhead loved it. I invited him to Randall's party. I got him
drunk and walked him home. We stopped at the patients' shitter. As we sat comfortably close with the erotic aroma of shit
and kerosene billowing about us, I peered out the door. I saw
no flashlights bobbing toward us in the drizzle, so I placed my
hand on his bared thigh. He puked on my arm. That ended the
evening. He had ripped out his stitches. I carried him back to
his ward and returned to the party. I thought I'd been discreet,
but every queen on the compound had been following the courtship with great interest. I refuse to be aware that my name has
been bandied about with knowing smiles.

Randall left for the States this morning with a hangover. I
already regret never having put the move on him. Although
Randall was neither handsome nor graceful, he had a lean hard
body and a magnificent schwantz hung between his long legs.
Every day after work we would go to the beach, where Alf
and Bernie lay in the sun while Randall and I joined the other
off-duty corpsmen for rousing games of touch football against

the SeaBees. Randall played a solid, if rough, line; I played center. (My natural positions are offensive end and defensive safety, but man-to-man contact can't compare with pile-ups on the line. We play our games in the nude, and our quarterback, a glorious creature, tickles my balls as his signal to hike.) After the game, Randall and I would swim and sun before climbing the cliff for a shower. Wet and naked, we'd retire to his cubicle to chat, knee to knee and schwantz to schwantz. But I never made a pass. You can't be a buddy to a straight guy with whom you've fucked.

Last night at the party, one of the guests uttered a smirking innuendo directed toward Alf and Bernie. Alf, after satisfying himself that Bernie hadn't heard, looked at me and shrugged philosophically. Randall, however, took violent exception and admitted to having once cornholed a gay guy. He said he enjoyed it. I had to leave the party immediately afterward to go to work. Randall left this morning, and I'm left with the dubious consolation of knowing my buddy returned to the States with his energy unsapped for wooing and "Woo wooing."

Relentlessly,

Kurt

First Medical Battalion
Chu Lai, Vietnam
28 October 66

Chloe dear,

Dau quá, bác sĩ translates from the Vietnamese as "It hurts, Doc." *Lôn* means "cunt." A doubtful vocabulary in most situations, but I am working to enlarge it with one of our patients, a stinky local. In turn, I tutor him in English. He is as eager as I to expand his knowledge of our language, so I have begun his lessons with an alphabet he can understand.

> *A is Amputation*
> Cutting off a leg or arm
> Streaked with suppuration
> Ere the body comes to harm.

B is for a Bedpan:
A bowl of silvery tint
Wounded gooks can sit on
To void their excrement.

C is ma belle, Camille
Of the shattered belly;
She copped a painful feel
That turned my knees to jelly.

And so on.

After Daddy died, Mother gave his clothes, his rifles, and his fishing gear to one of his brothers. She detested the Stroms, but felt Daddy would have wanted her to do it. The only possession of his still in our family is the diary he kept when he served in the South Pacific during World War II. He was an engineer's mate on an LST, a small ship used for landing troops during island assaults. I've read the diary several times, and I'm always disappointed.

9 May 45: Sighted the Battleship *North Carolina*.
10 May 45: Hot. Nothing sighted.
11 May 45: Hot. Nothing sighted.
12 May 45: Stood off Eniwetok. No shore leave.

And so on. Mother told me that she'd asked Daddy to keep the log so I would know him as a young man when I reached his age. Well, Chloe, I am his age now, and I'll be damned if I understand him one whit better than if he had never written it.

But I can identify. I'd thought of keeping a war diary for Neil and Ricky and the sons I hope eventually to beget; unfortunately, like Daddy, I have little to say.

23 Oct 66: Rained last night. Eleven patients—six American, one Korean, and four Vietnamese. Went to the beach.
24 Oct 66: Rained last night. Five patients—one American and four Vietnamese. Went to the beach.
25 Oct 66: Rained last night. Twelve patients—six Americans, two Koreans, and four Vietnamese. Went to the beach.

Posterity is just around the corner.

Later:

Stinky Lô Blô was waiting for me when I came on duty tonight. The doctors had finally amputated his gangrenous leg. He pointed to his stump with tears running down his cheeks. I sat next to the bed and held his scungy hand. I hated every moment. It's contagious, you know: mutilation . . . death . . . The poor gook will go to a Roman Catholic hospital in Da Nang.

Oglesby, who washed dishes next to me during Kitchen Patrol, lay two beds up from Stinky, lacking a left hand. In the two weeks I've worked on ICU, I've already seen two classmates from Corps School with holes through their abdomens and a pleasant guy who bunked across from me at Lejeune with his jaw blasted away.

And do you remember Mickey Wendell, who carried me by car to Atlanta? He was on patrol in the jungle when a sniper shot him through the head.

Relentlessly,

Kurt

PART TWO

★ ★ ★

THE
HANGED MEN DANCE

> On old one-arm, black scaffolding,
> The hanged men dance;
> The devil's skinny advocates,
> Dead soldiers' bones.

Beezlebub jerks ropes about the necks
Of small black dolls who squirm against the sky;
With slaps, with whacks and cuffs and kicks
He makes them dance an antique roundelay!

Excited jumping jacks, they join thin arms;
Black organ lofts, their fretwork breasts
That once beat fast at beauteous damsels' charms
Now click together in a perverse embrace

Hurrah the jolly dancers, whose guts are gone!
About the narrow planks they jerk and prance!
Beezlebub roars the rasping fiddles' song!
Hop! They cannot tell the battle from the dance!

Hard heels, that never wear out shoes!
They've all put off their overcoat of skin;
What's left beneath is hardly worth excuse—
Their skulls are frail and white beneath the rain.

A crow provides a crest for these cracked heads,
A strip of flesh shakes on a skinny chin;
They swing about in somber skirmishes
Like heroes, stiff, their armor growing thin.

And the breeze blows for the skeletons' ball!
The gibbet groans like an organ of iron;
In violet forests the wolves wail;
The distant sky flames with hell's own fires!

Oh, shake me these dark commanders down!
Who slyly rake through broken fingertips
Love's rosary across their pale ribs:
This is no monastery, you dead men!

And there in the midst of the danse macabre
One wild skeleton leaps in the scarlet clouds
Stung with madness like a rearing horse
With the rope pulled stiff above his head.

He tightens bony fingers on his cracking knees
With squeals that make a mock of dead men's groans,
And, like a puppet flopping in the breeze,
Whirls in the dance to the sound of clacking bones.

> On old one-arm, black scaffolding
> The hanged men dance;
> The devil's skinny advocates,
> Dead soldiers' bones.

—ARTHUR RIMBAUD

96

Arch,

A gangly lieutenant j.g. who regularly holds surprise personal neatness inspections of disbelieving and highly affronted battalion corpsmen called me into his office late last week. "William Kurt Strom, Hospitalman, service number 2438429?"

"Yes, sir."

"You are to report to the Second Infantry Battalion, Seventh Marine Regiment."

"Yes, sir."

"You push off tomorrow at sixteen-thirty for the lines," he said bravely. "Pack your seabag, sailor."

I went to my hut to pack my seabag. My hoochmates watched me; when I looked up, they lowered their eyes—they had appraised my ability to survive out there. I considered throwing myself at the feet of my commander to beg for mercy, but that would have embarrassed both of us; besides, I had no idea what he looked like. Instead, I wrapped myself around the pee-pipe and refused to let go. They pried me away and dragged me down to Motor Pool. A jeep awaited me, complete with driver and guard. I climbed in. As the driver turned the ignition key, my friend Alf tore off the St. Christopher's metal he always wore around his neck, ran to the jeep, and hung the medal around my neck; then, he stepped back and crossed himself. The driver released the brake, and the jeep lurched forward.

I hung on for dear life as the jeep swerved and skidded along the muddy road going inland toward the mountains. Several miles past civilization, we reached a crossroads. The jeep slowed down to make a U-turn as the shotgun threw my bags onto the road. I jumped out after them. I watched the jeep hurtle into the gathering twilight. Darkness fell. I heard a noise in the bushes behind me. I turned around. A tall marine stepped out of the shadows. His red eyes burned. "Follow me," he said gravely. He turned and vanished into the jungle. I saw a seedy movie marquee above the trees, missing several letters and blinking on and off: AL HOPE ABA DON, YE WH ENT R HERE.

Relentlessly,

Kurt

2ND BATTALION, ECHO CO.
7TH MARINES
2 November 66

Chloe dear,

Remember when we'd come by in the station wagon on Saturday nights to pick you up on our way to a "Horrorama" at the drive-in? Karen would have filled several huge bags with popcorn, the boys would have filled a washtub with Cokes and ice, and you'd have hidden a couple of family-size Hershey Bars in your purse, which you and I would surreptitiously gorge upon as we polished off a fifth of rum in the front seat. Karen would set up a lawn chair next to the car, so she could hold court without disturbing us. Neil and Ricky would rotate between the playground and a harassment of Karen's beaus. You and I would be getting plastered. Then the movies would begin: *Two Lost Worlds, Bucket of Blood, The Naked Jungle* . . . By the end of the evening, all of us would be huddled together in the car with the windows rolled up and the doors locked, certain that everyone at the drive-in was a zombie and unsure about one another.

Cadaverous gentlemen welcomed naive travelers through the creaking doors of ancient castles. In cobwebbed hallways, misguided heroes told their girl friends to "Wait here" as they went to investigate some bump in the night. A dizzy blonde wandered away from the protection of a group in the most Godforsaken places, only to be found three shrieks later cowering in a shallow hole as a pair of dinosaurs locked in a death grip rolled back and forth over her. Molten lava flowed down a mountainside to envelop the screaming brunette. Ghoulies and ghosties and longlegged beasties would haunt our dreams for weeks.

Giant tarantulas and giant scorpions and Ramar's walking through the rain forest with a tiger on his tail held us spellbound. Natives bind Tarzan's friends to two trees tied together at the top; the ropes are cut and the trees go whap! and the people split open. Pythons drop from branches and spook the safari. Zebras and elephants stampede and trample a few niggers. Fire ants go on the march, eating everything in their path and crawling all over the face of the drunken mestizo as he shrieks "My eyes! My eyes!" (Neils' special nightmare.)

We'd be uneasy after the last movie concluded in the wee hours of the morning, but the cavalcade of cars driving through the exit gates would bring us back to reality. Although we'd conjure up terrifying fantasies that always began with a breakdown of the car somewhere near a fog-shrouded Dead River and a subsequent journey by foot through the swamps to get home, we knew we were in these United States and safe.

Chloe, I'm no longer in those United States, and I've learned that we hadn't been viewing backlot "B" productions. Nosireebob. I'm on location now. What we thought were movies were newsreels. They were Tru-Life Adventures. They were where it's happening.

I suppose I must write home to tell them all about it. I could never deprive Mother of catastrophe.

Relentlessly,

Kurt

2ND BATTALION, ECHO CO.
7TH MARINES
3 November 66

Dear Mom,

I am assigned to a line company that goes into the jungle to look for the enemy so the captain can report the enemy's location to the people with the big guns. It's sort of a tattletale company. My job will be to repair the bruises of careless tattletales. Actually, I have two jobs. The second is to keep myself from falling into the yellow claws of the Viet Cong. And not necessarily in that order. It is all very interesting.

I know you'll worry. Don't. I'd wondered whether I should tell you if my future seemed bleak. I discussed the question with Karen. I know the two of you are on the outs, but Karen respects you. She felt you would be hurt if I were to lie to you and that I would have far to go before finding anyone with whom to better share adversity. I had to agree. So I am on the lines and find that the speculation about my safety was unwarranted. I am in a battalion of six hundred men, dug in and well fortified. Several battalions of Viet Cong would be needed to infiltrate our defenses, and the VC prefer to operate in smaller groups.

The casualty rate in the newspaper can be deceptive. Two hundred thousand troops are scattered throughout Vietnam, sixty thousand of them marines. I'll be a needle in a haystack.

Love,

Kurt

2ND BATTALION, ECHO CO.
7TH MARINES
4 November 66

My dear Paul,

Tom-toms throb with a message from Kurtala, the Jungle Queen. "BWANA! GET ME OUT OF HERE!"

Paul, this howling wilderness is hardly a nice place to visit, much less live, if you can call this living. I haven't an inkling of where I am located in relation to anyplace else in Vietnam but then, I haven't an inkling of where anyplace else is located either. I don't know where I am or where anybody else is. And nobody else knows where I am. If I weren't surrounded by hundreds of people, I might think I was lost.

High in the treetops and wrapped snugly within the mighty arms of the ape-man, Lord Greystoke, I might rest content, but I fucking doubt it. I am less afraid of the Cong than of finding a foot-long centipede wrapping itself around my toes as I pull on my boots in the morning or feeling some slithery, scaly, nameless thing dropping out of the trees upon my head. I have struck up an intimate acquaintance with my bowels, which insist upon being moved at the goddamnedest times, and you wouldn't believe the set-up here for that.

Other parts of my body have begun to intrigue me, too, and I examine myself daily and thoroughly for symptoms of plague and scourge. The monsoon reigns. My clothes mold upon me. Leathernecks stink, feeling as they do that changing stockings and undergarments are vexations to the spirit. People I have just met disappear into the rain forest and never return. Those who come back charge about the camp yelling "Rape... maim... kill!" "C"-rations make me nauseous; the drinking water smells suspiciously of a nearby latrine. And worst of all, Mommy isn't nearby to kiss my bruises and to tell the bogeyman to go away.

On the other hand, the jungle brings back memories of the swamps of home; nursing jarheads can be no more oppressive than rearing turkeys; and I am surrounded by six hundred ruthless and horny youths. All in all, it's not half bad.

Relentlessly,

Kurt

2ND BATTALION, ECHO CO.
7TH MARINES
8 November 66

Chloe dear,

Pay no attention to whatever I wrote to you last week. I was suffering from hysteria. I learned that in a book my chief corpsman lent me: *Psychological and Physiological Dangers to the Individual during Conflicts with Guerrillas in Semi-Tropical Southeastern Asian Nations Divided by Opposing Political Idelogies.*

Yes, dear heart, I am in the jungle. Aba daba daba. I suspect skulduggery by the owners of nine American League clubs to prevent the Detroit Tigers from reaching the World Series throughout the 1970's, sparked by that incredible superstar at third base, Kloutin' Kurt Strom.

Actually, it's not too bad out here, should you be anxious to meet your Maker. Chances are good that I might step on a land mine and get both my arms and both my legs blown off; then I can be used *as* third base.

I'd like to tell you where I am located, but it seems to be the secret beyond the grave. Don't think for a minute that I'm downhearted. Who, me? Never! GO TEAM GO!

> *Kick 'em in the funnybone.*
> *Sock 'em in the jaw.*
> *Put 'em in the cemetery.*
> *Rah! Rah! Rah!*

Into the Valley of Death rode the six hundred. When I have fears that I may cease to be before my pen has gleaned my teeming brain. It is only when the moon is full that the were-wolves howl.

Nuts to such a pessimistic view of life. I shall think happy and sunny thoughts. Sunshine . . . daydreams . . . wet dreams . . . wet . . . rain . . . monsoon . . . Vietnam . . . doom . . . defeat . . . despair . . .

Speaking of wet dreams, I heard a story the other day about a prince who can be turned back into a frog only when a wrinkled, black-toothed, disease-ridden mamasan gives him head.

Mother has often told me that to be happy, a person must think interesting thoughts. I'll forget about such happy people as Swift, Strindberg, and Rimbaud, and I'll think interesting thoughts. What lies behind the door to the Inner Sanctum? Who knows what evil lurks in the hearts of men? Where was Moses when the lights went out?

I saw a Japanese movie once in which several people were shipwrecked upon a damp, misty island. They turned into fungi.

> *Relentlessly,*
>
> *Kurt*

Arch,

I survived my first patrol. Thirteen of us were to infiltrate deep into "Viet Cong territory." What they kept referring to as a "suspected concentration of VC" had built up in the vicinity, and we were to try to find it. They just couldn't leave well enough alone.

We slogged along in the dark, the rain dripping upon us through the jungle canopy high overhead. As we were on a secret mission, the trails were taboo, so we pushed through eye-high brambles, chin-deep mud, and chilly streams up to our armpits. They warned us to be careful of quicksand. I was more than willing to comply, but how ever does one go about being careful of quicksand?

After four hours or so, we reached our first objective: a thorny thicket. I sat down on the thorns. What's a scratch on the ass? Besides, I was distracted by my crawling skin. I had tried while hiking to ignore the sensation of hosting company under my greens; I'd hoped that creeping flesh was just another symptom of terror. As I sat on the thorns, my curiosity got the better of me, so I rubbed my chest. My hand touched something slimy. A dab of mud? I tried to wipe it off. I couldn't. It wasn't mud; it was alive. I scuttled over to Sergeant Pinkerton, who led the patrol. "Excuse me, Sarge, but I have some sort of slimy tropical infestation upon my chest."

"What?"

"Something's on me and it's gooey."

"It's just a leech, Doc."

Just a leech!

"They're probably all over you."

All over me!

"You'll get used to them."

Get used to them! My God! Babich was right. War is hell. Jesus Christ! Leeches! Suddenly I heard a scream. My mouth hung open. Did I do that?

"Something's crawled up my pecker."

I clutched my crotch.

"Gawd Damn it! Help me, Doc!"

It wasn't me. What a relief! I looked around. It was dark. I couldn't see anything. The sarge pushed me, and I landed atop a huge mass of shrieking grunt. "What seems to be the trouble, buddy?" I asked.

"My pecker!"

"I see. And what ever were you doing when you first noticed this problem?"

"Pissing."

"I see."

"It's probably a leech, Doc," whispered Pinkerton into my ear.

A leech! In his pecker! "It's probably just a leech," I said to the grunt.

"Yeah," he replied. "I was taking a leak and my pecker hit a leaf."

And a leech slithered inside his penis. It's simple, once you have the facts. The grunt shrieked again; in pain, I reasoned. The sarge put in a request that the grunt hush before the gooks heard him and fell upon us. The grunt ignored the sarge and continued to bellow. Corporal McGrath, the company sharpshooter, threw him a left hook in the jaw. The dude unconscious, everyone waited for me to take over.

"What am I supposed to do, Sarge?" I wondered.

"You got me by the balls, Doc," he replied.

Hmm. I tried to remain cool. How does one treat a patient with this complaint? I pulled the tiny flashlight from my three-pouch, waterproof, unfolding medical corpsman's kit and shone a minuscule beam of light on the grunt, a pockmarked bear of a guy. I unzipped his trousers and pulled out a clammy little prick. I pushed back the dangling foreskin; under it were hundreds of white flecks of smegma. The stench was terrific. I wiped my hand convulsively across my pants. I opened my handy navy blue corpsman's manual and thumbed pages frantically. I looked under "L" for "leech." Nothing. I tried "P" for "penis." "U" for "uretha," and "A" for "amphibious insect." Nothing. Wouldn't you know—my first day on the job, and something like this turns up.

I held my breath and peered closely at the reeking appendage. It had no opening. How ever could a leech crawl into it? How ever could the grunt piss? He began to moan. I turned away for another breath before peering at his penis again. I lifted it up. The opening was a gaping hold on the underside

104

of the shaft. No wonder the leech had found a haven; A Sherman tank could have driven into that hole and parked overnight.

He began to regain consciousness. I rummaged desperately through my medical kit: razor blades, straws, Band-Aids, and morphine. I thought about slitting the underside of the penis with a razor blade to dig out the leech, but I discarded that notion quickly. I spent even less time on the idea of sucking the leech out of the hole with a straw. My Band-Aid technique could win prizes, but it wouldn't get a leech out of a penis and my audience carried no trophies; I did, however, make a mental note to cover the opening of my own precious as soon as I could. The jarhead screamed again, so I shot him full of morphine. Uneasily suspecting the injection to be inappropriate, I did find the resulting silence soothing.

At dawn we moved to higher ground, called for a med-evac, set up a protective perimeter, and hustled the grunt aboard a chopper that had come to take him far, far away.

Relentlessly,

Kurt

2ND BATTALION, ECHO CO.
7TH MARINES
10 November 66

My dear Paul,

I am a member of an infantry company. An infantry company sends patrols into the boonies (no-man's-land) to attempt contact with the enemy and, hopefully, kill him. I didn't much want to kill anybody. Our captain saw this as a bad attitude. The iron-souled hardass introduced me to several puberty-stained post-adolescents whom I was to accompany into the unknown for three days and nights. I had one hour to prepare.

I fled to my tent. I checked the contents of my three-pouch, waterproof, unfolding medical corpsman's kit, the last legacy and largest remaining remnant of my predecessor. I pulled on two olive-green T-shirts, two pairs of olive-green undershorts, two pairs of thick olive-green socks, a heavy olive-green shirt, a pair of olive-green pants, a pair of black and olive-green jungle boots, a thick olive-green bulletproof chest armor, a heavy olive-green coat, an olive-green raincoat, an olive-green helmet, and finally, I strapped an olive-green gun belt containing a .45 pistol around my waist. I stepped out of my tent looking like a fat Peter Pan.

My sergeant strolled over. He is a nice-looking fellow with an easy grin. He was grinning. "Hey, Doc, you might get real tired lugging all that stuff on your back. It's going to be a long patrol. You better just wear your jungle greens."

I protested. "If I don't wear my raincoat, I'll get wet."

Pinkerton liked that. "You had it easy back at the Med Battalion, didn't you, Doc?"

Now I did not, in point of fact, have it easy back at the Med Battalion, but in retrospect, the Med Battalion looked pretty good: pots, Stinky Lô Blô, and all. Regardless, I was determined above all to be brave and butch, so I merely asked, in my roughest and deepest voice, "Okay, Sarge, tell me what to do."

"Strip down," demanded my lean, hard sergeant. I removed my .45, my raincoat, and my flak jacket. "Strip all the way down," ordered my bronzed, blue-eyed sergeant. I stripped. Several jarheads gathered to watch the action. Pinkerton went to his tent. By the time he returned, I was naked and shivering in the cold night rain. He poured insect repellent into my hands. "Rub this all over your front side, Doc; I'll take care of your back side." We finished that all too soon. Pinkerton stepped back to admire our handiwork. He stood musing for a minute. "You're in pretty good shape, ain't you, Doc?" He looked at the soggy pile of my clothes. "Put on your jungle greens, socks, and boots." I put them on. He ripped the caduceus from my shirt. "Charlie likes to kill corpsmen, Doc."

Pinkerton's tentmate, Corporal McGrath, brought me several packages of "C"-rations and an M–14 rifle. "That forty-five ain't worth jack-shit," he said.

Pinkerton told me to pack an extra pair of socks and hang a couple more canteens of water from my belt; then we went to his tent, where the sarge painted my face black and green for camouflage. The paint was smelly and greasy but with Pinkerton's face a foot from mine, I was too distracted by those intent blue eyes to notice. When he had completed the task, I was ready to travel: light, chilly, and vulnerable. We joined our platoon by the entrance to the jungle. Hi yo, Silver.

The patrol ranks high upon my top-ten list of experiences

better forgotten. Several hours out, a grunt found a leech sucking his dick. My ultimate solution to the problem was to knock him out with morphine and strap a tourniquet around the base of his cock, so the leech could slither no farther inside than it already had. Pinkerton worried that gangrene might result; but I remembered tales of the queens who cruised Third Avenue in New York. My "Uncle" Ralphie had told me that before the queens crawled out of the woodwork, they masturbated themselves into erections, which they maintained by wrapping rubber bands around the bases of their pricks, advertising their baskets. Ralph never told me about any of them developing gangrene, and the ugliest walked those streets for hours. I could hardly explain all this to the sarge, so I assured him that such technique was often used at the Med Battalion.

When we returned to camp three days later, I went to the battalion doctor to ask him what procedure I should have followed concerning the leech. He said, "Don't worry. It won't happen again."

Relentlessly,

Kurt

2ND BATTALION, ECHO CO.
7TH MARINES
11 November 66

Dear Mom,

I'd always considered you a good woman and a marvelous grandmother, but a crack has appeared in the porcelain. You're gullible. From you, I've learned gullibility. You have always believed everything you've read, and you've taught me to do the same. Oh, Mom.

You see, before I left Boston, I checked Ivan Sanderson's *The Book of Great Jungles* out of the public library. I checked out Kipling's *The Jungle Book,* too, something I oughtn't to have done; Mowgli the Jungle Boy meets some fearsome creatures in his travels, which haunt my dreams—creatures like ravenous tigers, malevolent pythons, and albino cobras. Mr. Sanderson consoled me, though. He made jungles seem such pleasant places, you wanted to rush right out to find one and buy a lot with a view. He said that once you get through the impenetrable thickets surrounding a jungle, the forest floor is free of underbrush, as the canopy of leaves high overhead keep the plants from receiving the sunrays needed for their nourishment. According to my observations, limited but on the spot, underbrush receives enough nourishment to cover the jungle floor with a hideous density. Then, I may be located smack-dab in the middle of the exception that proves the rule. Another lingering impression from *The Book of Great Jungles* is that rain forests tend to be flat. Then again, I may be laboring under a misapprehension.

At least, I have yet to come face to fang with an albino cobra.

Love,

Kurt

2ND BATTALION, ECHO CO.
7TH MARINES
15 November 66

Arch,

I survived my second patrol. They called it a combat patrol. We were to look for the enemy and try to kill him. I was loath to join the expedition. The collective persuasion of the chief corpsman, the lieutenant, and the captain—the enemies within—forced me to go.

The entire company, 160 men at our present strength, left the compound just before dawn. "At least," I rationalized, "in the daylight I can see leeches crawling over me and kill them." On second thought, I realized that the VC could see corpsmen crawling over Nam and kill them. I decided to refrain from thinking.

We traveled heavy, laden with flak jackets, packs, helmets, and extra rounds of ammunition. All morning I looked in every direction for VC, booby traps, and cobras, and I stepped carefully in the footsteps of the man in front of me. After lunch ("C"-rations packed in 1942), the rains ceased, the sun came out, and it got very hot. I began to look less carefully for danger. We were soaked with sweat, and the red dust we kicked up settled upon us and turned into mud. I got to where I didn't look anywhere for anything.

Following a hike of miles and miles, we reached the foot of a rugged and very high hill. We climbed it. At the top, we could see a narrow valley on the other side, dotted with villages and rice paddies. We descended the monstrous precipice. At the bottom, the company realigned in the formation held throughout the morning: The First Platoon advanced down the road; my platoon hiked through elephant grass and rice paddies parallel to the First Platoon, about a hundred yards to its right and another hundred yards behind; and the Third Platoon flanked the road on the left. Lieutenant Halderman informed us that we were crossing the valley so we could climb the hill on the far side of it. Good thing I had stopped thinking.

We approached a hamlet. Peasants waded in a rice paddy with their water buffalo. I thought it picturesque and was idly wishing I had brought my camera, when all hell broke loose. Bullets everywhere! Ambush!

Actually, ambush is too strong a word. A single sniper had fired upon us. How could I know? At least I didn't faint. I dropped to the ground and babbled.

As I lay hugging the ground and hoping vehemently that no one would require my immediate services, the villagers and their water bison had been withdrawing from the encounter. One of the buffalo trod upon the stomach of a distracted grunt. I crawled listlessly toward his cries and opened my navy blue corpsman's manual to "W" for "water buffalo." I turned the pages to "H" for "hoof." I sighed. The book was uninformative and left me completely at sea, where I longed violently to be. I dove into my unfolding corpsman's kit and broke out the morphine. Lieutenant Halderman called for a dust-off, and my patient was carried away.

We continued across the valley and up the hill. The First Platoon took several casualties from mines along the road. Chicon mines. They blow after a man steps on them. Blasts shredded legs and seared bellies, asses, balls, and peckers. The nasty things delayed us, and we reached the top of the hill after dark. We slept under our ponchos. The rains poured down. It was nifty.

The next morning we retraced our steps. When we arrived home, I limped over to Battalion Headquarters to ask the doctor what procedure I should have followed concerning the water buffalo. He said, "Don't worry. It won't happen again."

Relentlessly,

Kurt

2ND BATTALION, ECHO CO.
7TH MARINES
16 November 66

My dear Paul,

A vow of celibacy should be easily honored here. I am being punished for my derogatory remarks about gay bars; God is everywhere and always watching. My ability to fantasize will be challenged by my surroundings. Even if I were to make a congenial acquaintance, privacy is neither within my tent nor without it, the rest room is al fresco, and balling in the jungle is unimaginable. I live without hope. I may never cum again before I die.

Three corpsmen share my tent and company duties and are, in order of their undesirability: 1) fat, 2) black, and 3) near-sighted. Although I must assume they have sexual yearnings, I prefer ignorance to whatever bliss they could offer. I should hate to encourage them in any way.

Fats is a bulbous-nosed, bad-tempered blond, lacking eyebrows, eyelashes, and probably pubic hair. I doubt that he's changed his underclothes since coming into full growth which like his stench, is considerable. He tries to act like "The Meanest Mother Fucker in the Valley." He would rather kill gooks than treat wounded grunts. Medical aid is woman's work. I've asked him for advice. He sneered and grunted. I think he wants me to respect him as a hardass.

Soul Brother goes by Splib, a nomenclature I'm told those of the persuasion find inoffensive, but that I wouldn't use on a bet. Splib speaks only to his Brothers. He has stacked boxes around his cot, behind which he disappears for days on end. I resent the crowding the boxes cause, and I find his isolation impenetrable. No advice from him; besides, have you ever tried to get directions from a nigger?

The bespectacled one never goes on patrol; he has an understanding with the chief corpsman. Queenie passes her days tastefully decorating her corner of the tent with silk scarves from Bangkok. Despite her friendliness, Queenie can give me little counsel, and her back issues of *Contemporary Living* are uninformative.

Several hundred yards down the trail is the Battalion Headquarters. The battalion medical officer lives there. An internist, the doctor seems preoccupied with his investments in Florida real estate. He did show enthusiasm in demanding that I join his crusade to stop marines from smoking cigarettes.

The chief roosts at Batt. Hqtrs., too. He is a bulky and ugly man. His bored replies to any questions of procedure apparently derive from the doctor's attitude which translates as: "A lot of corpsmen have come out here during the past months. Most of them have returned to the States in boxes. I feel I'm wasting my breath, saying the same things over and over. So blow it out your ass, fellow."

Relentlessly,

Kurt

2ND BATTALION, ECHO CO.
7TH MARINES
17 November 66

Chloe dear,

You grew up in Bonifay; you never underwent the trauma of changing schools. You never were the new kid. Everyone shared a history. Whenever anyone tried to impress the new kid with bullshit, his ignorance forced him either to believe everything told him or to relinquish all trust and withdraw. Everyone knew more than he, and everyone seemed bigger. At six foot three, two hundred pounds, and twenty-four years of age, I find myself a little kid again.

I want to learn as much as I can for survival's sake, so I hearken to the grunts' conversations. They tolerate me, but I hear little of practical value. And they don't converse. They trade unpleasant anecdotes about dismemberments and deaths. I think they're trying to frighten me with these tales. They

111

needn't go to any trouble. As things stand, I could shit my pants on a card trick.

Mother, assuming I am doomed, sends, with great regularity, tear-stained apologies for her failings as a parent. She seems racked by the certainty that we shall never meet again.

And Mother's always right.

Relentlessly,

Kurt

2ND BATTALION, ECHO CO.
7TH MARINES
18 November 66

Dear Mom,

Do you recollect the story you told us about the rich brother and the poor brother.

"The rich brother goes to visit his poor brother, who has many children and whose house smells like number two. The rich brother sniffs and sniffs and says, 'Heavenly days, Poor Brother. How ever can you bear that awful smell?' He says this several times. The poor brother grows annoyed. He secretly rubs number two inside the rich brother's hat; then he hands the hat to the rich brother, who puts it on his head and leaves.

"A month or so later and still wearing his hat, the rich brother visits again. He sniffs the air and turns to the poor brother to say, 'Congratulations, Poor Brother! I can't imagine how ever in the world you did it, but that awful smell is gone!' The poor brother smiles; he knows his house smells as it always had.

"And the moral of that little story is *you can get used to anything.*"

Your fable is indicative of reality. When I arrived at Echo, the first thing I noticed was that everything smelled. My tent contained a musty odor, the jungle gave off a rotten one, and the marines stank to Heaven's gates. In a couple of weeks, I have got used to everything. Oh, I'm still revolted by such outrageous stinks as that of a grossly overweight tentmate, but on the whole, my helmet substitutes right well for the rich brother's hat.

I have no special requests for Christmas. The only thing I'm standing in need of is a cold beer or a tall glass filled with cornbread and buttermilk. Drenched as I am by this continuous rain, I shouldn't be thirsty all the time, but I've always been a child of perversity.

And there I go again, calling Mother names.

Love,

Kurt

2ND BATTALION, ECHO CO.
7TH MARINES
22 November 66

Arch,

I survived my third, fourth, fifth, sixth, and seventh patrols. It's terrible, Arch, just terrible. It's always dark and we're always wet and there are mines everywhere blowing legs and heads off and the captain is a maniac and whenever we survive one mission he sends us out to try again and I can't believe I'm not dead and there are bugs everywhere and people screaming . . .

Boy Howdee, that felt good. Now I can be rational. It is bad, Arch. It's always dark and we're always wet and . . .

Back at the Med Battalion, a kind of peace prevailed. The patients were in pain and minus hands and stuff, but they were safe. They had survived. They would no longer go through every day with a terrible uncertainty. But here, it's different. Two days ago, for instance. Patrol Number Six.

We left camp just before dawn, at the hour when people die. The hopeless hour. The hour of dread. I gritted my teeth and I bit down on the grit between my teeth and marched into that rain and cold and muck and terror. We stumbled along in the dark.

The Cong are out there. We know it. They know we know it. But there are usually too many of us, and they wouldn't show themselves unless there were too many of them. Although that is something to think about, it hasn't happened. Not to us. Not yet.

We walked through the drizzle and the cold and the muck and the terror. We walked all morning. Toward noon, the drizzle ceased and the sun came out. We sweltered in the wet, itchy heat. I ran up and down the straggling line of men, handing out salt tablets and looking for the swimmy-headed; I wanted no cases of heat exhaustion among my men, or worse, someone's brains boiling because of heat stroke.

We stopped for lunch. I opened my "C"-rations to find turkey loaf. As I bargained with a jarhead who had a more palatable dish, I heard a loud boom, the ground quivered, and I saw a cloud of dust by a fence several yards away. Three men had been near the fence. Farrow, a good-looking guy from Iowa, had sat down and, apparently off guard, leaned against a fence post. Attached to the fence was a land mine. Farrow's head was blown off, and his arms were separated from his body. We couldn't find his trunk from the tits to the stomach. The pelvis remained, with the legs still attached to it. The legs were kicking.

His best buddy and lifelong friend, his cousin Douds, stood looking at what there was of Farrow, and he screamed. He continued to scream until Corporal McGrath clipped him in the jaw and knocked him out.

I worked on the third man, Monroe—a strapping and good-natured black from Chicago. Blood gushed from the holes where his eyes had been.

When you look at eye sockets filled with blood instead of eyeballs, you feel a sledgehammer hit you in the guts, pushing up shit to clog your throat. You want to fall to the ground and beat it with your fists. You want to vomit. You want to scream. You want to lie still in a warm, soft darkness.

But you can't. So you forget your horror, your revulsion, and your helplessness. You put a tourniquet around Monroe's arm to stop the blood pouring from the stump where his hand had been. You put a compress against Monroe's gushing eye sockets. You apply pressure to the artery in his neck that carries blood to the brain, hoping you don't overdo the pressure and kill too many brain cells by robbing them of oxygen. You shut out his squeals of "Mama! It hurts, Mama! Help me, Mama!"

You keep Monroe alive, somehow, through a profound shock until a dust-off comes to take him away. Him and Douds and what pieces of Farrow can be found. You eat your turkey loaf and continue Patrol Number Six.

Relentlessly,

Kurt

2ND BATTALION, ECHO CO.
7TH MARINES
23 November 66

Chloe dear,

It's the pits, Honey. I should have listened more diligently at Lejeune; I could be causing permanent damage to some of these guys. My only excuse, and it's no excuse, is that I had no idea it would be like this. And I'm scared. Like Susan Hayward, I want to live. I'm moody, querulous, and unkind. Unadulterated terror makes me that way. I'd developed fears in the past that I've conquered. How ever did I do it?

When I was four or so, Mother took Karen and me to a movie. It scared me so bad that Mother had to spend hours with cotton balls and fingernail polish to rid my groin of chewing gum. For years I was haunted by a scene that began with a girl's taking her clothes from a closet to pack them in a suitcase on a bed. While her attention is directed toward the suitcase, the camera pans to the closet and focuses on two eyes that peer out of the darkness. A scream.

My solution: Inspect all suspicious closets for eyes.

Current ideal: Avoid dark places where eyes may peer at me.

Current reality: Don't think about it.

When I was ten, I went with some friends to the next town to see *Dracula* and *Frankenstein*. (Chloe, those movies marked me for life.) Afterward, I felt obliged to respond to a dare and walked along a lonely creek, across a deserted railroad yard, through a scary woods, and up a dark alley before I reached home, pissing my pants at every rustle in every shadow.

My solution: Never respond to dares.

Current ideal: Refrain from walking through scary woods at night.

Current reality: Don't think about it.

When I played for Sundown in the Desert League, all home games were held in the late afternoon. The sun set in a line with third base. In the first game of the season, a ground ball bounced up and smashed into my Adam's apple. I'd lost the ball in the setting sun. I spent three days in a hospital and saw yellow for two weeks. I was scared shitless that I would be hit in the throat again. For the rest of the season, I played halfway up the line toward home plate whenever the sun was setting. I have good reflexes; I set a league record for assists and double plays. The fans loved my arrogance.

My solution: To avoid seeing yellow, crowd opponents.

Current ideal: To avoid seeing yellow, give opponents plenty of room.

Current reality: Don't think about it.

I felt I should enlist, but I had qualms about dying for my country. I didn't want people to shoot me.

My solution: It seemed unlikely that I would be a good target if I were hidden away on a big ship, so I enlisted in the Navy.

Current ideal: Get my ass on a big ship. Until then, I shall refuse to think about reality.

Relentlessly,

Kurt

2ND BATTALION, ECHO CO.
7TH MARINES
24 November 66

My dear Paul,

The chief corpsman holds classes every Sunday after dinner. The fifteen corpsmen in the battalion attend required seminars such as "Dental Woes in Combat," "The Corpsman and his Commanding Officer," and "Tiger Bites." I'd felt guilt at seeing the woebegone faces of grunts who court inquiries on patrol without a doc to put them to right, so I'd played truant until this past Sunday when I really needed a respite; besides, the

116

chief had been getting on my ass. And who ever do you think sat demurely in the front row, pencil poised and eyes radiant with the joy of learning? I'll tell you. It was Miss Priss, one of the four corpsmen assigned to our sister company. (Do you like that appellation, too?)

I walked her home after class. Her company has endured the same routine as ours: No actual combat, but casualties every day from mines and booby traps. We chatted about old friends, and Miss P bragged of locating Stokes, who had already been wounded twice. "Minor dings," breathed Miss P, as she raised her eyes toward Heaven. Nevertheless, she worried. "Kipp seems different. He's so far away, as if he were in a different world." While she mourned for the old Stokes, I was idly surveying the local talent. I learned nothing about a couple of beauties I casually pointed out; Miss Priss is somewhat insipid, with only good to say about people. I could see what was good about the men I pointed out; I wanted to know a little of the bad. Finally, I gave up trying to pump for information and let her gush on about Stokes.

"What was he like in Boot Camp? In Boston? At Lejeune, before I met him?" I decided to lay a few cards on the table and asked her, if isolated for years on a desert island with Stokes, she would ever consider having sex with him. "Oh, no!" cried a shocked Miss P. She looked at me with disapproval.

"It was only a theoretical question," I hastily asserted.

"I should hope so," replied Miss P.

I pleaded a full bladder and withdrew to a pee-pipe, where I was joined by a ferret-faced jarhead who made no secret of his desire to come to grips with my precious. (Paul, they're everywhere. Why ever do they always lack sex appeal?) I returned unsullied to Miss P, who was busily brewing mint tea over a sterno and cutting slices from a fruitcake sent by Mumsie.

Sergeant Pinkerton and Corporal McGrath walked up to the tent to fetch me home for a patrol; they had followed my route from battalion. Miss P invited them to join us and, to their amazement, served the tea in tiny china cups. As we traversed the six hundred yards of trail between Foxtrot and Echo, McGrath asked, "Is that old sissy a buddy of yours?"

"Merely a friend of a friend," I replied courageously.

McGrath cast me a suspicious glance. Yesterday I caught

117

him staring at me several times. I felt just like a tall dyke in drag.

Relentlessly,

Kurt

2ND BATTALION, ECHO CO.
7TH MARINES
25 November 66

Dear Mom,

No, Vietnam is hardly as I pictured it. I'd thought to pass the time of day lying in a hammock by a blue lagoon with palms to fan me and an occasional bare-breasted native girl to bring me pineapples and coconuts and refreshing concoctions based on rum. That's how I pictured Vietnam, rather unreasonably, now that I think about it. I certainly imaged nothing like this continual cold drizzle. And where ever are those native girls?

It could be worse. Daddy told me about seeing a native on some island in the Pacific pushing a wheelbarrow that held a giant testicle several feet in diameter and still attached to the man. Yaws. I have yet to see that. No piranhas swim in local streams, ready to strip the flesh from hands and feet dangling in the water, as they do in the Amazon River. Nor do worms crawl into one's feet and burrow through the body to eventually erupt from the arms and neck, a hazard of wading in Lake Tanganyika, if I am to believe the slides I saw at age eight that were shown at the Christian and Missionary Alliance Church Bible School. Islands in the Caribbean are inhabited by the ferdelance, a snake which will chase down people and animals to inject deadly venom into their flesh out of pure malice. And I still haven't seen an albino cobra.

I have a lot to be thankful for.

Love,

Kurt

Arch,

The Marine Corps seems to be preparing for an operation, and we have moved north, I think, and farther inland. Last Wednesday morning, giant helicopters carried us for twenty minutes and set us down in a small clearing ostensibly guarded by ARVN (Army of the Republic of Vietnam). As the expeditionary force, my company had the duty of establishing the campsite before the rest of the battalion arrived over the weekend. We would be vulnerable to a VC attack while we were working, so the ARVN troops disappeared into the jungle with a promise to patrol the surrounding area. ARVN vows are written on water; nevertheless, we unloaded the choppers and set to work.

The First and Second platoons dug a trench six feet deep that surrounded a perimeter 320 feet × 160 feet; then they laid barbed wire outside the trench, cut down trees, and cleared away the brush beyond the wire. The Weapons Platoon built six watchtowers from rocks and sandbags, one to a corner, and one at the midpoint of the longer sides of the rectangle; afterward, they set up machine-gun emplacements and the chopper pad, and they laid minefields outside the wire. The Third Platoon, my team, chopped down trees and cleared off the land within the perimeter. We dug a protective trench four feet deep and two feet wide, which meanders through the encampment. We dug a latrine for the enlisted men, built a shithouse for the officers, and erected the colonel's bungalow and his private outhouse. After three days, Regimental Headquarters were ready for occupancy.

Sixty thousand grunts are stationed in Nam and attached to regiments of the First and Third divisions. A general in Da Nang commands the First Division; a colonel commands the 7th Regiment. Three battalions and a headquarters company constitute a regiment: one hundred officers and two thousand men. The colonel's staff includes three majors who head Operations, Intelligence, and Personnel and three captains in charge of Supply, Communications, and Medical Service.

Over the weekend, we cleared a path through four miles of jungle to chop down trees, dig trenches, etc., on a smaller scale for Battalion Headquarters. A lieutenant colonel commands 2nd Battalion, an infantry battalion of twenty-eight officers and six hundred men. A doctor and a chief corpsman provide my only contact with the battalion level.

On Tuesday the entire regiment arrived. We were sent to clear several hundred yards of trail that would lead to our company campsite. Echo Company is commanded by a captain with four lieutenants on his staff. Three of the lieutenants are in charge of platoons of forty men, divided into three rifle squads. I am attached to Lieutenant Halderman, although I go out on patrols with the other two rifle platoons. (The Fourth Platoon is Heavy Weapons, which rarely goes on patrol.)

I am writing this letter as I sit on a three-foot-high wall of sandbags separated from our tent by a four-foot-deep foxhole. Unlike the grunts, who live in low two-man tents scattered about the compound in shallow and soggy pits, we corpsmen share a large four-man tent in which we can stand erect. Inside the tent, odors of wet canvas, unwashed bodies, and damp earth prevail. Esmé would love the squalor.

Relentlessly,

Kurt

2ND BATTALION, ECHO CO.
7TH MARINES
30 November 66

Dear Mom,

A mile from our camp is a hamlet populated by the elderly, the very young, and women whose husbands are either dead or off fighting with one side or another. We invaded it with peaceful intentions, and I found a woman willing to wash my clothes for 25 cents a load. I am trying to encourage one of my tentmates to avail himself of her services, but he remains deaf to my hints. I've done everything but tell him outright that he smells like a stool specimen; he thinks he is tougher that way. Remember how Dad would enter the house after working all day with the turkeys? He'd stick his nose in his armpits, inhale deeply, and say, "Ah! That's how a man smells." This guy has something of the same mentality.

I read your copy of *Jubilee Trail* when I was ten. An incident within the book has stayed with me. A filthy, naked Ute Indian sits on the ground, staring at nothing. Suddenly, a lizard flashes by. The Ute grabs the lizard, bites off its head, spits the head out, and stuffs the wriggling remainder into his mouth. As only that Ute Indian could relish the food served us in the battalion mess, I eat as often as possible in the hamlet. The food tastes good, I receive excellent service, and I take a worm pill once a week.

Speaking of resorts, have yourself a good time on your cruise to Nassau. Fawn appeared spritely, and she seemed to enjoy playing games. Don't gorge yourself with goodies. You have a fine figure that you shouldn't lose, unless you plan to become the last of the red hot mamas. On second thought, eat as much as you like.

Love,

Kurt

2ND BATTALION, ECHO CO.
7TH MARINES
1 December 66

My dear Paul,

Marines doubt the masculinity of corpsmen. To silence malevolent asides, I accompanied several grunts to a nearby ville for my first taste of slant pussy. I am not particularly eager for that sort of thing, but as chaste as I've been lately, I could probably get it up for a water buffalo. Although I should prefer to slake my lust with a little more romance, I've a history of sacrificing inclination to social approval. And I've always held a slight yen to meet the Dragon Lady of "Terry and the Pirates." So I went.

First of all, we dropped off our laundry at the local washerwoman's; then we stopped at a tiny inn to eat a passable dinner of chicken, rice, and tapeworm. I drank several beers, hoping they would screw up my courage, and I let my boisterous pals lead me to a ramshackle hut of straw mats. A dull-eyed mamasan squatted before the open doorway. Red betelnut juice smeared a mouth filled with black teeth. Flies circled her head in a buzzing halo. Dragon Lady.

So eager were the jarheads to initiate me into the delights inside the hut, they pushed me through the door and withdrew to await sloppy seconds, thirds, etc. Dragon Lady followed me. So did the flies.

The odor inside the hut resembled that of the mamasan, a smell halfway between rotting fish and pigshit. "Be a man," I said to myself. Sensing her impatience, I decided to get down to the business at hand. I took off my clothes and lay on her pallet, thinking more of parasites than technique. She jabbered at me in her native tongue. Empathizing with her desire to consummate the act quickly, I set to the task of working myself up. Dragon Lady waxed wroth. Unknown to me, custom decrees that one must remain fully clothed during intercourse because of unscheduled inspections by various political groups. My misunderstanding was numba ten. (Bad!) Dragon Lady shrugged her scrawny shoulders, spit out a red hawker, pulled down her scrungy black drawers, squatted in a corner of the hut, and peed on the earthen floor; then, through the space between the straw mat and the ground, she swept her residue outside with a bare, dusty foot. I jumped up, pulled on my clothes, threw a fistful of piastres on the pallet, and walked out the door. The next man in line brushed past me, pulling at his cock with his hand and showing his wide-spaced and unbrushed green and yellow teeth in a lewd grin. Sweeney brags of his talent for eating pussy. To avoid picturing his putting that talent to use, I hurried to the bar for several more beers. Sweeney and the others joined me, one by one, bragging of their prowess. I bullshitted as grandly as they.

On the way home, we passed by the mamasan who squatted in the dust, flies and all, smirking at us.

Was this the face that launched a thousand ships?

Relentlessly,

Kurt

122

Chloe dear,

One of the more stupid jarheads in our company has been oddly scarred by the zips. Gemelas was determined to get off the lines for a couple of weeks, so he applied for a circumcision. After the operation and with his stiches still unhealed, the leering Greek accompanied several other patients on a search for pussy. They found some, and Gemelas reinfected his slashed penis with a raging dose of something nasty.

He returned last week after a two-month convalescence at a hospital in Japan, and I saw him yesterday in the showers. His prick stands out, swollen and fire engine red. His medical record reports that the deformity is permanent. He'll always fire blanks: no little Gemelas will ever exist. The Greek Geek blames iniquitous treatment for his condition; he should thank modern medicine for his escaping a lifetime on the Island of the Red Rose.

A virulent strain of venereal disease resistant to wonder drugs has been spread by Vietnamese prostitutes who believe penicillin pills contain magic powers. The glad girls pop the pills into their mouths before every sexual encounter. Their unlucky partners are reported Missing in Action and sent to a concentration camp on a remote island in the South Pacific.

Picture the island in long shot. A smoking volcano dominates a spirochetes-shape coral reef surrounded by lagoons rife with man-eating sharks. Huge leathery turkeys flap through fern-ridden swamps, gobbling mournfully.

A boat glides through the thick fog covering the lagoons. Men in decontamination suits row toward the island with muffled oars. The boat lands, and its passengers step ashore. The deceptively healthy-looking young men huddle together as the boat disappears into the fog. From a group of tattered tents come several men to greet the newcomers. They lack noses. Pus-filled holes have replaced their genitals. Red, white, and blue lesions cover their bodies. One of the deceptively healthy-looking young men begins to whimper.

At the next full moon, the gruesome and mutilated beat on tom-toms and chant "Rape . . . Maim . . . Kill . . . !" They grab one of the newcomers, the whimperer, and tie him to a crum-

123

bling stone phallus. At midnight the moon disappears behind a black cloud, the fog rolls in, and a huge nameless thing creeps down from its lair near the volcano to pick up the whimperer and carries him through the fern-ridden swamp to the other side of the island, far away from everyone else, where no one can hear him call.

You pays your money and you takes your chance.

Relentlessly,

Kurt

2ND BATTALION, ECHO CO.
7TH MARINES
6 December 66

Arch,

We set out on a fifteen-mile patrol last night. I hate night patrols of any length. We tread warily upon the trail in the blackness, maintaining a distance of several yards from one another. I would rather cling to the belt of the man in front of me, but prudent orders discourage such childishness. If that man accidentally trips a booby trap, only he shall be blown away. And vice versa. I hate vice versa.

So I maintain my distance of several yards and feel mounting panic at the irresistible notion that I could easily make a wrong turn in the darkness and become lost in the jungle. With my contact lenses tinted green, I see less than nothing everyone else sees. Jesus Christ Himself would be spooked.

> *Like one that on a lonesome road*
> *Doth walk in fear and dread,*
> *And having once turned round walks on,*
> *And turns no more his head;*
> *Because he knows a frightful fiend*
> *Doth close behind him tread.*

As I walked along in fear and dread, thinking of the war in my own way, a flare exploded above us. Shots from everywhere! An ambush! I hurled myself to the ground, my favorite position at a time like this, and waited for the hills to come

124

alive with the sound of "CORPSMAN!" As the Marine Corps Creed demands that the grunts charge an entrenched enemy to wipe it out of contention, I could count on a couple of deaths and several really discouraging injuries. Throughout the sylvan glade, my name resounded monotonously. I refuse to answer to the alias of "Doc!" as the Cong, by no means slow witted, have bumped off several distracted medics who took no notice of a slight Oriental accent while making house calls. Assured that the cries came from red-blooded Americans, I reluctantly crawled forward. I never forget for an instant that some sort of deadly, disgusting creature may be skulking underbelly. I never forget for an instant that a VC may be lurking behind the next clump of bushes. I will never, ever forget any of this.

Bullets whined over my head. A grenade exploded nearby. "Doc!" A cry several yards from me, in a voice too deep to be of gookish origin. I crawled to the wounded man.

"Where you hit, buddy?"

"My chest. Help me, Doc."

I ripped open his shirt and found two holes, front and back—a bullet through the lung, collapsing it. I opened my medical kit to pull out some Vaseline gauze to cover the holes. As I taped the gauze to the man's chest, someone crawled up to us.

"Where you hit, Ace?" he asked.

"It's okay," I told him. "I got it."

"Who are you?" asked the new man.

"Doc Strom."

"Where'd you come from?"

"Over there. I was working on Maroni and I heard Linkhogle yell for a doc . . ."

"Who's Maroni? Who's Linkhogle? What is this?" The mysterious stranger caught on first. He yelled, "Stop! Everyone's American!"

And so we were, including the seven wounded and the three dead.

Will there really be a morning?

Relentlessly,

Kurt

Chloe dear,

It gets closer to home. The VC infiltrated our sister company under cover of darkness; the guard on watch had apparently fallen asleep. Along with eight other men, including all four corpsmen, he was hacked to death by machetes.

One of our patrols got into a fire fight near camp. Two choppers coming to support the Americans collided in the darkness and fell in flames just outside our perimeter. Everyone aboard each was burned beyond recognition.

A nondescript and quiet little grunt, teased and envied because of an outrageously long prick, went barefoot to the latrine in the middle of the night and was bitten by a tiny but deadly viper called a krait. His death must have been instantaneous; he was found the following morning in the trough. New orders are out to wear boots to the latrine.

Everything else aside, the rains are letting up, I am relatively safe, and the last thing I would want is for you to worry.

> *Relentlessly,*
>
> *Kurt*

Dear Mom,

You know how you picked up those ten pounds and so do I. "Here's something sweet to finish up the meal," and you bring out the strawberry shortcake or the lemon meringue pie. And you eat too much bread and jam. Drink a glass of orange juice before every meal; that should cut down your craving for sweets.

If you're eating to forget Howard, I'll throw myself on a grenade. How can you care? Of course he would marry a woman like that. She may have money, but anyone could see that she's up from trash. Howard showed good sense. He probably felt he would be more comfortable with his own kind; you have too much dignity and breeding for him. He may have been company for a social event, but God knows I've dated girls I would never have married. And Howard looked like a lousy kisser.

Chloe told me that during the time it took her date to get around the car and into his own seat after closing her door, she always thought three things:

1. How ever will he make his first pass?
2. Will he be a good kisser?
3. What ever would the children look like?

That would be a good objective, Mom, that I feel Howard would have had difficulty in attaining. You could present us with a new grandfather who is a gentleman and a good kisser.

If you wish to marry well, marry an equal.

> *Love,*
>
> *Kurt*

2ND BATTALION, ECHO CO.
7TH MARINES
9 December 66

My dear Paul,

In the past couple of weeks, I've seen several devastated human bodies, but I've yet to see an injury that looks like the rubber wounds we played at Lejeune. And unless my memory has failed me, they never mentioned leeches.

Did you know what leeches were like? I didn't. My grandmother broke her leg when I was a little kid. She has told me how leeches were placed under her cast to suck out the infection; she could feel them on her all the time. And, of course, I've seen *The African Queen* and remember Humphrey Bogart getting leeches on his back as he tried to pull the boat through the bayous.

In Nam, leeches come at you in assorted sizes and shapes. The long, black aquatic worms are ubiquitous. You wade through a bog, you become a leech feast. Before purifying the drinking water hauled up from village wells, you must pick out the leeches.

Smaller brown and red leeches live on land. You sit down to rest or eat lunch during a patrol, and the leeches come at you from all sides, undulating across the ground like tiny cobras. As you trudge through the jungle, misery has company—slimy globs hang from your skin, glutted with your blood.

I wear expanding metal bracelets around my ankles to keep leeches from my legs. I wear a rubber around my dick. If I could buy them in a local store, I would stuff Kotex up my asshole.

Every time I return to camp, I strip, burn off the leeches and ticks, and scrub myself thoroughly under our cold-water shower. After I dress, I join the grunts in group therapy, an event held nightly upwind of the latrine. We sit in a circle, chanting, "Kill the Gooks! Kill the Gooks!" After two or three hours of chanting, each man tells the rest of us how many days he has left in Nam. Short-timers expect envy as their due; new men accept disdain. This is followed by show-and-tell time. True tales of death and mutilation are enacted with roaring gusto by those who saw it happen, or who did it. A rousing chorus of "Kill the Gooks!" closes the session. Then we trundle off to bed for a pleasant night's sleep. Perchance to dream.

Relentlessly,

Kurt

2ND BATTALION, ECHO CO.
7TH MARINES
13 December 66

Dear Mom,

My fifteen thousand is in cars, tractors, land, and beach houses; it is in everything but my name. Mother said I would receive interest for my investments. I figured the accumulated interest would be around five thousand dollars, had the money have been left in my savings account. I wrote Mother that I wanted the five thousand sent to Karen. Put in a defensive position, Mother atttacked. "I won't be a partner to your throwing away the money for your education. Karen's made her bed; she can lay in it."

128

Although Karen would never dream of borrowing penny one from me, I know she's bad off. She has no social life except for nurses, prospective nurses, and Reggie. She goes to school all day, works under the bitches in white every evening (and I can imagine how those dragons treat aides), and comes home unable to kick back with a beer. Reading between the lines of her letters, I've developed the impression that Reggie doesn't wash a dish or sweep a floor in his consuming passion to find himself; instead, he saves up profound thoughts to throw at Karen as she walks through the door. Reggie chooses the nights before Karen's tests to become deeply depressed, and he demands that she empathize with him until the wee small hours.

What a joy Reggie must be to come home to—a real barrel of laughs. I've often reflected upon why Karen would marry a man with no sense of humor. Perhaps clichés are true. Opposites attract. Of course, Reggie may feel that I have no sense of humor. In my present frame of mind, he'd be absolutely correct.

I swear to God, I wonder we're all not schizophrenic. You believe we can do no wrong; Mother is certain we're on the road to ruin. Mother told Neil and Ricky that she yells at them so much, because she's afraid they'll turn out to be losers like Karen and me. She tells them that she loved Karen and me too much; therefore, Neil and Ricky will do better if she doesn't love them.

Sometimes, I envy orphans.

                                                    Love,

                                                    Kurt

                              2ND BATTALION, ECHO CO.
                              7TH MARINES
                              14 December 66

Chloe dear,

My recollections of North Carolina hinder my envisioning the state as a vacationer's paradise, but your plans for the cabin seem splendid. I read somewhere that the Appalachian Range once towered nine miles above sea level.

Closer to earth, I have been a quivering mass of righteous indignation. Orders came down last week that corpsmen would stand watches with the grunts. I was only mildly offended and took little notice; then I saw my name formally posted on the watch list. No other corpsman was listed. As I average twelve to eighteen hours every day on patrols and ambushes, often very informally, I went to the chief.

Our relationship, never strong to begin with, broke down completely. I pointed to Queenie, who goes on patrol only when the captain does, which is once in a blue moon. I told the chief that I felt it unfair that Soul Brother could sandbag patrols by accusations of racism, pleas of the miseries, and hiding behind his boxes. I wondered why Fats and I were unfairly manipulated into taking up the jigaboo's slack. I elaborated upon the incompetence of those in charge who allow such injustice. I lost my head and said several other things which have no bearing on the case in point.

The chief remained calm. He said Sambo's transfer was imminent. He told me that Queenie had been trained for important duties as head corpsman in Echo and wasn't to be wasted. I took this to mean that my duties were unimportant, and I was fit to be wasted. ("Wasted" is Grunt for "obliterated.") I lost my head once more.

The chief whistled tunelessly throughout my diatribe. After I had wound down, the chief spoke. "Are you through now, Strom? Then I'll tell you a few things. One: I don't have to give you one friggin' reason for anything I do. Two: I'm putting your ass on report. Three: If you miss so much as one watch, I'll break you to an E–1. Now shove off."

I went beserk. "Listen, you fish-faced scumbag. My Uncle Carl is a Navy commander stationed in San Francisco. He told me to act like a man, but if I were ever treated unfairly, I was to call him and he'd break the son a bitch that fucked me over." Actually, Uncle Carl, like the rest of the Stroms, hadn't even bothered to send me a Christmas card, and he's certainly never told me to count on him for anything. But how could the chief know that? "Don't believe me? Call one of your satchel-assed friends in California. There can't be too many Commander Stroms. I'll tell him about your shafting me so you can use safety as pogey bait for Queenie. Uncle Carl will have a watermelon up your ass for the rest of your Navy career. He'll have brass laying for you wherever you transfer. You can kiss

off easy duty, Numbnuts, so you'd best cut me some slack."
I stormed back to Echo.

The next day my name was struck off the watch list.

There's them that kiss ass and there's them that beat ass and
there's them that merely shake it from side to side.

Relentlessly,

Kurt

2ND BATTALION, ECHO CO.
7TH MARINES
15 December 66

Arch,

You develop the guilts for the goddamnedest reasons. Why
ever do you feel you should enlist? You've not failed a sanity
test recently, have you?

I come from a long line of worker ants, horses with blinders,
and patient oxen. I enlisted because I'm an animal. Basically,
I'm half-sheep and half-goat.

Jesus, Arch, you quit baseball because you disliked the
rinky-dink shit of curfews and the like. You'd hate the rules
and regulations of the military. And if you thought the manager
and coaches in the minors abused power, you'd go insane here.

Other than doctors, who as a rule could give a flying fuck
as long as you're capable, it's my opinion that officers are
intensely aware of every little star and stripe and don't for a
minute allow anyone who ranks below them to forget their
status. I'll admit my contact with officers is limited. At the
regimental and battalion level, I can only recognize the colonel,
whom I loathe; the rest all look alike to me.

The grunts take barrels of shit daily; as a corpsman at company level, I receive little hassle from officers: They never
know when their lives may depend upon me. Queenie handles
all intrigue on the compound and puts up with the fussiness of
our captain, who will decide of a morning that the huge brown
rats with which we share our home carry bubonic plague.
Queenie will set out poison and traps. The captain remembers
his little mangy mutt, a zip dog which gets into everything we
own, and orders the poison picked up. Or the captain will get

131

a wild hair up his ass about malaria, and Queenie must put oil on standing water. The monsoon comes in again and the puddles become rivers; we walk around looking like a gusher just came in. Scuttlebutt has it that a seed catalogue has arrived in the captain's mail; we'll eventually be planting a garden and standing watch as scarecrows.

Under the captain is Lieutenant Kline, executive officer, commander of the Weapons Platoon, and an alcoholic. Whenever I see him, and it's seldom, Kline seems friendly, if dazed.

Officially, I am assigned to Lieutenant Halderman's platoon. I respect him, although some of the men resent his adherence to the rule book. Halderman holds daily inspections of rifles, bayonets, packs, and radios, and demands that our uniforms be regulation and as clean as circumstances allow. He often calls us out for physical training, while the other platoons are lounging. I grumble, but I am becoming fairly adept at hand-to-hand combat, knives and bayonets, and rifling—deadly pursuits in which I now find amusement. Halderman has apprenticed me to the radioman to learn grid lines and coordinates; I call for all dust-offs and must know how to direct the choppers to wherever in Hell we're located. I think Halderman wants us to be the pride of the Marines.

Whenever Fats is unavailable, I attend the First Platoon, led by Lieutenant Donlevy. Less conservative than Halderman, Donlevy gets more kills and more booty; he also loses more men. Donlevy is dashing in appearance, his men wear eccentric additions to their uniforms, and his patrols often run to high drama.

I hate to accompany Lieutenant Sanford's platoon. Sanford is a skinny, nervous chain smoker likely to be mistaken for a Keystone Kop. The weapons belonging to his sloppy platoon frequently misfire because of improper maintenance; his men smoke and talk loudly during ambushes—when they aren't asleep. They're losers only because of their leader, and they show their latent intelligence by refusing to heed Sanford's orders when he goes to pieces during emergencies.

All things considered, I'd rather be in Philadelphia.

Relentlessly,

Kurt

My dear Paul,

Isabella Stewart Gardiner, a wealthy lady from Boston with an affinity for art, made a grand tour of Southeast Asia toward the end of the nineteenth century. After visiting the hidden ruins of the Angkor Wat, she was invited for an audience with the King of Cambodia. He expressed grave concern that a white woman should travel alone in the jungle. I wish my captain felt the same.

He's begun to insist that I learn to play a game called "Night Ambush!" The rules are simple. A squad embracing fourteen men goes into the woods after dark. They hide, hoping to surprise the opposing team, which may be hiding, too. Should the opponents appear, everyone fires his piece. Whoever gets killed, loses.

We play the game whenever the captain begins to brood about becoming a major; subsequently, we stroll into the twilight. When the patrol arrives at the eeriest, most Godforsaken spot possible, everyone pairs off with a buddy and retires, widely spaced in a rectangle along the trail. As one partner sleeps, the other keeps watch; on the hour, the roles reverse. At dawn, if the opposing team has failed to show, we hurry home to play daytime games. I play all of these games badly.

Still, excitement is infectious and I decided to look my best for the evening's event. I wore a snazzy olive-green ensemble with a matching helmet, two-toned jungle boots which are "in" over here, and contrasting khaki knapsacks. My date picked me up in front of my tent, Northwood McGrath, currently foremost among my erotic longings. McGrath is from Delta country in Mississippi, a tall, lean, mean blond, whose rugged good looks are only slightly marred by old acne scars. The evening might have promised well had I been in any condition but that of total terror.

We roamed far into the rain forest before finding a spot so remote that if things went badly for us, no one could help us. I would have slept through the first hour of the watch had I not been busily building a little nest in the mud and wet debris. I wondered whether I should check the pebbles for the nasty little inhabitants that inevitably dwell thereunder or merely hope

133

skeptically that their motto, too, was "Live and let live." McGrath noticed my alert condition and began a quiet but fascinating discussion about cars and chicks, which filled the hour.

When his turn to doze arrived, McGrath ingenuously laid his head on my lap. I attempted to discourage a revealing bulge under the nape of his neck, while I fretted over the shortcomings of our civilization as compared with that of the Ancient Greeks. Then I noticed a constant, repetitive movement of his right arm.

"McGrath?" I whispered.

"Yeah, Doc?"

"If you've got a rash, you'd better report to the medical tent when we get back to camp. You should get it treated."

"I ain't got no rash, Doc. Just athlete's foot."

"Why ever are you scratching yourself?"

"Shit, Doc, I ain't scratching. I'm poundin' my pud."

I think the ensuing silence was mistaken for disapproval. McGrath reckoned that people who read books probably had too much to think about to be horny. I rejected that argument and allowed as to how circumstances subdued eroticism. He protested: Maidens without diseases and privacy in the encampment were nonexistent. Where else could be beat off frustration? I liked his reasoning. I swore silence on the matter, and our discussion petered out. For the hours remaining in the long night, we kept our hands upon our metal rods.

Maybe I should have worn my taffeta?

Relentlessly,

Kurt

2ND BATTALION, ECHO CO.
7TH MARINES
20 December 66

Arch,

We go into the jungle every day to look for VC. Because we go the same way every day, a couple of men trip the mines or step into the punji traps that the VC have set out during the night; the gooks know our route. The wounded and the dead are sent to the Med Battalion. The survivors return to camp. The VC emerge from hiding. They dig their punji traps and lay their mines. They go back to wherever it is they go. We go into the jungle to trip some more mines and to step on some more punji traps. It is really disheartening.

Even the captain realized that something more than coincidence was at work, so he has decided to catch the VC in the act of laying their traps for us boobies. We go into the jungle at night now to lurk in the dark. The VC don't bother to come where we are lurking. They know where we are. Most of the grunts are asleep and snoring, and they sound like a den of bears. No bears reside in these woods. Even if bears did reside here, do you think the VC would go where the bears are? Of course they wouldn't. But the VC know the noise comes from snoring marines rather than bears. And so it goes.

A quiet and nice-looking guy joined us recently as a replacement. He was encouraged to show us a picture of his wife. Cochrane was shy, but obviously proud. None of us could blame him; she was a honey. Cochrane and Honey were married a week before he crossed the Pacific. And a good thing they had that week. A couple of days ago, Cochrane tripped a grenade mine that blew off his dick and balls. Wait until Honey gets a load of what he has left. Come to think of it, Honey will never get a load from what he's got left.

Relentlessly,

Kurt

2ND BATTALION, ECHO CO.
7TH MARINES
21 December 66

Chloe dear,

Thanks for adding a new dimension to my fear. I'd never thought of lying in a hospital for weeks or months at the mercy of nurses. I'd be another anonymous body to interfere with their continual perusal of nursing notes and doctors' orders. I'd succumb to their indifference and become a passive, silent, undemanding ghost.

Perhaps I'm too hard on nurses. They seldom know their patients beforehand, and they probably have difficulty in identifying with the wounded men: All patients look alike. I'd have no such difficulty. Take Farrow, for instance.

Farrow was an attractive kid, blond, with an angelic face and, unique among the grunts I've met, fastidious in his dress. He hated wearing a dirty uniform and would spend hours scrubbing his clothes in a stream near camp. The tent he shared with his cousin always had laundry draped over it.

One night a red alert sounded (VC nearby.) Everybody dove into the nearest foxhole. When the alert proved false, Farrow emerged from his foxhole with a grim, shocked look on his face and his newly laundered greens in shambles. Some malignant bastard had shit in the hole.

A couple of days later, while on patrol, Farrow leaned against a fence during a lunch break and tripped a mine that blew him to smithereens.

Or take Zouralias, a pale, lanky, long-faced Greek who had no buddy and rarely spoke. He was among a group one day that was listening to a grunt who giggled convulsively after every earshattering revelation made about a life back home that he astonishingly felt was interesting. Giggles was barefoot, and I was irritated. I interrupted him to make a diagnosis of leprosy. Giggles never listens when anyone else talks, but I was talking about him. He asked me the symptoms of leprosy. I'd read *Hawaii:* Wu Chow's Auntie had examined her toes daily for half a century, looking for little red spots. As all the marines have diseased-looking feet from stagnant water, endless hiking, and rotting socks, I thought it a safe bet to elaborate upon those red spots. I noticed Zouralias, obviously worried, get up and drift toward the water buffalo, a tank on wheels that holds our drinking water. He sat down beside the buffalo, removed his shoes and socks (for the first time in weeks, I'm sure), and peered at each of his nasty toes.

The following day he stepped on a grenade mine and lost parts of both legs. I treated him the best I could, but he died. He shouldn't have, but he just lay there and died.

Staggs and Hitt were from Oklahoma. Staggs, a well-built half-breed, and Hitt, a moon-faced redhead, were best buddies, noisy, and utterly good-natured.

They sat one night among a group outside my tent telling ghost stories. I told my magnum opus, "The Monster of Dead River Swamp." Do you recall how everyone believed the monster nearly ate me when I was six? The story goes over big out here in the jungle; the jarheads have sat transfixed through several reiterations.

I had reached the part in which the monster first comes out of the swamp, and Little Kurtie sees the hairy, fiery-eyed creature from his bedroom window. Staggs jumped up and went into an ape-man routine, grunting and scratching under his arms: It comes natural to these guys. Hitt turned into Little Kurtie, running through the night to escape the monster's hairy arms and foul breath. The grunts loved it.

Hitt bought the farm during a fire fight. We retreated to one side of a rice paddy; the Cong fired at us from the other side. Hitt's body lay beyond a dike on the VC side. Staggs tried to cross over the dike, but he couldn't get through the intense fire. Suddenly, Staggs stood up and began blasting away with his M–14 as he ran toward Hitt's body. A bullet hit his shoulder, turning him completely around. Staggs continued to climb the dike. Bullets slammed into him, raising puffs of dust on his greens and knocking him down again and again. He never stopped trying to shoot his way to Hitt. At last, when Staggs could only crawl on his knees, a bullet blew his face apart.

And Sergeant Culpepper, a cheerful guy from Florida, an excellent marine, and rather debonair despite his olive-green togs. During a patrol, we stopped at a village suspected of aiding the VC. The people hid from us, but the grunts dragged a couple of old men from one of the huts for interrogation. The old men kept their heads down and refused to answer any questions. Restless jarheads began to push the old men. A woman screamed. People stepped out of their huts. The hostility was becoming murderous.

Suddenly, Culpepper put his helmet on the end of his M–14, which he held high in the air, and began to tap dance through the puddles in his jungle boots, while warbling "Singin' in the Rain." Before long, villagers and jarheads alike were laughing and clapping their hands. We obtained the information we wanted.

This morning a clumsy dude who talks compulsively in an inaudible voice, started to talk to another grunt. Eicheldinger is irritating; he expects answers, but you seldom hear what idiotic statement he's uttered. The other grunt was embarrassed by his proximity to the doofus, and he became annoyed. He repeatedly asked, "What?" and each "What?" was sharper as the grunt grew more annoyed. Eicheldinger got uptight, and in his agitation he began bouncing a grenade from one hand to the other. Somehow, he pulled the pin. The other grunt dove for cover. Eicheldinger, startled, threw the grenade. It landed ten feet away in the lap of Culpepper, who was writing a letter to his wife. The grenade exploded.

I'd like to thank all the little people who made this possible.

Relentlessly,

Kurt

2ND BATTALION, ECHO CO.
7TH MARINES
22 December 66

My dear Paul,

We held ambush in a swamp the other night. We were deployed in a semicircle along the path running around one side of a large pond. Mosquitoes settled upon us in droves. No one could sleep and everyone was just this side of madness come morning. As my partner for the evening was an ugly, boring boob, I was especially tense by the time McGrath joined Eicheldinger and me at our post.

"We packing it in, McGrath?"

"Damn straight. But first, we're going to do a little duck hunting."

An hour later a flock of ducks settled on the pond. Everyone had his long rod at ready and several ducks dropped. As Eicheldinger waded out to bring in three birds which had fallen near us, McGrath turned to me and said, "Wonder if he's got a soft mouth." He reached over and gently rubbed his thumb along my lips. "I bet you got a soft mouth, Doc."

The following day I cornered Sergeant Pinkerton in the medical tent. He and McGrath are both plagued by athlete's foot and undergo treatment whenever possible. It sounds leprous, I know, but both were twelve-letter men in high school.

And I find any physical contact desirable. Pinkerton soaked his feet while we passed the time with warrior chat. After disarming him with some sparkling repartee, I threw him my best curve.

"Sarge, I got a letter from home today that bothers the hell out of me. I'll be in a foul mood tonight with no patience for that dumb shit Eicheldinger."

"You on ambush again tonight? You been out a lot lately, Doc. One of the other docs could go."

"No! I'd rather stand watch. Really. Help me forget. I just don't want Eicheldinger around me." Tears fell that rinsed the Sarge's nasty feet.

"I got to stay with that cherry. I'll put the Dinger with the Geek. Hate like hell to put two assholes together. That leaves McGrath. Okay with you?"

"McGrath will do just fine, Sarge." I dried his feet with my hair.

That night, as clean as my fresh uniform and liberally sprinkled with Aqua Velva After Shave—for the Man's Man—I lay under a jungle moon next to the golden beast of the Delta. During a piquant conversation, we bewailed the unappetizing possibilities available to us in Vietnam for erotic maneuvers. I enthralled him with some sexual exploits (genders changed) from my past; McGrath enthralled me when he began to diddle himself.

"McGrath, are you poundin' your pud again?"

"Sorry, Doc. I'll stop."

"No! Go right ahead. I've half a mind to join you." Silence. "McGrath, I believe I will join you."

"Go to it, Doc."

Despite the companionable feeling, I wasn't satisfied. "Would you like me give you a few whacks, buddy?"

"I'd take to it kindly, Doc," he replied.

My hand replaced his hand upon his sex. "Would you mind giving me a little help?" I asked.

McGrath obliged with his easy grace. "Sure, Doc." His hand replaced my hand upon my sex. Before long, we stripped and each of us placed his sex in whatever orifices would accommodate. But when I tried to give him a little smooch, McGrath pushed me away.

"You can fuck a marine," he snarled. "But you can't fuck with a marine."

Well, shut my mouth. I was dismayed for a moment, but

139

oily persuasion repaired the rupture and white heat again warmed the jungle.

And a man's a man for a' that.

Relentlessly,

Kurt

2ND BATTALION, ECHO CO.
7TH MARINES
23 December 66

Dear Mom,

Is this you who worries about my "roughing it"? Who ever accompanied Dad, Karen, and me on expeditions to Glacier and Yellowstone parks, Jackson Hole, ghost towns, and ice caves? Who ever lived happily one summer in a cabin with no plumbing, no electricity, and no neighbors? No radio? No television? You loved it.

I believe with all my heart that Karen and I were in more danger chasing bear cubs along the Stillwater than I am here. We have no watchful mother bears in Vietnam, no rattlesnakes, and no rumors of marauding mountain lions. The food I eat tastes no worse and is less likely to be tainted by ptomaine and salmonella than the food in those greasy spoons in which Dad made us eat.

A man needs adventure, possibly to satisfy some primeval urge. Would you rather I caught some debilitating nigger disease while hunting elephants in Africa? I like elephants. Or would you have me prove my manliness by developing gangrene of the fingers and toes on top of Mt. Everest? Or should I squash against the ground as I wonder why my parachute didn't open?

What I should prefer your doing is to set up the projector and look at those slides of Montana. As you're looking, I'd like you to recollect that those were the best of times.

Love,

Kurt

Chloe dear,

I appreciated your gift. So did my buddies Pinkerton and McGrath. We mixed one bottle with cherry Kool-Aid and the other with lime Kool-Aid (for the holly and the ivy) and enjoyed lovely, rummy hangovers Christmas morning. I should have found it difficult to eat my turkey anyway.

My granny sent me a pair of binoculars. Binoculars! The better, I suppose, to see this fucking country. Mother and DT mailed two cartons filled with everything from soup to nuts. Karen sent *The Country Doctor's Medical Companion*. Neil opened a six-month subscription to the *Sporting News* for me. Ricky sent a record: "If You're Going to San Francisco, Wear Flowers . . ." which had melted in a Post Office fire in Mobile, Alabama. Grandma DeBarard, as always, gave me deodorant and after shave.

An old girl friend on her year abroad mailed a package of postcard replicas of paintings in the Louvre. Baseball groupies from Arizona and Oregon baked cookies and boiled fudge. And my grandmother's lady friend Fawn sent me her deceased husband's gold tie clip and matching cuff links. I must fit everything into ⅙ of a tent.

The *Acadian* listed my name among other hometown boys in Nam, and about forty people from Bonifay sent cards and letters. The strangest was from a lady professor of psychology at Evangeline, who sent two hundred questionnaires and asked that I get them filled out by marines and returned to her. She wrote that she prefers men on the front lines, but will take what she can get. Questions like:

Do you feel reverence for the American flag?
Do you hate your father?
Do you keep up with current events?
Have you ever desired a twin brother?
When you look at a *Playboy* pin-up, are you a) excited? b) merely curious? or c) indifferent?
Do you feel killing an Oriental to be morally wrong? A Negro? Someone of the Semitic descent?

I'm afraid I must disappoint her. I would be so embarrassed, handing those questionnaires to the grunts. I'll write her that the monsoon has ruined her papers; although I am sorry about that, most marines can't read anyway, and none of them would know what Semitic means.

Chloe, I think only you would picture yourself as a fat old shrew whom time is passing by. When you come to my mind, and you often do, I think of crushed velvet and dimmed lights, soft chamber music and slim volumes of poems, and nectar and ambrosia graciously served by a glorious Rubens woman.

Relentlessly,

Kurt

2ND BATTALION, ECHO CO.
7TH MARINES
28 December 66

Dear Mom,

That's a dandy pair of binoculars. I look through them everwhichaways and am the envy of the compound. Even the officers have asked to borrow them.

I enjoyed a pleasant Christmas. The mess hall overwhelmed us with a good dinner. I traded my turkey for a large piece of fruitcake.

I'll write a thank-you note to Fawn for her gifts. I'm uncertain as to how I shall utilize them, but I have little to do other than to think about things. Her presents will give me something to think about, so tell her I appreciate her thoughtfulness.

Would you do something else for me? About forty persons answered the notice in the *Acadian* and sent cards and letters. The nicest was from an old lady who wrote a very long letter about her son, the doctor, over to Houston, and how he had served in the Korean War. I enjoyed her letter and will write to thank her myself. Would you mind ringing her up to say that I appreciated her interest? Mrs. Ida Mae Fournier—LOngfellow 3–9171.

Mother and DT's preacher sent a Christmas card with an

enclosed snapshot of him and his dreary family—no note but the diamond on his pinky finger glittered. Although I applaud the use of Season's Greetings instead of angels singing and cattle lowing, I do think a minister of God should have religious symbols decorating his card instead of "Have a Merry . . ." You can take that in several ways, and it seems slightly obscene to me. And offensive, especially when there isn't a snowball's chance in Hell that I'm having a "Merry" over here, in any sense of the word.

Happy New Year to you, too.

Love,

Kurt

2ND BATTALION, ECHO CO.
7TH MARINES
29 December 66

Arch,

How refreshing to know that someone worries whether I'm as snug as a bug in a rug. And in my glorious eiderdown waterproof sleeping bag with its matching goose-feather pillow, I shall be. Thank you, buddy.

As long as you're leaving the Land of the Chili Shitters for Aspen, why ever don't you visit my old pal Paul? He lives in the mountains near Boulder, teaches at the university, and skis frequently. Paul's brilliant and elegant and will make you feel as if you were the wittiest and most charming person he's ever met. I'll include his address; I think you'd have a good time.

The Tigers sent me last year's yearbook and this year's roster for Christmas. Among the infielders is:

Strom, Wm. Kurt L–R R Military Service 6'3" 205
    3/15/42 Tarentum, Pa   Bonifay, La

I'm in the big time at last.

I refuse to regret the three seasons I'll miss. Better players than I'll ever be lost years of their careers to World War II and Korea. I'm in good company.

143

Of all the guys we played with, only that asshole Puzio made the roster. And he'll be doing right well to make the Detroit outfield.

You'd have made it, too, buddy. You were the best pitcher I saw during four years in the minors. God damn it, but we were hot stuff.

We have heard the chimes at midnight.

Relentlessy,

Kurt

2ND BATTALION, ECHO CO.
7TH MARINES
30 December 66

My dear Paul,

I was just saying to one of the marines the other day, "Jarhead," I said, "wouldn't it be pleasant to relax for a week in a warm, dry library?"

"Duhhh," said the jarhead, "what's a library?"

Mail call came before I could reply. Four boxes for Doc Strom from Paul Carroll in Boulder, Colorado. They were heavy. They were wrapped securely. I borrowed a machete from a marine of the Latin persuasion and hacked off the strings. I opened the boxes. Books! Forty-seven books. The complete works of Anthony Trollope.

Who the fuck is Anthony Trollope? Perhaps he's an expert, if little-known, pornographer; at least, I can think about it. I read *Can You Forgive Her*. Now I'm reading *Phineas Finn*. And Fanny Hill be damned, I'm enjoying myself. How ever can I thank you? I know. I'll send to the Library of Congress for their pamphlet "Where to Find Cowboys."

Speaking of mail, I've confirmed that the battalion's censors send corspmen's mail on without reading it. Now I can really dish the dirt. And is there ever a sensation within the perimeter! A gorgeous number from our sister company has returned off R&R with his mouth full of astonishing news.

Have I told you about R&R? Rest and Relaxation. It's a nice invention. As the soldiers during the Civil War returning to their farms for a couple of weeks to plant their crops, we get a vacation from the conflict to sow a few wild oats. Midway through a thirteen-month tour of duty in Vietnam, everyone gets a respite in an Oriental city of his choice: either five days in Bangkok, Singapore, Taiwan, or Hong Kong or, because of the distance, seven days in Tokyo, Sydney, or Honolulu. Most of the guys I've known who survived long enough to get R&R have gone to either Hong Kong or Bangkok. They blew several hundred dollars on fancy hotel rooms, liquor, and women. It's rather pleasant, considering that back home the niggers only get a fish fry.

Anyway, the nifty number next door chose Taiwan. He arrived at noon, rented a hotel room, arranged a date that night with a Chinese fox, downed a few beers, and rented a Honda for the afternoon. As he explored the countryside, he was joined by another American cycle nut, and they played motor games for a couple of hours; afterward, over a drink at his new buddy's exotic pad, Visconti recognized him. Guess who it was. Your favorite movie star! The hot man himself, currently filming on the island. They polished off a couple of fifths before getting down to the nitty-gritty. It's getting so you can't trust anyone. Eat your heart out.

Although Visconti is a rugged hunk of masculinity, he boasts of the affair. Grooving, and I gather provided for, he saw no need to return to his hotel and his fox; he spent the rest of his holiday in a nest of unnatural bliss. At the airport, Visconti was asked to encourage other "Groovy Studs" with upcoming R&R's to accept the dynamo's hospitality. Visconti has returned to pass along the invitation. Every grunt in the regiment seems amenable to be wined, dined, and perverted. Stars in their eyes, they have descended in a frenzy upon the R&R office. It would turn your stomach to look at some of the men who fancy themselves "Groovy Studs."

An old buddy of mine might call upon you. Arch McFarland. We were roommates for three years in the minors. I've told you how I loved the guy. Funny and easygoing with natural macho, Arch slept in the same bed with me on road trips for three years. I wanted him desperately, but never touched him—too afraid of losing his friendship. God, the fantasies I had. Only summers I didn't spend all my free time reading.

Arch got married and decided to quit baseball. And a damn shame, too. Divorced within a year, Arch now paints sawmills every summer, relaxes in Mexico during the winter, and writes a letter to me every week.

Friends make salt sweet and blackness bright.

Relentlessy,

Kurt

2ND BATTALION, ECHO CO.
7TH MARINES
3 January 67

Dear Mom,

What a surprise! A basket of goodies from Grandma. I thought it was supposed to be the other way around. I invited all the Southern boys in my platoon to a New Year's banquet of pickled pig's feet and blackeye peas. Eyes rolled, lips smacked, hands rubbed stomachs, and belches resounded. Such gratitude poured forth that halfway around the world, your ears must have burned.

I'm glad to hear you enjoyed your cruise; I'm sorry that Fawn felt too poorly to accompany you. I'm planning my holiday for the end of the month; I'm going to Tokyo for R&R. Cherry blossoms and geisha girls, Fujiyama and the Golden Pavilion, sumo wrestlers and geisha girls . . .

Sayonara,

Kurt

2ND BATTALION, ECHO CO.
7TH MARINES
4 January 67

Arch,

A break in the action occurred when the captain followed the colonel into Da Nang for a week of in-country R&R. The lieutenant left in charge preferred booze to glory and divided the company into four sections, each section standing two days of perimeter watch and making economy-size patrols for local surveillance. The powers that be have returned, and once again, we are pawns in the colonel's crusade to rid Vietnam of the Communist scourge. But while he was gone, we lived: They can't take that away from me.

I slept through the first day for eighteen uninterrupted hours. The second and third days, I read. I caught duty the fourth and fifth days, so I held sick call for the company: treating sores, trenchfoot, and clap; dispensing medicines; and recommending the jaundiced and the malarial visit the battalion doctor. The jaundiced and the malarial never saw the doctor; as usual, he was out of his office, and Christ alone knew where he had gone. His office hours rarely coincide with any opportunity a grunt may have to visit him.

The sixth day, I accompanied two buddies into Chu Lai. Along the road into town, we passed several wrinkled mamasans with black teeth. They offered us number one boom boom for ten dollars. We countered with an offer of one dollar for number ten boom boom. They hissed at our ungallant appraisal and turned away to await those with less acumen.

We spent that afternoon on the beach. The wind had a bite to it, and the sea was chilly; nevertheless, we tore off our clothes and dove in. We swam. We rolled in the sand. We swam again. We played "Monster from the Deep," a variation of tag that took us to the far end of the beach. We raced back to where we'd left our clothes. Someone had gone through our pants and stolen our money.

There's always a nigger in the woodpile.

Relentlessly,

Kurt

2ND BATTALION, ECHO CO.
7TH MARINES
5 January 67

Chloe dear,

Last week and against my will (the story of my life in Vietnam), I visited the Vegetable Garden, a special hospital for hopeless cases who refuse to die after their brains do. My buddies Pinkerton and McGrath refused to enter any of the gray, concrete buildings set in long, forbidding rows. They waited outside, while I dropped off some personal effects belonging to members of our company in residence.

I found Negley in the first ward I entered. Before he tripped a grenade mine that shredded him, Negley had been a big, clumsy guy—enthusiastic but lacking smarts. I tried hard to save him. I shouldn't have bothered. Somewhere along the line he died, and too much time passed before his heart beat again; the temporary cessation of blood flow had irreparably damaged too many brain cells. The surgeons removed both legs, both arms, and one eye. His remaining eye was open; I doubt he saw me. I left his Christmas present on the bedside table: a photograph of his family framed in silver.

I had more difficulty finding Rogers, asking for him in ward after ward. The wards were identical: a nursing station in the middle of each guarded two long rows of beds holding men swathed in bandages and attached to IV bottles, catheter bags, and jugs holding ominous-looking liquids.

At the seventh ward, the skinny, bespectacled nurse on duty glanced up as I entered; then she turned back to her *Modern Screen* magazine. I walked over to her desk. "Excuse me, ma'am. Do you have a patient named Rogers?"

She tore herself away from the magazine and looked at me. Her eyes widened; she took off her glasses and set them on the desk beside her. "Hi, soldier. What brings you here?"

"I'm looking for a man from my company. Rogers."

"Are you from out there in the jungle?"

"Yes, ma'am. We were in the same company."

"In the jungle?"

"Yes, ma'am. That's where he got hurt. Rogers."

"The jungle."

"David Rogers."

"You have a good tan, soldier. Isn't it raining out there, too?"

"Yes, ma'am, but not during the afternoons."

"I never get to the beach. I'm stuck here all day."

"I'm sorry, ma'am. Rogers?"

"What?"

"David Rogers. Is he one of your patients?"

"I think so. Sit down, soldier, and take a load off your feet."

"Thank you, ma'am, but I have Rogers' Christmas presents here and—"

"Sit down. He's not going anywhere. Would you like some coffee?"

"No, thank you, ma'am. I just want—"

"Sit, soldier!"

"Yes, ma'am." I sat down on a chair next to the desk. The nurse reached for the coffee pot behind her, spreading her legs. Her dress covered her knees. She poured coffee into a paper cup.

"You men must get lonely out there in the jungle. Cream?"

"No. We're together most of the time." She reached behind her for a container. Her dress had pulled up. I could see her kneecaps.

"Have you been on R&R yet? Sugar?" She leaned backward again. I saw thigh.

"No. Not yet. I'm planning—"

"You can tell me. You're too good-looking not to have a couple of slant-eyed chippies on the side. One lump or two?"

"No, ma'am. None." She gave me three, leaning farther back and spreading her legs wider with every lump. I could see yellow panties. She handed me the coffee, light and sweet, just the way I like it.

"How long have you been in Vietnam, soldier?"

"Almost four months now. I—"

"You must be lonely. So lonely." She laid her hand upon my leg. I stood up and spilled the coffee all over my greens. I suppose the situation was a marine's dream, but a skinny little nurse, for Christ's sake.

"Listen, ma'am. I've got two buddies waiting for me outside and it's coming up a cloud and I just came to see Rogers and—"

She stopped smiling and put her glasses back on. She glared at me through them; then she snapped her magazine open and went back to reading it. I set the empty cup upon the desk and walked between the long rows of beds looking for Rogers among the Vegies. Each was wrapped in bandages like the Invisible Man; the only way to tell one from the other was by the names taped on the charts hanging from the beds. I found a chart with "Rogers, David" taped on it. I set down his presents, one a football by the feel of it, and leafed through the chart to learn what had been done to him. The nurse ran up and grabbed the chart out of my hands.

"What do you think you're doing?" she asked.

"Reading that chart."

"You have no business reading that chart."

"I took care of this man when he got hurt. His buddies and I would like to know what's to become of him."

"You should have asked Nurse. She would have furnished you with any prognosis she thought you should know."

"Excuse me, ma'am. What's his prognosis?"

She looked around at the patients, aghast that I should be asking such a question in front of them, as if the mummies could hear. They just stared at the ceiling. "Have your commanding officer write to the hospital, and he'll be furnished with the proper information."

"He could care what happens to anybody. Let me read the chart, I'll be gone in three minutes, and you can go back to your movie magazine."

"Don't get snotty, soldier. Remember, I'm an officer. And you should know better than to come on a hospital ward in a muddy uniform."

"As if it makes any difference in this place. Are you for real? Give me the goddam chart."

"You'd better leave this ward."

By this time, she was screaming, and so was I. The Vegies paid us no mind. The nurse clutched the chart to her scrawny bosom.

"The next time somebody comes in here, you might get off your skinny butt and give him a little help, instead of playing the whore."

"I could have you court-martialed for that remark."

"Scare me, bitch. It would get me off the lines."

"Get out of here!" she screamed as she ran to the telephone, still clutching the chart.

I got out of there and made tracks. She'd hardly blow the whistle on me, though. She must know what little chance a line corpsman has of making it. All she has to do is wait.

Relentlessly,

Kurt

My dear Paul,

I've been thinking it over as I snuggle within the brand-new eiderdown sleeping bag my buddy Arch sent me. I've really appreciated your letters; I know you're hardly one for sitting at a typewriter when snow bunnies and ski bums in all their glowing glory swoop down nearby mountain slopes. And you've been a good friend over the years. The least I could do is to drop by your favorite movie star's and fuck him silly for you. The very least I could do.

After I came to that decision, I wandered over to our sister company to get every last detail from Visconti. He was lying on the ground in front of his tent, elbow propping up his head, a portrait of lean, easy grace. I had no little trouble separating him from a flock of lesser mortals jabbering their nonsense. (All right, I followed him to the pee-pipe. And what he whipped out there would put half of New York on its knees.) He replied coolly to my impertinent, but subtle, questioning; apparently he has been a victim of cruel badinage because of his honesty concerning carnal matters. Nevertheless, my considerable empathy thawed him to the point where he was nothing averse to giving me every last detail. I can't imagine your being interested in his exact words; it suffices to say I was intrigued. Visconti could tell.

"Shit, Doc! You ought to go to Taiwan. He'd like you." I lowered my eyes modestly and smoothed out a wrinkle in my greens. I glanced up to find the curly haired centurion looking at me critically through eyes the color of a rain cloud. "Yeah, he'd like you for sure."

Paul, you couldn't believe how much I was enjoying this conversation, but all good things must end; my eyes, which are the color of doggy doo, began to smoulder and that bodes no good for my reputation. I bade Visconti adieu and tripped back to Echo, my brain seething.

The next day I hitchhiked into Chu Lai with Pinkerton and McGrath. The first place I hit was R&R headquarters, located at my old home, the First Medical Battalion. The travel agent, a jungle bunny wearing eyeglasses, let me know that certain indiscretions early in my Oriental sojourn made my inclinations

151

known to him. Anyway, he had heard rumors. He propositioned me. I declined. Unwilling to believe that I might be objecting to her ugliness rather than her color, the Queen of Spades accused me of prejudice. She tried to blackmail me. I countered with my own rumors. Scuttlebutt (Alf) maintains that the dark lady has ghoulishly substituted herself for corpsmen who had been killed before they could go on R&R. Jemima has rested and relaxed in foreign ports five times in the past nine months. Grunts and line corpsmen are lucky to go on one R&R; even officers and chiefs rarely go more than two or three times. I threatened to raise hell. I fly to Tokyo in a couple of weeks. (Taiwan is booked up until July.)

I took Pinkerton and McGrath with me to ICU, so Alf and Bernie could see how it was with me on the lines; I knew my fairy friends would be stunned. And they were, gratifyingly so. (If rumors must be spread about me, let them be beautiful.) After applauding my victory over the African queen, Alf invited us to spend the night and then took us to the ville where he treated us to a gourmet dinner of something or other. He camped outrageously all during supper: Mae West and Bette Davis brightened one dark corner of this wretched nation.

The next day a jeep carried us over the river and into the woods before the bogeymen emerged. Nevertheless, Ho Chi Minh got some revenge; the something or other we had for supper had us squatting and squirting over the honey pit, drunk and disorderly, side by side, time after time.

Relentlessly,

Kurt

2ND BATTALION, ECHO CO.
7TH MARINES
10 January 67

Arch,

I have survived eleven patrols this week. "So," you say, "Kurt embarks upon many patrols, but they must be short. He must endure no all-day patrols anymore."

"Unfortunately," replies Kurt, "not only do I go on dawn-to-dusk patrols every day, I hump the boonies several nights a week on dusk-to-dawn ambushes."

"What ever could they be thinking?" you ask. "Such a pace could kill a man."

Yes, buddy. It does.

I recall going out for football in the eighth grade. The coach would run us ragged during the first week so he could cut the pussies off the squad. At the end of practice, we would walk on rubber legs to the locker room. We'd collapse with the dry heaves and try to vomit through raw throats. Guys would fall down exhausted in the shower room, and despite the rumored possibility of catching athlete's foot of the body, they'd just lie there. Nobody laughed. I feel like that most of the time.

Yet we continue to go out. I never get more than three consecutive hours of sleep. The mind stops functioning. You know you must be alert to snipers and booby traps, but you forget. You are so tired you forget. And suddenly, resoundingly, finally, you cease to live.

If the gods are smiling and the darkness has yet to cover your eyes, you come back to camp. One of the lieutenants walks up to you. He asks you to accompany a night patrol that he will command. He apologizes. You look longingly at your damp, sandy sleeping bag. You fill three or four canteens. You resupply the three-pouch, waterproof, unfolding medical corpsman's kit. You lick your contact lenses clean and replace them in burning eyes. And you go blindly into the night.

Those grunts have it no easier than you. While you endure a patrol with another platoon, they stand watch or rearrange the shape of the compound according to the colonel's newest whim: dipping trenches, restretching concertina wire, laying minefields . . . The colonel watches the grunts sweat and strain, occasionally snapping off an order to our captain, who relays it to the gunny sergeant in charge of the jarheads; after a few minutes, the colonel turns an abrupt about-face and marches off. Our captain and a couple of other sycophants diddly bop along behind him to his bungalow at Regimental Headquarters, where they guzzle Scotch and play bridge under a framed motto: BETTER THEM THAN ME.

Relentlessly,

Kurt

Chloe dear,

Lieutenant Halderman reamed my ass last night. My speaking ill of the colonel, said the lieutenant, demoralizes the troops. I denied badmouthing the colonel. Halderman said my imitations of the colonel were sufficient slander. He admitted that the colonel employs tactics and procedures incomprehensible to us at times, but we should respect his rank and his superior knowledge. "You have a little imagination, Strom. Instead of walking and talking like the colonel, maybe you should put yourself in his shoes. Try to see things his way."

I respect Halderman. I agreed to try to see things as the colonel would. And I tried. I put myself in the colonel's shoes, and I looked this way and I looked that way. I had no success. Although I've my peculiarities, I'm not a pompous homicidal asshole. I took off his shoes and ran barefoot through my imagination. And I conceived a plan. I would get to know the colonel by interviewing him.

Q. What is your name?
A. My name is Judson S. Grant.
Q. Where were you born?
A. I was born in West Egg, Long Island, with a mouth in which butter would not melt.
Q. What is your education?
A. I attended St. Salome Grammar School in North Egg, Long Island; the Henry Hawk Military Academy in South Egg, Long Island; and Rhode Island A&M in Awfuckit, Rhode Island.
Q. Are you married?
A. Yes. The little woman is the former Angela Saxon of Main Street, U.S. of A.
Q. Have you any children?
A. Yes, three. Junior, Ulysses S., and Sister.
Q. Why ever did you make the Marine Corps a career?
A. To abuse power, to knock a few heads together, and to get away from a wife who's an ice cube with a hole in it.

Q. What ever is your feeling about the Vietnam conflict?

A. I thank God on my knees every night. I thought those damn politicians in Washington would never get around to holding another war.

Q. Wouldn't you rather be stationed at a safer location?

A. No! To make rank, one needs points. I get a point for each six months I command an infantry regiment; besides I'm safe enough.

Q. You feel safe in the middle of a jungle teeming with enemies?

A. Certainly. We are well fortified, and I rarely leave Regimental Headquarters except by helicopter, which is relatively safe, although heroic.

Q. Do you miss the luxuries of the rear?

A. Of course, I do; nevertheless, I've tried to make myself comfortable. My troops erected a portable bungalow I designed myself, according to plans I was given of a Swiss chalet I once saw near Blitzberg, Vermont. I have a personal shower and toilet, also designed in the Swiss style. Three orderlies clean my bungalow, attend to my wardrobe, and serve the meals cooked by my personal chef in the regimental mess. I have laid in a good supply of liquor and have adequate bridge players among my staff.

Q. Sounds nice.

A. It's all right.

Q. Do you miss sex?

A. With my wife? Don't make me laugh. I've found power more than a substitute.

Q. Since your troops live like animals, they must resent your self-indulgence.

A. Tough shit!

Q. Why ever do you keep rearranging the perimeters of the compound? With patrols day and night, the troops must already be exhausted.

A. I admit that I have no strategy, but I must keep the men busy. When they dig ditches, they develop blisters. When they roll wire, they cut their hands. Makes them tougher. And distracted by minor aches and pains and by exhaustion, they don't wonder about my tactics. Idleness is the Devil's work.

Q. But these boys are dying . . .

A. So what?

Relentlessly,

Kurt

My dear Paul,

This is Paranoia Week. Since I've been on the lines, I've celebrated Fear and Trembling Week, Utter Horror Week, Great Dismay Week, Absolute Terror Week, Racking Despair Week, and now I'm in the middle of Complete Paranoia Week. Sex reared its ugly head, and I'm besmirched by its scarlet drool.

I've admitted to my little session in the jungle with McGrath, right? We made it straight on the up and up. The seduction was mutual. Perhaps I enjoyed the session more than I should have. And McGrath responded with little hesistancy when I initiated a repetition of the act an hour later. Yet he doesn't speak to me now. He glares at me. You'd think the intimacy would have cemented our friendship. I suppose I should be neither surprised nor hurt. In real life, fairy tales end unhappily.

Marines are trained to hate queers. Marines take great offense when they are called queers. Should a recruit be unable to hack basic training, he is known as a queer. Whenever a marine fucks up, he is an assumed queer. It's rock bottom to these guys. The pits. A queer has no reason to live, so he's best done away with. Kill a queer for Uncle Sam.

Lieutenant Sanford led a seminar in Homosexuality to celebrate Paranoia Week. He had the ultimate solution to the problem. "I believe the government should stand all faggots before a firing squad. If I ever thought that one of my men was a faggot, I'd shoot him in the back and call it self-defense." He looked at me.

Oh, Lieutenant Sanford, I thought, you needn't worry about defending your spindly body, your purple lips, your receding chin, and your two-inch pecker. I thought the aforementioned; I never said it aloud. What I said aloud was, "Oh, Lieutenant Sanford, you can do better than that. Fit the punishment to the crime. Pull the pin of a grenade and shove it up the queer's ass."

"Have him suck on a punji stick and ram it down his throat," yelled a grunt.

"Stick leeches up the queer's dick and they'll suck him to death," cried another.

"Tie him to stakes in the latrine and drown him with piss," a third grunt advised.

"Or we could shit on him until he smothers," added a fourth. What ever have I started?

Relentlessly,

Kurt

2ND BATTALION, ECHO CO.
7TH MARINES
13 January 67

Dear Mom,

We ate hamburgers today. With catsup. Brownies for dessert. Baked in 1953. And Kool-Aid. Lime.

Reggie has left Karen. She's upset. And ashamed.

A couple of months ago, Reggie apparently started to hang around the apartment of a wealthy buddy, a bachelor who entertained a continuous string of ladies. Reggie plucked a pearl from the string and brought her to the house to while away a few afternoons. Every night Karen would drag into the house to find dirty dishes, unswept floors, and unchanged diapers. She learned from a neighbor about Pearl. Karen confronted Reggie. He admitted to the affair. Karen asked him to choose between Pearl and her. Reggie moved out. That's how things stand at the moment.

What's with Mother? She sent Christmas presents, but she's written neither Karen nor me for a month. We've concluded that she has been brooding over her disappointment in us. If she's drawn a circle that has shut us out, she can expect only contempt. She's certainly not to expect letters. So don't keep asking me to write to her.

I miss you, too.

Love,

Kurt

2ND BATTALION, ECHO CO.
7TH MARINES
17 January 67

Arch,

You are just one among the many who have nominated me for the title "The Most Obnoxious Cardplayer in the World." I never took offense. But I should have taken heed. Because of my joy at *always* winning, I nearly drowned. I'll tell you how it happened.

Lieutenant Sanford has long desired an invitation to the colonel's bridge tournaments held in his Swiss chalet. As Sanford would be hard pressed to receive an invitation to attend services at the Jehovah's Witnesses, his attempts to climb the pecking order were in vain. If he couldn't be among the men, he apparently decided to become one of the boys; he invited the three best cardplayers in Echo to his tent for an evening of bridge. Sanford even provided refreshments: a can of warm beer for each of us and a fifth of Scotch for himself. His deficiencies as a host were as nothing compared to his lack of card sense. He bid with a reckless abandon that overwhelmed all attempts at collaboration, he mistook diamonds for hearts and clubs for spades, and he slapped his winning cards on the table with irritating glee. McGrath, obviously descended from a long line of Mississippi riverboat gamblers, looked at Sweeney, who worked one summer as a dealer in Reno, and Sweeney looked at me. I shrugged and began to glance at the bottom card before each cut, just for something interesting to do. I knew I displayed improper bridge etiquette, and my compulsion bothered Sanford. He'd declare, "If this was the Wild West, you'd be dead." I would have been irritated had he not been losing; instead, after each of his frequent misplays, I would smugly exclaim, "If this were the Wild Wild West, you'd be dead, too, sir." I could see him boil, but I am the son of my mother; I can't help picking at a scab. I said it once too often. Sanford squeaked, leaped behind me, grabbed my neck with both of his hands, and began to choke me. My chair fell backward. As I braced myself to keep my head from hitting against the lieutenant's footlocker, I blacked out. I came to with McGrath giving me mouth-to-mouth resuscitation. Sanford sat on his rack, weeping furiously. Sweeney stood over him, patting him awkwardly on the back.

But I promised you a near-drowning.

Sanford shook me awake this morning at 4 A.M. I almost shot him with the .45 pistol I keep under my pillow. I wish I had. He told me I was to accompany his platoon on a patrol. I protested; I had been out on ambush with Halderman's platoon until 1 A.M., and Sanford had given me no advance notice, which he was supposed to do. And where ever the hell was Soul Brother anyway?

"I'm ordering you to go, sailor."

So be it.

A VC prisoner had hinted under duress of a cache of weapons hidden in a series of tunnels near a village about seven miles distant. After two hours of hiking, we reached the village; another two hours passed before we found the entrance, a 3-foot × 3-foot hole in the ground hidden under a hedge. Sanford ordered a concussion mine thrown in the hole. We heard a muffled boom, the ground quivered, and the villagers ran out of their huts and disappeared down the road. Sanford turned to me, smiling.

"Strom, you've never gone in one of these set-ups, have you?"

"No," I replied.

"It's your turn."

I looked at the hole, a home for Viet Cong, deadly kraits, booby traps, and nasty odors. I looked at the lieutenant. I looked at the hole.

"Go to it, Strom. That's an order."

"It's an order for corpsman annihilation. If nothing else, the dust down there would choke me to death." No one had thought to bring gas masks.

"You're a pussy, Strom, a number one pussy." (I'll accept that.) "If you don't go down that hole, I'll put your ass on report as soon as we get back to camp." I shrugged. "You

159

damn corpsmen aren't worth the money it costs to bring you over here. You don't belong with real marines."

Slapping down on all corpsmen to get his revenge, Sanford scandalized his platoon. The gunny sergeant stepped forward. "Lieutenant, Doc's not trained for that kind of shit. We'd do better to send down one of the men."

Sanford looked at me, a sneer curling his lips. "Yeah. One of the *men*. Any volunteers?"

Everyone studied the hole. A long silence followed. I started giggling. The gunny glanced at me and said quickly, "Klima, you go down."

Klima, a short, blond, sunny-natured kid, looked up, his face white. Everyone else continued to study the hole.

"Snap to it, Klima," Sanford ordered, "we haven't got all day."

Klima stood absolutely still for a few seconds; then he sloughed off his pack, handed his gear to his buddy, pulled out a knife, and disappeared into the hole, headfirst. He reappeared immediately, feetfirst, followed by a large brown rat which disappeared into the hedge. Klima looked beseechingly at the lieutenant; Sanford stared impassively back. Klima scrambled into the hole. We waited silently for a few minutes; then we heard a muffled explosion and saw a portion of the rice paddy sink. A volley of shots followed. We had been tricked into an ambush.

Sanford screamed out five or six meaningless orders simultaneously. The jarheads ignored him, placed themselves in a circle, and fired back at an invisible enemy. I crawled to the center of the circle to wait for the inevitable cry of "CORPSMAN!" Sanford and the radioman joined me in the bull's-eye.

I hadn't long to wait. Eicheldinger, a particularly useless grunt, had wandered off before the attack. He was shrieking for help. "I'm hit! I'm hit! Doc! Doc!"

I raised my head to look at the bare patch of ground I would have to cross to reach Eicheldinger: thirty feet with no cover. "Bring him in," Sanford screeched.

"He's a decoy," I cried. "I'll be a sitting duck."

"Do your job, pussy," Sanford told me.

I looked at that bare patch of ground. I believe Eicheldinger to be worthless in every conceivable way, and were I given a choice, I might find a certain solace in his nonexistence. But my duty as a corpsman calls for tending to wounded jarheads, whatever their use to society. My duty as a corpsman also included living long enough to tend as many grunts as possible, and exposing myself on that bare piece of ground courted death. I was caught between the horns of a dilemma.

"Bring that man in, Strom, or I'll shoot your ass."

My dilemma was resolved. I crawled to a tree next to the bare piece of ground. Cringing behind it, I called to Eicheldinger. "How bad are you hit?"

"Blood! Blood! I see blood!"

Yes, Eicheldinger, that happens sometimes when you get shot. "How bad? Can you crawl this far?"

No answer. He was unconscious. Shit! I crawled toward Eicheldinger. Before I reached him, a bullet hit the ground inches away from my head, throwing up dust that got behind my contacts and blinded me. I took the lenses out of my eyes, licked them clean, and put them back in place. The entire procedure took only thirty seconds, but Sanford got impatient; he sent Mikkleson, a new man, to bring in the Dinger. As Mikkleson ran past me, bent over double, he caught a bullet in the head. The force of the bullet threw him on top of me. I slid from under him. The bullet had gone into his eyeball and blown his brains out the back of his head. I continued toward Eicheldinger. Bullets threw up dust all around me. Another typical day in Vietnam.

When I got to Dinger, I felt of him. I found no wounds. His pulse beat steadily. Blood covered his face. I spit in his face and wiped the blood off. He had apparently fallen to the ground during the initial volley and bumped his nose, causing it to bleed. He'd fainted when he saw the blood. I slapped him hard. He returned to consciousness. "Where am I?" he wondered.

"You asshole," I replied.

"Blood! Blood!" he screamed.

"Shut up," I said. He sat up and clutched at me. Bullets whined past us. I pulled him back down. "Follow me," I told him. I dragged Mikkleson's body to that distant tree. Eicheldinger followed. I should have preferred to gather my wits behind the safety of the tree, but the smell of Eicheldinger's fear drove me away; he had shit his pants. I duck walked around the perimeter, checking the rest of the platoon. The confrontation soon ended, with only two other men wounded.

I washed brains off my greens this evening. Mikkleson is

161

being hosed down by the dorks in Graves, as is Klima, who had drowned when the rice paddy caved in. Lieutenant Sanford has put me on report for disobeying an officer. Eicheldinger is resting comfortably.

We freeze on until the grave increases our cold.

Relentlessly,

Kurt

2ND BATTALION, ECHO CO.
7TH MARINES
18 January 67

Chloe dear,

I am sitting on the sandbags piled in front of my tent. Permeating the atmosphere is the smell of urine, the spore of a tentmate too fat and lazy to walk to the pee-pipe. Soul brothers dance together to jungle music that could make reverberations in ghettos across the sea. Chapped lips and a dry tongue caked with dust give a muddy flavor to food, trembling hands drop a pen I can't feel, and burning eyes closed in hopes of rest and relief wince at bright red flashes.

Discussion groups abound in my immediate neighborhood, but the topics remain the same tired protestations against doom, defeat, and despair. A few loners hide in their tents, writing interminable letters to a home they can't describe. A town is a town, a mother is a mother, and a girl is a girl. The jarheads idealize everything back home into clichés, especially their cars and their high school drinking bouts. Each man's car went faster than the next man's; each man drank more booze than the next. Cherished exaggerations are told and twice told in explicit detail.

The sole creativity here is a blatant cruelty. Baiting weaknesses is a favorite pastime, a search-and-destroy mission against another's self-esteem. To be touched by the death or mutilation of a comrade is to expose oneself to censure for a lack of machismo; style, hereabouts, consists of cool arrogance and a cold anger.

The jarheads have learned to tread warily when hurling insults my way. I just whip out my vicious tongue and the

162

hordes retreat, flayed by appropriate nicknames like "Crater Face," "Leper Breath," and "Blubber Butt." Nicknames are the rage here, but the troops prefer "Batman," "Mr. Cool," and "Cochise." Because I turn twenty-five in March, an ancient to these guys, disgusting attempts have been made to tag me with "Pops." I nipped that in the bud.

"Pops!" Can you believe it? To hell with them. No wise man ever wished to be younger.

Relentlessly,

Kurt

2ND BATTALION, ECHO CO.
7TH MARINES
19 January 67

My dear Paul,

I've put off writing. Why ever should I spread depression across the world? I'm so tense, I'm tempted to reveal myself to the ferret-faced queen in our sister company, just to have someone to dish with. Rumors fly that he blows the entire company regularly (and badly, I'm sure), and I'd enjoy hearing the details. What a dump this place is! What a goddam dump!

NEWS BULLETIN!!!

Sergeant Pinkerton dropped by for a chat. He pulled me over to the showers, away from everyone else. The sarge was obviously embarrassed. I endured a tense silence before he spoke.

"McGrath tells me you and him got it on."

So. Everything wasted. Suck on a punji stick, Kurt. Stick a grenade up your ass. McGrath has gone and blown the whistle, having apparently made up his mind to get away, honorably or not, from the danger I'd thought he thrived on. People have shot off their toes to get out of Nam; McGrath's is a better method and just as effective. Well, at least I wasn't pregnant.

Eicheldinger joined us. "What are you guys talking about?" he wondered.

163

"It's a private discussion between the doc and I," explained Pinkerton.

"Oh, yeah?" said Eicheldinger. He sprawled on the ground and looked at us.

There was a long silence.

"Get your ass out of here, Dinger," advised the sarge.

With a hurt look on his face, the Dinger pulled his loose bones together and got them erect; then he slowly walked away, ready at every step to accept our apologies and rejoin the conversation. The sarge and I watched as he sat down in the midst of several laughing grunts. The laughter ceased. One by one, the grunts left the group, until Eicheldinger sat alone in the dust. He looked at us. Pinkerton and I turned to each other. We looked away, embarrassed.

I decided to embark upon the defense casual. "We sure did, Sarge. I'm here to take care of y'all, am I not? You think you might like to try it? I'd be more than happy to oblige."

Pinkerton frowned; then he grinned. "You shitbird. If you had tits, I might think about it." He stopped grinning. "I know it's tough out here, Doc, and a guy who looks like you is probably used to a lot of pussy. We'd all like some pussy, and what you and McGrath done is just what we used to do back home when we was kids and didn't have no pussy. The Marine Corps, though, don't like it. They want you to be a man, and a man don't do kid stuff. That's what it is, Doc. It's kid stuff. You and McGrath should know better than that. I don't care that you done it. It's just that the Crotch don't like it. If they found out, they'd boot your ass to the brig. They'd think you was queer. I know you're not queer, and I know you're a good doc. I'd hate to lose you because of something dumb." He squeezed my arm and ran his hand through my hair. "I'd hate to lose you for any reason, you shitbird." He grinned and threw his arm across my shoulders as he walked me back to my tent. "You buy yourself some good pussy on R&R, Doc. Ain't nothing like pussy to make a guy forget about kid stuff."

Kid stuff, huh? Suffer the little children to come unto me.

Relentlessly,

Kurt

Dear Mom,

I leave for Da Nang tomorrow to catch my flight. Destination Tokyo. Don't worry. I'll come home without an Oriental wife, no matter how obedient those girls may be.

I bought several books about Japan from the PX. Whether any of the information I've absorbed will be useful remains to be seen, but I have practiced saying "Sayonara."

Two attractions of Tokyo I intend to bypass are the botanical gardens and the zoo. I've seen enough Oriental plant and animal life to discourage further curiosity.

I'm looking forward to the geisha girls and their tea and sympathy.

> *Love,*
>
> *Kurt*

TOKYO, JAPAN
24 January 67

Chloe dear,

Of all foreign cities, I should know my way around Tokyo; after all, I've seen Godzilla, Rodan, Mothra, and their spawn destroy the city time and again. And no wonder. It's a city of papier-mâché.

I spent hours walking in the rain as I tried to find a *ryukyu* (a Japanese inn) recommended in my guidebook. I asked directions from people on sidewalks. The Japanese were too polite to admit that my questions were incomprehensible. They were so polite that they refused to embarrass me with the possibility of my thinking they were embarrassed by misunderstanding me, so they sent me politely upon several wild-goose chases before I finally found my inn under a weeping willow tree, just as the guidebook had promised.

According to local custom, one removes his shoes upon entering a home or a hotel. The innkeeper took one horrified look at my shamefully large feet and begged me to put my shoes back on. The maid who ran my bath brought a friend to watch me splash about in the boiling water. I later realized that they were giggling at the blithe idiot who wasn't morified by his shamefully large penis.

The following morning, the maid served my breakfast on a tray decorated so prettily that to be polite, I ate every bite of a large raw eel.

I fill my days with sight-seeing and my nights with debauchery, but I promised myself back in Nam that I would spend a quiet afternoon alone. I sat in my room and tried to appreciate the solitude; after five minutes, I jumped up and rushed into the crowded streets. I'd realized that Neil and Ricky would never forgive my missing a possible appearance by Godzilla.

Relentlessly,

Kurt

TOKYO, JAPAN
25 January 67

Arch,

I came to Tokyo with the hope that I'd learn a few of the ninety-nine pleasures more than pain and the ninety-nine pains more than pleasure. When I grow old and fat and bald and ugly, I'd like the ladies to say, "Of course, Kurt is old and fat and bald and ugly, but he does know the ninety-nine pleasures more than pain, etc." I desired an erotic massage. I had an urge to feel a gorgeous geisha sticking a knotted silk scarf up my ass that she would jerk out at the moment of ejaculation. Did their pussies really slant? I was an Occidental with an Oriental yen for love.

Need I expound upon shattered dreams? No one peeped from behind elaborate painted fans. No one wanted to play the "Scissors, Rock, and Paper" game I'd read about in a James Bond book. The bathhouses were respectable. I found no bars filled with loose wild women.

Poor Broken Blossom.

166

So I played Pachinko, pinballs without the razzle-dazzle, gumball machines filled with silver balls. Pachinko parlors stand on every corner of downtown Tokyo. What pleasure the Nips find in playing the game lies without my understanding. As soon as I deposited my yen, I realized that Pachinko was boring. Unfortunately, I kept beating the machine. I won no money, just more little silver balls. Japanese crowded around me, evidently amazed at my prowess. I was bored stiff, but little balls continued to pour down the chute. I was trapped in a nightmare. Grinning Japs cheered me on. I smiled grimly and politely and continued to play. Silver balls rolled down the chute. I put them back in the machine. I won more. Finally, I cast politeness to the winds, left the lucky machine with a horde of little men fighting for it, and strolled into the night. It was raining eels. I went to my hotel and ate some.

Relentlessly,

Kurt

TOKYO, JAPAN
26 January 67

Dear Mom,

I'm hooked. Travel is my bag. I'd always thought so, but my first foreign country being Vietnam, the desire to voyage to distant lands diminished. As I have enjoyed myself in Japan despite rain falling throughout my visit, I've once again readjusted my thinking. When I escape Vietnam, I'll take the roads to Morocco, Zanzibar, Bali, et cetera, et cetera, et cetera . . .

I'd determined before arriving in Tokyo that I would mingle with the people, something I had thus far avoided among the Asians I have known. I'd worried about dressing correctly— the only civilian clothes in my travel bag were a pair of jeans, a sweat shirt, and a pair of cowboy boots. One of my guidebooks mentioned that the Japanese dress formally in the city. How ever could I mingle in cowboy boots? Fortunately, at the airport, I discovered a shop that rented suits. I chose a three-piece suit of Prussian blue. Wrong! Every Jap I saw wore a

167

black suit or jeans and cowboy boots. I was hardly likely to lose myself in the crowd, anyway.

I rented a small, chilly room in a pretty inn called "The Weeping Willow." They served me breakfast in bed: a raw eel, a fried egg, and what I supposed was a salad but could easily have been the Nipponese equivalent to parsley.

I ate lunch and supper in whatever restaurants appealed to me. The Japanese put sample plates in little windows in front of their restaurants, so I could point out my choices to the waiter. I ate lots of rice and seafood. I think it was seafood.

For all my research, I toured with little direction. I saw the Imperial Hotel, designed by Frank Lloyd Wright and the only building in Tokyo to survive the Great Earthquake of 1923. Across from the Imperial and in a great walled park was the Emperor's palace; I caught glimpses of it through tall, ancient pines. Mostly, I just walked.

Strong and content I travel the open road.

Love,

Kurt

TOKYO, JAPAN
27 January 67

My dear Paul,

I flew to Tokyo via TWA. Perspiring stewardesses spread joy among surprisingly well-mannered servicemen who either slept most of the way or watched Kirk Douglas grimace at Indians in *The War Wagon*. I preferred to cement a friendship with a dazzling, green-eyed marine in the seat next to me.

Kenny and I checked into a hotel together. Flagrantly misleading the simple grunt, I patted my guidebook and promised him a perfumed garden on the Ginza. I guided him into the most respectable massage parlors *Japan on Five Dollars a Day* could recommend. Stocky middle-aged mamasans walked on our backs as we lay side by side on mats. To drown his disappointment, I treated Kenny to gallons of potent saki. After we returned to our hotel room, I led him into a Greek embrace. As he understated, "It's better than nothing."

The next morning I woke up to find my jarhead gone, as well as fifty million yen (about five dollars) that I'd left in my pants pocket. (My wallet lay safely under my mattress; I like marines, but I'd never trust them.) I checked out of the hotel and into a Y; then I went to the USO, where I made an appointment in reply to an advertisement scrawled on a wall of the john. After strolling along the Ginza for a couple of hours, I returned to the USO and met my blind date, a pleasant soldier from Wisconsin. Naughtiness consumed the afternoon; that evening, we went to see *Gone With The Wind*, a movie that has been showing in Tokyo for years. After hearing Rhett not give a fuck anymore, we searched for a gay bar described in *Tokyo After Dark*. We never found it. Wisconsin decided to take a train to Yokohama, where he planned to cruise the docks for sailors. I returned to the Y to look for some ruthless Samurai or a few hot-eyed Kamikaze pilots. None. I soaked in the communal bath, willing to settle for gymnasts or skiers. None joined me. I wandered through the halls, looking for students or farmers. Nobody. I went to bed. I lay wide awake. I recalled a Nipponese tradition that has intrigued me for years: the insertion of a knotted silk handkerchief up the derriere withdrawn at climax. It seemed such a bother that I did the unthinkable— I masturbated on R&R.

The next morning at breakfast, as I chewed my raw eel, I got to thinking: Here I am in my very first foreign country (Okinawa and Vietnam hardly count), and what had I done? I'd fucked with two Americans and seen *Gone With The Wind* for the umpteenth time. What ever would I tell my grandchildren? I decided to go native.

I moved to a quaint Japanese inn, bathed again, and ate supper in a Korean restaurant where everything was pickled and stank. I followed a trio of giddy rice soup queens to a gay bar. I watched a horde of screeching, long-nailed faggots overwhelm the sound system. I realized that I would be returning to my *ryukyu* alone and wondered how in the hell I would be conjuring an apt fantasy, when I approached by one of those dreary, serious types in eyeglasses who are seldom realistic about the tastes of a stranger. Nevertheless, he spoke English and proved informative when a bespangled fairy sitting next to me jumped up and ran from the pub in tears. The fairy had been dishonored, said Dreary, by the villainous insinuation that he had a large prick.

My jaws tightened, and I left the bar. Dreary hurried after me with an offer of a ride home. I accepted, although I think he was disappointed when I jumped out of the car, bowed, said "thank you" in Japanese, and hurried into my inn. I was so turned off, I went to sleep immediately.

The maid brought up a message with my breakfast. I had a visitor: Dreary Eyeglasses. He invited me to accompany him to the Botanical Gardens. I demurred. I'd planned to attend the Kabuki Theater. Dreary sighed, but insisted upon accompanying me. From 11 A.M. to 7 P. M., we watched play after play, wild clanging pieces with magnificent scenic effects and actors who chewed the scenery down. Surrounding me in the audience, little old ladies in kimonos laughed, cried, and ate box lunches throughout the performances, while Dreary attempted to explain the plot of whatever playlet I was watching. As I had reasonably coherent program notes, I suffered through his scholastic English only from politeness. After all, he got no other pleasure; he said the plays drove him to distraction.

He began to get romantic during supper, but I had no desire to prove his distraction. I took him to a Western-style theater to see the Japanese stage version of *Gone With The Wind*. The first half of the book ran last year; we saw the second half, astounded by such tremendous effects as the burning of Atlanta and the ride of the Klan. I had no need of the little earphones that provided an English translation for foreigners; I know that book by heart.

I'd seen a lot of theater and felt no urge to watch performances by rice soup queens in drag, which disappointed Dreary Eyeglasses. He'd obviously hoped to get me drunk and clutch my Occidental flesh with his tiny fingers. I got him to drive me to the inn. We made a date for the morrow. He said he loved me. I hoped I looked inscrutable.

I gave Dreary five minutes before leaving for the Ginza. After an hour of prowling, I found a lost, lonely, and very drunk soldier on R&R. Two beds were in my room, and I dragged him to the inn to embellish one of them. He never knew what hit him. This morning, as he was leaving, he thanked me for putting him up.

"Man, I was so drunk last night. Wow. I could have been mugged. It sure was nice of you to take me in." He turned at the door with a word of warning. "Hey, man. Watch out for that saki. It sure does give a guy a sore asshole."

170

Soon after, I climbed into Dreary's Datsun, and we set out for Tokyo's environs and a closer view of Fujiyama. Honor decreed that I give myself to Dreary, but happily, his roommate's family was visiting until the next day. And I had an appointment with Uncle Sam at six. I ran into Wisconsin at the airport. As he should have returned to Nam two days before, he was AWOL.

"I'm in trouble, Seafood. No doubt about it. But holy cow, there's a booth in the john here that just won't wait. Glory holes on either side. I've been in there for the past two days. I've sucked off over a hundred guys. Incoming from Nam; outgoing from Japan. And not dragons or trolls either—these were studs. It's incredible."

I disapproved. I knew what kind of scungy pussies those "incoming" studs had been drilling in Nam, and God knows what diseases the "outgoing" studs had picked up here in Tokyo. Besides, some other queen had usurped the throne.

All that excitement only twenty feet away, and I scratch little marks on pieces of paper.

Relentlessly,

Kurt

PART THREE

✪ ✪ ✪

EVIL

While the red-stained mouths of machine guns ring
Across the infinite expanse of day;
While red or green, before their posturing King,
The massed battalions break and melt away;

And while a monstrous frenzy runs a course
That makes of a thousand men a smoking pile—
Poor fools!—dead, in summer, in the grass,
On nature's breast, who meant these men to smile;

There is a God, who smiles upon us through
The gleam of gold, the incense-laden air,
Who drowses in a cloud of murmured prayer,

And only wakes when weeping mothers bow
Themselves in anguish, wrapped in old black shawls—
And their last small coin into his coffer falls.

—ARTHUR RIMBAUD

BELLE OMBRE
DEAD RIVER ROAD
BONIFAY, LOUISIANA
31 January 67

Arch,

The captain called out for a formation of the troops. "All those men with mothers take one step forward. Not so fast, Strom."

I missed the funeral but have been granted twenty-one days of leave in the States. Sure never expected anything like this.

Relentlessly,

Kurt

BELLE OMBRE
DEAD RIVER ROAD
BONIFAY, LOUISIANA
1 February 67

My dear Paul,

I've returned to the States for twenty-one days. My mother died of cancer two days after my stepfather's mother died of diabetes. I've been writing regularly, so I didn't want you to think something might have happened to me.

Relentlessly,

Kurt

Chloe dear,

Ironic, isn't it? After all those years of carting that projector around Bonifay to show the danger signals of breast cancer, Mother was too frightened to see a doctor in time.

The boys say she seldom left her room after she'd returned from the hopsital. She refused to let DT touch her—said she was no longer a real woman. DT would awaken in the middle of the night to find himself alone in bed. Mother would be in my room, or Karen's, crying.

She made everyone promise to keep her operation from me; she thought I'd worry. When she didn't write (her arm hurt too much; they'd taken the right breast), I thought she'd been brooding again about Karen's marriage and my refusal to go back to college. The family begged me to write, but no one ever told me why. So I didn't.

I should have been told, Chloe. I bought a tape recorder at the PX and filled a couple of tapes with ramblings about my feelings and shit like that, stuff she'd have liked. When she never wrote, I erased the tapes. She would have listened to those tapes over and over.

> *Relentlessly,*
>
> *Kurt*

BELLE OMBRE
DEAD RIVER ROAD
BONIFAY, LOUISIANA
3 February 67

My dearest Karen,

It's been awful, Angel. I would never have guessed that it would hurt.

My name came over the loudspeaker at the military airport in Tokyo as I was chatting merrily with a soldier from Wisconsin. A man at the main desk sent me to wait in a small bare room. The Red Cross representative bustled in. He asked me if Mrs. Doyle T. DeBarard was my mother and told me that she'd died several days previously. The Red Cross, which had been attempting to find me since her death, had arranged for twenty-one days of leave.

As I waited in the little room for a departure time, I recalled that Grandma's name is also Mrs. Doyle T. DeBarard. She must have finally kicked the bucket, and Mother was using the similarity of their names to pull a fast one on the military. Although I was annoyed by her meddling, the leave sounded good.

I slept most of the way home. They'd put me aboard an Army casualty flight. The plane carried bunks filled with sick and wounded soldiers; I sat in the tail with a dozen other passengers. The stewardesses were nurses.

I called home from Washington. Mom answered the phone. "What the hell is Mother trying to pull this time?"

"Oh, Kurtie," Mom said, "she was so sick."

The family met me at the airport in New Orleans. All the way home, DT tried to tell me how the past months had been, but he would break down sobbing. Mom said, "I sat in that hospital every day and brushed her hair. Phyllis kept saying, 'Oh, Mama, I'm so glad you're with me. I'm so scared.' She was my little girl again." Ricky would twist down in front of me to watch me cry.

Whatever else I thought about Mother, I respected her efficiency in a crisis. Were I ever hurt, it was reassuring to know I would return to consciousness with her smiling down at me. Selfish, isn't it?

I'm so sorry to have missed you.

With much love,

Kurt

BELLE OMBRE
DEAD RIVER ROAD
BONIFAY, LOUISIANA
7 February 67

Chloe dear,

Ghosts swarm through the swamps. DT sat by Mother's grave again today. He begged for a sign to help him face life without her. A butterfly with unusual markings alighted on the tombstone before fluttering over to DT's shoulder. He felt at peace.

I don't know why. Mother would never reincarnate as a butterfly. She'd come back as a praying mantis. Or an alligator; they eat their young. Butterflies!

DT's wild grief appalls me. He says he resisted flying his plane into a suicidal tailspin because he promised Mother on her deathbed to look after the boys.

To cheer him, I took him to the drive-in, where we saw *A Funny Thing Happened On The Way To The Forum*. Throughout one interminable scene, the cast wept and wailed over a woman's corpse. When we returned home, DT pulled out a packet of photographs he had taken of Mother in her casket. To please him, I looked at them, too.

I've got to get out of this place.

Relentlessly,

Kurt

BELLE OOMBRE
DEAD RIVER ROAD
BONIFAY, LOUISIANA
8 February 67

Arch,

The weeping and wailing at home has yet to cease and desist, so to escape it, I spent an evening at the Outlaw's Tavern.

As Bonifay's answer to Ty Cobb, I'd never paid for a beer there. The regulars would set me up and ask for the straight scoop: Did I have a Baseball Annie waiting for me in whatever city I played? Had I ever met Al Kaline?

When I walked into the bar the other night, the regulars waved me over to their tables, as always, but I bought my own beer. Few people seem to be sure bets for major league stardom; anyone can go to Vietnam. I told them what I'd been doing; then I rhapsodized over intimacies with sloe-eyed, golden-skinned damsels and, God forgive me, with iron-breasted nurses. The denizens laughed, slapped me on my back, and rolled out yarns about their experiences during the Second World War. "That, my boy, was a real war, if you know what I mean."

Tonight I'm sitting home with a book.

Relentlessly,

Kurt

Belle Ombre
Dead River Road
Bonifay, Louisiana
9 February 67

My dear Paul,

Thank you for the note of condolence. Would you believe I received a card from Vietnam signed by everyone in the platoon? They knew about Mother's death before I did.

Were I weary in body and spirit, I suppose there would be no place like home; as it stands, I'm blessed with energy and motivation. My brothers have interests outside Belle Ombre and no longer provide the diversion they used to. My friends from high school have scattered. I've seen the movies offered on the Late Show. Bonifay is too small and my family too prominent for me to go thrillseeking. You would think I'd be bored.

Among the comforts of home, however, is a closed door behind which I climb on my magic bed to return to Vietnam. Paul, some breathtaking splendor trudges through the elephant grass. Glory flowers in the rice paddies. I'm aware of your impatience with "Mindless Machines," but the shape those "Robots" sometimes take would astonish you.

179

As I always do, I've compiled a list of ten favorites; lying on my magic bed, I make it with each of them. In ascending order:

10. Lieutenant Kline: Dozens of men within the battalion are sexier, but Lieutenant Kline of the Weapons Platoon turned me on one evening and I can't forget. I was sitting near the chopper pad writing letters when Kline wandered by with a large tumbler full of bourbon. I daresay he'd enjoyed several already. "Mind if I join you, Strom?" As darkness settled upon us, we sat shoulder to shoulder with our backs against one of the boxes surrounding the landing pad, very relaxed and talking desultorily. Of a sudden, Kline tensed and his voice choked as he asked, "Do you think any of the marines play around with one another? Sexually?"

I'd wondered about that myself. Why ever should Lieutenant Kline? I looked at him. Quiet. Pale. A teddy bear of a guy with a sexy walk—how ever could I have failed to notice his being such a cute lil' old thing. I decided to lie. "I know of at least two."

Short silence. "How do you know?"

"I saw them in the shower."

Kline's breath came in gasps. "What were they doing?"

"Butt-fucking."

"You've never told on them?"

"Shit! That one old boy had such a pretty pooper, I was tempted to join them." I casually lay my hand on Kline's leg. A rock-hard boner slid down his inner thigh. He jumped up and hurtled toward the officers' tents. I worried for a couple of days, but nothing happened, although Kline avoided me ever after.

9. Sergeant Pinkerton: terrifically nice guy—a good ole boy without the meanness. Cheerful, optimistic, Pinkerton wishes everyone well and is butch as all get-out. He's admitted playing around as a teen-ager. He must remember the pleasure.

8. Colonel Grant: I despise the man, but in his arrogance, he is sexy. Cold eyes, a cruel mouth, a small compact body . . . I've heard that he regularly drinks himself into oblivion and one of his orderlies must put him to bed. Were I his orderly, he would be undressed, put to bed, and thoroughly fucked. I'd like to figure out a way to spend the night at Battalion Headquarters. I sneak up to his room . . . You know.

7. Corporal Herndon: dazzling golden guy. Unlike many

of the marines, he displays perfect white teeth—the advantage of an upper middle class upbringing. Herndon has lovely blue eyes, a good complexion, and he reads occasionally; unfortunately, he's a sullen bore.

6. Lieutenant Halderman: Plain face and undistinguished coloring, Halderman owns the best-developed body in the company. He stands ramrod straight; veins of rope stand out in his muscular forearms; his thighs could break coconuts. I've been itching to see if his prick is as huge as his hands but Halderman, a private person, always turns away to take his leaks. Not only does he discourage any intimacy with the troops, he's a loner in camp among the officers, too. I can't help getting turned on by competence.

5. Private First Class Visconti: the type of tall, lean Italian-American who grows on a person and always remains masculine, despite (in my experience) being fabulous in the sack. Wolfish, with a graceful and powerful walk, he's recently transferred to our company from Foxtrot, but because of his notoriety as a bisexual star-fucker, I've been wary of establishing a close rapport. I will, believe me, I will.

4. Corporal McGrath: I've already had him, but he was damn good. I have yet to begin plumbing the depths of his sexuality.

3. Lieutenant Donlevy: a dashing Errol Flynn type. Always smiling, forever ready to laugh. The most popular man in the company. As he's everybody's friend, I'd seldom talked to him until one day when Fats, his regular corpsman, was gone with Sanford's platoon, and with Soul Brother hidden away, I had to accompany Donlevy's patrol. During a rest break, Donlevy asked for some codeine. "Tooth's killing me." I carried no codeine in my kit, so I promised to bring him some when we returned to camp. As we entered the gates of the compound, Donlevy reminded me about the toothache.

"Right on, Lieutenant."

"No hurry, Doc. I want to shit, shower, and shave. Go ahead and take your shower, too."

Half an hour later I tapped at the flap of the tent Donlevy shared with Lieutenant Kline, who was on R&R. No answer. I entered the tent to leave the codeine tablets on the lieutenant's cot. He was already sprawled across it, apparently asleep, naked, with his hand encircling the base of a very pretty erection. I was stunned and very nearly threw caution to the winds. What a dilemma! On the one hand, this was just a week after I'd approached his tentmate and the day after Lieutenant Sanford had sworn to kill any queer in his platoon. On the other hand, the lieutenant did appear to be randy.

So what did the chicken-livered, yellow-bellied Kurt Strom do? He set the codeine on Donlevy's footlocker and tip-toed out of the tent, shattered.

2. Private First Class Chauncey: When Miss Priss and the other corpsmen were chopped to death with machetes, Soul Brother was assigned to Foxtrot until replacements arrived. For three days, he was to be corpsman to 150 men, treating minor wounds, ascertaining that every jarhead carried medical supplies, and holding classes for a couple of grunts in each platoon who would be acting doc on patrols. He left for his new job late one afternoon but came huffing and puffing into our tent that evening.

"I ain't goin' back. Dere be's blood all over dat tent. I ain't stayin' weah dey be haints. Patrols ain't no wuss den dat."

Queenie looked at me. "You'd better go over, Kurt. I'll clear it with the chief."

I had no more desire to spend the night in a haunted tent than Soul Brother did. I ran along the darkening trail to Foxtrot as wide-eyed as the Black Sloth. After reporting to the captain, I went to the corpsman's tent. I shone my little flashlight upon the four cots; pools of dried blood were everywhere. I gathered up the blankets and sleeping bags and threw them outside; then I threw a poncho on the ground, stacked footlockers all around, and lay down, knowing as I closed my eyes that I'd never be able to sleep. Ten seconds later I was unconscious.

The next thing I knew, I was completely awake. And terrified. Something was in the tent with me. My hair stood on end; gooseflesh erupted all over me; my bowels went frigid. I could make out a dark shape. I smelled damp earth. I was petrified.

Another shape entered the tent. "Chauncey?" "Yeah?" I fought cramps and listened intently. I heard slurping sounds. "Turn over." A footlocker squeaked as one of the shapes apparently leaned on it. The sound of cloth against skin. The footlocker shook. Slapping sounds. The smell of shit. A sigh. Something wet hit me in the eye. Pants being pulled up. The shapes left the tent. I was awake for the rest of the night.

The next morning I was busy equipping several grunts with

corpsmen's kits and teaching them how to handle bleeding, breathing, and shock. I finally had a chance at lunch to ask after Chauncey.

"Mean mother fucker."

"Oh yeah? Which one is he?"

"Just left on patrol."

"What does he look like?"

"Big dude. Good-looking."

No girl could have awaited her sweetheart's return from battle more impatiently than I awaited Chauncey. The patrol returned late that night. The men scattered immediately for their tents. I'd not had the foresight to pinpoint Chauncey's. As it was known by then that I slept in the corpsmen's tent, I had no midnight intrusions.

The next morning I was up bright and early. I looked for big, good-looking mother fuckers. "Where's Chauncey?"

"You just missed him. He's gone on patrol."

I learned which tent the elusive Chauncey lived in. The patrol drifted in just before dark. As I loitered by the entrance to the trail, one of the company's lieutenants came over and began hassling me about going out on an early patrol the next morning. I refused, and he dragged me to the company commander, whom I reminded that I had been lent to Foxtrot with the understanding that I never leave the compound. The captain glared, but set me free. I ran to Chauncey's tent. His tentmate said Chauncey had gone to the showers. I hurried to my tent, stripped, threw a towel over my shoulder, grabbed a bar of soap, and hustled to the showers as fast as my flip-flops would let me. A couple of scrawny spades stood jiving under the cold water. I took a quick shower, my fourth of the day (I'd been curious about a couple of other beauties), and ran to Chauncey's tent. His buddy was writing a letter by flashlight.

"Where's Chauncey?"

"He's not here."

"Where is he?"

"Taking a walk."

"Where?"

"How the hell would I know? I ain't standing the Chauncey watch."

Fuck you, too, ace. I want prowling around the compound in the dark, but I never found Chauncey. The next morning he had gone on patrol again. The replacements arrived from First

Med. I briefed them on procedure and returned to Echo. I visited Foxtrot a couple of times afterward, but never did meet Chauncey. And I never learned who the other man was. It wasn't the company faggot, whom I delicately sounded out. Chauncey, if he survives, will be mine when I return to Nam.

1. The lieutenant from Foxtrot who hassled me, a cold-eyed blond with thick hairy wrists and the face of King Harold the Fair, a Viking King described by a medieval monk as "... the wildest, most beautifullest man who ever lived." My easy duty aggravated the lieutenant. When I declined an invitation to join his patrol, he threatened to put me on report. I told him that it was his privilege. He made loud noises about cocksucking, pansyassed pecker-checkers interested in nothing but holding shortarm inspections. I would have been a hypocrite to have taken offense.

My fantasy: I meet the lieutenant's price: e.g., money, a girl, captain's bars ... He agrees to do everything I demand of him. We make it in a room with mirrored walls. Behind each of the two-way mirrors sits a fellow officer: Kline, Halderman, Donlevy, and Colonel Grant. They watch us, and we do everything. After I'm sated, the four officers stand in a circle. The lieutenant blows each of them; then he sits at their feet and jerks off as they piss on him. End of fantasy.

Do you think I'm kinky?

Relentlessly,

Kurt

BELLE OMBRE
DEAD RIVER ROAD
BONIFAY, LOUISIANA
10 February 67

My dearest Karen,

I should prefer to leave the old plantation, but were I to do so, the guilts would begin in earnest. To get away from a house where I catch myself expecting Mother to walk into whatever room I'm in and where the Dobermans whine all day and howl all night, I've begun to visit Grandpa DeBarard. He's moved into that old cabin overlooking the bayou. I've never liked him, but he seems softened by Grandma's death. We sit on the bank, fishing in the rain. Occasionally, we talk. The conversation always turns back to Grandma, and he starts crying. I've gone to Dubois with him a couple of times to look at her grave.

DT makes me accompany him on his daily visits to Mother's grave. He sobs continually, dramatizing this, the great tragedy of his life, for all it's worth. Don't lecture. I'm aware that Mother was everything to him, and I'm certain his grief is real. It's just that he is such a little man.

Unwilling to be left out of the grief business, Mom has dragged me to the cemetery in town to talk about Dad over his tombstone. You are well out of this; it's enough to make a person morbid.

Mom comes over every day and follows me around the house, dishcloth in hand, wondering why I haven't found a nice girl with whom to share conjugal bliss. She sits me down over coffee and relives Mother's life, Dad's, mine, yours, and her own. She's always enjoyed rehashing the past, and at the moment, I'm willing to listen. It's an opportunity she has no intention of missing.

Neil says that DT was helpless during Mother's last weeks. When he wasn't running from room to room at the hospital, visiting Mother and Grandma, he'd lock himself in the ice-house, where he'd alternate between begging God to spare Mother and threatening Him for daring to cause her pain. The old black weed pullers were horrified, their kinky hair standing on end; several quit. Those remaining roll their eyes as they exposulate upon the enormity of DT's despair. Their great bulks heave with an empathy I am unable to share.

Neil has a girl friend. His first. I've relieved him of the responsibility of picking up Ricky after basketball practice. Ricky follows me everywhere and hero-worships me so unashamedly, he can barely talk.

I've just made up my mind. I'll arrive in Cincinnati by the end of the week. Expect me when you see me.

With much love,

Kurt

185

Dear Mom,

Karen's doing just fine, the babies seem healthy and happy, and you have no reason to worry.

Karen and I sit up every night, chatting until the wee small hours. We shouldn't. She's dead on her feet at work the next day, and the boys wake me around seven. Little Kurtie has begun the "Terrible Two's" and is into everything. Little Reggie has just completed the "Terrible Two's" but has yet to forget them. While I'm cleaning up one mess, they're making another. I volunteered. I deserve it.

Every once in a while, I can get them to sit down to go through their fairy tales. I overact outrageously during these recitations; the boys sit wide-eyed with their thumbs in their mouths. I taught them a game during which I can sit down, a game called "See":

> *See my finger?*
> *See my thumb?*
> *See my fist?*
> *You better run.*

Kurtie and Reggie love "See." They run down the hall to their room, shrieking. I have thirty seconds of peace and quiet before they creep into the living room, giggling and demanding more "See."

I took them to the zoo Sunday to give Karen a day to herself. We looked at every animal. I could understand why you love little kids so much when, without looking away from the animals, Kurtie and Reggie reached up to put their hands in mine.

Big Reggie called after we'd returned home. "Daddy! Daddy!" cried the boys.

"I can't stand it," muttered Karen.

After he'd hung up the phone, Little Reggie happily informed me that "I'm Daddy's Kid."

"Gurgle gurgle," added Little Kurt.

"I just can't stand it," said Karen.

I took the boys downtown this morning and bought them a farm set, a jungle set, and a dinosaur set. When Karen arrived home to find three hundred tiny animals occupying her living room floor, she gave me a very dirty look, but at the moment, the kids are happily immersed in their menagerie.

I've got to stop writing now to imagine the sound a brontosaurus would utter.

GHRRUNGH,

Kurt

1412 STEINFELDT STREET
CINCINNATI, OHIO
17 February 67

Chloe dear,

You've never met Karen's asshole of a husband, have you? He'd be a lawyer if he'd finished law school, he'd be in business if he had any ambition, and he could now be a salesman, if he'd work; instead, he prefers to be a student of life. Reggie's good-looking in a lean, blond manner perilously close to pale-eyed, pale-haired, hill-country white trash. Although Reggie's always been pleasant to me, he walks about with a perpetual sneer that I've mistrusted. To be fair, I must admit to his abilities as a mechanic and a handyman, his rapport with the boys, and his knowledge of biography and history. We've never lacked for something to talk about.

So perhaps I should have expected Reggie to drop by during my visit with Karen. He walked in the house as if he were still living there. "Kurt, old man. Good to see you. Feel like going out for a few beers?"

I was reluctant. He had interrupted Karen and me in the middle of a gleeful dissection of old schoolmates; besides, I felt vaguely that I should be loyal to Karen.

"Come on, Kurt. I told my old lady's roommate about you. All you'd need to get her into the sack is ginger ale and a card trick."

"Tempting, Reg, but I'm going to see too little of Karen as it is."

"You mean a marine on leave is going to sit home on a

187

Saturday night with his sister when there's all that snatch out there?"

"I guess so."

"Jesus, Kurt, what have they done to you? Karen, get me a beer." Reggie settled in his chair and looked at me. "So how do you like being one of Uncle Sam's killers?"

"Well, I've never thought of myself—"

"How can you possibly condone U.S. participation in Vietnam?"

"I don't exactly—"

"Surely you're not sucked in by that game of 'Dominoes'?"

"Actually, I—"

"You are defoliating millions of acres of land."

"The jungles could use—"

"You're dropping napalm bombs on innocent children."

"I've only—"

"People are starving!"

"I suppose—"

"Would you want your mother and sister whoring?"

"No, I—"

"What's going to happen to all those babies with American fathers?"

"You've got me there."

"Can you sleep at night, knowing you are emasculating the entire male population of Vietnam?"

"It's not easy."

"Every time I talk to a Vietnam vet, he tells me how awful it was for him. Do you ever stop to think how bad it is for the Vietnamese?"

"No."

"Of course, you don't. It makes me sick. GREAT BIG Americans with their GREAT BIG guns oppressing the poor little Vietnamese who want nothing more than to be left alone. I'll tell you one thing, killer; before they send me over there to make money for the industrialists and to put medals on the generals, I'd emigrate to Canada."

Karen looked up from her sewing. "You couldn't leave soon enough to suit me, Reg. Don't let the door slam you on the ass on your way out."

Reggie left in a huff, but more congenial folk wandered by a little later. They seemed to want to hear about Vietnam, so I told them a couple of stories about leeches and of injuries

I've treated. I got no applause, so we talked about baseball and babies for the rest of the evening.

Relentlessly,

Kurt

1412 Steinfeldt Street
Cincinnati, Ohio
17 February 67

Arch,

I'm at my sister's. We've been retelling old tales. You come off well in many of them.

I flew to Cincinnati by way of Lakeland, Florida, and New York City. Spring training is in full swing at Tiger Town. I'd forgotten how important baseball had seemed. Nostalgia hit with a fury. Puzio talked the trainer into letting me dress out, so I spent the day hitting fungoes and taking infield practice. They timed my wind sprints; I'm still the fastest white man in the Detroit organization.

Puzio considers me a fool. "You had it made, Strom. Everybody knew it."

I didn't. And Puzio doesn't remember a manager who crawled up my ass for every mistake, who put me down at every opportunity, who accepted a good fielding play or an opportune hit as good luck that was bound to turn. I remember very well.

In New York I decided to drop by the coffee shop where an old friend works as a counterman. I freaked him out.

"Kurtie baby, you took ten years off my life. I knew you were in Vietnam. When you walked in the door, I figured you'd been killed and your ghost had come to say good-bye."

I refuse to consider that as an omen.

Relentlessly,

Kurt

My dear Paul,

The old itch set in, I had a week before reporting in at Travis AFB in San Francisco, and I planned to fuck myself silly from coast to coast.

My better self said, "Don't do it, Kurt. You needn't knock out your front teeth in grief or gouge out an eye, but you should maintain some decorum. Think of your duty as a son."

My worse selves said, "Kurt, you have lost fifteen pounds in Vietnam and are now 185 pounds of solid muscle. You are lean, hard, and bronzed. Spread it around."

I brooded about it for a day, before I finally said to myself, "Kurt, old boy, you deserve it."

One week to spend however I wished. And plenty of money. I thought about running up to New Orleans and the French Quarter, running down to Florida where the Tigers have gathered for spring training, flying to New York to really do it up big, or visiting my sister in Cincinnati. I did all of the above.

In New Orleans I'd determined to go to bed with the best; several bars and thousands of queens later, I went to my hotel alone. In Lakeland I drank my buddies under the table, but I took no advantage of their prone position, despite a long-standing lust for two—I was too busy drowning my regret for having thrown away three years of my career in baseball. I passed my time in New York drinking wine as my "Uncle" Ralph told me that I hadn't wasted my life. "Baby, there are pretty boys playing baseball and pretty boys playing war; this way, you have access to that many more pretty boys."

It's one way of looking at it.

Relentlessly,

Kurt

Dear Mom,

I returned to Nam reluctantly, but a man lives up to his obligations. And did I really have a choice?

Reggie, of all people, wrangled a first-class seat for me at half-fare on an American Airlines flight from Cincinnati to San Francisco. His accomplice, a long-legged stewardess, plied me with liquor and good food. Too much liquor. While waiting for a bus for Travis Air Force Base, I nodded off and someone stole the marine cap off my head.

Don't be alarmed at any news of my being wounded. I just received a mild concussion suffered in an auto accident, something which could have happened in the States. I could write no letters were I badly hurt.

My first purple heart, and no VC within miles.

Love,

Kurt

First Medical Battalion
Chu Lai, Vietnam
23 February 67

My dear Paul,

I'd planned to stop by Denver to spend a day or two with you, but as they say, the road to Hell is paved with good intentions.

I did pass a dreary evening in San Francisco with a couple of homely queens recommended by an acquaintance whose name I've already stricken from my address book. The dismal creatures expressed an unreciprocated interest in consummating our friendship; I hinted at an exposure to hideous Oriental social diseases. I shouldn't doubt the sheets I slept on having been thoroughly washed in Clorox.

I spent two days in Okinawa, waiting for a flight to Nam. They put me to work in the inoculation shed. Naked marines passed by in a long line kept tight by continuous cries of "Nuts to butts." When I wasn't watching strong men faint at the sight of the needles in my hand, I was prowling the barracks. Marines were everywhere: in bunks, heads, showers, corridors ... everywhere. And they had nothing to do but sit and wait. I discovered a dozen or so hiding away in odd corners, passing their time by beating their meat. Two were well worth joining, and one stalwart beauty seemed delighted by my company. I never learned whether he was coming or going.

I'm at such an impasse myself. The 7th Battalion had moved north while I was in the States. Intensive interrogation of satchel-assed office personnel divulged their location, I hitched a ride on a jeep, the jeep hit a mine, and I'm back at First Med with a broken collarbone.

Relentlessly,

Kurt

Arch,

I know it's trite to despise officers, but they seem to go out of their way to provoke a person.

After disembarking from an air-conditioned jet liner into the wet heat of Da Nang's airfield, I thumbed a ride on a truck into the jungle. I hopped off it along a lonely stretch of road outside a small Vietnamese village. Nearly an hour passed before a jeep bounced by, carrying three men. It stopped several yards down the road. I ran up to find the driver arguing with a captain who sat in the back seat. I recognized the driver: I'd dug several pieces of shrapnel out of his leg that he'd gotten when a buddy stepped on a mine and lost a foot. The captain obviously resented my presence, but was bright enough to know that should he ignore a corpsman in distress, the corpsmen of the 7th Regiment might very well ignore a captain in distress.

The captain was making a tour of the countryside: ostensibly to inspect facilities; actually, according to his driver, to shoot the shit with cronies. His last stop lasted until late evening, and against everyone's better judgment, the captain insisted upon returning to 7th Regiment after dark. (As soon as the sun goes down, the VC plant booby traps along Vietnam's roadways.) A marine joined us as a guard, and I had to squeeze into the small space between the backseat and the spare tire. The jeep hit a mine, killing the driver instantly. The adjutant lost one leg and the guard both legs. I got a couple of badly bruised hips, three broken ribs, a broken collarbone, a concussion, and a deep cut along the side of my head. The captain suffered a separated shoulder.

So I'm back on SICU at First Med. The adjutant "Rests Comfortably" in the bed next to mine. My doctor remembered me and agreed with Alf that my injuries necessitate my remaining for a few days in the recovery room.

When Alf informed the captain that he was to be transferred to one of the wards, the man waxed wroth. He preferred to remain on ICU because it's air-conditioned. His surgeon helped Alf carry the captain to the ward and Alf reports that they took great pleasure in bumping the stretcher with its ranting burden into every obstacle they passed.

Relentlessly,

Kurt

FIRST MEDICAL BATTALION
CHU LAI, VIETNAM
24 February 67

Chloe dear,

I refuse to go back to the jungle. No way. Perhaps I'm a coward, or maybe I've finally come to my senses.

I was a passenger in a jeep which hit a mine. I remember a thunderous explosion; then I was crawling toward someone moaning. My breath had been knocked out of me. My arm hurt. My chest hurt. I couldn't see anything. I cut my leg crawling over sharp metal. I reached the moaning. Face okay. Head. Neck. Chest. Belly. All okay. Arms. Lift him up. Back okay. Leg okay. Leg! Wet with blood, shattered bones sticking out of ripped flesh. I tore off my belt to make a tourniquet and my shirt to cover him. I crawled on. What was I scared of? What happened? A mine. I'm scared of crawling on another mine. A man lying very still—no pulse, no rise and fall of the chest. I couldn't see in the dark, so I stopped, listening for breathing. I heard breathing, close to me. A knife in my throat.

"Who?"

"Me! Doc! Doc! Kurt! Me!"

A hand in my hair. "Anyone else?"

"One dead. One leg—bad. Looking for the others."

We finally found the fifth man. One leg off, one mangled all to shit. I took off my pants. "Knife," I whispered.

"Never!"

"You asshole! I've got to make tourniquets out of my pants."

We dragged the wounded off the road. "Strip!" I said.

"Wha . . . ?"

"They're in shock. We got to keep them warm. Somehow."

We covered them with the light greens. Not much good.

"You lay up against that man; I'll try to keep this guy warm. You okay, by the way?"

"Yeah."

I felt my man's pulse grow weaker and weaker. It took him all night to die. All night we listened for VC. It hurt to breathe.

They finally found us, just before dawn. Americans.

I'm not going back, Chloe.

Relentlessly,

Kurt

FIRST MEDICAL BATTALION
CHU LAI, VIETNAM
28 February 67

Dear Mom,

I have a comfortable home, practically to myself, next door to the hut in which I lived when I first arrived in Nam; almost everyone who was here then is gone now. Last fall the monsoon poured down; this spring, the sun shines steadily. Nine men were crowded together; the two men with whom I now share the hut work in-country with one of the Battalion-Aid stations and seldom visit us here.

They transferred me back to Med Battalion and I'll begin work on the Surgical Intensive Care Unit tonight. That's where

I've been staying, except for two days on a ward, when I was told to report to my ward corpsman four times a day and to abide by the rules governing patients. The ward corpsman, one month in Nam, tried to tell me that I must never leave the ward between 9 P.M. and 9 A.M. and that I must ask his permission to go down to the beach. My friend Alf let me rant; then he arranged my transfer back to his ward, SICU, and found living quarters in the hut.

DT hardly deserves all the blame for the trouble between him and Ricky. I'm aware that you think of Ricky as practically perfect in every way. He's willful, spoiled, and can be inconsiderate. I love him, don't get me wrong. Just remember that DT gave Mother many things she'd always wanted, and he helped raise four stepchildren. He still writes long letters of dogged grief, enumerating the recurring appearances of Mother's ghost. He takes little pleasure in life. Ricky could make good use of this time to practice consideration.

You are unlikely to dishonor the memory of Dad by marrying again. I'm sure he'd have wanted you to be happy. I dislike your writing, "I'll never love another man after Dad." What's wrong with loving someone else? You have plenty of affection left under those bosoms. Those who would say anything nasty are envious. You could hardly consider them friends.

I think that Mr. Hebner is attractive, a gentleman, and carries himself with dignity. I look forward to talking with him again and I wish you both lots of happiness.

And never put yourself down; you're still a sexy baby.

Love,

Kurt

First Medical Battalion
Chu Lai, Vietnam
1 March 67

Chloe dear,

A VC nurse had part of her foot shot off. She developed gangrene, and the surgeon had to amputate everything below the ankle. After her operation, she was brought to the recovery room, only half-conscious because of the anaesthesia. The nurse was attractive enough to inspire lechery; we passed a motion to take a gander at her pretty. As her black pajama bottoms were being removed, she protested feebly, but this is war and war is hell. A shapely bush was exposed. We were surprised; most Vietnamese women pluck out the few hairs Buddha grants them. We probed deeper, only to find her vagina caked with shit.

Working on ICU that night with Alf was a strapping hillbilly from West Virginia, a corpsman who had cracked up on the lines.

He cracked me up here.

After Alf took the midnight vital signs, he turned off the overhead lights and sat down at the desk to read. Hillbilly made a great show of checking bandages and IV bottles. I knew something was in the air, so I feigned sleep. Hillbilly filled a basin with soapy water, douched the nurse's pussy, and proceeded to perform an act of cunnilingus upon her as he whacked off.

The following day I came back from the beach to find the enlisted men's quarters in an uproar. Hillbilly had gone berserk and torn up several huts: slashing cots and blankets, overturning footlockers . . . He now raves in the nut ward.

Hillbilly's frenzy inspired Alf to hide my chart and make an agreement with the head corpsman of the recovery room to announce my being a worker of SICU until my injuries heal, which Alf has prognosticated will be the day before my year in Nam is over.

"Just keep a low profile, Kurt, and we'll get away with it."
And who am I to quarrel with good fortune?

Relentlessly,

Kurt

196

Arch,

I thumbed a ride on a casualty flight to the hospital ship *Sanctuary*, on which my buddy Babich serves as a corpsman. I hadn't seen him for several months, so we rehashed old times over a few beers. Same old Babich.

He had been wounded last October and carried to the *Sanctuary*. After a minor operation, he was given two weeks to recuperate. Nurses what they are, Babich wasn't allowed to enjoy his convalescence; they set him to work. His initial annoyance soon gave way to a feeling of gratitude. As he limped about the ward, Babich noticed a patient with an infected wound; he dipped cotton swabs into the wound and rubbed the swabs into his own injury. Result: another month aboard ship to recuperate.

When his transfer to the lines again seemed imminent, Babich infected himself once more. Result: the doctors were astounded. It took two more reinfections before the doctors realized that they might have a case which could make medical history, so Babich was assigned as a corpsman aboard the *Sanctuary*, where they could study him.

He could hardly write about this; all I received were letters from the ports where the *Sanctuary* berthed, such as this one from Subic Bay in the Philippines:

> Dear Kurt,
>   Great port. As soon as the liberty bell rang, I ran to the red-light district and fucked a great-looking whore. Then I thought of my buddies in the jungle, so I fucked her again for Stokes and once more for you. Did your dick itch? Great port. Etc. Etc.
>
> Jim

He meant well. Anyway, as soon as we were pleasantly high on the beer, Babich took me to his cabin so he could watch me drool over his vast collection of Oriental pornography. It included Polaroid snapshots of every prostitute with whom he has enacted the doublebacked beast. Babich allowed me to read a collection of letters that Stokes had written. Stokes was wounded for the third time a few weeks ago; the three purple hearts got him Stateside.

"I worry about you guys," Babich said.

"Put that in the past tense, buddy. We're safe now and out of it."

Babich just looked at me.

I doubt that I'll visit him again.

Relentlessly,

Kurt

FIRST MEDICAL BATTALION
CHU LAI, VIETNAM
3 March 67

My dear Paul,

My daily constitutional leads me past Triage, where naked young men lie passively on stretchers. Prurient thoughts are stifled by blood, stench, and moans of pain.

> *The many men, so beautiful!*
> *And they all dead did lie;*
> *And a thousand thousand slimy things*
> *Lived on; and so did I.*

It's like old times. I'm back on SICU amongst the machinery. I'm working informally from midnight to noon with the ward supervisor, Alf, a capable operating-room technician slumming unwillingly on ICU. Kraft and Hilgendorf, also OR techs, constitute the day crew. Kraft is a jolly, lumbering fellow who has shown me photos of his nude wife. Hilgendorf is a skinny, ladylike gentleman who loves taking nursing notes and is breathlessly awaiting R&R in Hawaii, when he will marry his well-stacked sweetheart. I wonder viciously who will do what and to whom.

No ghosts remain. Even the odor of old Stinky Lô Blô has dissipated. Alf tells me that ICU gets few zips nowadays; Americans fill all the beds. My thoughts about that are paradoxical: I hate to see those boys lying wounded and in pain, but they sure do brighten up the room.

198

Unlike my previous tour on ICU, when I carefully avoided naughtiness, I have been grabbing every opportunity that has presented itself. The patients come onto the ward directly from the operating room, nude, half-conscious, their pricks engorged by the anaesthesia into a semierect succulence that delights the eye. My eye, anyway. I make a halfhearted attempt to keep a level head, but sooner or later, these lucious temptations will get me into trouble.

The other morning, with the ward crowded with doctors perusing charts, I grabbed a bottle of lotion and began to massage a virile beast with a shattered knee, a procedure carefully described in my navy blue corpsman's manual. Shoulders. Arms. Chest. Legs. Thighs. My hand drifted. As the marine lay grinning, the message evolved into a highly unprofessional climax.

Last night we admitted a yummy blond with a broken leg and covered waist to toes with a spica cast that left only his groin exposed. I began combing the plaster flakes from his pubic hair. He erected.

Time for lights out.

I took temps, felt pulses, and harkened to respirations. I injected morphine where needed and checked the IV drip rates. I adjusted oxygen rates, dabbed petroleum jelly at the point where catheters enter urethras, shone a flashlight into the eyes of concussed grunts, and examined bandages for seeping blood. I peered through a little window in the door between ICU and the operating rooms, making sure the OR was inactive. I ascertained that Alf remained immersed in his book under the night lamp. I was ready.

I returned to Yummy so I could finish brushing away the orthopedist's debris, as instructed in the manual. When he erected again, I indulged in some erotic lingual procedures. He softly moaned, "No . . . no . . ." although he didn't try to push me away with his muscular and undamaged arms. I stopped anyway; I had forgotten to rinse off the Phisohex soap I had used to wash him.

Havoc and spoil and ruin are my gain.

Relentlessly,

Kurt

Chloe dear,

We've had a string of odd injuries. A grunt lighted a cigarette while pouring kerosene in a shit barrel, and the resulting explosion fried him. A pair of the more stupid gooks on record planted a minefield (for our side) and, too lazy to walk around it, tried to take a shortcut home; they lost all their legs. A grunt jumping off a truck caught his wedding ring on the tailgate and tore his finger off.

This morning a soldier was enjoying some target practice on a firing range. A helicopter flying overhead accidentally discharged a rocket that wedged in the soldier's leg. The round failed to explode. No one understands yet why it didn't. An ambulance transported the soldier over several miles of bumpy road; the driver, the shotgun, and the medic courted death the entire trip. Preparing the soldier for surgery endangered another medic. In the cramped operating room two doctors, the anaesthesiologist, and two OR techs risked getting mangled as they removed the soldier's leg. Upon dismantling, the round was found to have been capable of blowing everyone to Kingdom Come. Such courage stuns me.

And how does the soldier feel about it? He lies on a bed in ICU, smiling and smiling. "Doc, I'm so goddamn happy to be alive."

The whole episode was a nine days' wonder on base, and nearly everyone came to see the soldier. Curiosity even brought the Protestant chaplain to the recovery room. I hadn't seen him since my first week in Nam. To Alf's knowledge, the chaplain has never before visited SICU, but then, we don't haunt his particular temple. Alf and I have deduced that his consolation is directed toward predestined officers.

I'm hardly anti-religion. No one could admire the Roman Catholic chaplain more than I. Father Kerry meets every dust-off on the landing pad and has been known to hitch rides to the battlefield. He's usually to be found on Triage, X ray, or ICU. Father Kerry's is a beautiful religion, filled with compassion and pity. He's always consoling the maimed and the dying, whatever their faith. I like him, although I'm of no faith myself. Kneeling bags my trousers.

Relentlessly,

Kurt

First Medical Battalion
Chu Lai, Vietnam
8 March 67

My dear Paul,

I've just come back from the beach. I spend my morning in the surf, before the sun becomes maddeningly hot. Bronzed marines cluster naked on the sand; I lurk among the rocks hoping to snatch up strays. I believe there's classical precedent for that.

Paul, I'm certain you mean well with your warning. And I appreciate it. But you're being hypocritical when you accuse me of "...living for sex to the detriment of better things." Wasn't it you sitting next to me in Sporter's throughout all those charming though wasted evenings, oblivious to my repartee as you stared holes through some blushing Fragonard with a face of porcelain. I can recall paintings left incomplete, brushes and oils drying out despite your many tears as you writhed melodramatically over another sad ending. And can you accuse me of bad form, when you showed no compunction over seducing your more attractive students? Hmmm? One can advise comfortably from a safe distance.

I'm surrounded by steel-eyed, swashbuckling, ruthless, sexy, and stupid men. I shall bait my hooks well: These fish will bite.

I'm beginning to sniff out my competition on the compound. Alf had told me about a couple of corpsmen who lurk in the shitters and take lengthy showers, but moles and ducks have seldom appealed to me. Another corpsman has been known to stage elaborate if unsuccessful seductions of the marines of Motor Pool with such props as vodka and Mickey Mouse orange

201

juice, a plot based upon pornographic snapshots from Japan, and a shattering climax: "I'm sorry, but I love you."

Our Catholic chaplain, Father Kerry, visits ICU every day. He sits next to the beds of the more attractive patients and murmurs soothingly, wiping their brows with his right hand as he rubs their lower abdomens with his left. His perversity dismays me; we share the same taste, and as he cruises the ward during the day, he can usually get to my favorites before I can.

I suspect several others among the corpsmen, one of them even attractive, but I prefer men from the lines. And I'll never have to ask Dear Abby where to find them.

I worked with Kraft last night—he of the great stocky body and the tiny sore feet. Alf had stood duty for Kraft the day before, when the colossus complained yet again of the miseries. Kraft vaguely promised to make up his absence on some future date, but Alf had put in twenty-four consecutive hours of duty. He said, "Never put off until tomorrow what you can do today," or words to that effect. Kraft whined, Alf proved adamant, and I got to spend the night with the behemoth.

Hilgendorf usually works with Kraft and has, I believe, an incomprehensible crush on the dinosaur. Hilgendorf pampers Kraft more than he does the patients and apparently believes patient care to be less important than continually reviewing nursing notes. Alf and I have made it a habit to drop by the ward after supper to make an unobtrusive check of the machines and IV bottles.

Last night the ward was full, relieving me of any obligation to hold a literary discussion with Kraft. The mammoth, you see, is a reader. As the pain felt by the patients could hardly compare to the anguish his delicate feet cause Kraft, he rests them on the desk throughout his work shift as he reads novels by the ladies who write short stories for *Good Housekeeping* and *Family Circle* magazines. He sneers at my interest in the classics; they hold only snob appeal. The novels *he* reads have much more to do with life as he lives it. No doubt.

Alf took me around the ward to explain the patients, and I was dreaming up projects for Kraft when I found myself face to face with a gorgeous marine lieutenant with a broken arm. I endured a parting longer than the last act of an Italian opera, before Hilgendorf finally tore himself away from Kraft and allowed Alf and Bernie to escort him home. I cajoled the giant sloth into napping, an effort that took about three seconds. I battened down the hatches. I set to.

First of all I plugged the lieutenant full of morphine. Then I staged an MGM production of Florence Nightingale: patting his bandages, smoothing the tape, and adjusting his sling. I chatted of events and exploits at 7th Infantry, while waiting for drowsiness to overwhelm him. The lieutenant's deep Georgia drawl slowed until he finally fell asleep. At intervals, I timed his pulse, always resting my hand upon that little bulge under the sheet, but to my annoynace, he woke up every time I did it. About the twenty-sixth time I held that patrician wrist between my fingers, I felt a flutter under my other hand. Lifting the sheet as I had every right to do, I uncovered a wee, timid, cowering erection. I did what had to be done.

You'd think one of these little dramas that intrude upon my duties would be enough to satiate me. Not a chance. At the other end of the ward lay a nice-looking boy who'd been shot through the shin. Fatty tissue in his bloodstream had formed an embolism which was moving steadily and inexorably through his veins to his heart; if the embolism remained intact, he would die.

The boy's temperature was 106.4°. I hesitated. He lay in a bed across the aisle from Kraft's. I checked the leviathan's respiration: loud, rasping, and regular. All clear.

I tore off my clothes and crawled into the blazing boy's bed. In his delirium, the boy alternated between an impassioned acceptance as he caressed me and a sudden clarity, when he would hiss, "I'll get you for this, faggot." Like his consciousness, his erection ebbed and flowed. Father Kerry had been performing ablutions when I arrived on the ward and had apparently relieved the boy's less critical congestion.

When I returned from the beach this afternoon, I stopped by ICU for a glimpse of last night's prey. The lieutenant sat in his bed: haggard, red-eyed, and stunning. The boy with the embolism had died. I took a shower; then I went to see our gay doctor, whom I'd hitherto avoided. Dr. Schiller is much loathed by the better-looking patients for his clap inspections. "Skin it back. Now milk it. Milk it some more . . ." I laid the whole sordid story before him.

"Did I kill the kid?"

Dr. Schiller looked out the door, he looked over at his bookcase, and he looked down at his desk. He played with his pencil. Finally he sighed and looked up at me. He said that nothing I had done could have made any difference. Then he got up to close the door and inspected me for clap.

Relentlessly,

Kurt

First Medical Battalion
Chu Lai, Vietnam
9 March 67

Arch,

I like my friends for what they are; I could never dislike them for what they're not. And I would never question a man's courage should he try to escape his military duty; on the contrary, I would question his intelligence should a man enlist.

Nevertheless, I could never wholeheartedly respect anyone who shirks his responsibility to his countrymen. Emotion, not reason, rules; perhaps Mother's disdain for 4F's during World War II dictates such an attitude. Only a percentage of active military personnel serve in Vietnam; only a small percentage are assigned to the lines. Your personal safety should not be considered in whatever decision you make.

Even if I were a dove, I could give little advice on how you could avoid the draft. A bad back? Feigning homosexuality? Schizophrenia? What about that old neck injury you got playing football? Forget about Canada or Sweden—you lose too much, Arch.

My subscription to the *Sporting News* got lost in all the moving I've done, but I've been catching up on baseball through the *Stars and Stripes*. The Tigers could take the pennant. If they lack anything, it's a fireballing pitcher and a hard-hitting third baseman.

Karen will appreciate your asking after her, but she would enjoy a letter more. Why don't you write her? You were involved in too many adventures with me for Karen not to feel she knows you. And I still remember the electricity which flowed when you met.

You're my buddy, Arch, whatever you do.

Relentlessly,

Kurt

Dear Mom,

Karen has filed for a divorce.

Reggie began to come by the house with his girl friends while Karen was at work, occasionally using it as a motel. When Karen learned of it, she told Reggie that a divorce seemed imminent. Reggie agreed, with the condition that he got the house and Little Kurtie; Karen could have Little Reggie and the car.

"Kurt, I thought I'd stopped loving Reggie when I found out about his girl friends. I knew I'd stopped loving him when he wanted to split up the boys."

As Reggie still lives off his family's largess, he has no money, so Karen will ask only for child support.

Perhaps you might visit her for a few days. Your quarrel's silly when set against something so serious. You have a way of making a body think he's right; Karen is filled with doubts, and I believe she's absolutely right. And you've wanted to see the babies. I think you're needed and you'd certainly be welcome.

You wouldn't believe how cute those little boys are, Mom.

Love,

Kurt

Chloe dear,

A Marine Corps ever on the alert for complacency suddenly announced that all Med Battalion personnel were to load their belongings into trucks headed for Da Nang, sixty miles to the north. According to rumor, an amphibious invasion of Haiphong, the seaport of Hanoi, was imminent. A skeleton crew of eight men were left behind to set up a temporary casualty reception area. We waved good-bye to the convoy while transferring patients to airplanes bound for Cam Ranh Bay. (In my limbo, I thought it in my best interest to stay near Alf and Bernie.) Around noon we boarded a truck bound for Fever Hospital, our temporary quarters.

Fever Hospital is a lazy little compound on a beach south of Chu Lai. Approximately forty patients linger through bouts with malaria because they'd either forgotten or refused to take their yellow pills each week. As seriously ill men were treated at First Med, the twelve corpsmen who share duty on Fever's four wards have had little exposure to the badly sick, the badly wounded, and hard work. Two doctors, a Medical Service Lieutenant, a chief, and a lab technician complete the personnel roster.

We'd no sooner arrived at Fever than reports came over the radio that the Viet Cong had hit hard throughout the Chu Lai area. The casualty rate among Americans was high.

Consternation and alarm!

Both Battalion-Aid stations (emergency rooms on the lines) were disassembled and moving north. The hospital ship *Sanctuary* was berthed in Manila; the hospital ship *Repose* was at sea and far away. The Army hadn't yet moved into our abandoned complex. All casualties would be coming to Fever.

Alf took charge. He set Hilgendorf and Kraft to scrubbing and baking (sterilizing surgical instruments) in a quartet of operating rooms hitherto utilized only to show porno flicks. He assigned two ward corpsmen to Bernie, who would head Triage, and handed me the last pair.

"Kurt, you'd better pull together a recovery room." He disappeared into the OR.

I looked at my corpsmen. Moritz could be adequate; he'd

been bored by the routine of ward duties and had taken to visiting ICU on his breaks, hoping to learn something. The other man, Cifax, was bald at twenty-three. At least he looked mature. They followed me into the shed allotted for an intensive care unit. Twenty cots covered with twenty blankets. Nothing else. I told Moritz to scrounge up some sheets and went looking for the chief.

I found him in the chow hall, drinking coffee, his wattles wagging as he yakked with one of the cooks. They ignored me, so I interrupted the conversation.

"Wait a minute! I worked my corpsmen pretty hard, getting ICU ready just in case. You got cots and blankets. What more do you want?"

"Oxygen, suction, several cases of IV fluids, weights for amputees, hospital beds—"

"Hospital beds!" exclaimed Chief Turkey. "Sure had it fancy at First Med. My grunts in Korea never asked for no hospital beds. They was tougher in those days, huh, Cookie?"

"You're not going to give us what we need?"

"Hell, no! You got twenty cots and twenty blankets. You don't want 'em, cram 'em up your ass." He turned away to sip his coffee. Cookie giggled.

I went to the heli-pad. Choppers landed, threw out patients, and flew away to pick up more. Marines from Fever's Motor Pool acted as stretcher-bearers, carrying their burdens to Triage. A lull in the activity. I walked over to a group of men lighting up cigarettes.

"Anybody here can drive me up to First Med?"

"No, man. We got to hump these litters."

"We need the equipment and the supplies that's left up there. If we can't get it, some of these marines you're carrying are going to die."

The men of Motor Pool melted away. I watched a chopper land and discharge several wounded men. One of the Motor Pool sidled up to me.

"Doc, we'd like to help you and all, but we stand to get our asses reamed if we leave the compound without permission." I looked at him; then at the chopper, which was rising in the air. "Doc?"

"Yeah."

"Doc . . . like it could be me or my buddy on one of those choppers. I . . . Don't look now, but a key's on the ground.

207

Right by your foot. Wait 'til I leave. You might look for truck number ten forty-two."

I maneuvered the truck through hordes of zips on bicycles and stopped at the SeaBee battalion, where a lab tech and an X-ray tech agreed to take off immediately for Fever; then I drove to First Med. As I wrestled an iron bed through the door to ICU, an Army captain appeared by the truck, rifle aimed at me.

"Cease and desist!" he ordered.

I'd barked my shins on the bed and my collarbone ached. I ignored him.

"Cease and desist, thief, or I'll shoot you in the knee."

I ceased and desisted. "Listen, doggie, you're barking up the wrong tree." I explained the disorder at Fever. The captain helped me fill the truck and followed me to Fever. When we carried in the first of several dozen cases of IV fluids into Triage, Bernie was clamping an artery gushing blood.

"Thank God! We were out. Kurt, would you mind setting up a couple of salines on those two guys in the corner?"

Fifteen grunts lay on the floor awaiting surgery. Thirty grunts lay outside Triage, wounded badly enough to need treatment. On the other side of the building, several dead bodies awaited disposition. Bernie was doing a nice job under the circumstances: six experienced corpsmen would have been busy; Bernie had two ward corpsmen who had never been in an emergency medical situation. They'd done nothing in Nam but take temps and dispense pills. Four doctors would have had their hands full; the OR could spare only two, one of them inexperienced.

The Army captain held a brief conference with one of the doctors while I finished unloading supplies; then he left the compound. I parked the truck behind the recovery room. Groaning and unconscious men lay on bare canvas cots. Moritz rushed over to me.

"Where the hell have you been? Post-ops pouring in, doctors screaming for suction and oxygen..."

"Why are these men lying on bare cots?"

"The ward corpsmen wouldn't give me any sheets. Said they needed written authorization."

"Unload the truck that's parked outside. I'll be right back."

"This isn't my duty station," said Cifax. "The guys from Fever should be working here instead of me."

I looked at Moritz, who shrugged. "I could have told you he was like that, Kurt."

"Cifax, I couldn't agree with you more. I walked past a bunch of Fever dudes playing basketball. I felt like kicking each and every one of them in the ass. I'm in an asskicking mood. If I were you, I'd unload that truck."

I brought back sheets and ordered Cifax to cover the cots; then I ran through the doctor's orders and put the men on the correct machines. Moritz was quick to pick up the procedures, so I hurried over to Triage. Father Kerry had just arrived, having heard of the casualties while on the convoy. He'd thumbed back down Highway 1. He was staring at the bodies, thirty or so by this time, lying in rows outside Triage, and turned to me with a stricken face.

"Father, I know you want to give last rites, but we've got a hundred walking wounded who haven't eaten, have no place to sleep, and just can't be gotten to."

"Right."

"And could you send some sandwiches up to the OR, Triage, and ICU? And tell the cook we'll need the coffee pot going all night."

"I'll take care of everything."

I knew he would.

The Army captain returned that evening, bringing with him several doctors, six OR techs, and four medics. I told Bernie to keep the four medics, who seemed well trained, and took his two ward corpsmen back to ICU to help Moritz; then I carried some supplies down to the beach, where the walking wounded were bivouacked, and began treating them.

Moritz interrupted me an hour later. "We're full up, Kurt. I'm putting men on the floor and the doctors are pissed."

I emptied two of Fever's wards and returned to ICU.

"I'm not going to move anybody," said Cifax. "This isn't my duty station."

I kicked him in the ass as hard as I could. "Next time I'll kick you in the family jewels. Start humping those litters."

Moritz and I reviewed the patients and decided who should stay and who should go. (It was real easy to decide; those on machines stayed and those off, went.) I ran through the machines, tipped Moritz off to some shortcuts, and adjusted weights on amputees; then I returned to the walking wounded. There were nearly two hundred by midnight. I was the closest thing to a doctor they'd seen. The choppers started churning in again. Bernie interrupted me this time.

"Kurt, I'm swamped."

I hustled up to Triage with him. "Those doggie medics looked good. What's the matter?"

"It calmed down in Triage about midnight. The Army doctors went down to the officers' quarters to get some shut-eye. The four medics and I climbed on stretchers to catch a few winks ourselves. Next thing I know, the Medical Service Lieutenant was shining a flashlight in my eyes. He said, 'All right, sailor, which of these men are soldiers?' I told him that they all were. The lieutenant woke them up and ordered them to follow him. Before he left, he ordered me to scrub down Triage and get it in shipshape. While I was mopping, the choppers started coming in, and it's worse than the first time. I've already woke up the doctors and the OR. Jeez, it looks bad."

We worked all night and into the next day, pushing patients into the OR and throwing the dead outside. No one from Graves came to pick them up and the smell was overwhelming. Periodically, I checked on a near-hysterical Moritz, who was working well. I peeked into the wards; Cifax was dozing. I burst into the officers' quarters. Eight wounded men and the Protestant chaplain looked up from coffee and do-nuts.

"I need two officers who give a shit about their men." Only the chaplain didn't stand up. I looked at their bars. "Which of you ranks highest? I can never figure it out." A man about thirty-five raised his good arm. "What are you?"

"A major."

"Then you'll be in charge. All of you come with me."

The chaplain appeared horrified, whether at my officiousness or at the officers meekly following me out of the hut, I didn't know. I knew they would follow me—when you're hurting, you're nice to Doc.

"What's the problem, Doc?" asked the major.

"We've got some mighty sick grunts, and nobody to take care of them."

"The chaplain informed us that our men were being well looked after."

"Was that before he kissed your ass or after?"

I took them to one of the wards. Badly wounded men lay everywhere: on cots, on the floor, outside on the ground. I showed the officers how to read the doctor's orders, give shots, and take blood pressures. They learned how to mix penicillin with water, watch IV bottles, and empty bedpans. I left four of them there and led the major and the remaining officers next door to a ward as crowded as the first. Cifax sat at the desk, his head on his arms, sound asleep. I woke him by kicking his chair over.

"This is Cifax," I said. "He's a poor excuse for a corpsman, but he's all we've got to spare. Everyone else is on Triage or in the recovery room. If you have any questions about procedure, wake Cifax up. I don't trust him to give medications at the right time, so you'll have to give them. Lay the morphine on these guys generously; they hurt a lot worse than you. They should be on ICU, but we're filled there with critical cases. If Cifax tries to sneak away, shoot him. Okay, you know what you have to do. I'll come back whenever I can."

I didn't have many opportunities. Triage was a nightmare— two Army doctors, Bernie, me, and two hundred wounded. Late that evening the Medical Service Lieutenant wandered by. Idly viewing the activity, he noticed a small group of Vietnamese in the corner, squatting around an ancient mamasan.

"Why isn't this woman receiving treatment?" he asked.

"Because we're too shorthanded to take care of the Americans," I snapped, "much less dinks."

"I wasn't aware that I was addressing you, sailor."

I looked up from a grunt with severe respiratory difficulty. "Oh, Doctor, it's you. I apologize. With all this work, I was plain distracted. I would never have expected to see you here."

"Not with all this work," added Bernie.

The doctors chuckled. The lieutenant peered at the marine I was working on and another that Bernie prepped for surgery, a man with shrapnel dangerously near the artery in his groin; then the lieutenant looked closely at the mamasan. "In my opinion, as far as their wounds are concerned, the Vietnamese ranks higher on the priority list than these marines."

I was too angry to say anything. A Medical Service Lieutenant usually earns his bars by majoring in chemistry or biology in college; he may have dissected a frog or two, but would know little beyond basic first aid, if that. Bernie was shaking with anger, too, and drawled out, "Why don't you start right in working on them, Doctor? With your vast medical knowledge and your bleeding heart, you ought to have them in tip-top shape in no time at all. Sir."

The lieutenant said, "Come with me, sailor. I don't have to take guff like that."

One of the Army doctors took the lieutenant aside, talked to him briefly, and gently prodded the man into leaving. The doctor then turned to Bernie. "Look, sailor, no matter how justified you think you are, you should remember that the man is an officer and, as an officer, entitled to your respect."

Bernie said, "You think so? Go down to Motor Pool. Find out what your fellow officer did with your Army medics that we need so bad. Then you come back and tell us again to respect that asshole."

Everyone was a little hot under the collar, so we worked silently for a few minutes; then Bernie took advantage of a brief respite to visit the shitter. After he'd gone, one of the doctors said, "What did happen to those medics?"

The other doctor didn't know. "I'd thought they went back to the base." They looked at me. "You going to tell us, Kurt?"

"Nope. Like Bernie said, go down to Motor Pool."

We worked for a couple of minutes. "Okay, I'll bite. Where's Motor Pool?" The doctor returned within five minutes, grabbed his flak jacket, and strapped on his .45. "Jack, I'm getting out of this insane place. You coming with me?"

The other doctor protested. "Dave, you can't. It's night. There'll be booby traps all along the road."

"Fuck a bunch of booby traps. Those four medics are sitting in the back of a truck, a marine guarding them with a rifle. They're under arrest for the crime of handling Navy property without authorization. Sailor, you can call that lieutenant anything you want to, but if you ever address him as 'Doctor' within my hearing, I'll see you court-martialed."

Doctor Dave tore out of Triage. Doctor Jack leaned against the wall and covered his eyes with his hand.

Casualties trickled in for the rest of the night. I caught up with the walking wounded and checked how my officers were doing on the wards. Cifax had disappeared soon after their arrival, but the major and his men had done a damned good job. They were proud of their work. I commended them, patting the major on the ass. He glowered at me.

The following morning I was able to relieve Moritz on ICU; we'd been up for over forty-eight hours. Chief Turkey moseyed on the ward with a coffee cup in his hand, belching, farting, a smile on his face. He waddled up to me while I was changing the colostomy bag on a black marine.

One becomes frustrated when changing a colostomy bag, a plastic sack taped around the end of an intestine protruding through the patient's stomach because of a bowel obstruction. The sack fills with runny shit and smells awful. You peel off the bulging sack, clean around the intestine to prevent infection, and just as you get ready to put on a clean bag, the intestine lets go with a glop of shit and you must begin all over again. You try hard to maintain sterile technique and the patient has no control so he's embarrassed and you're trying to hide your dismay and he keeps shitting . . .

"Gobble gobble!" said Chief Turkey, as he plucked at my sleeve. I ignored him. "Gobble gobble!" Chief Turkey attempted to squeeze his huge bulk between me and the patient. "Gobble gobble!"

I finally completed the colostomy change and turned to the chief. "You get in my way one more time, and I'll shoot your ass."

Chief Turkey opened and closed his mouth in indignation. I pushed the dressing cart to the bedside of another patient. Chief Turkey waddled along behind me. I removed a blood-soaked dressing.

"Strom, you know that only doctors are allowed to change dressings." I ignored him and cleaned the wound. "Strom, if you persist in ignoring me, I'm putting your ass on report." I walked over to my gear, pulled out my .45, and started to load it. Chief Turkey waddled out of ICU at a rapid clip. Five minutes later he returned with the Medical Service Lieutenant. They came over to the bed where I was adjusting the weights on a double leg amputee.

"What seems to be the trouble, sailor?"

"No trouble. Just keep that worthless bag of shit away from me."

"That's what I mean, Lieutenant. He ain't got no respect. He ought not talk to you like that. Just because he's been out on the lines don't make him special. He's been like that ever since he got here. Instead of going through the chain of command, he thinks he's the CO. Instead of coming to me for sheets, he goes through the wards ripping sheets off beds and threatening to wipe up the floor with anybody what stopped him. And he goes to the wards, telling our patients that no one at Fever cares about wounded grunts, that if they care about their wounded buddies needing a place out of the night, they'd pick up their gear and find a empty bed somewheres else. And he left the compound at least three times that I know of without permission in a truck he stole. And bringing the Army in makes the Navy look real bad, Lieutenant. The Navy takes care of its own."

The lieutenant watched me irrigate a stomach tube. "You appear to be in deep trouble, sailor."

"And he stole both coffee urns from the chow hall and set one up in Triage and the other down on the wards. And he drove over to the SeaBee barracks in the truck he stole and announced over the loudspeaker that every SeaBee was ordered to come give blood at Fever and—"

"You'd better come with us, sailor."

"I'm not about to leave thirty men in critical condition."

"I could call marine guards to remove you by force."

"At least let me wake up someone to replace me."

"Do you want disobeying an officer added to the charges?"

As we passed a group of off-duty corpsmen from Fever playing basketball, the marine major rushed out of one of the wards. "Strom, we have a boy hemorrhaging. Get up here."

With the major having been shot through the arm and my ribs hurting like a bitch, Chief Turkey and the lieutenant, prodded by the major, had to carry the boy up to Triage. As Bernie and the doctor worked on him, I told the major to wake up Moritz, that ICU was unattended. "I'm under arrest, you know."

"What for?"

I referred him to the lieutenant, who told the major of my crimes.

"I can't believe this shit," said the major. "Where's a telephone?"

"Don't forget Moritz," I called out over my shoulder as I was led away.

I spent a couple of hours dozing in the back of the truck. The Army medics were quiet and very polite. When we were released, I returned to ICU, where Moritz was grinning from ear to ear.

"Boy, did you miss a show. A marine general flew in from Da Nang. They called us all into Triage. The general's aide was taking down names of witnesses for your court-martial.

It would have been funny, if I wasn't scared shitless. There was Alf and the doctors from the OR, blood all over them; Bernie and the Army doctors, blood all over them. The lieutenant and the chief were looking real important. Dr. Minter said, 'General, I think you should give these two men medals. Or maybe Ho Chi Minh should. They're better at killing Americans than any Cong. We lost three men in the operating rooms because we couldn't get to them fast enough. Nobody's fault on Triage. They didn't have the personnel and no cooperation from these two bozos.'

"The Army doctor said, 'We lost another seven men out here we shouldn't have because these idiots had locked up my Army medics, leaving us with no personnel. Because of these morons, ten mothers sit back in the States, wondering how their sons are faring. Ten girls dream about the day their husbands or boyfriends come home. Fathers proud of their sons . . . sisters . . . brothers . . . teachers . . . All of them with dead dreams. And there would be another dozen dead men if it wasn't for that boy they locked up.'

"Everybody got into the act. Dr. Minter said, 'Two dozen.' Bernie said, 'Three dozen.' By the time it had gone through the major and Alf and a couple of other OR doctors and got around to me, you'd saved nearly a hundred men. That's when Father Kerry came running up, pissed as hell that you'd been put under lock and key. He knew the general and blessed him out. Nobody had ever seen Father Kerry mad. The general finally said, 'Release them all' and left for the chopper pad."

The general apparently had the casualties rerouted to Da Nang because we had no more that night. Triage and the OR closed down, but Moritz and I were still humping on ICU. The next morning the lieutenant came on the ward with several men from Fever.

"Strom, take your men and report to the docks immediately."

I protested. I wanted to ascertain that the new men knew how to work the machines and to tell them about the patients—every man on the ward was hooked up to something, but the lieutenant got huffy and Moritz dragged me away before I could land myself in the brig. As we left, the ward corpsmen were standing around the desk, reading their navy blue corpsman's manuals. They didn't have the least idea of what the hell they were supposed to be doing.

We found Cifax sitting on the dock, whistling and swinging his legs over the water. Moritz kept me from kicking him off. We spent the rest of the day sitting there, waiting to board.

> *Relentlessly,*
>
> *Kurt*

FIRST MEDICAL BATTALION
DA NANG, VIETNAM
15 March 67

Dear Mom,

The Marine Corps has moved north; the Med Battalion followed. The Viet Cong have been eradicated in the area of Chu Lai, supposedly. The Army will keep it clean.

We sailed to Da Nang on an LST, a Landing Ship Tanker—the type of ship on which Daddy served. Because we traveled by night, we saw little, but as we arrived in Da Nang, dawn broke over the harbor. The sun shone, the blue sea glittered, the hills around the bay appeared green and lush, and the hospital ship *Repose* gleamed white against the water.

We live in buildings erected with more of an eye to comfort than those in Chu Lai. I work in the sunshine where I can look at the bay on the one hand and, on the other hand, at a steep hill that rises above the encampment. I suppose it's not volcanic.

Happy Birthday to me.

> *Love,*
>
> *Kurt*

FIRST MEDICAL BATTALION
DA NANG, VIETNAM
16 March 67

Arch,

Even at my most romantically irresponsible, I've never considered a career in the Navy, which is a good thing, because the events of the past week might have otherwise dismayed me. After an incredible four days of insanity, the invasion of Haiphong no longer hangs imminent. At least I've heard nothing more about it, and Rumor with his cloak of tongues finds eager ears at First Med.

It all seems like the rerun of what was once an interesting movie. The Med Battalion lies next to a busy, dusty road. We look over a large bay where the hospital ship *Repose* is at anchor, a great red cross contrasting with the ship's white surface and the deep blue of the water. A beautiful establishing shot, don't you think, calling out for a full orchestra and a throbbing exotic beat. But then the camera pans slowly landward and suddenly, buddy, it's another film.

Beyond the dusty road as it winds northward along the bay stands Monkey Mountain, where marines get killed day and night. To the south the road passes the PX and the air base, skirts the city of Da Nang, and heads toward Marble Mountain and more fireworks. As I have no intention of visiting either Monkey or Marble mountains and the city of Da Nang is off limits, and as I've seen no maps, that's the world as I know it. Your travelogue is over, and the house lights go up a bit too fast.

Within the compound itself, I live in the last house on the left, a hooch wider, longer, and sunnier than the hooch in which I lived in Chu Lai, and set apart from the other huts. The Garbage Detail lives there, corpsmen who prefer emptying garbage to bedpans. I incurred the enmity of a wattle-necked chief for a bit of sass and now spend my days picking up cigarette butts and candy wrappers strewn around the compound. I am fit only to associate with the Garbage Detail.

And a person is known by the company he keeps.

Relentlessly,

Kurt

My dear Paul,

I have good news and I have bad news. First the good news.

We've moved to Da Nang and a mile down the road from First Med stands the Marine Corps PX, a complex that includes a USO, a cinema, a library, and a barbershop. The well-stocked library provides luxury in the form of flush toilets. Continually overflowing bowls make for discomfort; apparently, the grunts forget to flush the toilets—if they ever knew how. Still, I take a certain perverse enjoyment in using the facilities. And I could hardly help noticing a huge glory hole between the two stalls. Grafitti mark the walls:

> YOUNG AND CLEAN
> STRONG AND LEAN
> 6′ 1″ OF RUGGED MARINE
> HAIR OF YELLOW
> EYES OF GREEN
> HERE AT 1500 EVERY TUESDAY TO FUCK ASS

> THE HORNIEST MOTHER FUCKER IN NAM
> DROPS BY EVERY WEDNESDAY MORNING
> TO CHECK OUT WHAT SOME OTHER
> HORNY MOTHER FUCKER
> MIGHT HAVE IN MIND

> DEAR ABBY,
> I DON'T LIKE QUEERS,
> BUT I DON'T WANT TO CATCH
> DISEASES
> FROM SLANT-EYE PUSSY NEITHER.
> WHAT SHOULD I DO?
> HARD ON AND UP

It was all very friendly and familiar, even in Arcady. Unfortunately, I visited the library this morning, a Friday, and all good little Catholic boys are supposed to eat fish. No Protestants appeared either. Like MacArthur, however, I shall return.

Now for the bad news.

When I left Cincinnati, I flew to San Francisco and stayed overnight with a pair of dreary things who could talk only of drapes and soufflés. They pressed on me the address of a GI in Cam Ranh Bay, and in a moment of weakness for which I may never forgive myself, I wrote him a note.

I received a reply this morning, from the Army stockade in which he is held prisoner. "Why didn't you write sooner... I was so lonely... My sergeant was so desirable."

Jesus Christ! They censor the letters of psychos. The fool! Any minute now, I expect a huge furry paw to clamp down on my shoulder and a gruff voice to growl, "Come with me, boy."

Relentlessly,

Kurt

FIRST MEDICAL BATTALION
DA NANG, VIETNAM
21 March 67

Dear Mom,

I've just enjoyed a pleasant weekend of R&R in Saigon, thanks to a couple of Air Force pilots who fly a supply shuttle between Da Nang and the capital. Saigon is busy, crowded, noisy, and dirty. I'd like to send a report describing my attendance at the city's tourist attractions; I should lie were I to send it. I saw the airport where I landed, the officers' club where I ate and drank, and the hotel in which I slept.

I ate and drank like there was no tomorrow. (That's an omen if I've ever come across one and I certainly have.) Saturday supper: Texas cut steak, baked potato, green salad, and apple pie. Saturday night: several tankards of Scotch. Sunday brunch: Bromo Seltzer and a hair of the dog that bit me. Sunday supper: Texas cut steak, baked potato, green salad, and apple pie. Monday: Bromo Seltzer and aspirin.

I've been trying to learn the Vietnamese language in my spare time and hoped to practice it in Saigon. I tried in a couple of shops, but the salespeople were too busy for chat, offering services to the Services, if you know what I mean.

Love,

Kurt

FIRST MEDICAL BATTALION
DA NANG, VIETNAM
22 March 67

My dear Paul,

When I was on the lines, I missed the Bob Hope Christmas show. I stood duty so that others could see Martha Raye in *Hello, Dolly!* when the show passed through Chu Lai. I have no regrets; after all, I've seen Broadway. The men talked long and loud about Miss Raye and Mr. Hope, who are greatly beloved in these parts, as they should be. But I am the only person at Med Battalion who has seen Saigon, and I can't tell a soul.

It began with a visit to our local library. (Paul, that place is a gold mine. You'd hardly believe the legions of studs who wander into the bathroom for reasons that would shock the Pentagon. Although I presume the studs make it with one another, my only steady competition comes from a buck-toothed soldier who inquires daily whether I've yet had an officer.) Bucky was at the library last Friday afternoon. I saw nothing worth outmaneuvering him for, so I retired to the reading room. As I was perusing a weekly Fascist rag (*Time* magazine), a dashing hard-eyed air jockey wearing a flight suit walked in. He sat down and stared at me over his own magazine. I walked into the stacks. The jockey passed by me, smiled, and continued out the door. He obviously had too much class to get down to the matter in six inches of toilet overflow. I followed him outside. He stood by the doorway.

"Where can a guy get a cup of coffee?"

I guided him to the USO. We talked for a couple of hours. I'd forgotten how enjoyable talking with someone could be, as opposed to being talked at. Steve apparently felt the same. A former illustrator for an advertising agency in Los Angeles, Steve now crews a cargo run between Da Nang and Saigon and invited me to fly down with him for the weekend. As I'd been vainly racking my brains for a place to bed the blue-eyed, hairy-chested air jockey, the invitation seemed a godsend. I accepted with alacrity.

Although I was flirting with a charge of AWOL and several weeks in the brig, I let Dr. Schiller milk me down, got an excuse from work, and reported to the air terminal bright and early Saturday morning, prepared to be disappointed. I needn't have worried. As I've said, this boy had class. He'd left a note for me at the flight desk.

Kurt,
    See you here at 0900. Looking forward to it.
                                                    Steve

At 0855 Steve walked into the waiting shed, dazzling me anew. He said that the crew believed me to be headed for Saigon to accompany the body of a naval officer to his home in the Canal Zone. I waited while Steve joined the crew for debriefing; then, as the only passenger aboard the C–141, I was off for a hot time in the city. I'd hoped to get a good aerial view of Vietnam, but Steve strapped me into a basket contraption that left me an inch off the floor of the plane. I slept most of the way.

When we arrived in Saigon, we went to Steve's hotel. As he showered, I took note of the double bed, a comfortable couch, and heavy drapes—a fitting seraglio. I trembled with anticipation. Steve came out of the shower wearing only a towel. My fairy godmothers had outdone themselves this time. I enjoyed the hot water, scrubbed myself carefully, and entered the bedroom drying my back. Steve, dressed in a captain's uniform, was leaning over the bed laying out a second uniform. He looked at me.

"Hold it right there." He moved to a desk and picked up a sketch pad. "The face grabbed me as soon as I saw it. I had to sketch those bones. But I never expected the body. Holy mackerel! Don't move." Steve walked around me for twenty minutes, flipping pages over as he filled them. I stood stunned. A captain! As I got used to the idea, and as I measured Steve's happy intensity, a carnal reaction set in. Steve saw it, blushed through his deep tan, and motioned toward the bed. "You'd

221

better put that on. It should fit." He noticed my perplexity. "We're eating at the officers' club." A shy one, huh? They say still waters run deep.

I respected his shyness throughout supper, as we talked of First Med, the lines, advertising, baseball, art, Louisiana, California, Steve's wife and kids, etc. Steve was fascinated by my stories about Paulette Carroll (I hope you don't mind my putting you in drag) and gently inquired whether I preferred older women. As Steve is about thirty, I was studying the question carefully, when we were interrupted by his copilot, a major, who expressed amazement at my rapid advancement through the ranks. Steve explained that we were old friends.

"Why didn't you tell me, Stevie boy? Any friend of yours is a friend of mine. You know that." He joined us for brandy. Steve seemed glad to see him, and I wondered what Heaven had in store for me. Don was a short wiry blond dude on the right side of devastating. A ménage à trois? Can one have too much of a good thing? Although he had no need to convince me of his maleness, Don embarked upon a series of tales that suggested an overwhelming heterosexual prowess.

"... and this one was when I was stationed in Omaha. I stopped at a drugstore to buy a pack of rubbers; I'd used a week's supply the previous night on a hot little blond bitch built like a brick shithouse. This redhead was at the counter, looking at makeup or something. Jesus, she was built. Like a brick shithouse. I winks at her and says to the salesgirl, 'Give me a dozen packs of prophylactics.' The redhead raises her eyebrows. God damn was she built! Anyway, she gives me the old up and down and says, 'Sure of yourself, aren't you, Major?' I says to her, 'Ain't heard no complaints yet.' Well, we gets to talking and I takes her out for a few drinks and we have a few laughs and she invites me up to her apartment ..."

They were all like that. I enjoyed looking at the two pilots; otherwise, I feigned enthusiasm. Don paid the checks and insisted we accompany him on some carousing; he had more memories he wanted to share. I'd gathered by then that his sexual preferences didn't include the likes of me, so I looked at Steve and conjectured ungratefully about the wedded state of Don's parents.

He took us to a spade bar where we stood out as the only honkies. Through five rounds of drinks, Don regaled us with boring variations of the same story—his utter irresistibility;

one look at him and a woman's legs went up in the air; on every corner, that old V for Victory stared him in the face. "Yeah," said Don, "that's a good way of putting it." I chalked one up for myself and tried to avoid looking paranoid under the glares of sixty blacks. Don merely lighted another cigar and droned on about a life as boring as a pornographic Frankie and Annette movie. It took another round before Steve could talk him into leaving.

In the stuffy hotel room, we stripped to our shorts and Steve hung his uniforms in the closet. Don brought a bottle of Scotch from his room and, after pouring very stiff drinks, settled upon the couch to tell yet another tale. I refused to listen anymore and interrupted his monologue with a story of my own.

"When I played ball in Kentucky, I had to make do in some down-home hick towns. One night my buddy Arch and I went out to get snockered, and we ended up drinking embalming fluid at a little redneck joint. Hobo Annie's. Bunch of hayseeds on cycles, chicks in leather jackets. Ugly as King Kong, all of them. Except two: a redhead and a brunette. Long thick hair. Blouses unbuttoned to their waists. Big firm tits. Nipples pointing straight out. Legs from here to there. We were slobbering into our beers. Those women were dynamite. Arch decided to give his left nut for a chance to ball them. I was drunk enough to say to myself, 'What the hell?' I went over and asked the brunette to dance. She looks up from under a ton of mascara..." Don sat rapt. "...so I'd eat out Lorrie while Darlene went down on me; then we'd switch. For hours I had a pussy to suck, a pussy to fuck. They were really lezzies, but they liked to make it with a guy every once in a while."

I leaned back and sipped my drink. Don pounded the arm of the sofa. "Holy smokes! I'd love to make it with two chicks. Jeezus Keerist!"

"Another time," I continued (and continued and continued, always with at least two chicks and mixing in violence and perversity whenever possible.) "...so that hard sexy blonde looked at me with one of those 'You can look all you want, Buddy, but you ain't touching it' looks. I was so excited, I could hardly catch my breath. I sat on the sofa, watching them on the floor, watching the little schoolteacher diving into the stewardess' muff. My knees shook. My head burnt. I shivered. I never wanted any chick so much as I wanted that hard sexy blonde. She watched me, her eyes half-closed. Finally, she said real low in her throat, husky, growling, 'Come on down, Tiger!'"

Don sat wide-eyed, his hand cupping his groin. "Gawd damn!" he exclaimed. He stood up, swayed, fell back on the sofa, and passed out. I crawled in bed next to Steve. He got up to turn off the light. I was asleep before he made it back to the bed.

I woke up the next morning to find the sofa empty and Steve asleep on top of the covers. I gently reached into his shorts, pulled out a lovely cock, and began to make ado with it. Steve stirred, sighed, and moaned softly as he stroked my head. It was wonderful. Until Don walked out of the bathroom.

"Holy Jesus!" he exclaimed.

Steve opened his eyes, looked at Don, and then looked down at me: "Oh shit!" he said.

Don wheeled out of the room. Steve's face was a study in misery. I sat up. "What will he do?"

"Tell everybody. Write my wife. Ruin my career." Steve got up and walked around the room. He struck his fist against a wall. He walked over to the door. He pressed his head against it. He looked at me with a resigned smile. I sat on the bed, uncertain. Steve walked over to me, grabbed my hair, and drew back his fist. I didn't try to defend myself. He dropped his fist and, with the other hand, released my hair and cupped my chin in his palm. He looked at me for a long time; then he flopped on the bed beside me.

"Hey!" he said, real low in his throat, husky, growling. "Git on down there, Tiger."

Relentlessly,

Kurt

FIRST MEDICAL BATTALION
DA NANG, VIETNAM
23 March 67

Arch,

The Garbage Detail invited me to join their ranks after a week of watching me pounce upon cigarette butts and candy wrappers as if I'd spied the red shoes that would transport me

224

out of OZ. I conjectured that anything would be better than crawling in the dust on my hands and knees while a fat chief gobbled in the shade, so I jumped at the chance to join the GD. It wasn't better. They crawl, too, under outhouses to remove huge drums of kerosene in which bob turds of varying sizes, shapes, and colors. (One thinks, against his will, of apples and Halloween.) We wrestle those drums to a honey pit, where we pour the contents, set the kerosene afire, and step back briskly. I won't revolt you by describing my inability to do any of this without splashing myself until I look like something that would have sickened the Marquis de Sade. I won't offend you with the language I used when I learned that the showers had broken down and would be shut off for several days. But I'm getting ahead of my story.

I empty shitters from eight to twelve. After an hour for lunch (I couldn't eat a thing), we pick up garbage. That is caviar to the morning's work, and I welcome the change. When we collect a truckload of trash, we drive to a big dump several miles past the air base. Eagerly awaiting us are a thousand children and a million rats. The GD amuse themselves by taking potshots at the rats and (I'm willing to swear to this on my navy blue corpsman's manual) the children.

Home again, home again, jiggety jog. Our workday ends after we empty the rat traps. Huge gray and brown beasts over a foot long and in a mood as ugly as themselves await disposition. As shooting our pieces on the compound is number ten, we (or I, being the new man) must club the rats on their heads until they are sufficiently dead. This extermination is a part of preventive medicine. Rats, you see, can carry bubonic plague. When I was a tiny tot, Mother read me to sleep with *Forever Amber*, which indelibly impressed upon my dreams those purple nodules suppurating and bursting in the armpits and groins of Cornel Wilde and Linda Darnell.

Now I know why they never sent the niggers back to Africa.

Relentlessly,

Kurt

Chloe dear,

Mom's hooked another husband. He's very patriotic and apparently a Republican: Portraits of Eisenhower and Nixon are set atop his television set; Hoover, Dewey, and MacArthur are set atop his desk; and Mr. Hebner and Mom will tie the knot July 4. A retired postmaster from North Dakota, Mr. Hebner is seventy-five. His wife died last winter, and he went into a decline. Taking no chances with the competition, Mom cooked his meals, cleaned his house, and nursed him back to health. He's the loyal type, I guess. Or cowardly, and by dating Mom, Mr. Hebner could evade the geriatric tigresses prepared to stalk him. When the bleary-eyed femmes fatales of the cane-and-corset set learned about the wedding plans, they trilled in cracked sopranos, "Poor Nedra not cold in her grave . . ." Mom and Mr. Hebner felt guilty, so they went to their preacher, who dispelled any doubt.

"At your age, you'd better make hay while the sun shines."

And that is exactly what Mom wanted to hear. They plan to honeymoon in Rio de Janeiro. And Neil tells me that despite Mr. Hebner's advanced age, Mom has every intention of starting off with a bang.

The invasion of Haiphong has been postponed. The Army took over Fever the day after we left, and Fever's personnel flew up to join First Med here in Da Nang. Grateful doctors had Alf and Hilgendorf permanently assigned to the operating room. Kraft complained so much of his sore feet and rested them so often that, according to Alf, the surgeons refuse to have him in the OR here; like Moritz and two of the basketball players from Fever, Kraft is a shift leader on SICU. Cifax lazes on a medical ward. The Medical Service Lieutenant sits in the personnel office and makes little marks on sheets of paper. Bernie and I were assigned to policing the battalion compound; for a week, we picked up candy wrappers and cigarette butts every day from eight to four while Chief Turkey watched us, coffee cup in his hand, smiling and smiling.

Relentlessly,

Kurt

My dear Paul,

Received quite a shock last Friday. Moritz came running into the mess hall while I was eating lunch. "Two Air Force officers are waiting for you on ICU."

"They say what they wanted?"

"No. Looks official."

I doubt that I could have eaten my dessert anyway. As we hurried to ICU, Moritz conjectured aloud as to what the officers could want from me. My own conjectures were silent: a full confession, names and dates, a psychiatric examination . . . Moritz said they'd asked him what kind of a fellow I was. "Kurt, I told them you were the best corpsman in Nam, but I couldn't truthfully say that you were a nice guy. I hope that's all right." Poor Moritz. He thinks only good of me.

When we entered the ward, I saw Don and Steve talking to a couple of patients. Don nodded curtly; Steve walked up to me and shook my hand.

"Hello, Captain." I nodded to Don. "Major."

Steve appeared ill at ease. "We thought we'd drop by and check out your company. How about a tour?"

"Sure." I showed the two pilots around the compound. At one point, as Don chatted with a doctor on Triage, Steve took me aside.

"Can you get away for a couple of hours and come to dinner with us?"

We stopped by Steve's room at the airport BOQ, where I changed into one of his uniforms. Don never left us alone. At supper, he sat quietly and watched me. Steve seemed nervous and said little. I did my butch act: cars, chicks, raping, maiming, killing . . . I got no applause.

After supper, Don stood up. "You'd better get him back, Steve." He nodded to me gravely and walked over to the bar. Steve followed him. They talked for several minutes; then Steve beckoned to me, and we left the club.

"Did I pass the test?"

Steve laughed. "Yeah."

"What if I'd flunked?"

"You didn't."

"What if?"

Steve sighed. "Don's got an exaggerated notion of masculinity. He . . ."

"He hates queers."

"Yes. But you're not . . ."

"And . . . ?"

Steve turned away. "He was going to turn you in for approaching an officer."

"Why did you come to see me?" Silence. "Why, Steve?"

"Don didn't want to get me in trouble. I'm his buddy. He was going to give you the opportunity to kill yourself first."

"Out of shame?"

"Kurt, I couldn't let that happen."

"It wouldn't have."

"I wasn't about to take the chance." We entered the BOQ, and I took off the uniform. Steve looked me over. "Let me sketch you one last time."

"Is that an order?"

Steve put his hands on my shoulders. "One last time."

I stayed the night. And, among other things, we talked. We never had in Saigon.

"I had to justify what I was doing. Oh, I know I didn't do much but lie back in Saigon but . . . I wanted to . . . do more. It was too new. I'd never even thought about . . . I was afraid. I couldn't justify what I felt. I wasn't sure what I felt. Then I decided that my aesthetic judgment was the key. Don appreciates getting it on with a beautiful woman, but he feels that any woman is better than no woman. I happen to disagree. I refuse to make love to a woman who's ugly or whom I can't respect. I'm an artist . . . a sold-out artist maybe . . . but I can still appreciate beauty. And you are, my friend, except for that scar along your head. Hey! Look at me." He ran his hand through my hair and traced the scar. "It might be too provoking if you were flawless. Kurt, I'd like . . . I'd like you to be the one who lies back. One last time, okay?" He slid down on the cot, took my precious in his hand and stared at it; then he looked up at me with a weak smile. "And one first time."

I left Steve asleep the next morning and thumbed back to the Med Battalion. I had just nodded off when Steve showed up and shook me awake.

"Not again."

"Get up. You're going to Saigon."

"No, man. I gotta sleep."

Steve pulled my sheet off and dressed me. When I refused to get up, he slung me over his shoulders.

"All right. I'm awake." I was awake until I climbed into a jeep. I was awake when I climbed aboard a plane. I was really awake somewhere over the South China Sea. Was I being transported into white slavery? I've heard interesting things about Arabs.

Steve came back from the cockpit. "Lonely?"

"Why . . . ?"

"Because I like you. Don't worry. I told your boss that you were needed in Saigon as a witness for a court-martial. He believed me. I'm a captain, remember?"

"Where's Don?"

"Up front."

"But . . ."

"He suggested you come."

"You're kidding?"

"He respects me. I'm a good pilot. He brought it up at breakfast. He figured it out, he said. Since I'm so wild, I was willing to try anything once."

"What did you say?"

"What could I say? I agreed with him."

"Why does he think you're wild?"

"You don't?"

"Of course I do. Jesus Christ! But why does he?"

"I'd taken him to a couple of far-out parties in Saigon and Manila. Crazy bars in Sydney. Things like that." Steve smiled. "Nothing like this."

"Why did he suggest I come to Saigon?"

"I don't honestly know. He asked me if I'd ever made it with a guy before. I didn't have to lie. He said, 'Why Kurt?' What could I tell him? The right time? The right place? The right person? Who knows?" Steve looked hard at me. "I know why. The right person. You have no idea of how goddam disarmingly sexy you are, do you?" I squirmed. Steve shook his head. "I'm catching myself staring at good-looking guys, comparing them with you. Their faces, their bodies, the way they walk. I think, 'My God! I'm turning queer.' But I don't want them in the sack. They don't look like a pure and terrible Viking prince. I'm in a fucking frenzy. Last night at dinner,

229

while you were talking to Don, you rested your hand on the table. I happened to look at your wrist. I couldn't catch my breath, I wanted you so suddenly, so much. I had to hold myself back from ripping that uniform off you. I want you now." His hands dug hard into my thighs.

"Okay."

Steve grinned and released his grip. "Not yet." He laughed uncomfortably. "You know, when you went to the john last night, I held the uniform you wore up to my face and smelled it. I . . . uh . . . it's crazy."

"What else did you tell Don?"

Steve blushed and looked away. "That you gave the best head I've ever had. You don't mind?"

"No."

"I thought not. He asked if I'd like to do it again. I said, 'Why put a stop to a good thing?' So he suggested I come over and pick you up." As he got up to return to the cockpit, Steve grinned wickedly. "So you would do it right here if I agreed." He shook his head and left the cabin.

Shit, I would have done it the night before in the officers' club.

When we reached Saigon, Steve and I went straight to the hotel. He encouraged me to talk about any obscenity I'd ever done or have wanted to do. "Would you have done this to Pinkerton? Does he like it?" or "I'm the colonel. I'm drunk. You're my orderly. Put me to bed." To quote the soulless Lola, "He makes me feel girlish, and I'm a hundred and ninety-seven years old."

Steve left Sunday afternoon for the air base and a two-day med-evac to the Philippines. "I could probably sneak you aboard, but we'd both be in big trouble if you got caught. I'll set you up with a buddy of mine; he'll show you Saigon. Be down in the lobby tonight at eleven. I'll be sitting in the cockpit thinking of you all the way. And stay away from Don while I'm gone."

I strolled through the city. You've seen the newsreels. Add noise. And stench. I did enjoy the streets filled with outstanding examples of American manhood and of interbreeding between the French and the Vietnamese. I strolled for hours and was getting tired when I saw the USO. I went in and sat down on a large leather chair. A soldier joined me, a dark, curly haired, good-looking guy.

230

"Howdy, pardner. Don't see many marines down this way."

"They're a dime a dozen where I come from."

"Where's that?"

"Da Nang."

"How did you get your heart?"

"Accident."

"Bad?"

"Bad enough."

"Yeah. Can I buy you some coffee?" Coffee is free at a USO.

"Sure." He brought a cup back for each of us.

"Thanks, buddy."

"Anytime. Name's Greg."

"Kurt."

"Sounds German."

"Swedish."

"Yeah? How long you in Saigon?"

"Couple of days."

"Where you staying?"

"Friends. A couple of pilots."

"Say, this coffee doesn't make it. Can I buy you a beer?"

"Be much obliged." We went around the corner to a little cafe. We drank our beers and watched people pass by.

"How are the chicks in Da Nang?"

"Not so good as Saigon."

"Found any yet?"

"Ain't had time."

"But you're looking?"

"Ain't everybody?"

"I suppose so. I never get enough pussy."

"I never get any."

"No?"

"No."

"You must be horny."

"Real horny."

"Hey! I just remembered. I've got some good Scotch in my apartment. Would you like to finish it off with me?"

"Might."

We walked a couple of blocks to a small hotel. He had a nice layout: living room, bedroom, and a bathroom down the hall.

"Nice layout."

231

"Thanks. The damned air-conditioner is broken. How do you drink your Scotch?"

"Straight."

"Only way. Damn, it's hot in here." He took off his clothes. "I hope you don't mind. It's too hot to wear anything. Damn air-conditioner. Strip down yourself, if you like."

Greg had a nice hairy body and a big piece of meat. I sat back in my chair. "Does this work?"

"What?"

"The whole set-up." I informed him of my sexual inclinations and hummed a few bars of "Somewhere Over the Rainbow" and "Strangers in the Night" to convince him. Greg turned on the air-conditioner, and we spent the rest of the afternoon trading stories and polishing off the Scotch. Greg's forte was picking up soldiers at the USO. They come in from the Delta looking for action, with no idea of where to find it. Overnight accommodations are at a premium, and as the military police maintain a sundown curfew, the boys need a place to hide after dark. They're lonely, Greg explained with a grin, and horny, and afraid of being tossed out on their ass should they prove unamiable. The set-up was hard to resist. Greg wanted me and was willing to share his spoils to get me.

Before we could leave for the USO, the door opened and an apparition walked in, a limp-wristed, hip-swaying, eye-rolling queen so nelly they could have heard the swish across the Mekong River. When she saw me, she gave a little scream, lisped "Excuse *me*," and slipped back outside.

I turned to Greg. "What ever was that?"

Greg groaned. "My roommate."

"Ah!" I said.

"Leigh makes himself scarce," Greg pleaded. "He'll stay down in the TV room until we've gone to bed."

Despite my misgivings, we returned to the USO. Greg grabbed a seat by the window and I sat down by the magazine rack. Five soldiers munched cookies. Three of them were strictly from hunger, one was a total disaster, and the fifth was black. What a blow! Greg and I looked despairingly at each other from across the room. Then a soldier walked in the door. *The* soldier. Nice-looking without being movie star handsome. Brown hair, brown eyes, tan, lean, rangy, uniform sleeves rolled above sinewed wrists, cap at a slant, rifle slung loosely over his shoulder. I avoided looking at him. He glanced around

the room, saw the magazines, and strode fearlessly into my
clutches. I sat for a minute, pulling my wits together. I glanced
at the soldier. He was looking at me. I cleared my throat, the
better to speak in a basso profundo. He grinned at me. Cute
grin. White teeth. He spoke.

"Hi. Don't see many marines this far south."

"They're a dime a dozen where I come from."

After I pulled that tacky coffee routine, Greg casually
walked over to the magazine rack.

"Howdy, pardner. Don't see many marines down this way."

The three of us went around the corner for a beer. We went
up to Greg's. We stripped to our skivvies. We drank until dark.
Greg invited us to crash overnight. I allowed that the offer was
mighty decent, and with the curfew and the MP's, I felt obliged
to accept. Our soldier had been uninformed about the curfew.
Greg painted him a horrifying picture of the local brig, reciting
almost word for word an article I'd also read in the *Reader's
Digest* about the Black Hole of Calcutta. The soldier decided
to stay, too.

Greg took one twin bed, and the soldier and I crowded into
the other. I "fell asleep" immediately. After a few minutes,
Greg crawled across the floor and lifted the sheet. I needed no
foreplay. He set to work. I writhed dramatically. I "awakened."
I waxed wroth. Greg apologized.

"I'm sorry. I don't know what came over me. It won't
happen again." He returned to his bed.

Silence.

I growled, "Okay, faggot, that felt good. You may as well
finish what you've started. And take care of my buddy, too."

Buddytoo had been lying quietly during the production. He
was soon a member of the company. I've always wondered
why you have no desire for straight guys. Besides the excitement of fucking virgin ass, they've never heard the rumors that
it's supposed to hurt.

After a couple of rounds of excellent sex, I remembered the
blind date Steve had set up. I had fifteen minutes to get back
to the hotel. Greg and I agreed to rendezvous the following
afternoon, and I hurried to Steve's hotel, keeping a wary eye
out for MP's. I showered quickly, changed into my jeans and
boots, and rushed downstairs. A tall, skinny, hawk-nosed, and
very ugly dude slouched in a chair against the wall, facing
away from the window.

"Call me Flak."

I followed Flak through reeking alleys as he led me through the underbelly of Saigon. We drank a couple of beers in a bar filled with pasty-faced young men with brown teeth and vacant eyes. One walked up to our table.

"Hey man! Got some change?"

"Fuck off, freak."

"You got it. Gimme some change."

Flak pulled a switchblade. "You want cut, freak. Fuck off." The guy whined, but scurried away when Flak made as if to stand up. "Goddam smack freaks. I hate 'em."

"What's a smack freak?"

"Ever hear of heroin?"

The next bar contained several sleazy round-eyes. "Tramps. They prowl through Asia. They make good money here." Shades of Sadie Thompson! The dead-eyed men who sat in silent groups of two and three ignored us studiously. They appeared as mean and angry as Flak.

"Killers. AWOL. They hire out: Americans, French, Chinese, Cong . . . Don't matter who."

It was all very interesting. I declined Flak's offer to show me an opium den, so he guided me to the last stop on the tour, an elegantly appointed villa in the suburbs. Gook houseboys in mascara attended sixty or so guests who were dancing, playing "Botticelli," or necking in corners. The guests, all male, wore uniforms, business suits, or full drag.

Flak whispered in my ear. "Feel at home, sweetie?" He sneered as he moved to the bar. I danced with whoever asked me, but I met no one who turned me on. After an hour or so, Flak walked over and, his nose an inch from mine, said, "I bet you dig the hell out of dirty sex." I let him lead me into a back bedroom. I smoked a cigarette that laid me open to whatever Flak wanted. He pushed me back on a chair, straddled me and, with his arms around me, brushed my lips with his own and promised to fuck me if I drank his piss. I couldn't quite bring myself to do it but, somehow, his proposition seemed attractive. The low point of the evening came as I lay on my back, Flak sitting on my face and inviting several guys I couldn't see to punkfuck me. I loved it.

I woke up around noon with someone gumming me. I pushed him away and returned to Steve's hotel where I douched myself thoroughly with Coca-Cola and rinsed my mouth with Listerine. At three-thirty, I met Gret at the USO. We picked up a sexy little soldier whom we bedded within an hour. After Greg treated us to supper in Chinatown, he bought another fifth of Scotch, and having sent the soldier on his way, we returned to his hotel to plan the evening's strategy. We walked into the living room where Leigh was entertaining an incredibly humpy beast, a monkey-faced number so ugly he was cute, and as butch as he could possibly be. Leigh allowed us one drink before he pushed us out the door. "Thanks for dropping by, guys. See you later. Oh, wait a minute." He stepped into the hall and closed the door behind him. "He's drunk a pint of sloe gin. What do I do now?"

"Put him to bed before he pukes," Greg and I whispered simultaneously.

"How?" Leigh's eyes were wide and pleading.

"Tell him it's late. He's too drunk to know."

We went down to the television room.

"I can't believe it," said Greg. "Leigh hasn't had sex during the eight months we've been here."

"You're kidding."

"I thought he was asexual. I can't believe it."

Leigh rushed into the room. "He's in bed. What should I do now?"

"Offer him a back rub," advised Greg. I liked the way this man thought.

Leigh rushed back out. Greg and I looked at each other; then we followed Leigh upstairs. The bedroom door was closed; we could see nothing through the keyhole. A few minutes later, Leigh wafted out. "I gave him a back rub and he went to sleep. Now what?"

Beside ourselves, we pushed past Leigh and entered the bedroom. The youth lay spread-eagle on the bed, his muscular arms crossed over his face. He was clad only in jockey shorts, and the white cloth outlined an obvious erection. Greg carefully lifted the waist band. We stared in wonder. Leigh hissed, "He's *mine! Mine!*"

Greg gave him five minutes to get with it, or the soldier was *ours*. We gulped down a couple of triples to steady our nerves. Suddenly, we heard a shout in the bedroom. Leigh flew through the door and slid down the wall into a heap. "Oh, God! Oh, God!" he wailed.

"What's the matter?" asked Greg.

"I'm ruined," cried Leigh, as he swayed to and fro. "Ruined." We rushed past him into the bedroom. The soldier stood in the middle of the room, pointing his rifle at us with one hand as he tried to pull up his pants with the other.

"What's going on, soldier?" I wondered. Greg grabbed at the wavering gun, careful to stay to the side of it.

"Fucking faggot," replied the soldier gravely. "Leggo my piece."

"Calm down," I said, beginning to grow frantic.

"Fucking faggot," he went on. "Gimme my goddam piece so I can get the hell away from here."

"You can't go outside after curfew," Greg interjected. "Be reasonable."

"Fucking faggot," the soldier reasoned as he yanked the rifle from Greg's grasp. He lurched out of the bedroom, glared fiercely at Leigh, and stormed out of our lives.

We carried Leigh to his bed, put cold compresses across his forehead, and gave him a sedative. It took several minutes of sobbing and hiccoughs before we could understand what had happened.

"Leigh," said Greg sternly, "you're never supposed to kiss them."

I had another appointment with Flak, so I returned to the hotel for a shower. Prowling through the room, I found letters to Steve in one of his drawers. I settled down to read. Don knocked at the door; he'd come to keep me company. I'd been having a fine time, but I invited him in. He poured some drinks from a bottle he'd brought. The talk was desultory until Don brought up the topic of homosexuality. He wanted to know about my first time. I felt like a hooker with a john. As the truth is unremarkable (Uncle Gus when I was six), I embroidered a tale in which Pinkerton held a .45 to my head and forced me to go down on him. ". . . and I liked it."

The major seemed intrigued. "You know, Kurtie, I always thought a medic got a bum deal, but considering you're a queer, it ain't too bad.

"Okay, I'm in a far-away country, the only man with a couple of hundred thousand nineteen-year-old chicks. I bunk in a room with a dozen or so. They're lying in their bunks wearing nothing but undies. I take a shower. A dozen chicks are soaping themselves down and scrubbing their sweet little snatches.

"I'm a medic, alone in a room with several young chicks lying naked in their beds. They need somebody to put his arm around them and tell them that everything is all right. I give each one a bath, soaping down their titties and washing out the inside of their pussies. I rub then dry with a soft towel. I pat their titties dry, very gently. I pat their sweet clean little pussies dry, very gently."

Don winked. "Sure does get a guy turned on to think about it from that angle, doesn't it?" He sat across from me, his legs wide apart, an erection poking out of the bottom of his shorts. It looked as big as a baby's arm.

"Yeah. Hey, Don, I've got a date tonight, so if you don't mind . . ."

"I've been thinking, you know, head's head, no matter who gives it." He grinned.

"Yeah. Well, lock up when you leave." I went to the door.

"Kurtie baby, you understand what I'm saying?"

I understood. I just mistrusted him. I looked at that hard bronzed body, those hairy muscular legs, and the mushroom-shape dong. My pilot sat grinning at me. "Major, if you only had a gun pointed at my head, you couldn't keep me off it. Ciao."

Flak took me to a Chinese restaurant where we ate sweet and sour dog, and to a cockfight, after which I barfed the dog up. We went to a sex show to watch two zip ladies do unspeakable things to each other, while little girls sucked off whichever of the soldiers in the audience asked for such favors. I smoked another of Flak's crazy cigarettes (heroin!), and we attended an orgy: two dozen military officers and three beautiful Vietnamese call girls. Although I had difficulty getting hard, several of the officers found my passivity to their liking. I saw Flak accepting money. What ever was I doing?

I felt like hell, but Flak made me smoke another of his cigarettes and I felt a lot better. We stopped by a squalid bar, where Flak picked up two smack freaks, and we brought them back to the hotel. They looked like fallen angels. I paid them twenty dollars to perform various perversions in front of us. They needed the money; they even drank our piss.

And this morning, Steve came back. I doubt that you'll believe me, but I was glad to see him.

This afternoon, Don flew me back to Da Nang. During the flight, he left the controls to the copilot and came back to visit

237

me. I was buckled into a little mesh hammock-type seat, my ass an inch off the floor, and my eyes level with Don's crotch. He pulled a water pistol from his pocket and squirted me in the face. He grinned and unzipped his flight suit.

I'm just a thing of impulse and a child of song.

Relentlessly,

Kurt

FIRST MEDICAL BATTALION
DA NANG, VIETNAM
29 March 67

Arch,

A few days on the Garbage Detail convinced me that I had little affinity for shit, trash, or rats, so I applied for ward duty. After two more days of wrestling, splashing, dumping, and clubbing, I was transferred to the Clap and Other Viruses ward. The head corpsman is a hysterical albino faggot from Bogotá, Colombia, and what he's doing in this man's Navy lies beyond my comprehension. As I refused him obeisance, I was left with a sickening choice of jobs: the garbage detail, tidy time in the sun, or a month of KP duty. I lay all day today on my cot in a perplexity, racked with indecision, and liberally applying English Leather cologne upon everything nearby. Happily, my buddy Moritz wandered by this evening to dangle my old job on ICU in front of me. I jumped at the chance and will begin emptying bedpans tomorrow.

Despite rising above my former level of "untouchable," I will continue to make my home with the GD. Call it sloth, ennui, or what you will, but here I stay.

I suppose the chief man in the hut is Howdy. I've never asked his last name; I prefer to think it's Doody, of whom he is the spirit and image. A rural rustic from North Carolina, Howdy has been in Nam for ten months and worked on the GD the entire time. The others often gather around his rack at the far end of the hooch as Howdy drawls out homespun philosophy. My hoochmates seem to regard the pompous boob as wisdom incarnate.

238

Sleeping across from Howdy is a fat little moron who calls himself the Green Hornet. When he is not hearkening to Howdy, the Green Hornet is cleaning his piece. Occasionally, he turns it upon us at midsection level and bursts out with an "ack-ack-ack." He thinks a machine gun sounds that way. "Ack-ack-ack."

In the next bunk over lies a sullen redhead who never smiles. He spends every evening determinedly writing in a notebook. Do you want to know why he never smiles and what he writes in the notebook? I'll tell you. It seems he hates his father, who he says is a faggot, and he is devising elaborate plans for killing said father when he returns to the States.

Tonto, our token redskin, is next, and I complete that side of the hut, my rack pushed in the corner as far from everyone as I can get. Across from me is Larson from North Dakota; his mother's letters contain transcriptions of the sexual infidelities of the bitter Larson's wife. Next to Larson lives a hairy little Italian from New Jersey, who is desperately in love with our pregnant house girl.

The hut, Vermin Hole, has been like some mad melodrama lately. Howdy and Larson have become great friends with Tonto; every night they invite him to join them at the Punji Trap for a few beers. After the Trap closes, they bring him home. A loud discussion begins with Howdy's conviction that Indians are a blight upon this good earth and end with Larson's allusion to the death of Tonto's father while he lay drunk in a gutter. How they obtained this information and whether it's true is up for conjecture. I do know that threats fly back and forth as both sides grab up guns and knives. The Green Hornet's stereo, meanwhile, blares out, over and over, "The Saga of Billy and Sue." (Billy, at war, receives a "Dear John" letter from Sue; he thereupon rushes into certain death.) I recline upon my rack reading Montaigne's *Essays* and loftily ignore the conflict. The crisis finally subsides when Tonto collapses onto his cot in tears. Like the Indians of cliché, he cannot hold his liquor.

Everyone says his prayers and turns in. I drowse fitfully, kept awake by the rats clicking across a rafter over my head; a monstrous beast fell upon me one night, and my wild shriek of terror had everyone in the compound grabbing up his piece. And the ants stop to munch on me as they crawl over my body all through the night.

There had better be a mighty welcome when Kurtie comes marching home.

Relentlessly,

Kurt

Chloe dear,

Moritz strolled into my hut yesterday. His distaste for the environment antagonized my hoochmates, but he ignored them and came straight to the point. Did I prefer the Garbage Detail or would I rather return to ICU? Does a bear shit in the woods? Once he ascertained the falsehood of scuttlebutt apparently spread by a fat chief that I was happier as a janitor, Moritz moved fast; he collected recommendations from several doctors and went straight to the top.

Part of the problem has been the question of my status: patient or corpsman. As my ribs give me no trouble and my collarbone seems to be knitting, I have only two or three weeks before a return to the lines. One of the reasons I've put up with the bullshit of working is the hope they'll get used to my hanging around First Med; another is to assuage the feeling of cowardice at fearing the jungle, the Cong, and the mines, all of which appear imminent now.

Alf and I had lunch together today. He'd plucked his good friend Bernie off the paper-picking patrol immediately and had him placed on ICU, but had no desire to put me under a spotlight. That I'd been rather snappish with Bernie while doing janitor service had also put a distance between us. Anyway, we're friends again, especially as my unsettled position afforded everyone such diversion.

First of all, the commanding officer of First Med learned of my doing heavy work with a broken collarbone and severely reprimanded Chief Turkey for misusing a patient—corpsman or no. Although the debacle at Fever made no waves this far north, Chief Turkey blundered and tried to make his actions accountable by detailing my insubordination in the south. The

Medical Service Lieutenant was asked for his story and a court-martial appeared likely. A corpsman in Personnel peered under the cloak of secrecy and notified Alf of the conspiracy; Alf told Moritz and together with Bernie, Dr. Minter, and a marine major with a broken arm, they descended upon the CO. All hell broke out across the compound and I knew nothing about it.

So, temporary or not, I was welcomed aboard ICU. Not by everyone. Kraft put up a fuss, maintaining that he would never work with anyone so lacking in the social amenities. As Moritz is the power behind the throne, Kraft has been reassigned to the Protestant chaplain. Ostensibly, a second class I'd never heard tell of heads ICU; he's a ridiculous little man, seldom seen and nobody pays him much mind when he does turn up. I'll admit readily, however, to his devising an agreeable work schedule. Sixteen men are divided into four shifts. I work every other day from eight to eight.

The ward is newer, cleaner, and twice as large as ICU in Chu Lai. I am head machinist. Moritz didn't undergo all that hassle because of auld lang syne; no one else knows how to run the machines nor can they be bothered to learn.

But there is no gathering the rose without being pricked by the thorns.

Relentlessly,

Kurt

First Medical Battalion
Da Nang, Vietnam
31 March 67

Dear Mom,

I work on SICU now. A friend took a lot of trouble to get me the position, and with my foulest temper on instant recall, I seem to be trying to lose it. Sloth and ineptitude anger me. I snarl. The slothful and the inept dislike being snarled at. They protest. I'm too world-weary to care what anyone thinks. I try to be as agreeable as Mother always swore she'd have been if everyone would have left her alone.

I'm good at my job and I enjoy it. I work twelve hours

241

every other day: eight to eight with a three-hour break during the afternoons. Easy duty. I usually play basketball on my break. The guys accuse me of unnecessary roughness; they've obviously never played ball with hard-headed Cajuns.

After work, I attend the revels at our local spa: The Punji Trap. I used to play cards with my hoochmates, but I won every game. As I'm considered an obnoxious winner (see, I haven't changed at all!), the guys ganged up on me. They cared little who won, as long as I lost. I considered this unfair and quit playing cards. Now I usually grab a couple of beers, watch the night's movie for about ten minutes, and wander down to the wards to chat with wounded marines.

Today, my day off, I went to the beach across Da Nang. I returned this evening to help out on Triage. As Mother once said so elegantly about Ricky: "He can't sit still long enough to take a crap." If you'll pardon my French.

Love,

Kurt

First Medical Battalion
Da Nang, Vietnam
4 April 67

Chloe dear,

Every morning at seven Alf, Bernie, Moritz, and I meet for breakfast. The food in Da Nang is inexplicably bad; in Chu Lai, we enjoyed fine cuisine, and the cooks we complain about here are the same men we complimented there. Even the Kool-Aid tastes worse, and I should hardly have thought that possible.

I arrive on the ward at eight. First of all, I check the machines ignored by the night crew. They'd rather play pinochle or a rugged board game called Risk. (To win at Risk, one's pink, green, red, yellow, black, or blue army must destroy all the others. I always choose yellow and yellow always conquers the world.)

Secondly I check IV bottles. Intravenous fluids drip from quart bottles into veins, replacing liquids the body has lost. Proper procedure has IV fluids dripping at a steady rate. The night crew ignores the drip rates until the 0700 bustle; then, if they remember, they'll speed up or slow down the drips, according to the error. I've walked on ICU to find fluid pouring through the tube, missing the vein and forming a hematoma (a discolored bulge under the skin), or worse, an empty bottle, which signifies an air pocket within the vein that could, theoretically, kill the patient.

The lackadaisical attitude of the men appalls Moritz, too, but he says they're the best available outside Triage. "You ought to see the scumbags who work on the wards."

Unless we're busy, I get off at eight. I hustle over to the Punji Trap, buy a couple of beers, and go outside to watch the evening flick. Invariably, we watch Jerry Lewis, John Wayne, or Charlton Heston strut their stuff. After the movie, I grab a ringside seat for the fights. It's been blacks against whites lately. And then, as my granny would say, it's time for beddy-bye.

I live a rich, full life that will soon be over.

Relentlessly,

Kurt

First Medical Battalion
Da Nang, Vietnam
5 April 67

Arch,

When I was a patient with aching ribs, a good ole boy from east Texas told me his life story. He could hardly be ignored; he lay in a cot across the aisle and I lay on my back facing him for three days. A crew chief on a dust-off, Larry had been injured in the same crash that had killed his best buddy, a corpsman. And he had just received a "Dear John" letter from his wife. I gave him the sympathy he seemed to crave. And what thanks did I get? Larry tried to talk me into taking his buddy's place. I turned on my side and endured the pain.

That was in Chu Lai, however, when a productive, if indefinite, future seemed assured. After a week of picking up garbage of one sort or another in Da Nang, I went to see Larry.

"Kurt, I got a good man training with me now. Sorry."

Well, I tried. To tell you the truth, I was glad. Choppers

are spooky. You see nothing except the sky, unless you get next to the door; then you can see the treetops spinning below you. When I look, I'm prone to vertigo. As a member of the crew, I would often double as a guard and be forced to get next to the door and look down. I adjusted better as a garbageman.

I'd reconciled myself to a safe mediocrity when Larry dropped by the following day. His new corpsman had fucked up. While lowering Larry by an electric winch into a minefield so he could pick up two trapped gooks, the corpsman got distracted by a movement in some trees across the way. He lowered the winch too far. A mine exploded: One gook was badly injured and Larry took some light shrapnel.

"I can't trust him no more. Nobody else free I'd work with. You care to try it?"

"Okay," I said.

Mistake! I knew it the moment I agreed. Larry gave me little time to harbor regrets. He led me to his commanding officer. "No!" said the CO.

I begged, just for appearance's sake. The prick relented. My name was put on the "Volunteer Reserve" list.

I survived my first dust-off. Nothing to it. The fire fight had ended, the landing perimeter was well established, and the casualties suffered from relatively minor injuries. I never left the chopper; the troops handed in the wounded at one end of the flight, and I handed them out to the litter-bearers at the other. I was terrified, of course, but fear's an ingrained habit.

Med-evacs are rather interesting. The aircraft commander (an officer) and the PP pilot (a warrant officer) sit at dual controls in the glass bubble of the chopper. Behind the bubble is the main body of the craft, with an open door on either side. Between the doors are three litters stacked atop one another. Eight inches of floor space separates the litters and the open doors, providing a walkway for the corpsman. Behind the litters is a transmission (or bear bar) that connects with the main rotor. On either side of the bear bar is a canvas seat; two patients can sit on each seat. They call the area encompassing the seats "The Hell Hole."

Helicopters are fragile machines and extremely vulnerable to VC bullets, weather conditions, and mechanical errors, yet I've never heard of any of the men who constitute chopper crews refusing a mission, no matter how dangerous.

Larry and his buddies have told me some harrowing tales. For instance, Larry got shot down over Cambodia. Only he and the PP pilot survived the crash. They set off together for the coast. On the third day, they saw a troop of VC marching toward them. The two men separated, planning to flank the enemy by hiding in the jungle on either side of the trail and meeting after the Cong had passed. Larry made it, but the other guy never showed. Larry continued on and, aided by friendly villagers, tramped through the highlands for thirty-eight days before being directed to a Green Beret encampment.

Another time, Larry left his best friend, a corpsman, behind because of an overweighted chopper; in the heavy action, the corpsman was killed. And when Larry was broken up by the death of his friend and the "Dear John" letter from his wife, another buddy insisted upon going in first on a mission. Larry watched the chopper his buddy rode in explode, killing everyone aboard.

We sit over a few beers, and as Larry and his friends rattle off these tales, I tremble. What am I, some sort of masochist? These guys seem so matter-of-fact about their incredible courage. I've never felt less brave. How ever can you feel gallant crouching in a corner like a terrified rat? And after all this time, I should still like so much to picture myself on a huge black stallion, sabre raised, staring forward into a sea of wavering blue uniforms and shouting "CHARGE!" But it's the wrong pose and the wrong war. Even then, I should have been far in the rear, rallying the camp followers.

Relentlessly,

Kurt

FIRST MEDICAL BATTALION
DA NANG, VIETNAM
6 April 67

My dear Paul,

DA NANG: CITY WITHOUT WOMEN
And Seven Good Reasons for Living There.

1. EMPLOYMENT: Days pass fast on SICU. I arrive at work between 0730 and 0800, check IV bottles and the machines. The doctors make their rounds at 0830, when they designate which patients are to be flown out of Nam and which are to be transferred to the wards—few patients remain on ICU longer than overnight. We've got a good team and have admitted as many as sixty post-ops during a shift without fluster. Bernie takes down doctors' orders and injects narcotics. I set up the machinery, irrigate throats and stomachs, insert catheters, change IV bottles, run oxygen, change colostomy bags, and inject antibiotics. The other two corpsmen take TPR's and empty ducks, bedpans, and emesis basins. Either Bernie or I help the doctors change dressings. On occasion Alf will invite us into the OR to watch a surgery; the commander would disapprove, but most of the doctors seem to like our knowing what's going on, as long as we keep out of the way. Unless we're really busy, Bernie and I take a four-hour break from noon to four; the other two men on our shift take theirs in the evening.

A couple of amusing incidents last week. Bernie and I were alone on the ward with a dozen patients. As I took the blood pressure of an attractive grunt with a shattered leg, my crotch against his hand as I listened to his heartbeat, the dude groped me. I looked at him incredulously. He grinned, untied the string of my OR pajamas, pulled out my precious, and went down on me. My back was to Bernie, who appeared to be busily perusing nursing notes; the other patients seemed to be dozing. Later, when Bernie had gone to the shitter, I returned the favor.

"When ever did you start doing that?" I asked him.

"On perimeter watch with my sarge," he replied. "We all did."

I knew something was happening somewhere.

The following morning I made my penicillin rounds. (Every patient, unless allergic, gets four to six injections a day.) As I pulled the sheet away from a tall skinny jarhead from Sylacauga, Alabama, preparatory to injection, a fourteen-inch prick lunged up and the head smacked against his chest even with his nipples. Fourteen inches, at least. I paled, the jarhead blushed, and his buddies on either side guffawed.

2. LEISURE: I spend my free days at China Beach, a resort on the far side of Da Nang, which embraces a soda shop, a dormitory with two dozen bunks, and a huge, modern shower

room. The line companies rotate in-country R&R among their battle-weary troops. We swim in the warm water, play Frisbee, and enjoy long talks as we lay in the sand. As the boys are usually alone, it's devilishly easy for a sophisticated city slicker to strike up an acquaintance with the best-looking. At night the dorm is very dark. You'll drool over my photograph album.

During the days, I cruise the showers, which are used by everyone who uses the beach, and nearly a hundred thousand athletically-minded young men live in the area. Although I enjoy the rush hours with aesthetic detachment, I prefer the slower siesta time. I watch through the window for magnificent specimens who will catch me inflicting self-pleasure under the water. Embarrassment prevails for a moment or two, but where ever else can you do it? And a chat about our enforced celibacy leads as often as not to a quick upright of one sort or another. It's a sexual smorgasbord.

3. SHOPPING: I usually drop in at the PX down the road on my afternoon break. Should the johns at the library and the USO be quiet, I'll stock up on goodies and hit the movie palace. Should the movie be boring, I'll haunt the john there. I've yet to visit the PX without success of one sort or another, and believe me, I never take less than the best.

4. TRANSPORTATION: I travel everywhere by thumb. No one refuses to pick up someone standing alongside the road— except officers. Most of the time I'll hop onto the bed of a truck, but occasionally I'll ride in the cab. Should the driver strike my fancy, I'll pull out tales of my R&R in Sydney. (Thanks to Steve, I need never go there.) As often as not, the driver gets hot and bothered, so I help him out as best I can.

Steve and I enjoyed a pleasant day at China Beach last weekend. He was flying to Cam Ranh Bay that afternoon, so I went to the airport to see him off. Looking around, I noticed several lovely things waiting for flights which wouldn't be leaving until the next day. Just for a change, I decided to camp out at the terminal. Two out of three ain't bad.

5. SOCIAL LIFE: Not only do I make many new acquaintances, but I continually renew old ones. A Marlboro man from the showers at China Beach came to interrogate a Vietnamese amputee with a touch of the pink. An Arrow Collar ad who'd been aggressively insatiable in the dorm one night came through ICU with a bullet hole through his lung. And a "Navy Wants You" poster I'd wrestled with in the library tearoom turned out

247

to be a doctor from one of the Battalion-Aid stations. I respected their silent pleas for anonymity, but I dislike the hysterical faggot part of me having an address known to the lavender lads.

6. ATHLETICS: Once a week I stand duty at the med-evac chopper pad near the air base from noon to midnight. The hard-living chopper crews play baseball for recreation and one afternoon I was asked to stand in for a recently deceased warrant officer. The chopper crews recognized a professional; they marveled loudly and I was an instant celebrity.

I made two chopper runs that evening and decided to stay over. I joined the crew for a few beers and several stories in one of the huts. Ten men were jammed together under the blue haze of cigar smoke. My second baseman that day had played with grace and agility, and we struck up a friendship as we complimented each other. The watch ordered "Lights Out" at midnight. We continued to drink and talk and in the dark, I made subtle contact with my second baseman. (He wore shorts; I lay my head in his lap, his resultant erection protruded through his fly—come to think of it, I guess "subtle" might be too mild a word.) Still, I was surprised when he followed me outside for fresh air and a pee. As our streams of urine intersected, he said quietly, "I'd sure dig fucking your ass, Pretty Boy." No sooner said than done.

I bunked that night in my crew chief's corner. I used the guilt Larry feels about the death of his previous corpsman to get him to admit to wondering what it was like. So I showed him.

7. FUTURE: I returned Sunday from twenty-four hours of lust in the sand to find a note on my cot. "The CO wants to see you in his office. STAT." When I reported, he saw me immediately. He wanted to know why I'd never told him about my uncle, the marine general. My uncle, the marine general? "Oh, my uncle, the marine general," I said. "He despises nepotism."

"The general flew in yesterday from Okinawa just to see you."

"Oh, really? I'm sorry I wasn't here."

"He waited for three hours. I dispatched half the Motor Pool in an attempt to find you."

I was drained by an especially successful night and just not up to pretending that I knew what the hell was going on when

248

I hadn't the slightest idea, although after seven months of doing just that, you'd think it would be second nature. I knew for certain that my Uncle Carl, the commander, wouldn't masquerade as a marine general; furthermore, he'd never come within a thousand sea miles of danger.

This new uncle put me in a perplexity, but in the normal confusion of my existence, I forgot about it until today. A marine came on ICU wearing a full dress uniform—you know, those blue trousers with the pretty red stripes down the sides. He handed me a letter:

> *Wm. Kurt Strom, HM3, USN:*
>
> You and I have a mutual friend in Captain Timothy Fallon. Tim insisted that I get in touch with you, so I'd be honored to have you as my guest for a few days. I've arranged a seat aboard a flight for Okinawa on 1 May 67 and will meet you when the plane lands at Kadena Air Force Base.
>
> Have a pleasant flight. I will be looking forward to meeting you.
>
> > *Yours very truly,*
> >
> > *Vincent M. Santucci, Lt. USMC*

The only Tim I know in the military is a lieutenant stationed in Charleston, South Carolina. Someone could have sneaked a look at my wallet in Saigon or at China Beach, but that seems doubtful. I can recall no Marine Corps general among my tricks.

The world uncertain comes and goes.

> *Relentlessly,*
>
> *Kurt*

Dear Mom,

DT has never replied to my queries concerning my savings account, so I had Guy Perrone confront him. DT swore to Guy that he knew nothing about the fifteen thousand. Guy wrote that I had no case unless I had a receipt for the loan. How could I, when Mother just took the money? I have nothing. No money. No case.

You know of Mother's deathbed wish: Karen was to get the silver, the jewelry, the car, and the wedding ring from Daddy. We boys were to split among us the twelve thousand Mother got for our house in town when she sold it to marry DT. Otherwise, she wrote no will. Neil says that DT pleads ignorance of the ring, nor does he know what happened to the twelve thousand. "Your mother bought some expensive furniture."

Daddy worked all those years in the coal mines to earn that money.

DT pleads poverty because of hospital and funeral expenses: Neil will have to work his way through college. Mother carried hospital insurance and Grandpa DeBarard paid for Mother's funeral. "My son was a worthless alcoholic. Phyllis made a man of him."

Mother certainly didn't marry DT for his looks. No wonder he sees her ghost.

Love,

Kurt

Chloe dear,

We've had two shipments of fresh corpsmen within the past month. Consequently, we have plenty of hands; unfortunately, few use them. I don't mind drudge work: emptying smelly

bottles of blood or stomach contents, ducks of urine, and bedpans of shit. I just get irritated when the toadies sit around for
hours with coffee cups in their hands.

The worst of them is Winthrop, the only corpsman on the
compound besides me who has been on the lines. One day
when Winthrop was absent, a VC ambush wiped out his entire
company. He refused to return to the lines, and after he spent
some time on the psychiatric ward, they allowed him to remain
at the Med Battalion.

When I first came to work on ICU, Winthrop swooped down
upon me; he'd heard I was queer for reading.

"Wow, Kurt. It's just great to find somebody else who
reads. You know how it was on the lines. There's nobody to
talk with. God, it was terrible. My entire company was wiped
out, you know! Man, I couldn't go back out there. My head
was really fucked up, you know! Wow, it's so good to talk to
somebody else who digs philosophy, you know!"

I'm fairly certain that Nietzsche was German and Plato was
Greek, but beyond that, my knowledge of philosophy runs an
indifferent course. Nevertheless, after all those people who
thought I resorted to books from boredom, I found Winthrop
refreshing. He made frequent references to my sensitivity and
my wit. Coming from the scion of a Pilgrim family and a
sometime student at Wesleyan, it was all very gratifying.

Physically, Winthrop stands out among the proletariat. Bull-
dogs have pedigrees, too, and Winthrop greatly resembles one.
He has a huge, wrinkled head and a squat, thickly flabbed
body. You would never court damnation, gentle cuz, lusting
after Winthrop.

I have yet to see him soil his stubby fingers with work.
Winthrop is cultivating a mustache and lives for morning sick
call, so he can corner a doctor who owns a magnificent specimen to chat man-to-man about waxes. I'd already begun to
back off from his companionship; he had just one basic line.
All day I would hear him terrifying the newer men with the
traumas of the lines. "My entire company was wiped out, you
know!" By this time, I knew.

Then a shot-up grunt came through. As I was the only
corpsman who went near him, he started up a conversation.
During our talk, he pointed at Winthrop and asked if the bulldog
was any good at his job. I said I didn't know; I'd never seen
him working at it. The grunt told me that Winthrop had been

251

in his company on the lines. He'd finagled out of patrols by feigning illness and rejected overtures of friendship by the grunts in favor of courting the officers. For all that, buddy of the captain or not, Winthrop was finally forced to go on patrol. A mile down the trail, Winthrop sat down in the middle of the path and refused to budge. Four marines dragged him back to camp. The captain had him admitted to the nut ward and asked for a replacement.

I observed that some people have less nerve and more imagination than others and it's easy to make unfair judgments; then, too, Winthrop might have the gift of second sight. "After he left, his entire company was wiped out, you know?"

The jarhead giggled. "Is that what he tells you, Doc? Heck, yesterday was the first action we've seen in four months."

Winthrop has been in-country only two months. "Hey, Winthrop, here's a man from your old company."

The bulldog walked over, said "Hello," and skedaddled away as soon as he could. I doubt that I'll hear any more about his entire company getting wiped out, you know!

Relentlessly,

Kurt

FIRST MEDICAL BATTALION
DA NANG, VIETNAM
12 April 67

Arch,

I check through the logbook in Triage every once in a while, looking for the names of corpsmen and marines I know. I've run across a couple of dozen among the pages and pages of names which fill the thick tome. And written over and over is that hideous Vietnamese word: DOA. (Dead on Arrival.)

A patient came through the ward the other day. He'd been shot in the abdomen. As his kidney had been irreparably damaged, the surgeon performed a nephrectomy. I fished the kidney out of the garbage can, borrowed a microscope from the lab and, aided by Bernie, dissected it. We kept up a running commentary so that the patient could hear; his interest was even greater than ours. His surgeon caught us in the act, and old

Fishlips seemed indignant. He reported us to the CO; Bernie and I were confined to base for the weekend. We spent Sunday together at China Beach. What ever can they do to punish us? Send us to Nam?

Fishlips has always been a creep. A week after he'd arrived in Chu Lai, he put in a request that a corpsman be assigned to him: to wash his clothes, polish his boots, make his bed . . . The request was denied. Although in Da Nang we have Vietnamese girls who act as maids, everybody on the compound despises the Nazi bastard.

The All-American golden boy came through the ward yesterday, a former lifeguard and surfer dreaming of becoming a forest ranger, an extremely handsome guy with blond hair, blue eyes, a square chin, and well-developed chest and arms. Everything below a stomach rippling with muscles was blown away.

The boy gave me two letters to mail; I took them by the shitter to read. He'd written to his parents and had asked that they withdraw his savings and buy him a cabin in the mountains; he wanted no one to see his mutilation. In the other letter, he wrote to his girl and broke their engagement. I threw the letters away. Why trouble the folks at home? Within a week or two, he'll die of a massive infection or a renal shutdown. His folks will receive a telegram: DIED OF WOUNDS RECEIVED IN ACTION. That's succinct and sufficient.

One of the more decent doctors broke down on ICU yesterday. A couple of weeks ago, Dr. Minter treated a boy with a wounded leg. The boy begged Minter to send him home. He'd already served eleven months of combat duty; all of his buddies were dead. Minter declined. He patched the boy up and sent him back to the lines. Yesterday the boy stepped on a mine, and Minter removed that same leg. He cried for an hour.

The mountains are in labor; a ridiculous mouse will be born.

Relentlessly,

Kurt

Dear Mom,

I hesitate before asking this, but have you decided to marry earlier than you planned because you have to? Haven't we had enough of that in our family? Shame on you.

As I write this, I'm sprawled across my bed and sipping a thimbleful of the Southern Comfort your Mr. Hebner so thoughtfully provided me. A little Vietnamese woman washes my clothes outside, chattering gaily with the other girls while they listen to the jabberwocky of a Vietnamese soap opera on the radio. (Their soap operas are really that: The performers sing of their troubles.) Kee also polishes my boots, makes my bed, and sweeps the dust from my little corner of the hut. I pay her the regulation fee of four dollars a month.

The mess hall prepares our meals with less concern for the palate than we observed in Chu Lai. As the same chefs serve us, I shall blame the water.

Unlike the massive attacks by insects in the jungle, the local bugs stage lonely kamikaze missions, which usually end in their annihilation.

I wish I could be there to cry at your wedding. Remember: The third time is the charm.

Love,

Kurt

FIRST MEDICAL BATTALION
DA NANG, VIETNAM
14 April 67

My dear Paul,

New perversion: I was alone on the ward the other evening while the other corpsmen ate supper. One of the patients lay unconscious, with his muscular arm hanging over the edge of the bed. His hand clenched and unclenched in his pain. You'll never guess what I inserted within that clenching fist. To be fair, I rewarded him; even in their pain, they erect, although ejaculation comes hard. As I read over his chart to learn who he was, I noted that his surgeon had marked down "Continue penicillin injections for gonorrheal infection." When Bernie finally drifted in from supper, I ran down to the shitter. In a darkness that nearly defeated me, I shook my little bottle of penicillin, drew it into a syringe, and injected myself in the thigh. I try not to be superstitious, but Somebody's always watching.

I got orders today concerning my transfer back to Echo. My immediate reaction was dread; then I allowed a long-latent curiosity about Pinkerton and McGrath to surface—I'd enjoy seeing them again. And who knows what adventures lay before me? Yet I've seen so many mangled marines. What little enthusiasm I could muster was damped by the clerk who brought me the orders. He told me that fewer than three hundred of the eight hundred corpsmen with whom I left Lejeune still remain in Nam; the rest have been wounded or killed.

Late yesterday afternoon, Don and Steve walked onto ICU to invite me to the air base for supper. I went to ask a bulldog-faced corpsman who owes me if he'd fill in for the evening. He refused. I beckoned Steve and Don into Winthrop's hooch. With a hearty man-to-man approach, the two officers cajoled him into working. Winthrop was unctuously servile. He even tried to invite himself along.

We drove to the BOQ, where Steven had stashed an extra uniform in his room and, as a captain, I ate and drank far too much. After yet another superfluous Scotch, Steve insisted that I accept a couple of presents: a watch that set him back $150 and a solid silver St. Christopher's medal. (I had them appraised by a corpsman who had been apprenticed to a jeweler.)

"Going-away presents?" I asked.

Steve looked sad. "I suppose they'll have to be. I wish they were coming-back presents."

Don was dumbfounded by such generosity, but he brightened and said, "I've got a little present for Kurtie baby, too." He pulled a water pistol from his pocket, siphoned the rest of his vodka and tonic into it, and squirted me in the face; then he gently laid the pistol in front of me. Steve watched in bewilderment.

We deserted a protesting Don soon after and returned to the BOQ, where we enjoyed a couple of hours of bliss. I was awakened by a tapping on the door. I extricated myself from

Steve, who was asleep, and pulled on my pants. The tapping stopped, but I was worried. I unlocked the door and padded down the hall. Don opened the door to my knock; he had just gotten back from the officers' club and was reeling with drink. Yes, he had tapped. "No, don't go." He rooted through his flight bag for some Scotch, stuck a cigar in my mouth, and fell back on his bunk, where we passed the bottle back and forth as we traded war stories. The stories led to thoughts of friends robbed of their youth. We fell into a melancholy mood and, subsequently, into each other's arms.

Don passed out, his arm cradling my head. I loved the sensation, but I've never been able to sleep in that position; I just get randy. I lay there for an hour, thoroughly absorbed in Don's proximity, but I had to disengage myself and get back to Steve. It was four in the morning by my new watch. I padded down the hall once more, hoping that I could remember which of the rooms Steve was in. As people around here sleep with .45's under their pillows, an error in judgment could get my head blown off. I crossed my fingers and tip-toed into a pitch-black cubicle. I sniffed the man in the bed. I'd know that soft, clean, freshly ironed smell anywhere. I crawled in beside him.

"Where have you been?" Steve's hard voice lashed out of the darkness.

"The john."

"For three hours?"

I lay silent. Steve sat up and lighted a cigarette. I felt terrible. Besides the beginning of a gargantuan hangover, I was about to lose Steve, and losing him, I'd gain back the feeling that I should walk alone, tinkle a little bell, and cry "Unclean! Unclean!"

"Who were you with?"

"Don."

"Oh, Jesus, Kurt! You didn't try anything with him? He'll turn you in like a shot."

"I doubt it."

"What do you mean? What did you do?"

"Got fucked."

"Damn. Damn it to hell."

Steve said nothing more, so I drifted off to sleep. He woke me at dawn. He was already dressed. I grabbed my shirt and boots, and we tip-toed to Don's room to get my pants. They were on the bed under Don, and as I pulled them free, Don woke up and murmured drowsily, "Ah, Kurtie baby, good-bye. Good-bye." He pulled my face into his armpit. "Before you go..." He pulled the sheet away from himself. "Before you go..." He pushed my head down with one arm and covered his eyes with the other. I looked at Steve, who was standing in the doorway. He was looking at me. As I set to work on Don, Steve shut the door behind him and moved to the bed to watch. Don arched his back. "Ah, Kurtie, so-o-o good." Steve unzipped his flight suit, pulled out an erect cock, straddled Don's chest, pinned Don's arms with his legs, grabbed the struggling major's head, and pumped his mouth furiously. As Don had given me a very sore asshole, I proceeded to return the favor.

> "Drink now and love, Democrates: for we
> Shall not have wine and boys eternally."

Relentlessly,

Kurt

First Medical Battalion
Da Nang, Vietnam
18 April 67

Arch,

Last night the hueys on duty were bringing in a tremendous number of casualties from a battle south of Da Nang. A call came in from the north; a single platoon had established contact with the VC. Several wounded required evacuation.

We could see the problem from the air. The platoon held the top of a rocky hill; a company of VC held the bottom. The VC were making a mighty effort to gain the top of the hill. In this game of Risk, I would bet on yellow.

It seemed impossible to settle in and pick up the casualties. I felt sorry for the poor suckers, but I was grateful when my pilots retreated from the conflict. *Better them than me.* I was horrified when my pilots swung in to recklessly attempt a landing. Ping. Ping. The chopper was dead.

We landed hard, but the chopper didn't explode. Shaken, we jumped out to reconnoiter our situation as refugees. Coming up the hillside was a wild-eyed horde spurred on by a saffron

Satan. As Larry, my crew chief, put it, "We're in a world of shit!" We clambered among the rocks to get the feel of the place. The grunts seemed glad to see us—the more the merrier. Their corpsman handled his casualties with adequacy; they had no need of me. Yet I found it difficult to say good-bye.

I should like to brag of my grace under pressure as a remnant of good guys held off the Golden Horde. I should treasure a film of my old expertise at fielding bunts called into play as I scooped newly arrived grenades off the rocks and fired them into the VC with shattering accuracy. I should prefer to hear a nation's applauding my valor, my heroism, and my gallantry.

But fantasy must give way to reality, and as Mother always said, "Truth is best." Five minutes after our forced landing, a battalion of grunts emerged from the jungle, the Cong retreated, I crawled from under a rock, and choppers came to remove us from the field of battle. Your correspondent, Gentle Kurt, remains alive and in one piece.

But death has a thousand doors to let out life. I shall find one.

Relentlessly,

Kurt

FIRST MEDICAL BATTALION
DA NANG, VIETNAM
19 April 67

Dear Mom,

What the devil is happening back there? I got a note from Ricky with the letterhead "The Arkansas Military Academy." He says he's a prisoner there. What ever is he doing in Arkansas?

I want to know what's happening. No more secrets like Mother's illness.

Arkansas!

I feel so helpless.

Love,

Kurt

Chloe dear,

General Walt or General Westmoreland or General Patton or General Rommel (I'm uncertain just who is in charge around here) has taken over a civilian project and made it military. They call the project CAP: Combined Action Platoon. At first they called it Combined Action Company, but CAC means penis in Vietnamese. The zips loved the name; nonetheless, the designation was changed. General Walt or whoever didn't want his men referred to as a bunch of pricks.

Fifty groups of twelve to twenty men will be dropped into remote villages of VC sympathizers. These groups have three objectives:

1. To kill VC.
2. To train the local militia, the Popular Forces, to kill VC.
3. To bribe the villagers into killing VC.

A young, enthusiastic sergeant will lead each unit. The Vietnamese dislike officers—they believe all officers to be corrupt, so our leader is Sergeant Pinkerton, who had been Echo Company's guide.

Pinkerton has no idea why he was chosen for CAP. As he had two months left in Nam, he has had to extend for six more months of overseas duty. The sarge feels the extra $65 a month he earns as combat pay makes the extension worthwhile; besides, in December, his enlistment will be completed.

Pinkerton was to have carte blanche in choosing his platoon from the volunteers in Echo, pending the colonel's approval. And thereby hangs a sad tale. As everyone respects Pinkerton, he was able to fill his quota with the best men in the company. The colonel refused to approve the list; he countered with his own: a dozen douche bags inadequate professionally and socially. The sarge was left in a quandary. Although he could have complained to higher brass, such presumption is frowned upon by the Marine Corps. McGrath offered to plant a mine under the colonel's private outhouse, but Pinkerton hates scenes. He compromised. If he could choose six of la crème de la crème, he would accept six dregs. So be it.

I was a bit blue to arrive at Echo only to learn that my best buddies were leaving the company; then I discovered that the unit included a corpsman and . . . "I held the doc spot open as long as I could," said Pinkerton. "McGrath and I think you're a shitbird, but we wanted you for the doc and figured you might want to volunteer. You go tell the chief you want to come with us."

I flew to Battalion Headquarters. The chief sat in the medical tent, drinking coffee and playing solitaire. "About time you're back, Strom. The other corpsmen have had to pick up your slack while you been fucking around."

"I want to volunteer for CAP."

"Blane's going with CAP."

"Who's Blane?"

"New man. Good corpsman. He'll do the job for that outfit."

"But Pinkerton said he wanted me."

"Blane's going. Better get some shut-eye. You'll be humpin' the trail come morning."

I returned to Echo and repeated the chief's words. Pinkerton got angry. "That asshole," he said. He tore off for Battalion Headquarters; McGrath and I followed. The chief had begun a new game of solitaire. "Chief, I told you I wanted Doc for CAP."

The chief never looked up. "Strom wasn't here to volunteer. Blane was."

"I choose the men for my outfit."

The chief sighed and played a red seven on a red eight. "I'm responsible for the corpsmen in Second Battalion; Blane goes with CAP, and Strom stays here."

"I want Doc."

I felt good, being fought over like that.

"What the hell is this? You queer for Strom or something? He ain't that hot a corpsman. Remember how he fucked over that man with the leech up his dong?"

I didn't feel so good anymore.

"If he ain't that hot, why do you want to keep him here? He's the best damn doc you got and you know it." The chief snorted. Pinkerton continued. "And I asked two doctors at the Battalion-Aid station about that leech and they didn't know what the fuck Doc should have done neither."

I felt better.

"Blane goes and Strom stays. You don't like it, take it up with the colonel."

Pinkerton lacks finesse at getting around the immovable object. I've had more experience. I remember Mama. "You've got a red seven on a red eight, Chief," I said. He slowly digested that piece of information. "Chief, I don't have to take your shit. I saw my Uncle Carl, the commander, while I was home. He said he'd be glad to arrange for my transfer back to First Med anytime I wanted it."

The chief looked at me. "Strom, I am highly unimpressed by your Uncle Carl, the commander. I don't even believe there is such a person."

Frankly, I'm unimpressed by Uncle Carl, too; nevertheless, as I told the chief, he exists. The chief played another card, looked up at us, and sighed. "Strom, even if there is such a person and even if he does get you transferred, it takes a lot of time to go through the channels and to complete all the paperwork. In the meantime, I will work your ass off, and that's a promise."

Well, you can't win them all. Pinkerton and I turned to go, but McGrath just stood leaning on his rifle. He was grinning. "Hey, Chief."

"What do you want?"

"I know you ain't easily impressed and all, but when we go to Chu Lai next week, we're going to be briefed by General Walt hisself. When he asks us if we have any questions, I'm going to ask him why some ugly fuck of a chief is allowed to demoralize a CAP unit by pushing an inexperienced corpsman on it. And there's liable to be correspondents and civilian brass, and a question like that ain't gonna make the general happy." Pinkerton and I looked at McGrath in disbelief.

The chief sighed again; then he pushed the cards together in a pile. "Okay. Blane stays and Strom goes. But I sure as hell hope all three of you get your asses greased."

On the trail back to Echo, I asked McGrath if General Walt was really going to brief us. McGrath chuckled. "How the fuck should I know? I doubt it. Probably just some chickenshit telephone colonel. I made it up. I couldn't let my buddies down."

A hair perhaps divides the false and true.

Relentlessly,

Kurt

My dear Paul,

When I arrived in no-man's-land, a dear familiar face shone out from amidst the tents and the dust; McGrath was stringing wire around the captain's proposed chicken run. (The colonel apparently likes omelets.) McGrath let out a Rebel yell, grabbed my travel bag, and dragged me to his tent. Pinkerton joined us, and after the proper condolences (Remember Mother?), the sarge pulled several cans of warm beer out of his footlocker that he'd saved for my homecoming; I pulled two fifths of Scotch out of my travel bag that I'd brought for them. We mixed the liquids into some potent boilermakers. As I took my first sip, Pinkerton hit me with a bombshell. "Doc, you're just in time. McGrath and me are leaving the battalion forever."

O break my heart. Good-bye my fancy. Were I only more noble Roman than tacky queen . . . I casually inquired about their destination. My buddies jubilantly explained that Pinkerton had been put in charge of a platoon that would administer aid to Vietnamese civilians and terrorize the VC. I dragged myself over to the clerk's tent to report in before I was too drunk, and I planned to get very drunk. I stopped by the corpsmen's tent to change from my khakis into my jungle greens. My belongings were nowhere to be seen.

"What ever happened to my seabag? My sleeping bag? My tape recorder? My books?"

A fat, blond, smelly turd sneered. "Hell, we left all that shit back at the last camp. Ain't nobody here got the time to mess with all that shit. The VC are probably wiping their asses with your fucking books." He waddled out of the tent.

This was certainly not my day.

Queenie was redecorating his corner of the tent; the yellow and green scheme was being changed to red and lavender. He greeted me more cordially. "Don't worry, Kurt. Pinkerton and McGrath brought your stuff up. I stashed it in the medical tent to keep everything dry."

I thanked him and ran back to Pinkerton and McGrath to thank them, too.

"It was a hassle, Doc," admitted Pinkerton, "but we knew

how much you loved those old books. We figured you'd go traipsing into the jungle to look for them." (They overestimate my love of literature.) "So we divided them up, and all the guys in the platoon carried some. Now, listen, Doc. How'd you like to do something for us? Go over to Battalion and volunteer for our unit. We're supposed to have a doc, and we was hoping you'd be back in time to go with us."

The chief proved rather difficult about my leaving his jurisdiction, which surprised me; I'd been certain he disliked me.

"He does, Kurt," said Queenie. "He told me that you'd caused a great deal of trouble for an old friend of his. A chief. He wanted to make you pay for it. I'm glad you're leaving. I've always liked you, no matter what everybody else thought."

Late that night Pinkerton, McGrath, and I were singing "Red River Valley" for the third time when the VC sent in a mortar barrage that killed three men. Pinkerton pushed through a drunken haze to get to his duty station, but McGrath and I were too embalmed to do anything but tumble into an empty bunker. It was all arms and legs and roving hands for a minute or so, but shit, Paul, I had to stop. I could hardly do anything so base, not with a buddy.

I'm happy to say that McGrath had no such scruples.

Relentlessly,

Kurt

China Beach
Da Nang, Vietnam
25 April 67

Arch,

Most of the old faces remained at Echo, some new faces, a few missing: Sambo was transferred, Lieutenant Donlevy killed, my replacement lost a leg to a mine . . .

I stayed at Echo only long enough for a cup of coffee. The Marine Corps is developing a program in which they send a dozen or so grunts and a corpsman into a village out in the boondocks to teach the Vietnamese to appreciate American ways and be less zippy. And you know me—easily bored, always ready for something new . . .

We left Echo this morning and neither the colonel nor our

captain bothered to see us off. We were hardly surprised; no one expected them to show good form. Pinkerton commandeered a truck, which dropped us off near the air base, and we sat in the dust alongside the road all morning, watching zillions of slopes bicycle past. Pinkerton searched in vain for someone with authority, but was passed from office to office. When he returned in a mild despair to where we sweltered under a hot sun, I suggested we thumb over to China Beach and bivouac there.

So I write this, leaning against a tall palm and watching my new comrades frolic in the waves.

As I understand it, my duties will include caring for ailing jarheads (something new?) and treating the local populace for their injuries and illnesses. I lack training for this sort of thing, but I've come to regard doctoring as a combination of common sense and swift reactions.

We'll be living with the village militia. I hope none of the village militia are Viet Cong. I've treated both in my time and they look the same. They don't wear white hats and black hats in the Wild Wild East.

Relentlessly,

Kurt

CHINA BEACH
DA NANG, VIETNAM
26 April 67

Dear Mom and Pops,

As I write this, I am imagining your clicking castanets on the beach at Ipanema, or dancing the tango at the Cocacabana with a rose between your teeth. Or is that done in Mexico? Or the Argentine? Wherever, I know you are enjoying your exotic adventures.

I regret being unable to attend your nuptials. Was the wedding pretty? Karen wrote of her distress at missing the services. I'd throw some rice around over here, but I'd probably be inundated by three thousand starving zips.

At the moment, I am lying on China Beach. The sun shines, the water is warm, and the company is congenial.

I've been transferred to a platoon that will move into a Vietnamese village to live with the people and improve their lifestyle. Or so goes the brochure. My duties will include providing medical services for the villagers. I pity them. My cures may well be worse than their diseases.

Love,

Kurt

CHINA BEACH
DA NANG, VIETNAM
27 April 67

My dear Paul,

I'll miss the colonel. He had deficiencies of personality, character, courage, and judgment, but he was a lean, steel-eyed father figure. My friend Alf told me to forget the colonel. He had observed that I had much to admire in my little CAP unit. He issued a few words of unwelcome advice. "Think of CAP as a monastery, and you have just taken the veil."

My fellow monks have passed the days we've bivouacked at China Beach lolling in the surf. I'd never seen most of them without their scungy greens, and I've spent pleasant hours ranking them in order of sexiness. There is good news: Half the men are humpy. And there is bad news: Half of them are not. Actually, I suppose I must grade on the curve. Although all of the men have bronzed faces, chests, and arms, most are fishbelly white from the waist down. And everyone's feet look diseased.

A chickenshit telephone colonel came to lecture us today, accompanied by a couple of aides, each toting a case of beer. (A telephone colonel is a lieutenant colonel and ranks below a full colonel, yet answers a telephone with "This is Colonel So and So.") Colonel So and So sent the aides back to the jeep and, letting his hair down, opened a beer for himself. The buddy-buddy method. We drank in a spirit of subservient conviviality, while Colonel So and So lectured us on the ayes and nays of CAP.

DO: Bang down hard on the VC.
     Treat the villagers with respect.
     Conduct yourselves as U.S. Marines.
DON'T: Fuck the women.
     Trust anyone.
     Fuck the women.
     Belittle the Popular Forces (the village militia).
     Fuck the women.
     Trust anyone.
     Fuck the women.

I am to live in a remote encampment with some very horny marines who are specifically ordered to refrain from fucking women. Let's hear it for Colonel So and So.

Relentlessly,

Kurt

CHINA BEACH
DA NANG, VIETNAM
28 April 67

Chloe dear,

I shall be competing with witch doctors for five months. Waxen effigies of me with pins sticking into them will be thrown into fires and rivers. I have no protection beyond my solid silver St. Christopher's medal and *The Country Doctor's Medical Companion.* I plan to bury all cuttings from my hair and fingernails.

My friend Moritz at the Med Battalion tried to help me disguise myself as a powerful medicine man by sending me out with one of the doctors who holds sick call in a local hamlet. I learned only negatives. The doctor, a hearty chap, stood back and jawed with his driver, while a couple of corpsmen indiscriminatley handed out aspirin and Band-Aids to the entire populace, many of whom went through the line several times.

How ever would I hold sick call? I returned to ICU and told Moritz that there had to be a better way. What was it? Moritz had no idea. And I had been given no medical supplies. At last, a challenge Moritz could delight in. He stripped ICU and

266

bundled everything in sheets and pillowcases. I hid the contraband in the chapel.

A bit of bad luck. One of the men came to me with complaints of headaches, lethargy, and depression. He had yellow skin and yellow eyes. As he also had yellow hair, I found it easy to deduce that he was not Oriental. He'll be on a medical ward for a month or two with hepatitis. So we set out tomorrow for the Great Beyond, and I am the thirteenth man.

Relentlessly,

Kurt

PART FOUR

✪ ✪ ✪

THE BOY WHO PICKED THE BULLETS UP

The boy who picked the bullets up, Destiny's child
In whose blood flows the memory of an exiled
Father, now aspires to new stature of his own
And prefers bed curtains to the drapes of the throne.
His soft features, his exquisite face, were not made
To lead a Nation or to storm a barricade!
His toys are all forgotten, now he only dreams
Of things that are forbidden; from his face he seems
Overcome by an immense desire to grab it.
"Poor young man, I hear he has a certain habit!"

—ARTHUR RIMBAUD

My dear Paul,

It all began that season one fine day
In Chu Lai where upon the beach I lay,
Bags beside me and ready to depart
With a dozen jarheads, devout in heart
To Mom and God and Pie and M'rine Corps creeds,
For Bou Bou Phu, Vietnam, to do great deeds.
By talking with these grunts about the trip,
I soon was one of them in fellowship.
We rose up early and we picked our way
To Bou Bou Phu, as you have heard me say.
  But nonetheless, while I have time and space,
Before my story takes a further pace,
It seems a reasonable thing to say
What their condition was, their dull array.
And with the sarge, I think I should begin,
My sexy sergeant with the easy grin
From the Panhandle in far West Texas
Home of cowboys, LBJ, and Mexes.
  Great Granddad began the family ranch
Near Abilene, a town called Thorny Branch.
At six, Duane climbed on a leather saddle
And learned to ride, rope, whoop, and herd cattle.
Fifteen, he broke his arm while cattle branding;
At sixteen, he popped his cherry standing
With a hot-eyed migrant señorita;
His friends did, too; a fad they found neat. A
Hero on the fields of South Pecos High,
His All-State style dazzled every eye.
He ran the mile, swam, quarter-backed, shortstopped,
Played forward, threw javelins, and sock hopped.
He learned at A&M to cuss and drink;
He studied agriculture, but he didn't like to think.
So he wed the Yellow Rose of Thorny Branch.

271

They kissed, they hugged, they settled down to ranch.
They made three sons: Duane Junior, Bill, and Joe;
Duane Junior's five. Sarge yearns to watch them grow.

   My cowboy's hips are lean, his shoulders wide,
Legs slightly bowed, dark skinned, brown haired, blue eyed.
Cute ass, a dick that's tiny when limber.
(Trees that give sweet fruit need not be timber.)

   His best buddy is Corporal McGrath,
A stealthy panther on the jungle path.
Keen eyes, sharp ears, taut body, hand steady,
McGrath's fond of danger, always ready
To aim his piece with deadly precision.
He kills with glee; lacking inhibition,
He'll shoot niggers, commies, fairies, and zips.

   His shoulders, like his drawl, are broad. His hips
Are narrow. His face is fineboned and scarred
Slightly by ancient acne—not so hard
To look at, by golly. Golden hair
Gilds his head, chest, wrists, legs, and elsewhere.
I've had hand-to-hand combat with his prick;
It's long and spongy, succulent and thick.

   Hardly to my taste is the corkscrew dick
Of the Third Squad leader, Gary Frick.
I have been told, and I believe that such
Mutation comes from jerking off too much.
Perhaps so; it's a solitary sport.
And he keeps to himself, I must report.
Thin as a rule, quiet, a trifle square,
Innumerable freckles, dark-red hair,
He often speaks of tractors, derricks, cranes,
Buzz saws, cement, hammers, lumber, and planes.
Now this can be boring, as I have found,
But he's a handy man to have around.

   The man who adds to CAP a bit of class,
Schooled at Dartmouth and something of an ass,
Herndon's a Virginia aristocrat,
And a captain's son, frat rat, Navy brat.
He hates to listen, but he loves to talk.
He stomps with every step—a clumpy walk;
Otherwise he's gorgeous: hair strawberry,
Eyes blue, muscles rippling, softly hairy.
A nasty, hostile, secret guy, and vain.

Inside him, I feel hidden pools of pain.
He says people bore him with what they say.
Will I learn what ever turned Dorian gray?

  The man with whom I'll probably most pal
Is our translator/liaison LaSalle.
Trilingual—speaking English, French, and Zip,
He's pleasant, if distant, witty and hip.
He's pale, with dark hair and a soft deep voice.
I'd make it with him if given the choice,
Which would hardly be the case with LaSalle
And his long dong. Ah, *mon cher, c'est trop mal.*
He's from Vermont, but knows his way around.
He talks of Picasso and Proust and Pound,
Of Gustav Mahler and Gertrude Stein—a
Handsome bon vivant in Indo-China.

  Simpler and far less sophisticated
Is Barry, whom the marines have rated
A radioman; I rate him straight A's.
He shyly grins beneath my ardent gaze.
His mild manner and his horn-rimmed glasses
Protected him once from my subtle passes,
But on the beach, glasses off, nearly nude,
Kurt Strom saw Superman and desire stewed.
He's innocent, open, a little boy
About to burst with life and health and joy.
Raised in lonely deserts north of Phoenix.
I'd love to add him to my list of tricks.

  Thomas L. Sweeney is a ladies' man;
He lives to lay them whenever he can.
And he did, I gather, every night.
He tells often of his favorite sight:
A "V" for Victory lies on the floor
When he opens a lady's bedroom door.
He tells us that he likes to fuck a lot,
But Paradise is when he's licking twat.
We are constantly told of lusty deeds,
And I, for one, believe that he succeeds,
Though he lacks a gentleman's discretion
And is cursed with a pimply complexion.
He looks, I daresay, like pitted white shit;
Energy must make up his touch of "IT."
I never have understood women's taste:

Ham hock hands, pudding thighs, scarred face of paste.
But he's a good soldier, so I don't mind,
Though Heaven forbid that my love be blind.
    Despite Sweeney's loud self-advertising,
'Twas Visconti born 'neath Venus rising.
He was the one who balled a movie star,
A benefit of the Vietnam War.
(I seem to recall telling that story,
But if I have not, it will not bore me
To unfold the tale. I'm intrigued. A lot.
The romance, like Visconti, gets me hot.)
He's long and lean, a wolf from Old Roma;
I fancy he reeks with an aroma
Of methods that pleasure man, woman, beast:
A Borgia banquet, a Fellini feast.
When he's not in Nam or stars or Crisco,
He works construction in San Francisco.
    From Cleveland comes George Gemelas, a Greek:
A liar, suspected thief, and a sneak.
We have had to live with his constant whines
About discomfort we shared on the lines.
The colonel forced him on us. Onto CAP,
For which neither of them gives a good rap.
Curly hair and a mama's boy's dimples
Combine with greasy forehead and pimples.
He lets nothing we say in chat slip by
Without his favorite comment "You lie!"
He walks head thrust forward, eyes on the ground,
Hoping to uncover secrets around.
Gemelas is lazy and uncaring,
Lacking honor, a buddy, and daring.
    Unlike Gemelas, a constant shirker,
Tennessee is CAP's most tireless worker.
He's big and patient and strong as a mule,
Easily pleased by his ration of gruel.
His voice has a grating that hurts my head;
An ugly face hurts my eyes. And that said,
There remain some admiring things to say
About his courage, and about the way
He'll always lend a hand without a flap.
The sarge fought hard to get him into CAP.
    Fellow Louisianian from Baton Rouge

Is our token black, Ottimus Bluege.
Accused by Brothers as an Uncle Tom,
He bore their banishment with great aplomb.
Bluege likes all people, whether black or white;
He's fun to have around, and very bright.
Wiry, witty, runs fast, and dances well,
He sees this year as a season in Hell
And faces each day with terror and dread;
Each night he wears a stocking cap to bed.
Bluege does his job, as far as I can see
And's the only man in CAP scared as me.

    Oh yeah. Eicheldinger. The company boob:
Clumsy, gawky, hayseed, hick, rural rube,
A bore, a bother, an embarrassment.
His presence the ultimate harassment
By the colonel. Dinger's lean and lanky
With a dirty nose that needs a hanky.
Everyone loathes the company stupe.
The deadly fool. The ass. The nincompoop.

    Well, I hate to bring this poem up short,
But the Sarge is back. I've got to report
How sick call went. I hope you are not hurt
By my quick closing.

Relentlessly,

Kurt

CAP #25
Bou Bou Phu, Vietnam
3 May 67

Chloe dear,

    I have moved into high gear with my medical services. Prospects looked gloomy for a while, but dedication, inspiration, and the ability to knock a few heads together have paid off.

    My initial sick call was a travesty of the medical oath. LaSalle, our translator, helped me shoulder supplies, and accompanied by three members of the Popular Forces, we marched upon the main village. I set up shop near a well the villagers had sunk in their graveyard for some reason. (Probably because that's where the water is, Kurt, you dumb ass.) The entire populace gathered around to watch; sick call's a big event in this one-bullock town. I stacked my supplies in neat piles, poured water into my basin, added disinfectant, and bugled the charge. The villagers stampeded, wriggling around me to grab my supplies and make off with as much booty as they could. I yelled for help. The Poofs, doubled over with laughter, recovered enough to beat everyone back with the butts of their rifles. The people disliked being beaten with rifles; they went away. LaSalle seemed disapproving and was as curious as I to see what I would do next.

What I did next was to gather the remnant of supplies and hike down the road to the last hamlet. Its population was a tenth of the village's and the turnout was in proportion. I set up my traveling medicine man show; the Poofs gave my pitch and stepped to the rear, bayonets to the ready. The women and the old men held back, but the kids seemed game for anything. One little boy stepped forward amidst much giggling. He held up his finger to show me a small cut. I washed the cut with hydrogen peroxide and stuck a Band-Aid around it. He was so proud. All the other kids wanted to be proud. Pride was a new Band-Aid. As all the kids had bruises or cuts of some sort or another, I saw some validity in their desire; nonetheless, I refused them pride. A Band-Aid is to keep a wound clean. No one wanted his cut douched with hydrogen peroxide, and these people bathe only upon threat of dismemberment. "N-O spells no," I said. I wanted the zips to get used to washing themselves so that 1) I wouldn't suffer from their stench and 2) I could better see the scungy skin diseases endemic among them: ringworm, eczema, creeping Congo crud, etc. "Let's wash up," I suggested. Oh no! No one wanted to wash, but everyone wanted a Band-Aid. So we struck a compromise. I thoroughly scrubbed ten volunteers, applied the salve most likely to cure whatever repugnant scuzzies they had on their bodies (I was unsure), and if they endured that, they got Band-Aids. Pride was ten clean kids with Band-Aids. Every kid in town clamored for a bath, but I stuck to the courageous ten. I marked an "A" on the back of their clean hands with a red felt pen. (As the filthies clawed at me to mark them, too, I considered carving the backs of their slimy hands with a dull machete.) I followed the same routine in the next hamlet and the hamlet after that.

By the end of the day, I had 120 patients and the rift rang with the shouts of proud children.

If dirt was trumps, what hands I would hold.

Relentlessly,

Kurt

CAP #25
BOU BOU PHU, VIETNAM
4 May 67

Dear Mom and Pops,

As usual, I'm uncertain as to where I am. I've seen our location on maps. It appears to be twenty miles inland from Da Nang. But if I learn nothing else from Vietnam, I'll always know that appearances can be deceiving.

The scenery is beautiful. We live at the bottom of a butte near a corner of a wide valley surrounded by mountains. In the rift between the butte and the nearest mountain lies our sphere of activity, a velvet-green checkerboard of rice paddies and vegetable gardens. About two thousand people live in a dozen hamlets that dot the rift. Our job is to become acquainted with these people and protect them from themselves.

Most of the men find the hamlets ugly and barren of interest. I share their disdain for the filth in which the Vietnamese seem to be comfortable, but the hamlets are set below thick-leaved trees, perfect for shading a drowsy Caucasian in olive-green who wishes to sustain his torpor. (Where are those native girls?) The swarms of flies irritate me, but I've been conducting a fierce and bloody, if unreported, war with insects for years.

The flies breed in the public defecations of the locals, who bring to mind the niggers back home. With acres of fern and oak trees surrounding DT's workers, they preferred to tinkle on the tires of my truck, or against the tree nearest to where I worked. And like jigaboos, zips tend to congregate in loud idle groups.

To tell the truth, as I write this, my buddies sit nearby in a loud idle group. People in glass houses . . .

Love,

Kurt

Arch,

SATURDAY 29 APRIL 67

At dawn we skipped breakfast to carry our gear to the chopper pad, where we were to board our charter helicopter. At noon we finally crawled into the belly of a huge chopper that soared into the wild blue yonder. After twenty minutes, the big bird set down in the middle of an acre of bare, burnt-over ground where a hamlet had stood a month before. A company of VC had wiped out a platoon of marines in a nearby paddy, so vengeful Americans destroyed the hamlet and transported its surviving inhabitants to a refugee camp.

The village militia (PF's) welcomed us with big smiles and lots of chatter. They escorted us to the base of a small wooded butte and proudly displayed their little fort and our new home. We were alarmed by the prospect.

A bamboo fence within a stagnant moat surrounded two straw huts standing on 40 feet × 30 feet of bare ground. Flies gorged upon the human turds littering one corner of the little island. The sun beat down unmercifully.

The PF's prepared a stinky supper of God-knows-what that we washed down with warm beer. At sundown all the slopes who sleep in the fort arrived: thirty soldiers and twenty-three civilians set up housekeeping. We had enough room to pitch just one tent. We used the tent for storing our gear and threw our sleeping bags into the corner farthest from the hillocks of shit, which grew alarmingly as the evening progressed.

The moat protected us from an enemy that could hardly be so dedicated to its godless ideals that it would consider wading through the baleful muck to inflict nastiness upon us. In this disgusting ditch dwelt myriads of mosquitoes which left only to eat—us.

The whining of the mosquitoes was muted by the clamor of the gooks, a people who enjoy playing cards and drinking beer. Such diversion was hardly alien to us, but the gooks argued vociferously over every turn of the cards until the wee hours of the morning.

278

SUNDAY 30 APRIL 67

LaSalle, our translator, escaped with me into the main hamlet to search for a likely spot where I could hold sick call. The villagers avoided us. I saw no likely spot.

Barry, the radioman, set up a transmitter in one of the huts. He would run out of the flimsy structure at intervals, brushing at his clothes. Cockroaches and less identifiable bugs dropped on him from the straw roof. What fun it must be to study entomology in Vietnam.

Other grunts policed the compound. Pinkerton ordered them to remove the shit from the island. I heard several arguments about who carried off the most turds. Hardly a game I could care to win.

Eicheldinger swore that he saw a twenty-foot-long python swimming in the moat. Nobody believed him, but we looked and we wondered.

MONDAY 1 MAY 67

Because my primary duty is to hold sick call for the villagers, I am one of three men excused from patrols and ambushes; Barry monitors all excursions by radio, and LaSalle acts as liaison between the Vietnamese and the Americans. Pinkerton decided that the three of us should know the countryside, even if we stay home every night. Led by the PF commander, we hiked the width, breadth, and circumference of our territory, our realm, this other Eden. As we stumbled through the forest that climbed the mountain across the way, I got a strong feeling of déjà vu, which got stronger as we reconnoitred the hamlets and rice paddies.

The forest was damp, stifling, and rife with insects. The hamlets and rice paddies were dirty, smelly, and strewn with garbage. The fort is a noisy combination of the aforementioned.

TUESDAY 2 MAY 67

Someone rifled the medical supplies during the night. As the PF's stood watch, one of them had to be the culprit. I complained to Pinkerton, but he was hesitant about confronting the PF commander; loss of face is a serious matter in these parts. So is the loss of medical supplies. I stood watch all day, determined to lose nothing else.

Pinkerton said nothing about the theft. He did, however, suggest to the gook commander that his men use the latrine we dug outside the fort. The commander agreed, but after the platoon went on patrol, the PF's who remained at the fork snuck behind our tent. I heard them giggling, so I went to check the scene. They were shitting large piles of their wormy excrement. The sarge has Frick, one of the squad leaders, drawing up plans for a two-holer.

WEDNESDAY 3 MAY 67

The gooks kept everyone awake all night with their chatter and clatter. My supply of aspirin is running out. Much grumbling and dissension among the troops.

I held my first sick call. A fiasco.

Anything seemed better than another sleepless night amidst the stench of the fort, so I went on ambush with Frick's squad. The more fool I. At least in the fort, I could slap the mosquitoes; on ambush, one must sit quietly and be drained of blood.

Smokers hate ambushes, when they must silently endure their nicotine fits. Nor can we talk. Surely that's worse.

We returned to the fort at 3 A.M. to find the unit smouldering. Apparently responding to a dare, one of the zips pissed on McGrath's sleeping bag while the rifleman was in it. McGrath went after the gook with a Bowie knife. Tennessee, a huge mild dude, held him back. Pinkerton seems troubled.

THURSDAY 4 MAY 67

I held sick call this morning in the hamlets. Sick call was merely a semifiasco.

As I had the afternoon off, Barry and I followed the rocky road that winds past the fort and up to the top of the butte, where it ends at a crevice twelve feet wide and about forty feet deep. The crevice cuts the butte in two parts; Barry and I had to climb down to the bottom and back up to get to the other side. (Barry broached the idea of swinging across the crevice on vines, but I refused to consider it.) The top of the butte is otherwise flat and covers about an acre of ground. In the center, buried under malevolent-looking undergrowth, we found an old stone house without doors, windows, or roof. A possibility of vipers kept us from exploring the ruins.

FRIDAY 5 MAY 67

Two cases of "C"-rations were stolen last night. Pinkerton confronted the zip commander with our loss. Not only did the zips deny stealing anything, but they also suggested we look among ourselves for the thief.

Most of the platoon climbed to the top of the butte to sightsee. One of the guys suggested that we move up there and away from the zips. He won immediate acclaim. Pinkerton vetoed the proposition. He was booed. A discussion ensued. Frick, a construction worker in the States, thought that the house could be made habitable. Pinkerton argued for a policy that would appease grunts and zips: a larger fort, convenient shitters . . . More booing. As medical advisor, I advocated a healthy distance from moat and paddies. Others threatened to put in for transfers unless we had a change of living conditions. McGrath maintained a murderous silence. Faced with mutiny, Pinkerton capitulated to the majority.

And democracy is what we're fighting to defend, right?

Relentlessly,

Kurt

COBRA'S FOLLY
BOU BOU PHU, VIETNAM
9 May 67

Dear Mom and Pops,

Atop a nearby butte, we found a deserted villa, made some repairs, and moved into it. Our translator learned that a wealthy French family from Da Nang had abandoned the villa after the debacle at Dien Bien Phu. LaSalle says the older Vietnamese

281

hate the villa; they hint at a curse. I have little desire to know more.

A steady breeze blows across the butte, so the house remains cool most of the day. A main room of 30 feet × 40 feet opens onto a terrace and will be used as an all-purpose room. At either end, it opens onto smaller rooms 10 feet × 15 feet; three grunts will sleep in each. The two rooms face west, toward a bridge, a watchtower, and the highest side of the butte.

Three feet below the terrace is a courtyard. Off the courtyard and overlooking the swimming pool are the two rooms of the north wing. The three squad leaders and the translator share it.

Sergeant Pinkerton, Barry the radioman, and I share the south wing. Barry sleeps in the radio room, across from a storeroom, where we keep medical and food supplies, tools, and ammunition. My bedroom is 20 feet × 10 feet. Indented in one wall is a fireplace; Pinkerton has placed snapshots of his wife and his three little boys upon its mantel. My library fills a built-in bookcase next to my bed. A pair of bamboo chairs completes the decor.

I dreamed again the other night I was at Manderley.

Love,

Kurt

COBRA'S FOLLY
BOU BOU PHU, VIETNAM
10 May 67

Arch,

Life has risen from the pits to the heights. A plantation in the sky. Huge trees shade our house and a helter-skelter luxuriance that must have been extensive flower gardens. Everyone pitched in to make our home habitable, and every task uncovered another example of the original builder's taste for beauty and comfort.

McGrath's squad cleared vegetation and vermin from the villa—a one-story house with a small kitchen next to it. As the roof had fallen in, McGrath's men laid a bamboo frame across the tops of the stone walls and covered the frame with straw mats.

Herndon's squad cleared the butte of jungle and cleaned out the cobblestone trough running from a fountain in the courtyard to the swimming pool. (Apparently a spring flows continually with no need of a pump. As we drink the water, I can only hope it's pure.)

Our company engineer, Frick, designed a footbridge across the crevice, a watchtower at the house end of the bridge, and an outhouse across two lips of rock at the far corner of the butte. His men erected the structures, and with sheer drops on three sides of the butte, we live in a healthy and comfortable citadel.

Every man except Eicheldinger contributed to the house-raising; he saw pythons, cobras, scorpions, and tarantulas so frequently that Pinkerton sent him to the Poof fort to guard our supplies. He bumbled there, too; another case of "C"-rations was stolen while we worked. McGrath wanted to set fire to the fort and shoot the Poofs as they swarmed out.

Nevertheless, Pinkerton continues to stress cooperation, and he invited the Poofs to our housewarming party. He felt they would be hurt otherwise; a clatter of Poofs had climbed the hill every day to watch us work. Thirty of them came to the party, oohed and aahed at our improvements, got very drunk on our beer, and passed out on the living room floor. We locked everything of value in the storeroom and crowded together in the bedrooms to sleep. The next morning we awakened with violent hangovers and to a lot of noise. The entire contingent of Poofs sat in the courtyard, as well as several local villagers who feared the VC for political reasons. They had decided to move in with us. They'd brought everything they owned to the villa. They sat looking at us with big smiles. They looked like a swarm of grasshoppers.

Big pow-wow.

Pinkerton suggested that we share the villa with the gooks. Everyone protested. They'd steal everything. We compromised. The gooks could visit, but they must live in the fort. Stamping feet, fierce glares, and clattering discussion followed that announcement. One Poof pulled his gun. Ultimately, they marched over the bridge and back to the fort, leaving behind their possessions. McGrath wanted to hurl everything over the cliffs, but we just deposited their stuff on the far side of the bridge.

When I woke up the following morning, the zips were sleeping in the courtyard and the kitchen, their paraphernalia in a pile by the fountain. I returned from sick call at three o'clock; they were just waking up from siesta. Pinkerton asked for a little time to work things out.

At midnight, forty or so zips were loudly clattering over cards and beer. Even Pinkerton got pissed. He told them to go home. They were afraid to go down the hill in the dark. Forty of them, Arch. We were sickened by their shaking and crying. They held hands, their eyes widening dramatically as they clamored in their tinny voices. Bluege and I escorted them to the fort. No goblins got them. Or us.

This morning a barefoot Pinkerton stepped into a pile of shit. The courtyard looked like a field of potatoes. The sarge rescinded the invitation to visit. We would henceforth meet for patrols outside their fort. They're like pigs and monkeys; you can't housebreak them.

Relentlessly,

Kurt

COBRA'S FOLLY
BOU BOU PHU, VIETNAM
11 May 67

Chloe dear,

We have moved into an abandoned villa atop an impregnable butte and are living in tropical elegance. We even have a swimming pool. My special, self-imposed task was to clean it out so that we could swim. I spend my free hours now with a chalkboard, scrawling over and over: NEVER VOLUNTEER FOR ANYTHING.

Over the years, the water in the pool had transformed itself into a ghastly, semisolid gelatin. As the neglected garden evolved into a jungle, the vegetation crawled down to the pool for a drink; eventually it crept into the water to bathe. Mosquitoes raised generations in the turbid mire. Slithery, scaly, nameless things slid into the reeking slime. The inky glop bubbled with natural and unnatural life.

I had two choices. I could bail the glop out, or I could descend into the quivering pit, pull out the ranker plants, and grope about underwater for the drain. I decided to bail it out.

I gingerly dipped my helmet into the water and flung out a clump of plants, leeches, larvae, and Heaven knows how many unkissed Frog Princes. It took two days to get rid of what could reasonably be called liquid, and another hot, hysteria-ridden day wading in knee-high muck to shovel out what remained. I get the heebie-jeebies just thinking about it. (I went into near-convulsions in the ooze when Gemelas, in an unsuccessful attempt to be amusing, threw a small cobra on top of me. He'd killed it in the courtyard.)

But we have a pool. I was allowed to christen it myself. I recited a rhythmic poem of my own invention which began

> By the shores of Getcha Gooey,
> By the mighty Cobra's Folly,
> Stands the villa of the CAP men,
> Brave and fierce and gallant CAP men,
> Et cetera, et cetera, et cetera...

Having no champagne, I then peed in it.

Relentlessly,

Kurt

COBRA'S FOLLY
BOU BOU PHU, VIETNAM
12 May 67

My dear Paul,

I have little to say about love, sex, or violence, everything that matters, but, as usual, I have much to say.

Every day I awaken with the sun. I glance lovingly at Pinkerton, who sleeps across the room; having come home from ambush very late, he huddles under his blanket against the morning chill. I shiver. I peer out the door, checking the courtyard for cobras. I run down to the pool for a few laps. I examine my body for scuzzies. I shake out my clothes and boots, checking for scorpions, centipedes, and kraits. I dress and shave; then I drink a cup of coffee and eat a packet of "C"-rations as I study a medical textbook my sister sent me. "C"-rations and medical textbooks mix uneasily. The book has many illustrations in living color of horrible infections and diseases; I dream about them by night and see them in real life every day. An hour of trying to understand that turgid prose drives me to putting the book away in my room. The morning has become warm. Pinkerton has thrown off his blanket and sprawls nude on his rack. I shiver. I say good-bye to the man on watch by the bridge and amble down the road to the village about half a mile away.

Women, children, and old people inhabit the rift. With the exception of the Poofs, the younger men are either dead or in the jungle with the other VC. One would think the people would resist my ministrations, but it's usually like rush hour in the Tokyo subway system.

I took Sunday off to study rashes and ringworms in my medical book. I am getting rather good at separating the different species, although I remain uncertain as to which species is which, separated though they are. Yaws was easy to diagnose; its victims had faces like raw hamburger. A couple of penicillin shots cleared those unsightly facial blemishes and I was acclaimed as a powerful medicine man.

Mothers began bringing their babies to me. Every baby in the rift has sores covering his head from scratching mosquito bites. The mothers had hitherto treated the sores with applications of buffalo dung. This results in maggot-ridden infections. I disinfect such sores, I swab out pus-filled eyes, I squirt worm medicine down tiny throats, I look at the little harelips and cripples, and I move on. Zips have a cruel habit of laughing at the deformities of their peers and insist upon exhibiting the uglies for public ridicule.

The other day several kids led me to a hut outside their hamlet. I entered the dark, incredibly smelly hovel to come face-to-nonface with a leper. I maintained some professional decorum and refrained from barfing, but then I faced a quandary. Lepers should be reported—the disease is contagious—but would the rift people trust me again if I reported one of their number? I passed the buck to Pinkerton, who passed it back to me. I am to ask at the Med Battalion about leper colonies.

I'd been told that all zips have malaria, tuberculosis, and stomach worms. I have worm pills, but these folk have such filthy personal habits, I'd be throwing them away. Nevertheless, worms cause malnutrition and lower resistance to infection.

I shall persevere until all my geese are swans.

Relentlessly,

Kurt

COBRA'S FOLLY
BOU BOU PHU, VIETNAM
16 May 67

Dear Mom and Pops,

I think you've seen too many World War II movies; believe me, I have not written extra letters to be mailed posthumously. Should your questions go unanswered, just assume I have yet to receive all my mail. The Marine Corps' tiny collective brain addled by our move, weeks may pass before our destination is determined. Your letters of 16 and 19 April arrived via the Thursday morning supply chopper.

We've been ransacking the marketplaces for furnishings and knick-knacks. A couple of the guys have bizarre tastes; no one seems indifferent to his environment. Besides outfitting our home, we've surveyed an athletic field on the site of a burnt-over hamlet. Our radioman is a sports freak; he has talked us into helping him dig up tree stumps and pick up trash. Meanwhile, at the Folly, we've hung a basketball hoop that twangs most of the afternoon, and we've strung up a volleyball net. The volleyball bounces into a crevice next to the court several times a game, but a guy with coordination problems good-naturedly stands at the bottom of the crevice to throw the ball back to us.

Your grandson, the doctor, has developed a thriving practice with few of the problems that assail Stateside physicians; no worry about patients paying their bills, no insurance hassles, and no arousals in the middle of the night to make house calls.

In answer to your questions, I bought film in Cincinnati for my camera. The inoculations I got when I first came over remain effective. And I saw no reason to bring my white suit with me.

Love,

Kurt

COBRA'S FOLLY
BOU BOU PHU, VIETNAM
17 May 67

Arch,

All this itching and scratching over the meaning of life hardly becomes you, buddy. My brother-in-law could have written that last letter. I decided a long time ago that I'm not particularly bright, and as I'm incapable of improving the world with my brains, I must have been put on earth to enjoy myself. I loved playing ball every summer, I loved living in New York every winter, and I like the Navy. You've always done what you wanted. To regret your life at twenty-four seems perverse. As Auntie Mame said, "Life is a banquet and most poor bastards are starving to death."

At the moment, I've given over to the establishment: I work a five-day forty-hour-week, Tuesday through Saturday. The grunts work every day, but an equal number of hours: an eight-hour patrol one day, a four- to six-hour ambush the second, and six hours of watch at the Folly. Six Popular Forces attend each patrol and ambush. The militia prefers patrols when, in daylight, the VC are rarely seen; they lack any desire to meet fellow slopes from the opposite side of the political fence. They are terrible warriors. I call them Poofs.

Monday mornings we go to school with the Poofs down by the fort. McGrath conducts target practice, Pinkerton makes us go through the intricacies of hand-to-hand combat, and Herndon teaches boxing and wrestling. Monday afternoons I hold classes in first-aid, determined my grunts will be capable corpsmen should I be indisposed. I'm exempt from the Vietnamese language lessons LaSalle holds every day for the grunts; LaSalle is so impressed by my flair for Zip and Grunt that he demands we speak French during meals. I'm also exempt from Map Reading and Radio, which I can handle better than the teachers.

I swim every morning and usually endure a half hour of running up and down the hill every evening. In the afternoons I lie in the sun to read or write letters. When I get too hot, I splash in the pool. In the evenings we play basketball or volleyball or a little poker.

It all seems a wonderful life, but I come across cases at sick call daily that I lack the education and the experience to diagnose and treat. So I worry. When Frick hitched a ride into Da Nang on the supply chopper to pick up tools and construction materials, I accompanied him. I went to the Med Battalion to ask my friend Alf for advice. He introduced me to a Dr. Abstein, cherry and gung ho. He seemed interested in the CAP program and smiled at my confession of ignorance. In simple layman's terms (I am a relatively simple layman), Dr. Abstein described several diagnostic procedures I could use and wrote down a list of medicines I would need. I returned to Alf, who filled my orders at Supply and Pharmacy. Heavily burdened, I hitched over to Headquarters Company to rendezvous with Frick.

He had accomplished nothing. Our needs had aroused little sympathy and no one would release supplies without written orders. We needed an "Open, Sesame." I decided to go right to the top.

A patient on the Medical Intensive Care Unit had everyone at Med Battalion in a tizzy: a general with severe constipation. The corpsman on duty told me that the general was in labor. I went down to the officers' shitter, introduced myself to the general, and explained our problem. He said, "That CAP program ain't worth jack-shit." His face contorted and he grunted. I tried to look sympathetic and humble. Apparently I succeeded. He asked me for something to write on. The only paper I had in my pockets was covered with predictions of the final standings in the 1967 major league pennant races. (Barry and I have a wager on.) I reached for a piece of toilet paper. "I ain't going to write an order on asswipe," bellowed the general. I scurried up to MICU, grabbed an empty envelope addressed to the general off his bedside table, and returned to the shitter. The general hadn't moved. Neither had his bowels. He wrote on the back of the envelope, "Give HM3 Strom whatever he needs." He signed it. As I left the shitter, he was still grunting. Marines never outgrow it.

I took the magic words back to Frick. We got our lumber and replacements for the tools the Poofs had stolen. We also picked up roofing, whitewash, screening, chlorine, a set of lawn chairs, four hammocks, a trash can, four kerosene lamps, ten gallons of kerosene, two dozen bug bombs, a dozen cots and pillows, two dozen blankets and sheets, two transistor radios, a dozen reams of paper, chicken feed, two volleyballs, and a microscope. My old pal Larry commandeered a chopper that carried us and our booty back to Bou Bou Phu. I gave the precious note to Pinkerton, who placed it between the pages of his Bible in the Book of Revelations.

Relentlessly,

Kurt

COBRA'S FOLLY
BOU BOU PHU, VIETNAM
18 May 67

Chloe dear,

Pinkerton ordered each of the grunts to present a project that would help to better the economy or life-style of the rift people. Visconti won first prize: three days of exemption from patrols and ambushes. Son of a sanitation worker in San Francisco, Visconti put his heritage to work and found a spot in the swamp beyond the last hamlet that could be used for a garbage dump, replacing the piles of trash that dot the local landscape and breed rats, flies, and other nasty things. Visconti would have trash cans placed in every hamlet's marketplace. Local workers would transport the garbage to the dump at the end of the day.

Second prize, two days of exemption from patrols and ambushes, went to Bluege, who will explore the possibilities of penning up the stringy, diseased-looking local fowl and feeding them from U.S. Government seed. He has put a dozen hens and a rooster in the experimental chicken run he built in the far corner of the butte.

Tennessee captured third place, one day of exemption from

patrols and ambushes. Having established a rapport with the local bison and swine, Tennessee wishes to better their living conditions. He will build a pigpen in the swamp on the far side of the village from the dump, put all the skinny pigs that roam the marketplaces into the pen, and direct their feeding. He will try to obtain grain to feed the water buffalo. Envying Bluege his chicken run, Tennessee bought a piglet for the Folly. "Them's good pets. Kills snakes. Be good eatin'." He named her Petunia.

Barry and LaSalle shared honorable mention: dinner for two at a local restaurant on a night of their choice. Barry, who plans to become a Phys Ed instructor, wants to hold physical fitness classes for the children of the rift and teach the youngsters how to play football, softball, basketball, and volleyball. He'd brought bats, balls, and nets from the States. Unfortunately, these kids consider rules superfluous; they just grab the balls and run away with them. Barry was disconsolate, so I reminded him that "Hide-and-Go-Seek" and "Keep-Away" are American games, too. Barry had to agree, but prefers more organized sports. An altered plan calls for the kids to learn the rules by watching the CAP unit play. We use the burnt-over site of a treacherous hamlet as our playing field.

LaSalle is the company translator, a grunt who had been sent to language school in Taiwan to learn Vietnamese. He conducts English classes among the Poofs and Vietnamese classes among the grunts. He proposed holding English classes for the local kids and enlisted me as an instructor. One drunken evening at the Folly, Bluege and I had amused the jarheads by acting out ribald versions of children's classics, so I shall clean up my act and tell the stories in English and Zip. I'll practice on Barry; he's easily amused.

Frick won no prize. For the rift's biggest marketplace, he built a rest room, a wooden two-holer screened in front from the waist up and with removable barrels filled with kerosene under the holes. The Vietnamese, you see, have a tendency to shit where they stand. Despite the two-holer, the people still shit where they stand; after all, they have been doing it that way for centuries. Pinkerton thinks the people may learn by example, so he has ordered all of us to sit in the two-holer for five minutes every day, whether or not we must shit. This embarrasses us, as the zips crowd around the edifice to peer at us through the screen.

Sweeney has grandiose plans for transforming the village wells into fountains for sanitary and aesthetic purposes. He doubts that these wells have been cleaned out for eons, and only God knows what monsters lurk on their bottoms. Sweeney asked LaSalle to describe the fountains he'd seen in Europe, and our plumber seemed intrigued by the idea of a statue spouting water. I suggested a spitting cobra.

McGrath's mechanical mind has been hampered by the absence of electricity. He needs a generator and has been gathering practical reasons to set before the CAP committee in Da Nang.

Herndon wanted to hold swimming, lifesaving, and scuba diving classes in our pool. Everyone objected immediately, but Pinkerton feels uneasy about the unit's isolation and thought such a project would encourage community between the rift and the butte. I showed the sarge illustrations in my medical book of the skin diseases we would be likely to catch if we shared our pool with zips. He remained unconvinced until I drew graphic pictures of the tapeworms that would be likely to inhabit the pool after the gooks were finished with it.

Eicheldinger once attended a production of *Our Town* and lost his heart to the theater. Although he has never seen another play (much less acted in one) and he speaks no Vietnamese, the Dinger wants to direct a local drama group.

Gemelas secreted himself away to work for hours on his project, asking each of us our plans, but acting very mysterious. He finally unveiled it, proud as could be, with rough sketches. Gemelas proposed that we use Frick and Visconti's construction expertise to build a hotel. The Greek Geek hoped to attract military personnel throughout Vietnam to Bou Bou Phu and the best little whorehouse in the jungle. We studied the brochures Gemelas handed out; the stacks of pornography he had brought back from Japan had been cut up and pasted onto writing tablets with descriptions of the activities.

LaSalle was to recruit local lovelies who would work in four fucking rooms for pussy only; one fucking room for anal only; two cocksucking rooms; a cunnilingus room; and a jerk-off room. An auditorium would show porno flicks; Eicheldinger would stage nude tableaus, perhaps with fairy tale themes. Herndon would train village belles to hold bare ass water ballets; Barry would teach the girls to play volleyball al fresco. I'd always granted Gemelas a dirty mind, but nothing like the frenzied filth he poured forth: mechanical masturbators designed by McGrath; a special room for those into water sports or coprophagia. I was to man the penicillin pump. Bluege and Tennessee would handle the chickens and pigs. Although everyone had to admit that a market for his hotel existed, and it would undoubtedly improve the economy of Bou Bou Phu, Gemelas joined Eicheldinger and Herndon on a construction crew to work under Frick.

At the moment, I am searching through LaSalle's dictionary for the Vietnamese equivalent of "Rumpelstiltskin" and beginning to wonder just how difficult this fairy tale project is likely to be.

Relentlessly,

Kurt

COBRA'S FOLLY
BOU BOU PHU, VIETNAM
19 May 67

My dear Paul,

My medicine show rotates among the hamlets. I hold sick call in two hamlets each day. It's an assembly-line production, and I'm usually finished by two. I make rounds in my minuscule hospital: a straw hut with four beds and no patients. At three I hold a class in first aid for the Poofs and at four, another class for my nursing cadets—girls recruited from each of the ten hamlets whom I pay ten cents a day to attend.

LaSalle joins me for lunch and supper at our favorite Howard Johnson's. I endure his intensive drills in the Vietnamese language and am able to hold sick call now with no interpreter. After dawdling over a couple of beers, LaSalle and I return to the Folly, where Barry leads the entire platoon in rugged calisthenics for an hour. We exercise in the nude. I love calisthenics. Except for Bluege, our token black, and Sweeney, who has skin problems, everyone has developed a deep overall tan, and I never get tired of looking. Carefully, I scuttle to explain, but we're all men, right?

I met Barry for the first time when we left Echo for China Beach—he seemed eager to chat, if shy, and I was in an

293

expansive mood. Although he seemed pleasant, Barry wore eyeglasses, which turns me off. On the beach, however, he shucked those glasses and his clothes and displayed one of the most beautiful bodies I've had the pleasure of viewing. Had I not already come to know him as a friendly puppy dog of a kid, I would have been too much in awe of bronzed good looks, heavily muscled body, and glorious butch walk to speak to him.

Barry's got vitality in abundance, and the Marine Corps' making him a radioman seems perverse. Unless LaSalle or I condescend to relieve him, Barry must spend anywhere from six to twelve hours a day in our stuffy little radio room, always in contact with patrols, ambushes, and the Poof fort. Between calls, Barry sits at his desk doodling out plans for the physical education program he hopes to develop in the Arizona school system. (He played fullback at Northern Arizona for a semester; bad grades and a broken heart sent him to the Marine Corps, already tougher than the lifers.) He has great fun naming his intramural teams and choosing the colors of their jerseys— e.g., boys would be tan cougars or black bears and girls would be red foxes or pink panthers. He will have everyone playing games, he says, and have them enjoy doing so.

Despite his evident good nature, Barry has no buddies at CAP. Everybody likes him, but no one wants to sit in the stuffy radio room to bullshit; besides, the only entrance to the radio room is through the room I share with Pinkerton, and I discourage heavy traffic. As the kitchen has had blackout curtains draped across its windows and door, a lantern there illuminates continual card games, a pastime I burned out on during four years in the minor leagues. The only other night light is in the radio room, so I have taken to dragging a chair in to read Trollope for a couple of hours every evening. Barry shyly interrupted a companionable silence to chat about touchdowns and cacti. We became bosom buddies.

I hated to take advantage of his innocence, but I subscribe loyally to Marine corps Oath #69: A hard cock has no conscience. I had several advantages:

1. The other grunts were either playing cards, on ambush, or sleeping.

2. Barry had seen me play ball in Flagstaff several times and had been so impressed he had followed my subsequent career in the *Sporting News*. (And who among us is not, deep down, a starfucker?)

3. We usually wore only a towel, if anything, in the stuffy windowless room.

4. Barry's trustful.

The night was mine.

So after a butch, paternal, and medical harangue about sexual matters, I got Barry to confess to self-abuse. I elaborated upon the dangers of masturbation, only stopping short of prophecizing blindness. "If you always do it the same way," I warned him darkly, "you will depend upon a certain rhythm so much that you'll be unable to enjoy a woman."

"No lie?" he said gravely.

Rather than let him suffer in agonized guilt or painful celibacy, I offered to share the knowledge I'd gained in my travels. "Are you aware of the ninety-nine ways to jerk off?" I asked him.

"No," he replied.

Lesson number one: soft and easy, round and about. Barry watched me, but he couldn't quite grasp the technique. I showed him how to do it. He showed me a thing or two. We went beyond mere manipulation. Barry loved it. So did I. We enjoyed it even more the following night. He dug any variation I threw at him. I was pleased and amazed and joyous.

Nonetheless, I decided to cool the scene the third night. I remained in my room and in my jeans. But I had to relieve Barry at midnight, for his break. And he was perplexed, friendly, and as affectionate as a puppy. In the middle of a particularly lovely bit of pleasure, we heard someone in my room cough. Whether friend or foe, we were close to exposure, and VC bayonets stab no deeper than sharp tongues. Whichever, we had to pretend we'd heard nothing, and we had to hide the noise of pulling on our jeans. "I went to the store and bought an apple," I said.

"What?"

"Go to the store and buy an apple and a banana," I whispered.

"They don't have apples," Barry whispered back.

"It's a game." He understands such talk.

"What?" He misunderstood it this time.

"Say 'I went to the store and bought an apple and a banana.'"

Barry blinked. "I went to the store and bought an apple and a banana."

I zipped up my jeans. "I went to the store and bought an apple, a banana, and a cherry."

"What?" He's slow on the uptake, Paul, but he's pretty.

"You go to the store and buy an apple, a banana, a cherry, and a dildo."

"What's a dildo?"

Real pretty.

By this time, Barry had his rifle loaded and cocked. I handed him his eyeglasses and he said in a normal voice, "If whoever is in Doc's room is an American, you'd better say so or we're coming out with guns blazing."

"No! No! It's me, Gemelas."

The sneaky Greek. He needed an antidote for diarrhea. As neither Barry nor I whisper endearments, nor would we be so ill-mannered as to instruct each other in technique, I'm certain Gemelas heard nothing. But we're more careful now and lay elaborate booby traps for anyone sliding into my room in the dark. And we never screw around when Pinkerton's at the Folly.

And Barry is fascinated by the "Apple, Banana, and Cherry" game. We go all the way to "Z" every night. He considers the game as foreplay. It's a small price to pay, I know, but...All right. He's pretty. Real pretty. And you can't buy anything like him in any store I've ever shopped in.

Relentlessly,

Kurt

COBRA'S FOLLY
BOU BOU PHU, VIETNAM
23 May 67

Arch,

LaSalle and I were chatting merrily with the waitress at our favorite restaurant last Saturday, when we heard a chopper overhead. As the supply run had delivered on Thursday, we looked at each other and said "Inspection!" in the same breath. The unit had been dreading inspection. The Marine Corps disapproves of luxury, and we've feared a move back to the Poof fort. LaSalle and I had a more immediate dread of inspection, because I wore jeans, a T-shirt, and cowboy boots, and LaSalle wore thongs and black pajamas. And we carried no guns. Yet someone had to meet the chopper. We ran to the athletic field.

The helicopter set down before we arrived. As it set down without a perimeter, we were appalled by the pilot's foolhardiness and relieved to learn no inspection was imminent: An officer of inspector's rank is extremely safety-conscious when it comes to his own skin. The crew chief jumped out of the bird and ran over to us. "Are you guys marines?" he asked dubiously.

"Correspondents," replied LaSalle, in a French accent and with admirable presence.

"There's a CAP unit near here, ain't there?"

"Oui oui!" I said, shaking my head affirmatively. LaSalle smiled.

"Do you know if a Corporal Frick, Gary, is a member of that unit?" shouted the crew chief over the beating of the rotors.

Q'est-ce que c'est?" said LaSalle. The marine looked at me.

"Oui oui!" I affirmed. The grunt waved at the chopper. A marine leaned into the cockpit and kissed both pilots before jumping out of the craft. The crew chief accepted a big kiss before he jumped into the bird, which departed immediately. The marine waved good-bye and, hips swaying, walked toward us carrying a powder-blue suitcase. I looked at LaSalle, who was looking at me, and then we both looked at the marine with the magic lips. The marine smiled and said, "Hi guys." The marine was female!

She took off her helmet and shook out her long, dark hair. "Where's Gary?" she asked. I pointed at the butte. "Up there?" I nodded affirmatively several times. She smiled broadly, a questioning smile. I smiled, too. She smiled at LaSalle. He bowed.

"Suivez-moi, mademoiselle. Kurt, montez-vous sa valise, s'il vous plaît."

She smiled at me.

"Follow you him, young lady. I bring me the bag."

We marched her through a silent, staring village and past unbelieving Poofs to the Folly. The grunts in residence spilled into the courtyard, shuffling their feet and gawking. His sister attacked a stunned Frick with hugs and kisses. She turned to us, wiping tears from her eyes. McGrath stepped forward and introduced us all in turn. Even Eicheldinger. The perfect Southern gentleman. McGrath, not Eicheldinger. *Au contraire.*

"I'm dying for a cigarette. Do any of you happen to have . . . ?" She got four immediately. She accepted one. Lighters flared on all sides of her. She lighted up and took a deep drag. She smiled again. So did we. She'd like to visit for a few days. Did we mind? Could we spare a bunk?

"We can arrange it," said McGrath, as he backhanded a Gemelas full of suggestions.

One never knows in Vietnam what the day will bring.

Relentlessly,

Kurt

COBRA'S FOLLY
BOU BOU PHU, VIETNAM
24 May 67

My dear Paul,

We are entertaining the sister of one of the grunts. How she got here is a long story, but I wish she'd leave. My sex life is in shambles. Nudity had been the general rule at the Folly before Sheila arrived: calisthenics, swimming, and lounging. Now everyone wears cut-offs. McGrath had eased me over to the cliffs for a couple of pleasant little sessions; Herndon and I did a bit of nude wrestling which left us very aware of each other; Visconti had taken to sneaking up behind me and throwing a few wicked bumps and grinds against my bare butt; Pinkerton showed signs of having a bad case of the raging hornies, and I knew just the medicine. And now everyone wears cut-offs. Sheila's presence negates all my good work. It will take weeks after she leaves before things get back to normal.

As we never know when Sheila is likely to bounce into the radio room, Barry and I have had to be circumspect to the point of abstinence. And he's reminded of his lost lady of the desert.

Barry now talks about his desert flower quite often. How ever had he lost her? What ever had he done wrong? How ever should he act when he sees her again? Do I think he's a redneck? Uncouth? Dumb? As you know better than most, my advice to the lovelorn lacks delicacy: Fuck and forget or fuck and fuck again and again. I inferred that Barry would appreciate delicacy

298

so I told him that the break-up could never have occurred because of any fault in his sunny nature. A college girl, I opined, probably felt compelled to study life instead of living it. Perhaps some women found it necessary to pass through a couple of effete intellectual snobs before they could appreciate a decent and simple man. I said everything but what I really thought—that she was stupid beyond belief and her looks were the type which would fade fast. If he could just get that dumb desert cunt out of his mind, I think Barry would give me his class ring and ask me to go steady.

> *Relentlessly,*
>
> *Kurt*

COBRA'S FOLLY
BOU BOU PHU, VIETNAM
25 May 67

Chloe dear,

You've wondered several times about the tension among men without women. You must never forget that our women live here with us—in our imagination—or we live back home with them. Pinkerton never enters our room without glancing at the photograph of his wife. He'll lie on his cot for hours, staring at her and his three boys. Whenever I make a sound or a movement that brings him out of his reverie, he'll reminisce aloud, beginning at whatever point he'd reached in his memory. He's read me all the letters sweet Jeanne sends. I know his sons' birthdays. And Jeanne's. She looks like a Raphael madonna.

Nearly everyone has snapshots displayed. Visconti's harem is worthy of a Caesar. McGrath has a tawny tigress for a lady friend and a couple of dashing blond sisters. Other finalists for the title of Miss Cobra's Folly would be Bluege's dusky honey and Barry's insipidly pretty sweetheart.

I've thought of putting up that snap of you showing lots of cleavage, licking your lips and suggesting forbidden pleasures, but it would soon be sticky with white stains. And trying to attain envy by exhibiting Karen's looks would have some of the dreariest people on record dropping in on her in Cincinnati.

A very sedate portrait of her with the boys stands on the mantel, along with the rest of the family. I keep all those chunky chicks with eyeglasses who seem to find me irresistible hidden deep in my seabag.

Sweeney has a wallet filled with heavily made-up girls with shiny bouffants. LaSalle, the cosmopolitan, allows us to gaze upon some of the excessively exotic ladies in his past.

At the lowest level are Tennessee's bovine spouse, Gemelas' bullock-waisted fiancée, and Eicheldinger's mother and sisters. They all look just like him. Ugly as shit.

Herndon never shares his snaps.

Frick's sisters were never contestants, unless in the Amazon Olympics: three big, broad-shouldered girls with stern faces and short hair. Shows you how pictures can lie. His oldest sister popped in the other day and her hair is long and she smiles all the time and she's gorgeous. And those incredible long legs are not to be believed.

The sarge called off all ambushes the day she arrived at CAP. We gathered in a silent group, spread out across the courtyard under Frick's watchful eye while she bathed in the pool. She returned with an olive drab towel wrapped around her hips and another around her breasts. She hugged Frick for the umpteenth time; then she sat down on the terrace, crossed her legs, and lighted a cigarette. Nobody said anything. Sheila gave us a shit-eating grin.

"You guys look as if you haven't seen a girl for months." I don't think I'm going to like her at all.

Relentlessly,

Kurt

Cobra's Folly
Bou Bou Phu, Vietnam
26 May 67

Dear Mom and Pops,

Once upon a time, there was a big dumb swimmer who never had dates. Sheila ran faster, climbed higher, and swam better than any of her friends, all of whom were boys. She hated school; she felt it a waste of sunshine to be sitting in a classroom with a gaggle of silly girls, learning how to cook soufflés and sew drapes. Sheila hated sewing drapes. She flunked Home Ec. Twice.

The big dumb swimmer never had dates. She had several good buddies on the swimming team, but they dated silly girls who enjoyed cooking soufflés and sewing drapes. Her buddies couldn't invite her to Senior Prom because they dated those silly girls. Sheila wanted to go to Senior Prom. She got a date, thanks to her brother, Gary, whose best friend was a year younger than Sheila and smaller and dumber, but in spite of his horror of girls and dancing, he invited Sheila to Prom. She threatened to beat him up if he didn't. Sheila loved dancing. Her brother's friend refused to let go of the wall, but each of Sheila's buddies danced with her. Twice.

After she graduated from high school, Sheila swam in the ocean all summer; then she left home and went to college. She liked water, so she studied marine biology. Sheila loved college: It was located near the ocean, she could swim whenever she wanted, and there weren't any other girls in her Biophysics and her Biochemistry classes. She flunked out. Twice.

Sheila decided to become a mermaid. She swam every day in the ocean. Her father had no desire to have a fish for a daughter; he gave Sheila a job with his construction company as a secretary. Sheila hated working; she felt it a waste of sunshine to be sitting in a stuffy office with a gaggle of silly women, learning how to type letters and file correspondence. Sheila hated filing correspondence. She quite the job. Twice.

One day Sheila sat by the window watching the drizzle outside and half-listening to her mommy talk with a neighbor lady. "Heavenly days!" exclaimed the neighbor lady. "I don't know what to do. Linda wants to go sailing to Hawaii with her boyfriend and his parents, but I just don't know." "Perhaps it would look better if another girl went along," said Sheila's mommy, "a chaperone." "You may be right," said the neighbor lady. "I wonder whom it should be." Both ladies looked at Sheila. Thery didn't have to ask her twice.

Sheila went shopping with Linda. "You've got great legs and no boobs," said Linda. "You will wear short shorts and sweat shirts. I have frog legs and elephant udders. I will wear halter straps and sarongs. We will each buy two bathing suits— one very conservative to show our parents and one very bitching to show the guys on the beach." Sheila enjoyed shopping with

Linda. And she loved sailing. At Waikiki, Sheila swam, surfed, and sunbathed on the beach while Linda fought with her boyfriend. The couple broke up. Twice.

When her piggy was empty, Sheila became depressed. She called her parents. "I'm depressed," she said. They sent five hundred dollars and told her to enjoy herself. Sheila was a dutiful daughter and always obeyed her parents. She pulled on her tight white shorts, Linda strapped on her halter, and they went to the docks, hoping to find someone with a boat and headed toward Tahiti. They heard about three great-looking guys with a schooner and asked the three great-looking guys if a couple of cooks might be needed. Sheila kept crossing her legs and Linda kept bending over. They had no need to ask twice.

The schooner put in at Tahiti, Bora Bora, Samoa, the Fijis, and New Guinea. In Tahiti, the sailors picked up Margie, a pretty redhead from Australia. When the sailors decided to return to the States, Margie invited Linda and Sheila to visit her family in Australia. The girls went skin diving off the Great Barrier Reef; they saw koala bears and kangaroos in the Outback. Sheila loved Australia. In Sydney the girls met some Air Force officers who said that Saigon was the greatest party town in the world. The officers had a big plane with an empty hold. Would the girls like to come along for the ride? There was no need to ask twice.

The air jockeys showed the ladies a good time. They partied every night for three weeks. They dined on steak and lobsters, and they drank champagne and White Russians. They danced the reeling midnights through. The girls loved Saigon. But Linda fell for a really sharp Army captain, so she moved to Cam Ranh Bay. Margie fell for a really groovy Marine lieutenant, so she moved to Hue. Sheila wanted to visit her brother, so she's moved to Bou Bou Phu, which anyone in his right mind would never want to visit once.

Love,

Kurt

My dear Paul,

Nobody talks about Sheila's living with us against all rules and regulations. A projected two- or three-day visit has extended through a week with no sign of ending. I ask Pinkerton daily whether he's worried about our getting caught with a round-eye in camp; he says "No!" and walks away. McGrath hangs around her all the time; they spend hours at target practice and self-defense.

The guys try to treat her like a sister, but they can't quite forget she's got a cunt. She reports halfhearted passes by Sweeney and McGrath, and Eicheldinger cornered her a couple of times to sob out his sad story, embarrassing her considerably. But the only man she dislikes is Herndon. "I don't know why. Dave's such a good-looking guy and he likes to swim. Why don't I like him?"

"Because he's an asshole, Sheila."

I've tried a couple of times to get something started with Barry, but he shrugs me off. "Holy cow, Doc, what if Sheila walks in and . . ." He's really pissed me off with his coyness, so I refuse to play that goddam "Apples, Bananas, and Cherries" with him. "What's the matter, Doc? I thought you liked that game."

Petunia Pig has fallen in love with Sheila and suffers brisk scrubdowns in the swimming pool.

Why ever does she stay so long?

Sheila and I do have fun gossiping. She's very curious about LaSalle and his village queen. And she learned that Vietnamese women usually have no hair on their pussies: She's dying to know whether LaSalle's girl has any.

Steve wrote a long, warm, and very discreet letter in which he proposed to visit me. I put him in touch with Larry, my old crew chief on the dust-offs. Saturday afternoon I looked up from splinting a broken finger to see Steve standing behind a crowd of onlooking gooks and smiling at me.

He followed Sheila and me on our rounds—Sheila's initial

shyness soon giving way to a discussion of friends and experiences they had in common in Saigon while I tried to determine the nature of scuzzies my zippies exhibited and clattered about. We spent the rest of the day by the pool, surrounded by grunts.

Sheila took her duty as a hostess seriously and never left us alone. I had to lace a cup of hot chocolate with Demerol Saturday night to get her sleepy. No sooner had she toddled off to her cot in the kitchen than Pinkerton began talking noncom to officer of the problems of leadership. When he finally left for an ambush, Barry appeared in the doorway, wondering about radios in airplanes.

"Hey, Steve," I said. "Maybe I better show you where the rest room is, just in case."

McGrath stood up. "I'll show him."

They returned chatting of football (Steve had played second-string quarterback at San Diego State), a topic that caught Barry's interest and the three of them retired to the radio room. I went to sleep.

Steve was royally entertained the following day. We walked down to the ball field, Pinkerton and Sheila pointing out the wonders of Bou Bou Phu and the Folly all the way. We played a hard-fought game of football. Bluege cooked the most God-awful gumbo I've ever tasted while Frick showed Steve his bridge and his outhouse and laconically described the intricacies of his craftsmanship, McGrath and Visconti gave an exhibition of hand-to-hand combat, Sweeney and Tennessee of boxing, Herndon of diving, and everyone played a hard-fought game of basketball. Eicheldinger saw a cobra nobody else saw. LaSalle took Steve down to the fort to meet the Poof commander and the village elders; then Pinkerton invited him to accompany the late afternoon patrol. That night I mixed a huge batch of hot chocolate, but Barry discovered that Steve also enjoyed camping out at the bottom of the Grand Canyon, to Sheila's intense interest, and I didn't have the heart to numb their obvious pleasure in the ensuing discussion. Gemelas took Steve to the shitter and I fell asleep during a conversation about mountain climbing.

We walked down to the chopper pad bright and early Monday morning chatting about skin diving, Pinkerton's arm draped around Steve's shoulders. As Larry's chopper churned over the horizon, we all shook hands with Steve. Sheila, tears in her eyes, hugged him hard several times.

"What a great guy," she said, as the chopper disappeared over the mountains.

"Yeah," I replied.

Relentlessly,

Kurt

COBRA'S FOLLY
BOU BOU PHU, VIETNAM
31 May 67

Arch,

And now for the Wednesday Night Sports Special.

FOOTBALL

Johnny Rebs 42　　　　damyankees 24

1st Quarter: Damyankees take 18–0 lead behind the quarter-backing of Barry and the running of Visconti.

2nd Quarter: Rebel defense pulls their shit together. Led by Tennessee, Sheila, and McGrath, the defense holds the damyankees scoreless, while Pinkerton throws four touchdown passes to "Surehand" Strom.

3rd Quarter: Goddamyankees doubleteam "Surehand" Strom, so Pinkerton passes off to Bluege, who runs for three touchdowns. Barry runs for the final yank t.d.

Game called on account of patrol.

BASKETBALL

damyankees 52　　　　Johnny Rebs 50

LaSalle, Sweeney, and Visconti scored in double figures for damyankees; Pinkerton, Bluege, and Sheila led the Rebs. Game marred by fistfights between Gemelas and McGrath, McGrath and Sweeney, and Sweeney and Frick. Game also marred by the inability of "Stilts" Strom to get the ball in the fucking basket.

SOFTBALL

Johnny Rebs 23   damyankees 0

Tennessee pitched a three-hitter, backed by the splendid infield of Strom to Pinkerton to Sheila and a swift outfield of Bluege and McGrath. Those goddamyankees never had a chance.

"Kloutin'" Kurt lashed out seven hits, including one double, three triples, and three home runs, and knocked in thirteen runs for the victors.

In the very minor sport of volleyball, the yanks won 15–13, 15–12, and 23–21.

SIGNING OFF AND STAY TUNED FOR

"Slugger" Strom

COBRA'S FOLLY
BOU BOU PHU, VIETNAM
1 June 67

Chloe dear,

Although I have a nursing student from my class in each of the hamlets to help me during sick calls, Sheila has become physician's assistant and head nurse. She accompanies me every day, sympathizes with my professional problems, and insists that LaSalle speak English during our meals together.

She delights Barry with her athletic abilities; she plays guard on the Johnny Reb football team, center on the basketball team, and first base during softball games. In turn, Barry has taught her to man the radio; she monitors ambushes and patrols in her deepest voice, should anyone from outside tune in our frequency.

Sheila wants to do everything the rest of us do; I shouldn't be surprised if she tries to pee while standing. She's desperate to go on a patrol, but the sarge refuses to let her. She cries. "I'll have to go home and have babies and sew drapes for the rest of my life. Let me have fun now." Pinkerton shook his head, so she gave him the silent treatment. But silence bothered Sheila more than the sarge. I believe she's trying flattery tonight. I can hear the two of them splashing about in the pool amidst shouts and laughter.

Sheila believes CAP to be built upon philosophical quicksand. "I think it's dumb. You guys work hard all day, trying to make the Vietnamese like you; then you go out at night to kill their brothers and fathers and husbands and sons. I don't care what anybody does for me. If they try to kill my brother or my father, I'll hate them. I think it's dumb."

When you're with the marines, you never wax philosophical; you just try to avoid waning.

Relentlessly,

Kurt

COBRA'S FOLLY
BOU BOU PHU, VIETNAM
2 June 67

Dear Mom and Pops,

I thought you might like a picture. I call this snap "Snow White and the Seven Dwarfs." The tall girl in the middle, in the sweat shirt and the short shorts, is Sheila, the sister of one of my grunts.

Sheila hugs her brother with her right arm. BASHFUL is a man of few words; he prefers to work with his hands instead of his mouth. BASHFUL can usually be found in the little stone kitchen next to the main house: once our game room and now Sheila's bedroom. BASHFUL uses it as his carpentry shop. Whenever I tire of listening to the nonsense I'm sometimes subjected to, I mosey over to the shop to chatter my own nonsense. BASHFUL's replies are laconic when they are audible, so at one point I got oversensitive about forcing myself upon him. I avoided BASHFUL for a week, until one afternoon as I lay by the pool, he came down from the house and looked at the water for several minutes. "Doc," he finally said, "I'm finishing a table at the shop if you don't have nobody to talk to." His sister bends his ear now; she talks as much and has as little to say as I.

Standing on the far left is SLEEPY, our translator. At first, he and I were constant companions because I needed him to help me communicate with the rift people during sick call and first-aid classes. He would speak only Vietnamese; as I must talk or die, I learned a smattering of the language. Since those first hectic days, I have become more intolerant of the foibles of others; I prefer to relax after my day in the village, and SLEEPY's refusal to speak English reduces his effectiveness as a companion. I eat lunch with Sheila and Pinkerton now, and only see SLEEPY when he's waking up from another nap. He has, incredibly, chosen to live with the Poofs, but even a hardened exotic must sleep. And we suspect he spends many of those sleepless nights in the village with his lady friend, a woman of notoriety.

On the ground at the right is SNEEZY, a mean dude with innumerable allergies. He often tells us about the fistfights he's enjoyed, about every episode of a television program called "Get Smart," and about the bevy of beauties back home vainly dreaming of him. He's aware of his ugliness; he says it doesn't matter. ("When I worked for the riding school, I wore this scarlet-and-mustard outfit that dazzled those rich chicks.") SNEEZY interrupts his stories with wild laughter; when he laughs, saliva splashes through his wide-spaced green and yellow teeth, and he likes to hold on to his listener's shirtfront as he tells his stories. In spite of such shortcomings, which include an everlasting itch to do battle with either the Cong or one of us, SNEEZY is amusing and a good combat marine, if you ignore his wheezing during ambushes.

On the ground in the middle, leaning against Sheila's legs, is DOPEY. He's as goofy as he looks. No one likes him. I've felt guilty at turning away from his forlorn pleas for friendship, but he seems to thrive on irritating a person. The other day I noticed he'd received a couple of letters on the mail run, so I betook it upon myself to ask after his family. The conversation which followed wasn't too painful, so I thought maybe I could establish a pleasant if distant rapport with the fool, thereby assuaging a guilty conscience. That night, however, DOPEY stumbled into my room without knocking, sat down on my cot, picked up a letter from Chloe I'd left on my pillow, leaned back and, lifting his boots upon my blanket, began to read the letter. I was so stunned by his bad manners, I just stared at him and said nothing. DOPEY continued to read, flicking his cigarette ashes on the floor. I find it difficult to be civil to such a nincompoop, so I asked DOPEY to leave and threatened to make him a soprano, should he ever darken my door again.

GRUMPY sits next to DOPEY. Nobody likes him either. Before we discovered the Poofs were stealing our supplies, suspicion centered on the sneaky Greek. He never looks a person straight in the eye; rather, he stands slump-shouldered, head thrust forward, peering sideways. During conversations, he becomes argumentative and doubts every statement. He complains continuously. Envy, sloth, and rancor are mother's milk to GRUMPY.

And that's old DOC with Sheila's left arm wrapped around his waist. My arm's around HAPPY, a merry good-natured kid and my best friend.

Although none of us whistles as he works, we'll do our best to keep away all wicked witches.

Love,

Kurt

COBRA'S FOLLY
BOU BOU PHU, VIETNAM
6 June 67

Chloe dear,

As the evening is spread out against the sky, the advent of darkness forces the cessation of ball games, card games, and reading, and we must look to one another for diversion. We hear tell of CAP units with generators; they enjoy the finer things: electric lights, refrigerators, and stereo equipment. Bluege seldom turns off a transistor radio, which we dance to after a few beers, but usually we sit in the courtyard, listening to the fountain splash and singing along to Herndon's excellent guitar picking.

And we talk. Most of the conversation is meant to impress Sheila. I have a good time, but sometimes I miss good chat about books and movies and faraway places.

Bluege, the only witty man in the company, is forced to hold his tongue; his bon mots about the conditions under which we exist or may cease to exist antagonize the grunts, and they reply in badinage about his color. Visconti is bemused by life and very funny in his more serious moods, but the Neanderthals drown him out.

Pinkerton tells pointless cowboy stories and simple, though

convoluted, jokes. McGrath, when he's in his cups, drops his backwoods act and, trading his redneck rasping for a honeyed drawl, tells long stories of coon hunts and fishing trips. Sweeney and Herndon give every detail of television shows and movies they have seen and that I'll never have to see. Whenever Eicheldinger opens his mouth, everyone squares his shoulders and prepares to be mortified. I don't know how he does it, but he can reach inside himself to pull out a topic that has everyone writhing in revulsion. This talent is inexplicable; take it from me, you'd run screaming from the room.

Except for Gemelas, the rest of the guys just listen. Gemelas never adds; he just subtracts with his derision. He did get drunk last week and become sentimental over his grandmother—how little and bent and funny she was, the stories she'd told him of her girlhood in Greece, and how badly he'd taken her death. It embarrassed the hell out of all of us, but he continued his soliloquy, tears streaming down his cheeks. I saw a side of Gemelas I had no idea existed and that I think he should keep covered.

Any sympathy he might have gained was lost today. Sheila leaned against the fountain with McGrath at her feet, as she lapped up a compliment about her legs. Gemelas muttered, "Shit! Back home, nobody would look at her twice."

McGrath started to rise to do battle, but Sheila restrained him with a gentle hand. She took a drag off her cigarette, exhaled, and tried to look cool, but her eyes filled with tears. I threw the rubber ball I was squeezing at Gemelas, hitting the Greek Geek between the eyes, and said, "Toto, I don't think we're in Kansas anymore."

Relentlessly,

Kurt

COBRA'S FOLLY
BOU BOU PHU, VIETNAM
7 June 67

My dear Paul,

I should be content. I'm adored by a sweet and beautiful nineteen-year-old. I like my job, I enjoy the camaraderie, and I eat out for every meal. I should be content. But I'm not.

Oh, I'm happy enough; I have no desire to be anywhere else. I just wish I could enjoy the beauty of my buddies aesthetically, instead of wanting to reveal my appreciation by tactile, oral, and anal means.

Sheila and I sat chatting by the pool the other day, as we watched Herndon monotonously churn through a hundred laps. Suddenly, Herndon dove underwater and, with a large splash, surfaced just in front of us. His golden hair was plastered darkly against his head and chest. Muscles rippled in his heavy shoulders and thick forearms. He pulled himself out of the pool, his face lighted by a private smile. Sheila stopped talking. As we stared at him, Herndon noticed us; his smile disappeared and he clumped up to the house. Sheila and I jumped into the pool and played for an hour.

One evening, as most of us sat in the courtyard in the gathering dusk, Sheila and her brother began reminiscing about their old hound Strider, which had died just after Gary enlisted. I recited a poem about a little dog angel that doesn't play with the other little dog angels, but waits all by himself at Heaven's gates. Tears streamed down Sheila's cheeks. Swollen with success, I delivered "Little Boy Blue." Sheila sobbed louder. Bluege cleared his throat and intoned "God's Trombones" by some nigger poet. And then LaSalle took the floor. In a deep, rich baritone, he enthralled us with "Kublai Khan." The Canuck's been to Xanadu. He's met that maiden with the dulcimer. I'd wager he's fabulous in bed.

Visconti sat on the terrace that evening, his bare legs hanging over the edge; I sat on the ground between his legs. During LaSalle's performance, I leaned against Visconti's thigh. He gently stroked my hair and eased my head back against his crotch. In the hush that followed the poem, I realized that Barry was staring at us through the gathering dusk. Visconti apparently saw him, too; he stood up, adjusted his shorts, and disappeared into his room.

The following evening, at another get-together, McGrath lounged carelessly against the fountain, easy and graceful. Gemelas uttered inanely that all women were whores. McGrath's face and body tightened instantly, and his eyes glittered as he rose casually to his feet. Pinkerton immediately said, "Geek, why don't you go down to the Poof fort and bring back LaSalle?" Ordinarily, Gemelas would have argued the order, but he had seen McGrath freeze; the Greek Geek was only too happy to undertake the errand. After Gemelas left, McGrath strode up and down the courtyard, looking neither left nor right; half an hour passed before he ceased prowling and relaxed.

Larry, the crew chief, dropped by with a case of Scotch that Steve had bought for us as a thank-you for a pleasant weekend. We threw ourselves a party. By midnight, the entire platoon was strewn about the courtyard unconscious. (Sheila, who drinks very little, stood watch.) I staggered into my room and fell into bed. Pinkerton followed me. He made a huge show of covering me up, put a book representing a teddy bear next to me, and sat on my bed to croon a garbled version of "The Little Lost Dogie." Afterward he patted me on the head and hugged me. He sat up, looked at me, laughed, and leaned forward to kiss me gently on the lips. He stood up uncertainly, lurched toward the doorway, and puked into the courtyard. I passed out to his retching. And all's quiet on the Eastern front.

Relentlessly,

Kurt

COBRA'S FOLLY
BOU BOU PHU, VIETNAM
8 June 67

Dear Mom and Pops,

I read between the lines of your letters and sense an accusation of caring nothing for Ricky's banishment. It's difficult to get a straight story. I'm a long way from home, you know. Karen and I have been writing back and forth between ourselves and to DT, Ricky, Neil, and Guy Perrone.

Mom says A: DT physically mistreated Ricky.
           B: DT allowed Ricky to attend no social activities.
           C: DT made Ricky work thirty hours a week in the fernery.
Neil says A: DT has been unusually gentle with Ricky since Mother's death.
           B: Ricky has been driving Neil's car without a license.
           C: Ricky's grades have dropped sharply in the last few months.

DT says A: Ricky would wait until DT had gone to bed; then he'd sneak out and drive into town to party with his friends.

B: Ricky wrecked Neil's car twice, and he was working in the fernery to pay the repair bills.

C: Every time he tried to discipline the kid, Ricky would run into town to Mom, who gave him anything he wanted.

Ricky says A: A friend showing off a karate move kicked in Neil's windshield.

B: An elderly man pulled out of a parking lot without looking and rammed into Neil's car while Ricky was driving it. The man said, "What's the matter with you? Don't you know I can't see?"

Guy Perrone says that he learned through the district attorney's office that Ricky was running with a fast crowd known by the police to be buying and selling and probably using such drugs as marijuana, hashish, and LSD. He warned DT of an imminent crackdown: hence, Arkansas.

I do not want to see Ricky in reform school. I do hate to think of his being torn away from his friends, his girls, and his teams. So I sent Ricky bus fare to Cincinnati, where he'll spend the summer with Karen, work part time, and help her with the babies. I've already sent Karen three hundred dollars to help out.

Ricky loves Karen as much as he does anybody. Karen's talked with him steadily for several days. Karen says:

A: Daddy died when Ricky was a baby.

B: Dad, whom Ricky adored, died when Ricky was eight.

C: Mother died when he was fifteen.

D: Ricky respects me more than anyone else and is convinced I will die in Vietnam.

E: If something should happen to me, it would be best for Ricky to be with Karen—they will need each other. You'll have Pops and Neil; besides, you can handle things like that.

Putting such maudlin conjectures aside, I believe the main problem to be DT's continued derangement due to grief—Neil says he wanted to talk incessantly with the boys about Mother.

Two weeks of such talk drove me to drink. Although I cannot condone Ricky's turning to dope, I can certainly understand why he sought escape.

Mother's was a strong personality. It will take time for all of us to grow accustomed to its absence.

Love,

Kurt

COBRA'S FOLLY
BOU BOU PHU, VIETNAM
9 June 67

Arch,

You wonder if we ever make contact with the VC. Where ever do you think we are—Shangri-La? Actually, we haven't.

Daytime patrols see signs of Charlie: booby traps along the trail, although we've had no casualties. We know from informers in the hamlets that the VC come and go throughout the night, in spite of ambushes set out to trap them. They have informers, too, who apparently tell them where the ambushes are located. We can guard the road running through the rift. However, the VC descend the slopes of the high hills across the rift from the Folly. So Pinkerton has had a brainstorm: we will find the enemy's encampment on the other side of the hills. We will do this, he says, by being dropped by helicopter on the far side of the valley and work our way around the mountains, which will take two to four days.

I shouldn't say "we." Let the heroes roam. Doctor Dan stays here, scrubbing his scuzzies.

But with four men gone, our forces are depleted and everyone left behind does double duty. While the troops are on ambush, I must stand a four-hour watch every night. Sheila and I drag lawn chairs up to the bridge and drink a couple of beers as we chat. Petunia Pig hates to be left alone at the house and Barry won't have her in the radio room, so she comes with us to root happily around the watchtower. I suppose we sound unmilitary, and Pinkerton would disapprove if he knew; fortunately, he doesn't. The men cut the fool as they climb the butte. Sheila has time to grab the chairs and beer cans and run back to the house, Petunia trotting along behind.

Sheila disapproves of the troops' playing grabass as they come up the hill. I told her I'd rather have a fool to make me merry than experience to make me sad. Sheila likes my saying things like that. She doesn't understand the quotations, but is sure that they're quite profound.

"Where did you learn all that stuff, Kurt?"

"I've watched a lot of television."

Relentlessly,

Kurt

COBRA'S FOLLY
BOU BOU PHU, VIETNAM
13 June 67

Chloe dear,

My hospital is running at full capacity: twelve patients. Frick—architect, contractor, and builder—plans to construct an annex next month. The rift people prefer to keep the sick and wounded at home to get well or to die. I prefer to have the sick and wounded in the hospital, where I can see that they get regular treatment, good food, and adequate rest. I've got the guns behind me. The rift people will see I'm right. I believe in a benevolent totalitarianism.

Three kids found a VC mine and blew various parts of themselves away by playing with it; after surgery at the Med Battalion, they were sent home to recuperate. A teen-ager tumbled down the mountain and broke his leg. Two elderly ladies are dying of cancer, and another old lady has pneumonia. A baby is recovering from a serious eye infection. A Poof shot himself in the foot. Three farmers are recovering from gunshot wounds; they refused to go to Med Battalion, so I got to remove bullets for the first time. They tell the other patients that Americans shot them. I believe it. I also believe they are VC.

Mom's grandparents died of grief after they'd lost their life savings during the Depression. Vietnam is still pre-social security. These impoverished farmers either try to save money for their old age or depend upon their children to care for them. Should their children die young, the old people slowly starve to death in stinking huts. Frick is building a large airy house for the aged in each hamlet. He has completed one, shared by

315

twenty-two ancient people. We've begun a garden and a chicken run for it and furnished it with a transistor radio, filling the rift with the clanging and chirping of musical soap operas. I thought (correctly) that the radio would not only amuse the old folks, but would serve to stimulate friends and relatives into regular visits to help with the garden.

Each man in CAP chips in with four dollars a month to feed my patients; fifty-two dollars goes a long way over here. I pay my nursing cadets out of my own pocket and with "C"-rations and medicines I suspect go to the VC. Each girl is head nurse within her own hamlet, and at the moment, they work rotating duty at the hospital. Although the VC control the entire valley and the mountains surrounding it, head men from villages throughout the enclave have come to see our public works, expressed admiration, and talk about sending girls to study with me. Kurt Strom, director of a nursing school; Karen would shit her pants.

Every day after lunch, I teach an English class in the largest of the hamlets. As children and their grandparents sit in a large circle picking lice from one another, LaSalle and I tell fairy tales in Vietnamese; then we act the stories out in English. The audience seems to enjoy our histrionics; Sergeant Pinkerton has counted up to four hundred people applauding us. In "Fairy Tales II," our more advanced students tell us Vietnamese stories in English, and they act them out in Vietnamese. Lots of giggles, but a few have developed a rudimentary English vocabulary.

The kids love to hear the same stories over and over: "Yellow Hair and the Three Water Buffalo," "Little Red Cheongsam and the Big Bad Tiger," and "Cloud White and the Seven Tiny Men." Although the kids never tire of the tales, I sure do. Last week I decided to try a new story: "Little Girl-san Who Is Half-Fish." I usually ad-lib, so it wasn't until I'd arrived at such words as "sea witch," "castle," and "ballroom" that I realized I was in over my head; nevertheless, after entertaining Karen, Neil, Ricky, and their friends for so many years, I am nothing if not resourceful. "Sea witch" became "ugly woman with snakes for hair who lives under the river." "Ballroom" became "ball ground with a floor of stone, walls of beads, and a ceiling of fireflies." Unfortunately, the kids grew restless as I groped for words, and I knew I'd struck out with that story. Cutting my losses, I broke off in midtale, did a clown routine, apologized for the silly story, and switched over to "The Three Small Pigs," a surefire crowd pleaser.

Herndon attended the session that day. An engineering major in college, he was considering teaching a math class. "Fairy Tales I and II" are such successes that he thought to pick up a few pointers. I was ashamed of my debacle, so we said little as we walked over to the cafe for a beer. Herndon broke the silence.

"All right, Doc. I'll bite. What did the Little Girl-san Who is Half-Fish do when the Prince threw her over for the other chick?"

And I'd thought I was casting pearls before swine.

Relentlessly,

Kurt

COBRA'S FOLLY
BOU BOU PHU, VIETNAM
14 June 67

Dear Mom and Pops,

Thanks to the total immersion method of language study, I have acquired a mediocre fluency in Vietnamese. I can hold sick call without an interpreter, locate the pen of my aunt, and order dinner from a menu. As the sole cafe in the rift serves nothing but a daily special, I need only know "Sock it to me, baby."

I never inquire into the contents of my meals. I usually dine on fish and rice, but I've been served such delicacies as chicken eyes. They sound horrible, and they are, but chicken eyes are not terrifically difficult to eat if the serving wench has garnished them into near-invisibility. Some delicacies, however, would revolt a goat.

A week ago, I performed what passes here for a major operation on an eight-year-old boy. I could only clear up his infected leg by injecting massive doses of penicillin at six-hour intervals. His entire family came to the hospital and moved in for two days. With every injection, the boy screamed hideously. So did his sisters and his cousins and his aunts. When the infection cleared up, the boy's grateful grandmother extended

317

dinner invitations to me, my surgical assistant Sergeant Pinkerton, my chief surgical nurse Sheila Frick, and my three ward nurses, the Misses Dien, Kien, and Kyun. (They held the kid down.) Beaming with pride, Granny served eggs. "That doesn't sound too bad," I hear you saying. "What ever could they do to eggs?" I'll tell you. They prefer waiting until the eggs are ready to hatch; then they eat the baby peeps, soft-boiled, with their feathers, beaks, and claws completely formed. We smiled at our hostess, devoured the peeps, and murmured our compliments to the chef. I'd eat raw cockroaches before I'd forget the manners you so carefully taught me.

Love,

Kurt

Cobra's Folly
Bou Bou Phu, Vietnam
15 June 67

Arch,

I awakened last night to a loud boom. I know that sound—a Bouncing Betty—and it had exploded nearby. I grabbed my corpsman's kit and, naked, ran across the bridge. I found Pinkerton kneeling in the road by the wounded man. Herndon had been walking ahead of the men as they returned from an ambush and had tripped a Betty attached to the gate. His right leg was blown off at the hip; his left leg below the knee hung in shreds. Mercifully, he was unconscious.

Barry called for a dust-off. When I'd stopped the bleeding, we loaded Herndon onto a stretcher and carried him to the athletic field. By the time the dust-off landed, Herndon was regaining consciousness, but the chopper would have him at First Med within fifteen minutes; until then, the corpsman on board would care for him.

As the chopper rose, we heard a ping; the craft shook, veered, and dove into the ground where it burst into flames. Because of the heat, we had to back away and watch the chopper burn. At least one man roasted alive; we listened to his screaming. When the remains of the chopper cooled, we could identify Herndon. His charred body was still strapped to the stretcher.

He'll fear no more the heat o' the sun.

Relentlessly,

Kurt

COBRA'S FOLLY
BOU BOU PHU, VIETNAM
16 June 67

My dear Paul,

Steve made a deal with Larry and a couple of chopper pilots: If they would carry him to CAP for another weekend, he'd treat them to a three-day all-expense-paid vacation in Saigon. They agreed, so Steve arrived Friday afternoon, charmed my comrades anew, and seemed to have a good time. We were never alone. I think he preferred it that way.

I didn't. Steve led the damyankees to a victory in football over the Johnny Rebs. He was so fucking sexy, Paul, wearing only tennis shoes and a pair of shorts, dropping back for a pass, his muscles taut, a face noble in concentration . . . He found something to praise in the performance of each man. I deserved it; only by my knocking down several of Steve's passes were we spared a rout.

"It's easy to believe you're a professional, Kurt. Size . . . speed . . . agility. I enjoyed watching you. And those were damn good passes, you fucker."

That's as lovey-dovey as we got.

Steve brought several sketch pads and followed me on my medical rounds, sketching the zips, who were fascinated. He spent much of the weekend sketching: Sheila, the grunts, the Folly . . . He does nice work, Paul. Nothing like those globs of paint you sling on a canvas and call art. We talked about it at lunch.

"You do nice work."

"Thanks."

"You have a nice touch."

Steve smiled. "I've had good teachers."

319

"You've caught their innocence. A cold innocence."

Steve looked at me thoughtfully. Sheila spoke. "Why are they all so good-looking?"

"What?"

"Linda and me talked about it in Saigon. We'd seen servicemen in the States and they looked . . . sort of goofy. Like little kids pretending to be men. They talked too loud and they moved jerkylike. In Saigon, and here, too, the guys talk low and they move quiet and . . . they're cool."

She looked to me for help. "I know what she means, Steve. Take Pinkerton—in the States, he'd be some dumbass cowboy; here he's . . ."

"Sexy."

"Yeah. He's quick and cool under fire. McGrath's like a jungle cat. Back home he's trash from the Delta."

"Visconti's sexy."

"Back home he's a construction worker. Barry's a dumb jock."

Sheila looked at Steve. "As an artist, who do you think . . . ?"

"Kurt. Hands down."

Sheila looked at me and grinned. "You ought to see pictures of his brothers. And his sister. Gosh, she's beautiful."

Steve stared at Sheila. "You have an interesting face, Sheila. You look like a romantic's ideal of an Indian princess. Those high cheekbones. That long straight hair. Of course, no Indian really looks like you, although they should. There's a lot of animal comes through. I'd love to do a couple of nudes."

"What a man!"

"I'm serious."

"You think I'm not?" Sheila covered Steve's hand with her own. I wondered if it was raining in Portugal.

Steve cleared his throat. "The best facial bones here are the translator's. What's his . . . ?"

"LaSalle."

"He looks like a Plantagenet." I explained to Sheila that a Plantagenet was not a bird. "Tennessee has that big square body—primitive and fascinating. My favorite subject here is that awkward kid."

"The Dinger?"

"Sure. He looks like the offspring of a stork and an old hound that's lost its sense of smell."

"You could sketch me in my room," interrupted Sheila.

"Nobody comes in besides my brother and he goes on ambush tonight."

About nine that night, Jezebel left all of us in Big Bend National Park. "Yawn. Yawn. Boy, am I sleepy." She retired to her little kitchen of ill repute.

At ten Judas Iscariot left us in the Carlsbad Caverns. "Just want a breath of fresh air. Never get any in Saigon. Boy oh boy, it's just great to be able to walk outside and be alone." He walked out the door.

Eicheldinger started to follow. I passed through a moment of inner turmoil before saying, "Dinger, sit your dumb ass down."

The following day, Sunday, I got to shine in softball; then Pinkerton invited Steve on an overnight patrol. Barry, who adored the whoremonger, begged to go, too. Pinkerton was reluctant until I offered to monitor the radio all night.

Steve seemed disappointed. "I would have thought you'd have wanted to come, Kurt."

"You gotta be shittin' me."

After they'd gone, I tried to read, but that slutty whore Delilah wanted to run her mouth about some two-timing air jockey. A drunken Herndon lurched in the room, carrying one of the bottles of tequila Steve had brought with him. The lewd wanton, Maggie of the Streets, left the room for her crib; her back and other parts were sore from the previous night's adultery. I was left alone to endure Herndon.

The man was beautiful, no doubt about it: a strawberry blond with magnificent muscles and as handsome as a movie star. He was a bit too conscious of his looks, which were marred by a pounding, determined, overaggressive walk, athlete's foot, and hemorrhoids.

I'd first run into Herndon at Echo, when he began to drop by my tent to chat about concepts in physics. Or to rattle on about some Paul Newman movie or other. No matter that I'd seen them (and I tried to tell Herndon I had): He would talk the plot through, scene by scene. I would gather it was "Trade an Anecdote" time, but whenever I spoke, he'd peruse the book I'd been reading or get up and walk away. I hate to feel I may be boring someone, so I just listened and never tried to talk. When Herndon's repertoire of engineering tales ended, the friendship did, too. He moved on to another man. And the next man after that.

Here at CAP our paths seldom crossed except in company. So I was surprised when he flopped on Barry's cot, took a slug of tequila (with no lemon or salt), and began rambling on about his life.

"...Dad's a commander...flier...Navy base in Spain ...over six feet...so's my brothers...all good athletes...I'm only five feet eight...always sick as a kid...wore eyeglasses ...hated sports...thirteen...older kid...in the back of the garage...Dad caught us...psychiatrists...contact lenses... lifted weights...captain of the wrestling team in high school ...wrong crowd in college...tried to rip off a stereo...dishonored family...no mail in three months...parents disappointed...girls encourage me...naked in bed...tell her promiscuity disgusts me...I'd sleep on the couch...love to get them to the point of no return...then leave..."

Of course I had him. That very night. He passed out. I amused myself with his pretty for a fair period of time, careful to be too gentle to wake him—if he really slept. I'll never know. He was blown up last night by a Bouncing Betty.

A sniper shot down the dust-off come to fetch Herndon, and Pinkerton feels responsible, both for Herndon's tripping the wire of the mine and the death of everybody aboard the chopper. "I should have had them watching better. I should have set up a safer perimeter."

Sheila and I sat by the pool this afternoon; for once, neither of us had much to say. The silence drove her into the village to buy vegetables for supper. After she'd gone, Pinkerton returned from an inquiry at CAP headquarters. He'd been interrogated for the chopper crash and was officially cleared but unofficially condemned. The sarge came straight to the pool, dirty clothes, rifle, and all, and tried to tell me about it. He couldn't. I was unable to help him. He stood up, stripped off his greens, dove into the water, and swam furiously for several minutes. When he emerged, he slowly walked up to the house. I carried his clothes and rifle back to our room. The sarge sat on the edge of his cot, still wet, his head in his hands. I grabbed a towel and dried him off; then I sat down next to him and put my arm around his shoulders. Pinkerton shivered but didn't shake me off. I pushed him gently. He lay back on the cot and turned his face to the wall. I brought my left hand softly down his side. I put my right hand on his calf and brought it softly up his leg. I rested it on his thigh. The sarge never moved. I

322

got up to let the drapes down and nearly bumped into the lecherous bawd, who stood in the doorway. She put her impure hand on my cheek; then she looked past me at Pinkerton. I knew what she meant. I walked through the doorway and dropped the bamboo shades behind me. The last thing I saw in my sink of iniquity was a scurrilous nymphomaniac, her back toward me, pulling her T-shirt over her head. I went down to the pool and stared at the water for a long time.

The bitch. At least she could have let me watch.

Relentlessly,

Kurt

COBRA'S FOLLY
BOU BOU PHU, VIETNAM
20 June 67

Chloe dear,

The unit has been minesweeping the area for the past few days, another case of locking the barn door after the horse has been stolen. Herndon got himself killed tripping over a Bouncing Betty.

At Infantry, we lost an average of three men a week to injury or death. Worrisome, I'll admit, but the adversity gave those surviving a common purpose: to rape, to maim, and to kill. We have one death at CAP in two months and the unit is falling apart. I don't understand.

Pinkerton's always down at the Poof fort conferring with the Poof commander or hiding away in our room with Sheila. I never see LaSalle anymore; whether he's living with the Poofs in their fort or with his girl in the village is uncertain. McGrath and Sweeney lay mines in the crevice and patrol the base of the butte. Visconti and Bluege hide in their room, smoking marijuana. Barry plays football games with dice. Frick hammers in the kitchen. Gemelas sulks in his room. Tennessee talks to Petunia. Eicheldinger bumbles. Sheila swims. I read.

Sweeney got into a nasty fistfight with Gemelas and beat the shit out of the Greek Geek, which was fine by everyone until we felt bound to stop the fight when Sweeney began kicking Gemelas in the head. McGrath pulled a knife on Visconti, for an undisclosed reason. Bluege no longer accepts ribbing about his color. Whenever the sarge returns to the Folly, he's bombarded with complaints.

Sheila reports blatant passes, and she says that her refusals are taken with little grace. Sweeney finds difficulty in believing that she'd consider it a hardship to lay back and let him eat her pussy. McGrath, apparently exasperated after an arduous courtship, accused Sheila of fucking her way across the Pacific: Why stop now? Gemelas makes snide comments about her sucking up to rank. Visconti swims bareass, exhibiting a long erection. I think Tennessee is fucking Petunia.

The sarge feels guilty. He wakes me in the middle of the night to worry over his infidelity with him. Sheila worries about her brother's finding out. It's all very complicated. I like to think of Sheila's leading the troops over the ramparts, one breast bared.

And I think it's going to rain today.

Relentlessly,

Kurt

COBRA'S FOLLY
BOU BOU PHU, VIETNAM
21 June 67

Dear Mom and Pops,

Why ever do you continue to patronize Gloria if you are dissatisfied with her technique? She must be better than the girl who tinted your hair blue, or the girl who cut your hair so short that you looked like a lady truck driver. Ask the ladies whose coiffures you admire where they get their hair done.

I'm sorry to hear that you let public opinion keep you from having the "Hawaiian Wedding Song" played at your nuptials.

It's too soon to be quarreling with Mr. Hebner's children. I can hardly blame their thinking that you're after their inheritance; after all, you did cajole him into signing over to you everything he owned. When you're greedy, you must expect objections.

I've developed a compulsive need for order and have become as fussy as a bourgeois Midwestern housewife. After cleaning my room fiercely, I put a bug bomb in the middle of it, sealed the room as best I could, and set the bomb off. I lingered in the courtyard and listened to frantic vermin fleeing annihilation through our grass roof. A damage check showed I caused the deaths of five scorpions, a hundred cockroaches, and some gory-looking spiders. I got so homesick, I nearly cried.

Love,

Kurt

COBRA'S FOLLY
BOU BOU PHU, VIETNAM
22 June 67

Arch,

That cocksucker Pinkerton called a meeting in the courtyard. "I been hearing nothing but complaints about who's always going on Recon [Reconnaissance Patrols]. Frick, since you been building things instead of hoofing it, you lead. Bluege and Visconti been messing around with dope. You go. And Doc makes four."

I was aghast. "I can't miss three days of sick call."

"Sheila and the nurses can handle sick call. They've learned a lot."

"But I'm a corpsman, not a marine. I never even heard of Recon until I got to Nam."

"You're in better shape than anybody here or at Seventh. And you volunteered."

"Recon guys are trained to scuba dive. To jump with parachutes. To climb mountains."

"You ain't going to do nothing but hump the boonies, Doc."

"They walk with silent, fearless strides."

"So do you."

"They're dirty, loud, and coarse."

"You'll do right well, Doc."

Arch, it was awful.

A chopper picked us up around noon and carried us beyond the mountains on the other side of the plain. As it hovered five feet above a small clearing, we jumped out and ran into the

325

jungle. The chopper flew away, dipping and hovering as it pretended drop-offs in several other spots, to confuse anyone who watched. We were alone, the four of us, in mountains supposedly crawling with VC. The last thing I wanted to do was to go looking for them.

We had a dozen objectives, each several miles from the others, and all of them high upon rocky ridges. A VC base camp was rumored to be hidden somewhere in the vicinity; we were to try to find it. For three days, we walked and hid. No trails existed so high up, and we had to hike along the sides of the hills. As we walked, we slipped, and as we slipped, we slid. Blisters along the sides of my feet bubbled and burst. We slept behind rocks or in thickets. We saw hundreds of Vietnamese from our viewpoints, but the people were too far away to be recognized as VC; besides, they all wore black pajamas. Bluege and I were ready at all times to jump out of our brown and white skins.

At noon of the third day, we ate lunch hidden under a malignant-looking tree dripping with creepers and serpents. We were desperately in need of sleep, but we were still about eight miles of tortuous hiking from Bou Bou Phu, and we hoped to make it home by nightfall.

After lunch, we walked along the side of a ridge, about twenty feet below the crest. Frick led, followed by Visconti, me, and bringing up the rear, Bluege. Suddenly Visconti wheeled around and aimed his piece at me. I dropped in my tracks and groveled. Bluege followed suit. Visconti stared at the trail behind us. Frick had continued on for twenty yards, before he realized we weren't following him. He dropped to the ground and crawled back to us. I was wondering what I had done to make Visconti hate me.

Frick whispered, "What is it?"

Visconti continued to stare down the trail.

"Visconti," gasped Bluege, "you tell Frick what you see."

"Zips. Following us."

Frick crawled to the top of the ridge. He returned with a grim look on his face. "They're about a quarter-mile behind us. Ten of them that I could see. Up there ahead, where the ridge curves, are some more. Couldn't tell how many."

Arch, at such a time, you have two options: You can shit your pants, or you can close your eyes and pretend you aren't there.

Frick continued. "Open your eyes, Doc, and listen up. The other side of the ridge drops off pretty steep as far as I can tell, but it's wooded enough for some cover. There's a clearing about two hundred yards past the bottom of the ridge. We'll head for it. Those gooks are damn likely to spot us when we cross the ridge, so go over fast and get for the bottom. Doc, you hump the radio."

It was, as they say, a tight spot. Frick called in for a chopper to meet us at the clearing. I took the radio and strapped it on. One by one, we crossed over the ridge and ran pell-mell down the thickly wooded and very steep slope. Bullets pinged past; the VC had damn sure spotted us.

Halfway down the slope, we had to leap from one side of a crevasse six feet across to the other side, which was ten feet lower. Frick leaped with Olympian prowess and turned to make sure the rest of us made it. Although I was weighed down with forty pounds of radio, I nearly sailed over his head. When Visconti jumped, he twisted his ankle; Bluege broke his. Both groups of Cong closed upon us in a pincer movement.

I scrambled back to scoop up Bluege, as Frick covered. Bluege weighed only about 150 pounds but combined with the radio, my speed was cut down considerably. No matter. In Recon, rule number one is "Everybody stays together," and Visconti could only hobble. We reached the bottom of the hill and took cover in a pile of rocks. The chopper was still far away. Frick took the radio and called for help. For ten minutes, we tried to hold off what appeared to be about twenty Cong. All of a sudden, Frick yelled, "Get down!" I heard a chopper; then the world was full of explosions. Someone shook me. Frick. He was saying something. I was deaf. He mouthed, "Run for the clearing." I threw Bluege over my shoulder again, Visconti hobbled along behind us, and Frick covered the retreat. As we ran for our lives, Bluege commented on the action behind us.

"That old dragon never got all them suckers. There's eight, nine, ten still coming. C'MON, VISCONTI. I got a million-dollar wound, I gotta million dollar . . . Ooh, Frick dropped one of those lil' ole smallass mother fuckers. I gotta million . . . They's gettin' closer. Run faster, Doc. I gotta . . . Hey, there's one cuttin' us off. I'll get him, Doc. You watch." (The recoil knocked us both down; I scooped Bluege back up and continued to run.) "Pretty good shooting, huh, Doc? Dropped old Chuck like a bad habit, I tell you what. I gotta million dollar... Where's that chopper gone, I wonder. I gotta mil...Man, *that* was close. I gotta...Thought you was *so* fast. Doc! They's gonna get us, yo feet don't do they stuff. They's gettin' closer. Run, Doc, run!"

We reached the clearing and discovered it to be a marsh, where the chopper could never land. We ran another couple of hundred yards, bullets slamming into the trees on either side of us. Two choppers appeared, led us to a field, and one set down on the far side of it. Frick yelled at me, "Run around the swamp. The trees will give us cover." I thought shit on that; the brush was too thick. As the dragon above us was giving us cover fire, I zig-zagged across the clearing and splashed right into some quicksand. Bluege was madder'n hell. "You goddam dumb honky! Get me out of here!" We were up to our waists in ooze. Visconti pulled us out, while shots whined over our heads. We backtracked to the woods and circled the muck. I finally arrived at the chopper, threw Bluege past the machine gunner, flung the radio and Visconti after him, and clambered aboard myself. Frick followed me, the bird lifted off, and the four of us suffered the dry heaves all the way back to First Med.

Visconti got his ankle taped and I got some cuts and scrapes treated and cleaned. We said good-bye to Bluege, still crooning about the million-dollar wound that would get him back to the States. A chopper carried us back to CAP.

And the sun still shines on the wicked.

Relentlessly,

Kurt

COBRA'S FOLLY
BOU BOU PHU, VIETNAM
23 June 67

My dear Paul,

I limped back from three days of Hell in the jungle yesterday with Visconti leaning against my shoulder. No one but Barry and Tennessee was home, so Frick, Visconti, and I stripped off our grimy greens and hobbled to the pool. Frick fell asleep in one of the hammocks; I carried Visconti to his room so I could retape his sprained ankle. I massaged both his legs and, with Visconti's unspoken blessing, was aiming to massage higher, when I happened to notice Barry come out of my room. He headed down to the pool, obviously looking for me. I had turned Visconti over and poured oil on his back before Barry found us. He had many questions about the patrol we'd been on. My replies were short.

Visconti dozed off, and Barry followed me into my room. The angel assumed my bad mood derived from weariness. He insisted on relaxing me with a rubdown. As he massaged my legs, my precious reacted just as Visconti's had; Barry overcame his diffidence of the past month and began to do what I'd wanted to do to Visconti. While he was thus occupied, Pinkerton stepped through the doorway. I grinned at the sarge. He shook his head and went down to the pool. Barry never knew Pinkerton had seen us.

I shrugged it off. I mean, what else can you do? It's women who live to suffer and why worry and if you think today's bad, you're going to hate tomorrow. Pinkerton told McGrath. Of all fucking people.

Pinkerton went on an overnight patrol last night, leaving McGrath in charge of CAP. Although Sheila had stopped begging to go on patrols long ago, McGrath asked whether she wanted to sit in on the ambush. She could hardly refuse. An ambush was sent out. Only Visconti, McGrath, Barry, and I would remain at the Folly. I liked the arrangement; I could enjoy Barry without fear of interruption.

I was to stand watch until midnight, when McGrath was to relieve me. I stood watch until two, when Visconti showed up. I went to McGrath's room. He was asleep. I shook him awake. McGrath snarled; then he tried to pull me down on him. I was pissed, so I shook him off and went to bed.

McGrath woke me up when he walked into my room. "What time is it?" I asked.

"Where's Barry?" he replied. "Where's that cocksucker?" Barry came out of the radio room. "There he is. There's that old cocksucker. Hey, I got something for you, cocksucker."

I sensed trouble. "Fuck off, McGrath."

"Shut up, Doc. Barry, is it true what the sarge tells me? That you're a cocksucker?" Barry turned to stone. "The sarge

329

tells me you suck old Doc's peter. Is that true?" Barry can't lie. He said nothing.

"Pinkerton saw us the other day, Barry. It seems he told McGrath . . ." Barry looked very unhappy.

"You guys must do it all the time. You ought to be in good practice, Barry. Come on. I want to see how good you are. Get on down there, Barry. See, it's all ready for you." Barry stood very still. McGrath swaggered over to him. He put his hand over the front of Barry's cut-offs. "You hurt my feelings, Barry. Don't I turn you on none? I'll bet old Doc turns you on. He is pretty, ain't he? Git on down there. On your knees. I'll get you hotter'n a firecracker." Barry was a statue. "You want me to write to your daddy and tell him 'bout you and Doc? Git on down there, Barry." McGrath put his hand on Barry's shoulder. Barry sank to his knees. With that same hand, McGrath cupped Barry's neck and pulled it to himself. There appeared to be no resistance. Barry proved a good marine. He did as he was told. I know. I watched.

After McGrath wiped himself off with my T-shirt and left, Barry tried to look at me. He tried to smile. He could do neither.

"It's all right, buddy," I whispered.

"I'm sorry, Doc."

"Don't you pay it no never mind, Barry."

"I better let you get some shut-eye." At the doorway, he turned around. He refused to look at me. "I'm sorry, Doc."

This morning Sheila declared that she had learned what it was like to stand ambush and once was enough. Barry and I have yet to speak. He's on a patrol now; Sheila and I share the radio watch. We are members of the lonely crowd.

Relentlessly,

Kurt

COBRA'S FOLLY
BOU BOU PHU, VIETNAM
27 June 67

My dear Chloe,

As I'm the only one who can use a chit giving us anything we need, I must make a run into Da Nang every other week with the supply chopper. Everyone gives me his list of necessities to buy at the PX. Sheila's list included lipstick, panty hose, and Tampons. I got some stares with those goodies in my shopping basket.

As my family in Bou Bou Phu splinters into unhappy loners, my family at home breaks into far-flung fragments.

Mom and Karen maintain an old argument begun when Mom went to Cincinnati after Little Kurtie was born. Karen, still weak from childbirth, had to listen to Mom's continual assurances that everyone was out to take her (Mom). Karen took as much as she could before telling an offended Mom to cool it. Mom began putting down Reggie's family, which is Roman Catholic. Karen asked to be left alone. Mom became friendly with Reggie's mother and, somehow, gave the impression that Karen was a wild girl consumed by deviltry, which confirmed all Mrs. Repine's suspicions. And you know how false an impression that is of Karen. Anyway, they didn't even speak at Mother's funeral.

Mom turned to spoiling Ricky, who was getting into dope quite heavily. (All this is secondhand information.) DT sent the kid to a military school. Ricky's living now with Karen, and despite her setting firm rules for his conduct in front of the babies, she smells marijuana whenever she passes the closed door of Ricky's room. Karen doesn't like it, but at least she knows where he is and seems willing to wait until I get home in October.

I take no sides. I can understand Karen's anger over Mom's causing trouble, but Mom has always been that way and there's no changing her. I do protest DT's refusal to transfer Ricky's orphan pension from the government. What does DT need with $65 a month? And Karen does need it. I'm going to raise hell with DT when I get home. Mother once shocked us by bragging about DT's cheating on his income tax. The law may allow the rich to rob orphans, but the law allows no one but government officials to rob the government. DT and I may have a bloody showdown.

Relentlessly,

Kurt

Dear Mom and Pops,

Your plans for a tour through New England to view the fall foliage seem delightful. I may be there to welcome you. I've put in for Newport, Rhode Island, as my next duty station. Next winter, I want to be where it snows.

I have no plans for college. The older I am when I return, the better prepared I shall be. My only ambition at the moment is to get out of the Navy. Oh, and to make the Tigers. I'll be discharged a year come October. Detroit will probably place me with a team in one of the winter leagues of Latin America. I've got a good arm, I'm a natural hitter, and I'm the fastest white man in the Detroit organization. I should have little difficulty getting back into the swing of things. (Ha ha!) Who knows? I may be earning a major league salary this time two years.

Excuse me, but I had to stop for a moment to refill a small shot glass with a teaspoonful of Scotch. Just to gargle with.

Speaking of nationalities, I've decided that I'm mighty sick of gooks. I have given some thought to teaching English in Japan during the off-season, but no longer. I just want to get shed of slant-eyes. I see them everywhere.

Americans, too, come to think of it. I should prefer to see no round-eyes, either. Would you come to visit me if I decided to become a hermit?

Love,

Kurt

Arch,

Pinkerton was called into CAP headquarters to pick up replacements for Herndon and Bluege. The sarge returned alone. The colonel had sent the three biggest bozos left alive under his command. The first makes Eicheldinger look like James Bond, a guy so dumb he couldn't find his ass to wipe it. Strike one. The second is a huge, red-eyed black dude who hates white authority and was a ringleader among the 7th Battalion's uppity chocolate bloc. Strike Two. Pinkerton suspected the track marks on the arm of the third to be signs of a heroin addict. Strike three.

Sheila should be gone before any replacements arrive. As she can't leave the Folly anymore, it's boring for her as well as dangerous. I'll miss her.

I suppose the reason I rarely conjecture about the future is that I'm so bored by the postbellum plans continually expounded by the guys here. I'd hate to cause yawning in my correspondents. Still, you asked for it.

I'll be twenty-six when my enlistment is up—quite old to be striving for the majors, but unless the Tigers make a trade, their infield will be weak. I can play three positions and I hit for high average and with power. A winter in Puerto Rico should sharpen my skills and get me back in shape. I'll be ready for the '69 season.

That's it: baseball. And I'd like to read a few books. Oh, and I'd like to accommodate my yearning for faraway places. Like the States.

All this, of course, is conditional upon my getting out of here alive and in one piece. Has that occurred to you?

Relentlessly,

Kurt

COBRA'S FOLLY
BOU BOU PHU, VIETNAM
30 June 67

My dear Paul,

I couldn't tell Barry about McGrath and me. Or Steve. Or even Herndon. I hated to muddy our friendship with an admission of promiscuity. Barry would never have understood. But his shame was so ill-disguised that I decided to spill the beans. The opportunity never presented itself. Barry began to hang around with Eicheldinger, for God's sake, and the boob

333

refused to leave his new buddy's side. I was offended. And Barry looked so hang-dog. It really pissed me off.

Last night we went on a patrol. Barry was point man, a sort of nearby scout. We heard him shout a warning. The patrol froze. A grenade exploded. Shots whined by. I started to crawl to Barry, who was supposed to be fifteen feet in front of us. Pinkerton grabbed hold of me.

"Leave him be. You'll get killed."

I shook him off and crawled under the hail of fire, enemy and friendly. I found Barry ten feet up the trail. The grenade had disemboweled him.

"Is it bad, Doc?"

"It's real bad, Barry." I cradled his head with my arm and we lay close together under the crossfire.

"Hey, Doc."

"Yeah, buddy?"

"I went to the . . . store and . . . bought an apple."

"I went to the store and bought an apple and a banana."

Barry chuckled; then he coughed. My hand was wet with the slime of his bloody intestines. "I went to the store and bought an apple, a banana, and . . . a cherry." After I'd bought some ice cream, I realized that Barry would never go to the store again.

Pinkerton sorted through Barry's belongings today for the things he'd send to Barry's family. He brought me two sheets of paper he'd found. Letters.

Dear Mom, Dad, and Ginger,

Sure wished I had been there for Star's foaling. I miss that old mare.

Only eight more months to go. Sure will be glad to come home.

So Ginger liked that picture of the Doc. He keeps himself in pretty good shape. I don't know why he don't like basketball. He's about the best friend I ever had.

I was thinking we might put some sheep out there across the arroyo. The grass is there. I know you don't like sheep, Dad, but I have plans.

The Doc gets out of the Navy next fall and promised to come visit for a couple of weeks. I bet he'll make Ginger forget old Tommy Ross. I'd like to have the cabin fixed up by the time he comes. I sure will be glad to get home.

> *Your loving son and brother*

Dear Doc,

This is dumb, writing you a letter when I see you every day.

I'm sorry. I was so scared he'd tell my dad. When Gemelas and the Dinger were around, you'd look through them like they wasn't there. I thought about how I'd hate it if you ever looked through me like that. Gosh, Doc, your the best

Orioles	girls	orange
Hawks	boys	black
Cardinals	girls?	red
Robins	girls	red and brown
Doves	girls	white

And may flights of angels sing thee to thy rest.

> *Relentlessly,*
>
> *Kurt*

> COBRA'S FOLLY
> BOU BOU PHU, VIETNAM
> 4 July 67

Arch,

Jittery villagers. We've had two confrontations with the VC I go on patrols again. It's like old times.

The VC have apparently been harassing the villagers. Several people have disappeared, all of whom had been friendly with us. LaSalle's girl friend is among the missing; he's moved back to the Folly, where he sleeps all the time. No one attends classes; only the really ill come to sick call. The nurses have quit, the radios have been stolen, and the elderly have gone back to their hovels. We wash our own clothes. We eat "C"-rations at the Folly. The kids no longer scramble to touch

McGrath's and my hair. Always reluctant to go on patrol, the Poofs now quiver with fear when we stop by to make formation; they slip away from ambush under cover of darkness.

This is no time for the troops to be blowing dope, but four or five smoke marijuana all day. They lie by the pool, staring into space or giggling among themselves at private jokes. Their conversation, never brilliant, now seldom goes beyond, "Heavy, man" or "Far out." Its bad enough when they indulge their filthy habit at the Folly, but they go dazed and incoherent on patrols and ambushes. When I go on patrol, I want very suspicious grunts surrounding me. I am only too aware of shifty slant-eyes peering at me through the foliage. My desire for escapism goes beyond a temporary euphoria.

Punji traps seem to be in an especial profusion. Although the wounds caused by punji sticks are less disastrous than those caused by mines, what courage I own nearly deserts me at the thought of stepping onto seemingly solid ground and, with all my weight on that foot, plunging through the camouflage onto a sharp, shit-ridden stake. I think of the Little Mermaid; with every step she felt as if knives and swords thrust into her feet. And she never even got the prince.

Relentlessly,

Kurt

COBRA'S FOLLY
BOU BOU PHU, VIETNAM
5 July 67

My dear Paul,

I was lying on my rack last night and reading, when Pinkerton walked into the room and began to clean his piece. We never spoke, but I could tell he was watching me. I continued to read. After he'd finished with the rifle, he went into the radio room, where Sheila stood watch. I heard whispers; then Sheila came out and closed the door behind her.

"Watcha' doin'?"

"Reading."

"Oh." She sat on my cot with me and looked at the book. She rested her arm on my chest. Her hand played with the

336

button on my jeans. She turned to look at me. I pushed her away and stood up. She looked toward the door to the radio room. "Kurt . . ."

"Forget it, Sheila." I left the room and took a walk with Petunia. When we got back, Sheila had gone and Pinkerton monitored the radio. I fell on my rack and tried to sleep.

This morning I went on a patrol led by McGrath and including Tennessee and the Dinger. The whole day was shitty. Charlie was nearby, but we never found him. We were certain the Cong were on to us; we expected them to hit us at any time. All day we climbed up hills and slid down hills and pushed through thorny underbrush.

We ate lunch in a grotto hidden by a cluster of huge black boulders. Nearby, a brook tumbled down the mountainside. I dug up a couple of earthworms as big as cigars and fished for an hour in a pool covered with lily pads. We boiled my catch over a sterno; then I went to the stream to fill my canteens. When I returned, Tennessee, Eicheldinger, and the three Poofs who accompanied us were gone. McGrath explained their absence. "I sent them over the rise to check out the next valley. Thought we might get a little rest."

Sounded good to me. I lay back and closed my eyes. After a minute, McGrath said, "I've got something for you, cocksucker," and he stuck a wet finger in my ear. The guys do that to each other and giggle—queer joke. Get it? But McGrath has too much class to do it for any reason other than malevolence. I ignored the finger. "What's the matter, cocksucker? You got lockjaw? Shit, don't tell me you got lockjaw. I've got something you like a whole lot, and if you got lockjaw, you ain't going to be able to taste it." I continued to ignore him. McGrath rolled against me and squeezed my crotch. "Like the idea, don't you? I can tell." He slid up and I hate to admit it, but I did what McGrath apparently wanted me to do. No sooner had I begun than McGrath said, "You see. What did I tell you?" I looked up. Tennessee, Eicheldinger, and the three gooks were watching. "Don't stop, Doc." McGrath guided my head with his hands. "Tennessee, you want some action?" The big hillbilly tittered and shook his head negatively. McGrath grabbed a handful of hair and pulled my head back. "You ever seen Tennessee's pecker, Doc? Biggest one I ever seen. Bigger'n a nigger's. Pull it out, Tenn."

Tennessee snickered and said, "Mebbe another time." The

337

Poofs giggled. Eicheldinger watched with horrified fascination.

McGrath picked up his rifle and got to his feet. He said quietly, "You pull it out, Tenn. Right now." Tennessee pulled it out. It was gigantic. And at full mast. "Okay, Doc. Go to it." I went to it. McGrath stroked himself as he watched. He turned to Eicheldinger. "Okay, Dinger. Your turn."

Eicheldinger blinked and started blubbering. I got angry. This was going too far. "No way, McGrath."

The Delta Devil laughed. "You're right, Doc. Even a cock-sucker ain't as low as the Dinger." He looked at the Poofs, who were shuffling around, squeezing their crotches.

"No, McGrath."

The rifleman studied my face; then he grinned and winked. "Okay, Dinger, pull down your britches. Go ahead, pull down your britches. Old Doc's goin' to plug you up." Eicheldinger appeared terrified and on the edge of hysterics. McGrath pointed his rifle at the cretin. "Dinger, ain't nobody'd ever say nothing if I shot your ass. You ain't worth a shit, and I lost me a good buddy when you threw that grenade at Culpepper and murdered him. Ain't nobody but would be happier if you was dead. Pull down your britches . . . You too, Doc. I'll shoot your ass, too, you fucking cocksucker . . . Hey Doc. It looks like the Dinger don't turn you on none. I don't rightly blame you. Here, this always turns you on . . . Yeah. Yeah. Let's see. Okay. Climb on the Dinger." He put the barrel of his rifle against my head. I climbed on Eicheldinger. I was so excited I tore the dumb puke apart. After I'd finished, McGrath took sloppy seconds, followed by all three of the Poofs. I took on Tennessee.

When we returned to the Folly, LaSalle stood guard in the watchtower by the bridge. McGrath was in a jovial mood. "Hey, Frenchie. You know how to tell if a guy is a cocksucker?"

LaSalle rose to the bait. "How?"

"You look at his mouth. You can always tell a cocksucker by the shape of his mouth. Like old Doc. He's got a cock-sucker's mouth. Look at it." LaSalle looked and Tennessee giggled. Eicheldinger threw down his gear and ran for the shitter. I can't get a transfer soon enough.

Relentlessly,

Kurt

338

Dear Mom and Pops,

I may transfer from CAP. I like the work and the people, but it's time to give another corpsman the opportunity; besides, summer has begun, and I should prefer to spend it by the beach.

Caught a nasty case of Ho Chi Minh's revenge. Dirty hands or dirty food. Or both. I eat "C"-rations now. And your powdered soups and dried fruit. Thank you.

No, it seldom rains. Short tropical showers. It's easy to slip indoors.

I often look through the binoculars. Tremendous views from the butte.

Learning that Neil has enlisted in the Army depresses the bejesus out of me. No one should suggest within my hearing that it will make a man of him.

Love,

Kurt

Chloe dear,

The rift is haunted. As we approach the Vietnamese, they fade away, vanishing into their houses or the jungle. We hear no chatter, only echoes and silence.

I've called off my classes; no one attended them anyway. My bedridden patients have been spirited out of the hospital. Our little cafe is boarded.

The VC are building up. We've had several confrontations. We find traces of their presence on every patrol: mines, booby traps, and signs warning us to leave. We know they watch us.

It's strange. This used to be such a happy place.

Relentlessly,

Kurt

My dear Paul,

When I was a little kid, my mother made me go to bed at 7:30 P.M., despite my not being sleepy. I'd lie in bed seeing monsters in every shadow, certain a bogeyman lurked in the closet or under the bed. I'd only fall asleep after what seemed like hours, the covers over my head. I knew ghouls lived in the coal cellar and in the attic.

I got older and wiser, but my fears of the night were only given wider range: dark streets and alleyways, a haunted house at the bottom of the hill, and a friendly playground of a woods turned home at sunset for huge foul-breathed creatures.

The poisonous snakes, centipedes, scorpions, and black widow spiders near Belle Ombre never frightened me like those imaginary fiends of my childhood. Occasionally, I'd dream of standing in the middle of the road, unable to move as a car hurtled down the hill toward me. Or, wide awake and walking across a high bridge, fight an almost irresistible desire to jump off.

For the past four days I've endured all of these real and imaginary dangers and survived.

And where should I begin? With McGrath sticking his tongue out at me and grabbing his crotch? With Tennessee sitting in the two-holer for hours, waiting for me with a mammoth erection? With LaSalle avoiding me? With Visconti keeping his distance? With Gemelas and Sweeney sneering? With Sheila trying to figure out what the hell was going on? With Eicheldinger sobbing in his room? When Pinkerton decided on an overnight patrol and demanded I go with him, I jumped at the chance to get away from the Folly.

Pinkerton told me that we were only going to be a few miles from Bou Bou Phu, but the chopper he'd requested had flown a fair distance: at least thirty miles. We scrambled through the jungle all afternoon to reach our objective, a rocky promontory overlooking a valley supposedly used as a rendezvous point by the Cong. Darkness fell just after we arrived, so we dug in to await the dawn, when we were to make our observations and transmit them to LaSalle on the radio. As a chilly wind blew over us, we huddled together in silence. After an hour or so, Pinkerton spoke.

"Doc, you awake?"

"Yeah."

"Doc, why didn't you fuck old Sheila. She's good pussy."

"It was neither the time nor the place."

"Don't you like pussy?"

"Yeah, I like pussy."

"I thought you was horny."

"I just didn't want to."

"You was horny enough to do it with McGrath."

"Yeah."

"And Barry." Silence. "Doc, you ain't queer, are you?"

"Yeah, I am."

Pinkerton stiffened; then he relaxed. "No, you ain't. I seen you play ball. You're faster than any of us. And stronger. And smarter. Doc, you ain't queer."

I took Pinkerton's face between my hands and kissed him. He accepted it. I slid my hand under his belt. Suddenly, the sarge reached over and grabbed my head. He pulled it toward him and whispered into my ear. "Doc, something's out there. You wait here. I'll be right back." He pulled out his Bowie knife and crawled into the darkness. I lay silent, trying to follow his movements, but he had vanished. I waited an hour; then I pulled out my knife, left the rifles, packs, and radio on the promontory and crawled into the trees to look for him. After I'd accomplished some twenty yards, it occurred to me that Pinkerton might mistake me for Charlie. I decided to lie low and wait for light.

During the hours that followed, I heard rustling and movement all around me. When the sun rose, I crawled back to the promontory. Everything was gone: rifles, packs, and radio. No sign of the sarge.

I searched all day for him. I examined the area of the promontory, I descended to the base of the cliff, I backtracked our route from the drop-off, examining the ground for any little clue. I found no sign of a struggle. Nothing. I returned to the promontory, where I passed a lonely night. In the morning, I decided to get on home.

I hadn't the foggiest of how to get there. I had no rifle and no radio. I had no idea whether anyone knew where I was. *I* knew where I was—just this side of utter panic. All I could think of was that the VC prefer to keep officers as prisoners; enlisted men endure torture before being greased. I'd heard tales of patrols finding Americans in tiny cages, stakes driven

341

through their elbows and knees, eyes gouged out, toes and fingers cut off, tongues cut out, stakes driven into ears. I decided that if it seemed likely that I would be taken prisoner, I would slit my throat. I'd read where unconsciousness occurs after thirty seconds and death within sixty seconds. But I didn't want to die, whatever seconds it took.

I walked toward a mountain I thought I recognized. On its far side was the plain, Bou Bou, and the Folly; if not, at least the mountain was to the east, with the ocean somewhere on the far side. Unfortunately, when down in the jungle, I could see no mountain. Just trees. I waded through waist-high swamps. I avoided paths and roads because of mines and booby traps, and because any gook who saw me would have run for the nearest VC. That night I sat in a tree, swatting mosquitoes. The next morning I continued through the swamps. Snakes would sense my approach and fall out of bushes and low-hanging limbs into the murky water. Leeches covered me. About midafternoon, I came to a morass too deep to wade through. I backtracked and found a dry trail alongside the swamp. As I crept down the path, I turned a corner and nearly stepped on a little boy of ten or twelve setting an animal trap. He started to run away, but I called out softly in Vietnamese, "Do you want some money?" The boy stopped and looked at me. "Do you want fifty piastres?" He smiled. "I'll give you fifty piastres if you let me play with your prick."

"No!" He giggled and moved toward me.

"A hundred piastres?"

He giggled again and came closer. "More."

"Two hundred piastres?"

"Okay."

I pulled a fistful of money from my pocket. He held out his hand. I walked up to him, handed over the money and, as he was counting it, slit his throat. I threw his body into the swamp, covered the blood on the path as best I could, and hurried along my way.

I slept most of the day in some bushes and walked all night through a string of hamlets. Dogs barked at me, chased me, bit me, and tore my clothes. I saw no people; I guess they didn't want to know what stalked past their houses. The next morning I heard a fire fight about a mile to my left. I skirted the action, snuck through a shoddy rear defense, and walked up to the landing perimeter, where I passed myself off as a wounded grunt. Covered with blood from dog bites, mosquito bites, thorn scratches, and squashed leeches, my clothes torn, and covered with mud, I was told to jump aboard the next dust-off. It took me to the Med Battalion. Alf and Bernie took me to the showers and scrubbed me down. They burned leeches off me. They cleaned my cuts and bites and bandaged them. They injected tetanus vaccine. We decided to tempt fate and forget about rabies shots. I bummed a ride by chopper to Bou Bou Phu. Pinkerton hadn't come back. I keep wondering if he's squeezed into an iron cage in some backwater hamlet, bamboo stakes driven through his knees and elbows, eye sockets crawling with maggots . . .

Relentlessly,

Kurt

FIRST MEDICAL BATTALION
DA NANG, VIETNAM
14 July 67

Dear Mom and Pops,

The reports of my death are greatly exaggerated. If my wound were serious, I'd be in route to a hospital Stateside and probably unable to write this letter.

I shall have no facial scarring. Neither will women faint when they see me, unless I go about bareass. I got a bullet through my derriere. Lots of blood flowed, but my doctor says I'll lead a completely normal life. He did advise against putting that part of my body on public exhibition.

Please forgive the bad handwriting. I've misplaced my contact lenses and you know I can't see a foot in front of me without them.

I've fulfilled my line duty. A corpsman is considered having fulfilled his line duty after six months. There's no way they can get me to return to the boonies. I'm safe and shall stay within the Med Battalion compound for the three months I have left in Nam. You need not worry about me.

"After all," sighed Narcissus the hunchback, "on me it looks good."

Love,

Kurt

Arch,

They've wiped us out. Everybody's dead.

I was on a patrol with McGrath's squad up the mountain across the rift. Frick staked out an ambush near the garbage dump. LaSalle and Sheila remained on watch at the Folly.

The night was hot and the jungle stifling. About 1 A.M., McGrath decided to cut the patrol short. We dropped the Poofs off at their fort and were climbing the butte, when we heard revolver fire at the Folly. We broke into a run. McGrath ordered a dispersement and veered off to the left with the Dinger; Tennessee and I took the right side. Gemelas continued up the roadway and was cut down by machine-gun fire from across the bridge. I crawled over to him. Dead.

Although we were uncertain where Sweeney and McGrath had laid their mines, Tennessee and I elected to cross the crevice. He went down hand over hand; I continued along the lip to an easier place to cross. Gunfire sounded nearby. Tennessee yelled, "Oh, God! I'm hit!" I heard a heavy thud at the bottom of the crevice and a mine exploded. I decided against the crevice crossing. I badly wanted to find somebody I knew. After a long and scary search, I found McGrath near the bridge.

"I can't see to get a bead on them, Doc. You stay here and guard the bridge." He crawled away.

No sooner had he disappeared than Eicheldinger rushed out of the bushes and tripped over me. "Get down, Dinger, you fucking fool." He grabbed hold of me and started babbling. I knocked his hands off and got the hell away from him. I was five feet away when a grenade exploded where I'd been. I crawled back and felt of the Dinger. He was dead.

Grenades exploded all around me. The machine gun cut loose. I heard McGrath yell. I found him ten feet away. I said, "The Dinger's greased." McGrath said nothing. He wasn't breathing. I took a chance and shone my red flashlight on him. Almost immediately, I felt a sharp sting in my ass; then a big black mass of pain washed over me. But I'd seen McGrath's trouble. He was drowning in his own blood from a wound in his throat. I slit his windpipe with a razor blade and threaded an endotracheal tube down his windpipe. I heard no inward and outward hiss of air, so I breathed for him. I kept on breathing and feeling his pulse. That's all I remember clearly. Just fuzzy faces and faraway people talking and lots of noises.

I have no idea how I got to First Med. I came to consciousness with the Frankenstein monster looking down at me. It's unmanly to admit, Arch, but that's when I started to cry.

Relentlessly,

Kurt

FIRST MEDICAL BATTALION
DA NANG, VIET NAM
15 July 67

Chloe dear,

It's over. CAP. Over and done with. Everybody's gone.

I'm back on SICU with a bullet up my ass. Alf says that McGrath has been flown to the States; beyond that, and the fact that McGrath and I came through Triage with five DOA (Dead on Arrival), he knows nothing. "Really, Kurt, I think I'd have been told if one of the DOA's was a tall woman. What in Heaven's name was a tall woman doing out there? I'm keeping you on ICU until you tell me *everything.*"

This afternoon I was trying to examine my wound in a shaving mirror, to the amusement of my fellow inmates, when Sheila and Gary Frick walked onto the ward. I'd thought they were dead. Sheila wore a helmet, an olive-green T-shirt, tight white shorts, and jungle boots. She covered the length of the ward in a few long strides, knelt by my cot, and hugged me hard. She rocked on her heels, tears streaming down her cheeks; then she sat on the empty cot next to mine. Frick sat beside her. A pudgy bulldog of a corpsman waddled over to tell them to get off the bed, but I advised him to go away.

"You go on and get away from here, Winthrop, or I'll kill you."

He left.

Sheila wiped her face with her hands. "I'm dying for a cigarette. Damn, that's right; you don't smoke. Oh, thank you." She reached over to pluck a ciggy from the fingers of my next cot neighbor; then she leaned back and crossed her long legs. "Has anyone told you what happened?"

"No one knew."

She blew out a stream of smoke. "It was hot that night, remember? It was stifling in the radio room. When McGrath called to say the patrol was coming in, I had to get outside. I thought about going up to the watchtower to talk with LaSalle, but he would have tried to make me speak Vietnamese. I was too sleepy to go through that. Besides, I was supposed to stay in the radio room.

"Since nobody else was at the Folly, I decided to go skinny-dipping. I stripped and ran down to the pool. Petunia rooted around in the mud while I swam. All of a sudden she ran squealing up to the house. I figured the ambush had come back, so I hurried to your room to grab a towel. I was drying my hair when Petunia came tearing around the house, squealing her head off. She'd never done that; she always made you guys scratch her for a while. I looked out your back window and saw several shapes flitting through the trees.

"I was scared to death. You guys had taken the rifles with you, but I remembered your pistol. I rummaged behind your books, just knowing I was going to grab a scorpion. I found the pistol and put it under your pillow; then I pulled your cot into the moonlight. I didn't know whether those guys were Poofs or Cong. Whichever they were, I hoped they'd want to rape me before they killed me. That would give me a chance. I began singing and giggling real girlishlike, and when I saw them in the courtyard, I did a sexy little dance in the doorway, swinging my hips and rubbing my tits." Frick covered his face with his hand.

"I laid down on your cot, wriggling around and singing. One of the zips came through the door. I shot him; then I ran into the radio room and turned out the light. They threw a couple of grenades into the bedroom; that's why your books are sort of messed up. Sorry about that. Anyway, I screamed and gurgled like I was dying. After a little while, another gook came into your room. He peeked into the radio room, so I blew his brains out.

"I don't know what would have happened next if the machine gun hadn't started shooting. I heard some gabble outside; then I didn't hear anything. I wanted to load more bullets in the .45, but I forgot where you kept them. I just hoped you had six in it.

346

"I crawled out the window and peeked around the corner of the house. A gook was standing there watching the door. I dropped him.

"I crawled along the ground all the way to the watchtower. Scratched the hell out of my tits. Look!" She bared her breasts. They were indeed scratched all to hell, as any fool and every patient on the ward could see. Frick made her cover them. "And I just knew that a leech was going to crawl up my vagina. It was spooky, let me tell you. I was starting to think about cobras and kraits when somebody across the bridge screamed, 'Oh God! I'm hit!' I couldn't tell who it was, but it sure got to me. I crawled faster. It was awful. It must have taken me ten minutes to reach the watchtower. Two gooks were sitting in it, gabbling and chirping. They were looking toward the bridge, so I took a chance that your gun still had bullets in it. I snuck up behind and shot one. Then the gun went click. I was so mad, thinking of those shitty little bastards waiting to kill my brother and the rest of the guys, I jumped on top of the gook I hadn't shot and beat him on the head with the butt of the .45 and scratched his eyes and kneed him until he was unconscious. I grabbed his knife and stabbed them both in the chest and in the belly, over and over again. Goddam gooks. Anyway, I swung the machine gun toward the house and kept swinging it and shooting until it jammed. Hey, got another butt, buddy?"

Sheila walked around my cot to light the cigarette and chat with my neighbor. She continued up the aisle, cheerfully shooting the breeze with wounded grunts. Winthrop walked up to her, coffee cup in hand, stroking his mustache. She looked at him; then called back to me. "Hey, Kurt, this the bulldog?" At my nod, she gave him a withering look. "Get lost, creep." She turned to a marine with half his face blown away. "Hi there, guy. Mind if I snuggle up and you can tell how that happened?"

Frick took the opportunity to tell me his side of the story.

"Bad scene, Doc. Squattin' on ambush, mosquitoes dining on my splendor, I hear machine-gun fire. 'The Folly! Sheila! Dad'll kill me!'

"Poof fort. They're rubbing their eyes. 'Like what's happening, man?' Fuckin' gooks wouldn't come with us. 'We'll be up bye and bye.'

"I trip over Gemelas. Deader 'n shit. All I'm thinkin' is 'Oh fuck!' Then Sheila yells 'Come on over, guys. I got the gun.' And there she was, cursing the machine gun, sittin' naked as a jaybird on top of two dead Chucks.

"LaSalle's by the watchtower with a slit throat. Sweeney does a search-and-destroy. Found him by the pool, next to a carved-up Charlie.

"You and McGrath was right at the edge of the cliff. You were kind of delirious, sayin' over and over, 'Breathe, damn it. Breathe.' You'd both lost a lot of blood, so Sheila started IV's on you." I looked wonderingly at Sheila, who was sitting on the bed of the man with half a face, listening to him try to tell his story out of what remained of his mouth, squeezing the muscle in his arm, and interrupting him with "What a man!"

"The Poofs carried you to the landing pad. Sheila and me took turns making McGrath breathe through that tube you'd stuck down his throat and carrying the IV bottles high. Sheila was covered with blood and butt naked." Frick glowered. "Fuckin' Polack. I thought the whole chopper crew was going to jump out and live with us.

"The Poofs strutted up when the shootin' died down. Found two Cong in the shitter. Giggled the whole time they tortured them; then they pushed the poor suckers over the cliff. Visconti caught one Poof sneaking out of the kitchen with my toolbox." Frick lowered his voice. "The Dago shot that sucker right between the eyes."

Frick counted on his fingers. "Eight Cong. One Poof. Sweeney, LaSalle, Gemelas had a hole in his back a foot across. Tennessee was blown to hell. Took us a long time to find him. Oh yeah. And the Dinger."

We chatted until the three o'clock penicillin shot. As they got up to leave, Frick turned to me. "Hey, Doc. You comin' back to the Folly?"

I laughed so hard, I nearly broke my stitches.

Relentlessly,

Kurt

348

Dear Mom and Pops,

I find life pleasant as a convalescent: no responsibilities, no obligations, and plenty of company should I desire social contact. I don't. The operation was a success; my wound has responded to treatment and is healing nicely. It stings a bit, but I refuse to take pain medications.

Sheila and her brother brought my belongings to the hospital. After they left, I burrowed through the boxes and pulled out a couple of Trollopes. A friend sent me the *Complete Works* as a Christmas present. Have you ever heard of Trollope? He was a nineteenth-century British author who wrote quiet novels about a people whose passions were spent wondering who the next bishop was to be. Those books contain all the excitement I need at the moment.

Love,

Kurt

FIRST MEDICAL BATTALION
DA NANG, VIETNAM
19 July 67

Arch,

The bullet passed through both buttocks, rather evenly, and the scars may pass for dimples. Still smarts when I sit, though.

So I walk a lot. Today I walked over to Triage to check the casualty list. Everyone but Pinkerton is there.

14 JULY

McGrath, Norwood C. Corp.		T/T Neck,
		Jaw, L. Leg
		OR
Strom, William K.	HM3	T/T L.&R.
		Buttocks OR

LaSalle, Edward P.	L/ Corp.	DOA	Graves
Gemelas, George J.	Pfc.	"	"
Sweeney, Thomas L.	Pfc.	"	"
Perkins, Cecil P.	Pfc.	"	"
Eicheldinger, Ernest E.	Pfc.	"	"

Choppers were buzzing in and out like mosquitoes, so I helped out for a while. Although I could do no lifting, I could take records, prepare men for surgery, and treat marines with minor wounds. Hundreds of patients went through Triage; we worked nonstop from midmorning until late afternoon. When the casualty flow eased up, I went outside to escape the smells of dirty socks, unwashed bodies, and blood. Graves was overloaded and could take no more casualties. Fifty dead marines lay in rows alongside the walkway outside Triage.

I have no more stomach for this fight.

Relentlessly,

Kurt

FIRST MEDICAL BATTALION
DA NANG, VIETNAM
20 July 67

Chloe dear,

I am the most notorious corpsman in Vietnam. Everyone from the battalion commander to the lowest grunt in Graves pauses in awe as I pass by. I was asked to dine at a captain's table. A major would have polished my boots had I asked him; an admiral would have kissed my ass. Perhaps I'd better explain.

Alf and I were eating lunch in the chow hall today. Suddenly, the clamor of silverware against tin plates ceased. Utter silence. I looked up. Alf stared over my shoulder, his mouth open. As I turned around to see what was happening, I heard a loud shriek.

"Kurt!"

Sheila! In a dress! Accompanied by a slim, radiant redhead and a short blonde with the biggest knockers I'd ever seen. They breasted the waves of corpsmen like the Titanic accompanied by a sloop and a tug. Sheila hugged me hard, tears rolling down her cheeks; then she turned to her friends, who were studying me.

"Well?"

"The MP in Saigon," said the redhead.

"That lifeguard in Brisbane," the blonde sighed dreamily.

"Take off your shirt, Kurt," demanded Sheila. I took off my shirt. Everyone in the chow hall was looking at us. The girls regarded me critically.

"Okay," said the redhead.

The blonde shook her head. "The lifeguard in Brisbane."

"Put your shirt back on, Kurt," Sheila said. I put my shirt back on. "How's your ass?"

"It's all right," I mumbled. The four of us stood looking at one another. "Sit down," I said chivalrously. Sheila sat down immediately and lighted a cigarette; her two friends eyed the greasy seats with dismay. One of the doctors appeared by the table.

"May I escort you ladies to the officers' dining room?"

Sheila blew smoke in his face. "We prefer to dine with the enlisted men."

"No, we don't," said the redhead.

"We're here to see Kurt," Sheila said.

The doctor noticed me for the first time. "Bert! I didn't see you standing there. Why don't you bring your friends over to meet the commander?" Sheila's friends glared at me. I betrayed my comrades. The doctor stepped aside to let us pass by. As I passed by, he hissed, "Button your shirt, Bert."

After a pleasant lunch, we were invited to the officers' quarters for a drink. "Not me," said Sheila. "I want to hit that beach." We got up to leave.

"You must let me take you to supper," said my new friend, the doctor, who had watched Margie and Linda wander off with better-looking cohorts. "I know this little Vietnamese restaurant . . ." Sheila took my hand and leaned against me. The doctor sighed. "You come, too, Bert."

I suggested hitching to China Beach, but Sheila insisted on climbing down to the little beach on the other side of the chopper pad, where she swam back and forth among the sharks and sea snakes. I couldn't watch. After an hour, she returned to the blanket. We lay in a companionable silence, gazing over the blue water.

"God, it's beautiful here, isn't it, Kurt? So relaxing." Silence. "Do you miss the Folly?"

"Yeah."

"It's a shame. Gary wanted to keep the CAP unit going as a memorial, so that the guys wouldn't have . . . died . . . in vain." Sheila broke down and sobbed. "We moved everything down to the Poof fort." She raised her eyebrows. "I know. Disgusting. But we were scared."

"What about Petunia?"

"Oh, Kurt, you're going to be mad. We gave the chickens to some old people, but I knew how they took care of their pigs and . . . And I couldn't see Petunia being all skinny and starving so . . . Gary shot her. The Poofs cooked her. Oh, Kurt, she smelled so good, I had to eat a little of . . . You're mad, aren't you?"

"No."

"The inspection team came and went over the Folly with tooth and comb. They told us to pack and wait for orders. We waited for a couple of days; then they transferred Gary and Angelo (Visconti) back to Seventh. I went along, just to see how it was. Your old colonel liked me and invited us for dinner. I knew Gary felt pretty low so . . . I stayed overnight in the chalet. I never really believed it existed, but there it was, big as life, right in the middle of nowhere, just like you said. It wasn't near as nice as the Folly.

"Anyway, Jud wanted to know all about CAP and we talked about the Poofs and drank too much. After the guys went back to Echo, Jud and I had a nightcap." She gave me a look and lighted a cigarette. "Now, Kurt, you know me. I make my own impressions of people. I knew you guys all hated Jud, but I . . ." A long stream of smoke. ". . . I thought he was kind of sexy. I was sort of turned on and not turned on, you know what I mean? No, I guess you don't. When I got too sleepy to stay up, I asked him if I could make up the couch. He told me to go upstairs and sleep in the bed; he had paperwork and would be up all night. Did you know he had a double bed? You knew? My God, guys gossip as bad as women.

"I should have known. I woke up, and Jud was crawling into bed with me. Now you know, Kurt . . ." Another stream of smoke. ". . . you know, at a given moment, there's a very fine line between a yes and a no. I just needed to be turned on a little more. 'Please,' he said. 'Please. It's so long since I've

352

slept next to a woman. I won't do anything. I promise.' Then
he tried to cram his finger up my butthole. 'I'm not into this,'
I said. 'Please,' he said. By then I was turned off. I told him
it was my period. It didn't matter to him. I said it mattered to
me. 'Just give me a little help,' he said. He pushed my head
down toward his crotch. I got out of bed and went to sleep on
the couch. When Jud woke me up there with his pawing, I got
dressed and slept on the porch.

"I spent the morning trying to get a ride into Da Nang; then
I went down to Echo to say good-bye to Gary. He wasn't there.
Angelo told me the colonel had sent Gary out on a two-day
scouting trip with the biggest fuck-up in the battalion." The
stream of smoke was like dragon breath. "I went back to Battalion and told Jud I'd got off the rag and would he still like
some help. After he went to sleep—and believe me, that was
the *worst* lay anyone ever had—I snuck downstairs and set fire
to the chalet. Burned to the ground. The son of a bitch jumped
out the window, but he got burnt. Not bad, but I hope to God
it smarted."

We watched the waves for a few minutes.

"So the colonel wanted you up the old dirt chute, huh?"

Sheila giggled; then she touched the bulge in my Navy issue
swimsuit. She lifted the waistband and peered under it. I lifted
my hips. She pulled the suit off, careful of my bandages. She
took off her own. I doubt that she looked up and saw that the
entire chopper company watched the show through binoculars.

Relentlessly,

Kurt

FIRST MEDICAL BATTALION
DA NANG, VIETNAM
21 July 67

My dear Paul,

Bernstein's *Candide* runs through my mind. I identify with
the old woman: "I am so easily assimilated," "I'm homesick
for anywhere but here," and "I'm missing the half of my back-
side."

Sheila's leaving Nam. Steve's carrying her and two girl

353

friends to Australia. We ate supper at the officers' club. Steve told everybody he was entertaining a movie star, and Sheila autographed several napkins. We lingered over drinks for several hours. Despite the donut cushion I carry with me everywhere, my ass hurt like the dickens, and combined with the alcohol, my tongue wagged a little too much. At one point, I could have bit it off.

I'd mentioned having written the dead men's families.

Steve said, "I suppose without a CO, you were the best man to do it."

"Yeah, it would have been a bitch for the sarge, bamboo stakes through his elbows and his eyes gouged out."

Sheila blanched. We'd kept those stories from her because of her brother. I was miserable.

Steve said quickly, "They'll find him. Probably holed up with a couple of jungle honeys."

Sheila's eyes welled with tears. "You'll let me know, one way or the other."

"I promise. I'll check the casualty list in Triage every day. And I'll keep on writing his wife."

Sheila dried her eyes. "You think I did wrong, don't you?"

"No."

Steve looked bewildered. Sheila searched my face carefully. "Really?"

"It was a good thing, Sheila."

She smiled uncertainly, glanced at Steve, and lighted a cigarette. "What kind of stuff did you say in the letters?"

"A bunch of shit. Funny things they did. Why everybody liked them."

"What did you say about the Greek and the Dinger? And Herndon? Nobody liked them."

"I lied. Herndon's dad wrote back. I didn't tell you? He knows my Uncle Carl and was happy to know that his son died like a man. And Barry . . ."

"What about Barry?"

"Nothing."

"Kurt?"

"His dad wrote. Said they missed me. Told me that Dick Smith did this and Tommy Ross did that. I don't know who the fuck Dick Smith and Tommy Ross are."

"Kurt, people are watching us." Steve laid his hand on mine. Sheila took my other hand.

"Mr. Barry told me that he'd gone ahead and finished the cabin down in the cottonwoods and . . . and I can live in it when I come home."

Sheila wiped off my cheeks with a napkin. Steve squeezed my hand. Nobody said anything for a few minutes.

Sheila's makeup was smeared all to hell. She tried to repair it. "Barry made me promise not to tell you . . . I suppose it doesn't matter now." We waited. She would have to repair her makeup again. "Did you know that whenever you went to the village, either Barry or McGrath followed to make sure nothing happened to you?"

"I didn't know."

"You don't think I'd have gone down there with you without knowing someone was nearby with a gun?"

"I never thought about it."

"Barry liked you so much. McGrath did, too."

"Sheila . . ."

"Don't tell me, Kurt,"

"Alf told me that McGrath will be on a respirator for the rest of his life. That wound fucked up his spine."

Steve spoke very slowly and deliberately. "I could always draw. And I was good at it. I learned to paint and sculpt and I was good at that, too. I was going to sacrifice everything to art. But I met a girl and fell in love and wanted to get married. That meant I had to support her and the children we would have. So I gave up art. The kind of art I loved.

"I've never regretted it. I love my wife very much and I love my kids. But when I made the decision to give up painting, I made another decision. I decided that I would compensate by never being bored. I would enjoy to the utmost what I had left. And I have. I would hang around only with fun people. Alive people. Beautiful people. And you are two of the most beautiful, alive, amusing, vital people I've ever known. And here, tonight, with you, I am having such a lot of fun."

Sheila and I burst into laughter and for the rest of the evening we were careful to keep the conversation light.

When Sheila went to the ladies' room, Steve pressed his knee hard against mine. "Kurt . . ."

"Take Sheila. I'll be around."

"There's no way the three of us . . . ?"

"No."

"You're sure?"

355

"Yeah."

"I haven't seen Don for three months."

"He's not . . . I wondered."

"He's defoliating jungle in the Delta."

"That's too bad. I'm sorry, Steve."

"It excites the hell out of me to think about that morning. Kurt, I don't like leaving you alone tonight."

"I'm okay."

The next morning Steve and Sheila arrived at Med Battalion just before Frick and Visconti, who had hitched in from 7th. Sheila collected Linda and Margie, and we stood around the jeep, saying good-bye. Linda could only tear her eyes from Steve to look at Visconti.

"Holy Moses, Sheila, now I understand why you stayed in the jungle. These guys are dynamite."

Sheila looked at Steve, Visconti, and me; then she turned to Linda and smiled sadly. "You should have seen the ones that got away."

Relentlessly,

Kurt

Paul,

Please excuse the printing. Left-handed. I'll tell you.

Larry, my chopper chief, woke me up. "Come with me, Kurt." Through wind and rain and dark of night. A huey hit an aerial mine. Killed everybody on it and flaming gasoline burned up everybody waiting below—wounded grunts, litter-bearers, corpsmen . . . Eight dead. Three alive.

Larry and me hauled in the crispies and three other men. A head, a leg, and a multiple. We slid in the mud. Lots of shooting. Choppers have lights. Good targets. I got hit in the elbow. Larry strapped a tourniquet.

Our huey lurched and Larry fell out. I slid into a crispy. Skin like a turtle's shell.

I was scared of falling out, too. The head died. I left the crispies alone. What the fuck was I suppose to do with them.

Went through surgery. Moritz gave me morphine. A dark velvet cloud. No pain. No crisps. Nothing.

Woke up surrounded by crispies. 85–95 percent burns.

Prognosis 0 percent. Everything scorched but the soles of their feet. Their eyes disintegrated. A special plane took them away. I forget where. Doesn't matter. They had to die.

Father Kerry died. Giving last rites during a fire fight. Frag blew his hand off. Never stopped giving the rites. A mortar round finished both of them.

Vince something took me off the casualty flight in Okinawa. I don't think the nurses saw him. Vince said he wrote letters I never answered. I always answered letters. He carried me to a little house and left me there. I woke up and Joe was fucking me. He hurt me when he did it so hard. Joe made me take showers and my bandage got wet. He wrapped an old green T-shirt around it. Then he made me learn lines from a piece of paper and he slapped me when I couldn't remember them and pushed me against the wall but I finally did. I knocked at the door and he said come in son and I said Dad what does circumcized mean and he showed me and made me blow him. Joe said I favored his son.

I stayed there four or five days I think. It wasn't bad. I took lots of morphine. I stole it from ICU. Joe couldn't hurt me then. One day he came and then he went and I knew it would be a while before he came again so I didn't take any morphine and I walked but I couldn't see because Joe had hidden my contact lenses. I walked and my tote bag got heavy but it had my morphine so I carried it. I walked and threw up and my mouth was dry when some air jockies picked me up and wanted to take me to the hospital but nurses there so they took me to the airport and sneaked me aboard a flight to the States and a Green Beret looked after me.

The Green Beret is driving a car through Reno and back to his old Kentucky home where my sister just across the river in Cincinnati is close. He wants to camp out in the desert and the mountains and rough it. You know how Green Berets are. I told him you teach snow bunnies in Boulder and how I always have my own room wherever you live and he said I could go with him.

He don't talk much. Green Berets do doctoring so he gives me penicillin but he won't give me morphine. He doesn't know I've got my own. He calls me Spaceman.

He is getting the car now. Renting it. I'm at the bus station now. Waiting for him. We leave when he gets back. I won't take any morphine, but I feel pretty sick. He says we'll gamble in Reno tonight. And camp out in the desert. Then I can shoot up and be all right.

There's people all around me but I can't see them so good. They're all blurs. Sometimes they talk to me but I can't understand them.

We'll be in Boulder come Friday unless I get a karate chop in the throat because he's pretty sexy. Have a stiff drink and a warm bed and a cute little snow bunny for the Green Beret and you and me will go downstairs and sit in front of the fire and have another drink and I'll tell you all about it.

Relentlessly,

Kurt

VIETNAM

NOVELS WRITTEN BY
MEN WHO WERE THERE

THE BIG V William Pelfrey   **67074-7/$2.95**

"An excellent novel...Mr. Pelfrey, who spent a year as an infantryman in Vietnam, recreates that experience with an intimacy that makes the difference."

The New York Times Book Review

WAR GAMES James Park Sloan   **01609-5/$3.50**

Amidst the fierce madness in Vietnam, a young man searches for the inspiration to write the "definitive war novel." "May become the new *Catch 22*." *Library Journal*

AMERICAN BOYS Steven Phillip Smith   **67934-5/$3.50 US/$3.95 Can**

Four boys come to Vietnam for separate reasons, but each must come to terms with what men are and what it takes to face dying. "The best novel I've come across on the war in Vietnam." Norman Mailer

THE BARKING DEER Jonathan Rubin   **61135-X/$3.50**

A team of twelve men is sent to a Montagnard village in the central highlands where the innocent tribesmen become victims of their would-be defenders. "Powerful." *The New York Times Book Review*

COOKS AND BAKERS Robert A. Anderson   **79590-6/$2.95**

A young marine lieutenant arrives just when the Vietnam War is at its height and becomes caught up in the personal struggle between the courage needed for killing and the shame of killing. An Avon Original. "A tough-minded unblinking report from hell." *Penthouse*

A FEW GOOD MEN Tom Suddick   **01866-7/$2.95**

Seven marines in a reconnaissance unit tell their individual stories in a novel that strips away the illusions of heroism in a savage and insane war. An Avon Original. "The brutal power of defined anger."

Publishers Weekly

VIETNAM

A WORLD OF HURT Bo Hathaway　　69567-7/$3.50 US/$4.50 CAN

A powerful, realistic novel of the war in Vietnam, of two friends from different worlds, fighting for different reasons in a war where all men died the same.

"War through the eyes of two young soldiers in Vietnam who emerge from the conflict profoundly changed...A painful experience, and an ultimately exhilarating one."

Philadelphia Inquirer

DISPATCHES Michael Herr　　01976-0/$3.95

Months on national hardcover and paperback bestseller lists. Michael Herr's nonfiction account of his years spent under fire with the front-line troops in Vietnam.

"The best book I have ever read about war in our time."

John le Carre

"I believe it may be the best personal journal about war, any war, that any writer has ever accomplished."

Robert Stone (DOG SOLDIERS) *Chicago Tribune*

FOREVER SAD THE HEARTS Patricia L. Walsh　　78378-9/$3.95

A "moving and explicit" (*Washington Post*) novel of a young American nurse, at a civilian hospital in Vietnam, who worked with a small group of dedicated doctors and nurses against desperate odds to save men, women and children.

"It's a truly wonderful book...I will be thinking about is and feeling things from it for a long time." Sally Field

NO BUGLES, NO DRUMS Charles Durden

69260-0/$3.50 US $4.50 CAN

The irony of guarding a pig farm outside Da Nang—The Sing My Swine Project—supplies the backdrop for a blackly humorous account of disillusionment, cynicism and coping with survival.

"The funniest, ghastliest military scenes put to paper since Joseph Heller wrote CATCH-22" *Newsweek*

"From out of Vietnam, a novel with echoes of Mailer, Jones and Heller,"

Houston Chronicle